A Bloody Merry Murder

The Anonymums Series

By Emilie Castera & Eve Goodfellow

This is a work of fiction. Names, characters, places, and incidents either are the product of the author's imagination or are used fictitiously. Any resemblance to actual persons, living or dead, events, or locales is entirely coincidental.

Copyright © 2025 by Emilie Castera and Eve Goodfellow

The right of Emilie Castera and Eve Goodfellow to be identified as the co-authors of this work has been asserted in accordance with the Copyright, Designs and Patents Act 1988. All rights reserved. No part of this book may be reproduced, stored in or introduced into a retrieval system, or transmitted in any form or by any means (electronic, mechanical, photocopying, recording or otherwise), or used in any manner without written permission of the copyright owner except for the use of quotations in a book review.

First paperback edition September 2025
Book design by Patrick Knowles

ISBN 978-1-0369-2899-5 (paperback)
www.theanonymums.com

To our husbands,
who, absolutely, unfalteringly, steadfastly, faithfully,
never believed in our ability to write this book.

Prologue

How she loathes this time of year.

As hundreds of strangers are about to invade her kitchen, Gemma resentfully glares at the expanse of darkness outside the full-width glass doors. Standing there, she knows she is totally visible to the outside world, but being exposed is something she is very used to. She can't shake the thought that the black pool of anxiety has spread from the pit of her stomach into the garden. No sign of the moon or stars to light the lawn beyond the wooden deck. Just the endless night.

The clocks went back last week. It gets dark earlier every day and even the daylight is barely sufficient to take good pictures. And let's not mention what November does to her complexion. So much time and effort spent on maintaining her sun kissed glow. Thank goodness for fake tan and LED ring lights.

For the umpteenth time, she checks her expensively coloured blonde wavy hair and 'took ages to look like barely there' make-up in the imposing gilded mirror she carefully selected to decorate her kitchen family room. It is one of her favourite objects in her home and, along with meticulously curated Jo Malone Pomegranate Noire candles, will provide her with a glamourous vignette background on screen in a few minutes.

She has done so many Lives on Instagram; they have become second nature to her. And yet, this one is different. She triple-checks her phone settings, satisfied the battery is full. She sighs as she tears off a sheet of kitchen paper to wipe the marks her clammy hands have left on the screen. A lot of effort has gone into this evening, and she knows she can't fuck it up.

If she is honest with herself, it has felt like an uphill struggle lately. She knows she could give it all up and get a 'normal' job like all those school mums she only ever sees at the school fete or at birthday parties. But, from her previous career, she knows just how boring these office jobs can be, and she enjoys being able to pick Charlie up from school at 3pm, rather than leaving him at After School Club.

Also, she would hate to admit it to anyone, but the high from being recognised never gets old. Not sure you can get much of that from being a supply chain manager or an accountant.

And yet, Gemma is tired of it all sometimes. She draws a deep sigh and thinks of her comfy bed where she would like nothing better than to curl up with an episode of *Bridgerton*.

But her life is not a delightful period drama full of suitors and muslin ballgowns. She has a job to do, and she will do it right, even if it feels like selling her soul to the devil at times.

She is grateful for the few minutes of quiet to collect her thoughts before starting the Live event. Charlie and Matthew left around 6pm and the house feels weirdly empty. How can she feel so lonely when she will be talking to hundreds of followers in less than 90 seconds through the magic of Instagram?

Her heart skips a couple of beats as a loud bang startles her out of her thoughts. Stupid Bonfire Night. Someone is about to receive the full wrath of the Upper Huxley Resident's Association. Everyone knows that fireworks are only allowed during regulated hours (6-7pm) on Guy Fawkes Day and (6-8pm) on Straw Man parade day. All that for pets.

She poises herself on the brown leather bar stool at the kitchen island and downs the glass of Chardonnay she poured ready for casual sipping on camera. Damn. She is not usually much of a drinker, but tonight she needs to calm her nerves. She refills her glass, checks her lipstick has not bled, and that her cleavage is only showing the right amount.

With a last glance to the clock on the oven, she puts on her best smile and, with a shaking hand, presses the Live button.

'Showtime!'

Chapter 1

@gemma_cotswolds_mum Morning friends! Thank you all so much for the wonderful love for little me in my tiny Cotswold village. I've had so many new followers recently so let me introduce myself ~~yet again because people are too lazy to read bios~~. I'm a proud mum of my Charlie and married to the impossibly handsome Matthew. On my page, you'll find a bit of fashion, a bit of cookery, parenting, and ~~my fruitless attempts at~~ self-improvement. #humbling #mumsofuk #healthylifestyle #motherhood #honestmum #youdoyou ~~#slowpostingday~~

Mary

Tuesday

'Poison!' My voice is dripping with frustration and general exhaustion. I'm unprepared – again! – and trying to buy some time. Think, Mary, think! I close my eyes, wipe the nervous sweat that has appeared on my forehead with the back of my right hand and try to conjure up the contents of the cupboard. I just can't remember what's there! As quietly as I can, I sneak out of the utility room and back into the kitchen. They will smell weakness if they think the decision hasn't already been finalised and that's just suicide.

'I'm so hungry!' They haven't seen me yet as they can't be bothered to look up from the fast-paced game of snap they are playing on the dinner table.

'Ummm ...' Shit! Failure. Game Over. I made the fatal mistake of whispering it too loudly and they heard it. They will have clocked the uncertainty. I slowly pivot on my left heel to face them and there are four blue eyes staring right through my skull.

I summon certainty and confidence that I've never felt before, stare straight back at them and, with the blind conviction of a cringy *Hollyoaks* heartthrob, dramatically announce 'Spag. Bol.' I enunciate the two, already shortened, syllables for theatrical impact. It is such a cowardly choice – spaghetti bolognese is a firm Lamb family favourite.

Ben throws a fist pump into the air and Charlotte beams her approval. They are placated. For now. Crisis averted. For five minutes, at least. I turn back to the cupboard and google 'how to defrost beef mince quickly.' A cursory review of my Google history would tell you everything you need to know about how disorganised my life is.

I pride myself on the fact that I refuse to be one of those mums that makes three different meals every evening: pride that dances dangerously with smug. The cutlery and plates have been set (after a fair few times of asking) and I place the sauce and pasta in their separate dishes on the table and take my allocated seat (nearest the fridge, of course). I scan the faces quickly to see who might express gratitude, if not for the dinner, then at least for not having cooked roasted vegetables or, even worse, anything with aubergine! My optimism fades almost immediately as the requests begin to come in as though I'm a minimum wage short order cook in some roadside American Diner!

'Mummy, did you make me rice? You know I don't like pasta.' Charlotte.

'Mummy, you forgot the ketchup!' Ben – who is a strictly 'no sauce, only ketchup' kind of kid.

'May, could you please grab the Tabasco? You know I like it HOT!' Tom, with a rude wink that leaves me keener to kick him in the shins than rumble in the sheets! Twat.

'Oh, for feck's sake, you lot! It's spag bol! Just fecking EAT IT!' I scream – luckily only in my head – as I turn back to the fridge. And that's what I get for my smugness. Here's all the parenting advice you'll ever need: Do whatever you want, raise your children with your values, but Don't. Be. Smug. You can bet it will bite you in the fecking arse!

As I place the items on the table with just enough passive aggressiveness to make myself feel slight better, I feel that not only am I the only one in this house who eats normally, but I have also clung to my 'strongly held principles' by only my heavily gnawed fingernails. When there is drama about which fork Ben has been given, I am sorely tempted to issue notice that 'the character of Mum will be played by a different sucker today', thanks very much.

Before this chaotic version of my life, I was a travel writer, more Phuket and Nairobi than Fuck-it and Bath-Robey. I was getting paid to hang out in the coolest bars in Koh Samui and watch the Northern Lights display in Tromsø. I don't want to say I was cool because that seems like a saddo thing to say but – I was. The coolest. And, whilst it wasn't the original plan at all, I learned how to do it all by myself. But what I've learned in this new version of me is that the Anthropology and Geography students I used to hang around with were missing out. If they thought that wearing yellow on Monday to pay homage to the king like they do in Thailand or stories about Norse Trolls were fascinating, they should come watch Lorna peddle terrible cakes at the school gates or Gemma 'work the crowd' at a PTFA meeting. They would find this display of social fuckwittery utterly enthralling. I, on the other hand, do not.

The most interesting thing that's happened in Upper Huxley lately is the arrival of a new family who moved to the village in the *middle of term* (cue not-so-hushed whispers and the revving of gossip engines). As if that wasn't enough, the Mum, Rowena, with her long, naturally curly hair, chocolate-brown eyes, and wide engaging smile, is supermodel beautiful, but naturally, almost like it's by accident – the type of beauty that is infuriating to those who feel the need to work so hard at it.

Anyway, this is my life now and I do love Upper Huxley as a settled adult, even if it feels a little pedestrian sometimes. My days are driven by the rhythm of kids, work, eat, sleep, repeat.

Over the course of the evening, the children both get bathed and bedded (this happens every evening but still never seems a sure thing). Norman gets walked (luckily, as a farm lab, he's not bothered by the fireworks, even if they are out of regulated hours!) and he and I snuggle on the sofa in front of the wood burner whilst I read the latest Kate Morton and Tom watches an old *Dad's Army* rerun.

Tom's work mobile begins to vibrate and his obnoxious ringtone cuts through the quiet. Just another 'day at the office' for him – and my night, by association. As a policeman's wife, I'm used to the constant interruption and him always getting pulled away, but it's still annoying. He speaks to whoever is on the other end with a serious, clipped tone, and one-word answers that make me look up from my book. Finally, an 'I'll be right there. ETA 20 minutes max.' and rings off. Something is wrong.

'What is it?' I can see the concern on his face.

'It's Gemma Hatherley … she's dead.

Chapter 2

@gemma_cotswolds_mum Morning friends! Getting up in the morning ~~is only slightly less hellish~~ has just become so much easier since I started juicing with my @juicemaster. Even Charlie absolutely loves ~~playing with all the freaking buttons until it spits out spinach juice all over my floors~~ it. #ad #healthylifestyle #juicingislife #healthybodyhealthymind

Rowena

Wednesday

It's only 8.26am, but, as I am leaving the house for the school run, I can already see fifteen WhatsApp messages and several notifications from Instagram. Common theme: 'Isn't Upper Huxley the village where you moved to?'

I'm sure it's Karma, catching up with me after I endlessly repeated to our London friends my rehearsed 'We want to give our children a wholesome childhood like the one we both had. Free from crime and traffic. In a place with a nice community, in the country.'

Shut up, Rowena. I cringe as the memory of these conversations. New repetitive intrusive thought unlocked. The intent remains partially true, of course. But surely, it was like telling our friends that they were not making the right big choices for the sake of their children.

Truth is, I haven't had to wait for my friends' messages to hear the tragic news. I was up at 3am with a whingey Eloise and during my night-time scrolling as I fed her back to sleep, my Instagram stories were full of people reporting it.

It seems like Instagram was quick to take down any traces of the Live feed in which @gemma_cotswolds_mum was killed during an attack by an intruder. As a result, I, thankfully, didn't see the actual footage but the whole internet was ablaze with talks about the tragedy and there was no going back to sleep for me. Thoughts of a murder on our doorstep were enough to keep me wide awake despite my exhaustion, along with the memories of the handful of interactions I'd had with Gemma at school. The first time I spotted her on the playground, my initial reaction was to think, for a second, that we were acquainted in real life. But even if she hadn't been so familiar to me, I couldn't have missed her. She had a glossy shine to her and simply stood out on the playground. Everything about her was "very'. Very tall, very blond, very stylish, very expensive, very slim. And very popular. The few times we spoke she was never alone, always with an entourage of mums. My heart sinks further, imagining their shock and sadness waking up to the news this morning.

As I push the pram down the (totally charming on a non-traumatic day) wooded lane to school, my phone pings with an email from the school Headteacher. Mrs Mearle is informing us of the tragic news, requesting privacy for the grieving family, and letting us know that teachers will deliver age-appropriate communication to the different classes. And there I was fretting about our London friends' reactions to this sad business, when, all along, I should have worried about how Alfie is going to feel hearing the news. At the age of 5, my little boy has luckily never had to face the scary subject of death, and I suddenly feel the crushing weight of mum guilt for my terrible parenting skills. I know I am thoroughly unprepared to answer the questions he will have tonight. I will need to turn to my go to website, gentlerparenting.co.uk, for advice before pick up; once I have rung the plumber to fix the boiler that decided to die on us overnight, that is. Short of a recommendation, I have had to pick one online. I considered for a while the one whose logo is orange, i.e. my favourite colour, but decided to go with the one called Harry Something, his first name being that of my favourite cousin, which felt like a much stronger sign.

If I was still in London, such a shocking morning would definitely call for a pumpkin spice latte on the way home as emotional reward. No such luck here, and homemade coffee will have to do.

Entering the school playground via the double gates topped by a wrought iron arch forming the words 'Infants' feels like going through a time machine, as, behind the 19th century Cotswold stone facade, Upper Huxley Community Primary School boasts all the latest sport equipment, a little wooded area, a kitchen garden, and a modern glass extension. On Alfie's first day the PTFA 'welcoming party', with the late Gemma at its helm, were very keen to tell me about how their multiple fundraising initiatives had enabled the school to finance not only the purchase of 20 new iPads but also the creation of the little Forest School area. I couldn't help wondering why a village school would need to create a mini forest on their grounds, when there is an actual one only about 300 metres away, but I kept my reservations to myself.

Today, the playground is buzzing with parents (96% mums, 3% grandparents, 1% dads) huddled together in hushed solemn chatter.

My mission this morning is simple: drop Alfie while avoiding eye-contact with anyone. I'm desperate to run home with the increasingly upset Eloise, but also, deep down, I'm not sure how to behave. As a newcomer who barely knew Gemma in real life, I would hate to impose on anyone's grief or be seen as a voyeur or gossip.

I successfully slalom around mum groups, inadvertently catching some 'How awful', 'I cannot believe we won't see Gemma again', 'The poor kid', 'Live on Instagram"...

As I think I've got away with it and turn into the little lane leading back to our house, I jump out of my skin as the pram collides with somebody's legging-clad legs. The explosive cocktail of sleep deprivation, a distraught baby, and the news of a possible murderer on the loose has completely shredded my nerves and I let out an embarrassing shriek.

I vaguely recognise the petite blonde woman as a mum from school, but I cannot remember if our kids are in the same year.

'I'm so sorry,' we both blurt out, but I keep moving as fast as I can towards my front door as, by that point, Eloise is hysterical and probably needs a top up of Calpol.

Getting her out of the pram in the hallway, my heart sinks as I feel the dampness on her back. She is covered in yellow poo all the way to her shoulders. Her winter suit is ruined, and I want to cry too. But I can't, can I? I am the responsible adult and the only one in this house who can deal with it.

Just as I start undressing her in the bath (experience tells me not to attempt cleaning her or her clothes anywhere that is not tiled), my phone rings. It is James 'checking in for the morning!' in what is, at this very moment, a supremely irritating cheery voice. I put him on speaker as I tend to a furious (and probably very cold) Eloise with a whole stack of wipes since a warm bath is out of the question.

'How are you? School run, OK? Did they both sleep well?' he asks in an absent-minded voice, a sure sign he is already at work and going through his emails.

'Crap. Crap. And crap,' is my answer to all three questions. When I have calmed down, I will regret my snappiness and the swearing within Eloise's earshot. But it is the truth. He's caught me at a bad time, and I need to vent.

I unload about the broken boiler and Eloise's teething. I can hear he has stopped checking his emails and I now have his full attention and sympathy. As much as I feel like moaning, I know he is incredibly supportive. After all, I had to sell him this idea of relocating to the country, assuring him I would be fine on my own for three days (and two nights!) a week while he works in London. When Eloise came along, everything changed, and we both knew we needed a fresh start elsewhere.

He abruptly changes the subject from the exploding poo; his tone changed to grave. 'What's this about a murder in the village? It's all over the national news this morning.'

'Yes, one of the school mums was killed live on Instagram. Terrible. I mentioned her to you, she is … was huge on Instagram in the Motherhood community. Proper influencer.' I have now used up half of the wipe packet and still the cleaning operation is ongoing.

'Wow, so sad. So, she's got children at the school?'

'Yes, a boy, in year 3, I think. Poor child. Dreadful. I can't believe it.' My voice wavers as I mention the little boy. 'I only met her a couple of times on the playground, but I knew her from Instagram. It feels so surreal.'

'That's awful. Poor kid. Do they know what happened then?'

'An intruder, burglar or something.' I sound a lot more detached and unconcerned than I really feel.

'Scary, really.' He pauses. 'So much for quiet country life ...' His tone is back to light.

'James, it's not funny. Someone's died.' I chastised him, still feeling the guilt of harbouring these very thoughts only an hour earlier.

He apologises earnestly as the doorbell rings downstairs. Just before hanging up, I can hear him say something about properly locking the doors and windows tonight. As if I needed telling! All I can do is fasten Eloise's nappy, finally clean and dry, run downstairs, and open the door to the school mum I crashed into earlier.

'Hi, sorry to bother you,' she looks at Eloise's half naked state and my cheeks flush instantly. 'You dropped this when we bumped ...' Just then, we are interrupted by an ominously loud crash coming from upstairs.

Chapter 3

@gemma_cotswolds_mum Morning Friends! Watching Charlie flexing his creativity with @lego is one of the most rewarding parts of being a mother ~~except when you step on the little fuckers~~. I can easily imagine him becoming an architect or an engineer. Being an only child can be tricky but with Lego, I know that he will keep himself entertained for ages. #ad #lego #kidimagination #mumsofuk #motherhood #honestmum #youdoyou ~~#everyboxshouldcomewithshoes~~

Mary

Wednesday

Rowena is the embodiment of stress and anxiety, with flushed cheeks, messy top knot, (still accidentally beautiful) and worried, desperate eyes. Afraid or unable to speak (not sure which) she points an instruction for me to enter, acknowledging the comforter I found dropped in the lane, launches the baby at me and makes a mad dash upstairs to see what's happened. Looks like my half-finished article 'Cosy Autumn walks at Hidcote' for Wonderlust will have to wait a wee bit longer.

I'm aware that Rowena might think it odd that despite the fact we have never had a proper conversation, I know which house is hers. But if she is going to live in Upper Huxley, she might as well get used to it.

I choose one of the many 'in case' muslins (omnipresent in the modern baby's home) and wonder if I should follow Rowena upstairs but decide against it – it feels too personal. I figure she will call down if she needs a hand. Instead, I carry the baby to the 'lived in' sofa in the front room so that I can have a cuddle and a chat with her. She has a sweet disposition but is grumpy to say the least – my guess would be teething judging from the drool. I miss the baby phase of my two – they really do grow up so fast – but I definitely don't miss that shit.

In the brief time that Rowena is upstairs, I catch myself thinking again of Gemma. Tom didn't come home, and I didn't sleep a wink after the news. It all feels so surreal. The thoughts going through my mind last night reappear. What about Charlie? Was he there? Oh God, I hope not! If not, who told him? And how? How do you tell a 7-year-old that his mum has died?

I'm not going to be one of those people that pretends to like someone after they've died. Obviously, I don't want to think ill of the dead, but neither will I pretend that Gemma was a humble humanitarian. She was not an easy person to like – at least not for me. I just decided many years ago that she wasn't my type of people and I gave her a wide berth (well, as wide as you can in a tiny village like ours). In any case, I can't wait for Tom to get home so that I can find out what happened. I was even careful not to linger on the playground in case anyone thought I had info, which I don't.

Upper Huxley is a fabulous village, but it doesn't escape the stereotype of being a hot bed for gossip. When Rowena and her family arrived, amidst the usual bitchy whisperings by the school gates, you could hear the 'What kind of mother moves their child in October?' 'Where on Earth did they come from and why come here?' and 'Where is the dad?'. But I could see through their petty comments. Lorna was desperate for someone to share the cake sale duties with on the last Friday of every term. Vicky was on the prowl to find out if there was a rogue dad going spare and Louise was only trying to lose her newbie status after six years in the village.

And *Queen Bee* of them all, Gemma Hatherley, couldn't wait to be top billing of the Welcoming Committee. 'Oh Rowena, we are so happy that you and James have decided to call Upper Huxley home! I'm sure that Alfie will be so happy here at UHCP. I know that we are going to be best of friends.' Etc., etc., ad nauseum.

The thing is, Rowena is the most beautiful person I'd seen in real life but with kind eyes and an intelligent glint that Gemma was missing. Gemma was driven and savvy, but I wouldn't have accused her of being particularly intelligent. She perceived Rowena as a threat to her position on the throne and was keen to assert her dominance over the potential usurper with everything short of a quick piss around the perimeter.

As if on cue, Rowena reappears looking terribly frazzled, holding an adorable yellow onesie for the baby. "If only James had used the skills and time he dedicates to building those Star Wars Legos on building the Ikea shelves that hold them.'

Ugh. Poor girl. I try to take her mind off the clear-up she'll face later. 'Never mind, these things, erm, happen?' We have a bit of an 'FML' laugh, she formally introduces me to Eloise, and then is kind enough to offer coffee.

I have one rule: Never, ever, turn down coffee. I also wonder if Rowena might like some grown-up conversation. I've never seen her husband at collection and drop off. Does he travel for work? New village + small children + partner "in absentia" can't be easy for anyone. As I follow her to the back of the house and a beautiful open plan kitchen, I hear myself saying 'So ... how are you settling in?'

She turns towards the serious task of working her fancy Italian coffee machine. Is she a secret barista? She and I are going to get along great! Besides, the distraction is welcome as we seem to have made a silent pact to avoid talking about Gemma's death – clearly the elephant in the room. Somehow convention dictates that you can't talk about someone being killed in your first proper conversation with a new neighbour, at least not straight away.

'The village is beautiful. We're really enjoying the space and the fresh air. It's nice to be able to take Eloise for a long walk in the pram whilst Alfie is at school. I'm having to get used to the quiet of the countryside at night again. It's so easy to forget quite how loud total silence can be.'

She opens the cupboard to grab the coffee and I'm struck by the extensive range of vitamins and supplements. The interior is like a mini-Holland & Barrett! Soon she is expertly grinding the beans, twirling this knob and that, tamping the grinds. It's like magic! She seems so precise, so sophisticated. What must she think of our old-fashioned village? Or me? I mean, I'm still wearing my beanie to hide my hair that is massively overdue a washing day.

I can't stop myself trying to win her over. 'Ha! Well, wait until Bonfire Night – the village has a Straw Man parade. It's great fun and all *fifty* of us are out at the same time! It's utter madness!' I say with prevalent sarcasm, secretly hoping that she will think it's as cool as I do. 'And how about the children – are they able to sleep in the deafening silence?'

She gives me a look dripping with forced positivity. 'Not too bad.'

(I'm not buying it.)

'The last few days have been a bit of a challenge.'

(Mum speak for *'fucking shit.'*)

'James is away during the week and Eloise is teething, so sleep is elusive.' (*I really need a break!*)

And then it becomes blindingly clear, coffee is more than a caffeine hit for this ally in the trench; it's a life-sustaining prop and

I like her a little bit more for it. Even when she is obviously feeling so terrible and desperate, I feel a spark of common ground that I haven't felt in a while, and it feels great. Yep, we're going to be best friends. I can tell.

Chapter 4

@gemma_cotswolds_mum Morning friends! As you guys know, I've stopped drinking coffee and tea. And it's ~~been absolutely killing me~~ made the world of difference to my anxiety. I ~~cannot get used to the taste of matcha~~ am obsessed with my new matcha tea routine in my gorgeous @hipinteriors cup.
Have a good day! #healthymum #honestmum #healthybodyhealthymind #ad

Rowena

Wednesday

Mary and I settle into the living room holding our coffees. I still feel all over the place, but Mary's easy-going attitude and dry humour are starting to chip away at my nerves, and I can feel my shoulders dropping a few centimetres below my ears.

Thanks to our knackered boiler, there is an undeniable chill in the house and Mary shows no sign of wanting to remove her pretty Fair Isle woollen hat and actually pulls it down further her blonde shoulder length hair as she settles herself into the navy velvet sofa, holding Eloise on her lap. I apologise for the temperature. Our 16th century house, although recently renovated and now relatively well insulated, still doesn't feel quite as warm as our old 1980s flat. No heating certainly doesn't help.

Thank goodness for the wood burner. Still an exciting novelty for me, I am keen to make a good impression and feel the pressure to get the fire going. Once I've explained the broken central heating, adding that I got the chimneys swept yesterday is my way of saying 'Look, I am an adult and I have (some of) my shit together' to make up for dropping my baby's favourite comforter, handing my half-naked baby to a stranger, and having a husband who can't build Ikea shelves.

When the fire is blazing and radiating its lovely heat around the room, I am as proud as if I'd swept the flue or cut the logs myself.

36 years old and still worrying about what people think of me. And why do I still feel like I am playing at being an adult? If having two kids, a husband, a mortgage and three published books is not enough to make me feel like a responsible adult, I'm not sure what will.

'This is a lovely room. I have to admit I have always loved your house, but I hadn't stepped inside since I was a kid.' Mary tells me as she looks around the large and yet cosy room.

I'm not a huge fan of the pale-yellow walls we inherited but I don't feel brave enough to try the moody dark hues I admire so much on Pinterest.

'Oh, so you have lived in Huxley for a long time then?'

'Yes, all my life, really. I left for uni and lived away a few years after that but moved back fairly young for family reasons.' She twists her mouth, as if embarrassed.

'It is a beautiful place. We are so pleased to be back living in the countryside after fifteen years in London. I grew up in Wiltshire and James in Devon. Spending the odd weekends and holidays at the grandparents wasn't enough fresh air and outdoor activity for us. And when Eloise came along, we couldn't stay in our cramped flat in East London. So, when James' company introduced a remote working policy, it felt serendipitous.' By now, the official version of the reasons behind our move comes out more naturally, and I have presented it to so many people that I can almost believe it is the only factor that motivated our new life here.

Mary tells me more about the village and insists we will feel welcome if we attend the weekend bonfire celebrations. I feel myself relax further with the warmth of the coffee, the room, and Mary herself. She is lovely but not pushy like some of the school mums that pressed themselves on me when we arrived. It would be nice to have a friend here, and an adult to talk to on the days James is in London.

***

'Shhhh, don't wake Mummy up, Sweetie,' I suddenly hear Mary whisper to Eloise as my eyes jolt open.

'Oh bugg ... Did I doze off? I'm so sorry! How long was I asleep for?' I can feel my face turn beetroot-red in mortification. So much for making a good impression! I'm so tired from being awake for most of last night, restless after hearing of Gemma's shocking death, but I don't dare admitting it to Mary as I hardly know the poor woman.

'You barely slept for two minutes. Don't worry. I only had time to play a bit with Eloise and send my editor to voicemail.' She smiles kindly at me.

My instincts badly want me to grab Eloise, squeeze her tight, and apologise to her for being such a terrible mother today. How can I fall asleep when a relative stranger is holding my child? But I stop myself for fear of looking totally neurotic and change the subject instead.

'Editor? Do you write too? What do you write?' I discreetly check my face with my hand for traces of drool.

'Mostly travel, for a magazine. But it tends to be pretty local nowadays as jetting off to Thailand is no longer practical.' Mary chuckles and then remembers my words. 'Do you mean you're a writer too? A journalist, maybe?'

'Children's books. I trained in marketing, but that wasn't for me, really. So, I moved onto Children's Literature when I became an aunt to my brother's daughter.'

'Would I know your books?' Mary asks eagerly.

'Maybe. My first book did quite well. 'Lily and the Peapod'?' I venture self-consciously.

'Nooo! My Charlotte loves that book! I can't believe it!' She claps her hands once and looks genuinely impressed.

'Oh, that's nice. I'm glad she likes it.' Three books in and I'm still terrible at accepting praise for my work. I awkwardly change the subject. 'Shame that neither of us writes crime novels, hey? We would have the perfect premise with what happened last night. Did you know Gemma well?' Eurgh, well done, now she's going to think I'm a gossip.

'Kind of. Her son joined the school a year after Charlotte did. Mostly saw her at PTFA events. She was VERY involved. I try to mostly stay away from it all. Who's got the time? But I'm shocked and devastated for her boy, Charlie. And her husband, of course.' She adds in suddenly, as if she has just remembered to say the right thing.

'So tragic. Heard about it all last night on Instagram. Of course, I recognised her straight away on Alfie's first day.'

'What do you mean, you 'recognised' her? Had you met Gemma before?' Mary's eyebrows frown in confusion.

'Oh no, I mean from her Instagram account, you know.' I clarify.

'Oh, OK. Never really been on Instagram or Twitter. Facebook is as far as it gets for me and even that, I deleted two years ago. Was wasting way too much time on it!'

'Really? So, you mean you didn't know that Gemma Hatherley was huge on Instagram? @gemma_cotswolds_mum? Proper influencer.' I tell Mary, who looks confused and astounded.

'I knew she was on there, but I thought it was just a silly narcissistic hobby of hers. I didn't know she was so big that she could be recognised by actual strangers! I vaguely know you can somehow make a living on there. But I'm very unsure how, to be honest. And Gemma was doing that?'

'She was. From what I read, she was doing a Live Q&A on Instagram with her followers when it happened. I don't believe the intruder was caught on camera but people watching could hear it all happening in the background. They were the ones who called 999.'

'Wow. How awful. I guess it means she was home alone then. I don't want to think what might have happened if Charlie had been around.' Mary shudders at the thought.

'Indeed.' I get distracted for a second, as my watch buzzes with a message. 'Sorry, that's James, my husband. Says he is coming home tonight as he is too worried about us being on our own. Do you think we should worry? I'm sure there were tons of burglaries within a smaller radius when we lived in East London, but we just didn't know about it!' I try to play it cool, but I can hear my voice going all high-pitched, more hysterical than philosophical. I hate myself for feeling relieved that James will be with us tonight. I take pride in being independent and, as proven recently, I do not need my husband at all times.

'My husband Tom is a Police Officer in Stroud. So, I'm afraid I hear all sorts of horror stories, more than people would imagine in quaint Gloucestershire. But having said that, we don't live in fear and mostly forget to lock our doors, at least during the day. And this is definitely the most dramatic thing that's ever happened in Upper Huxley. Generally, pretty boring, I'm afraid.' She reassures me. 'I'm sure they are trying to assess if it was a targeted attack or a burglary gone wrong. I mean, she lived in a stunning big house ...' She stops as she looks around at my stunning biggish house. 'I mean, like expensive looking and big showy Architect-type pile ... I'm sure you will be fine.' She backtracks awkwardly.

'It's fine, don't worry.' More near-hysterical laughs. 'I don't have much time to worry about this anyway.' *But I will find some, no doubt.* 'And James will be home tonight until at least Monday. I'm sure it will all be clearer by then.' I try to sound carefree, but it's been an awful long time since I have felt that way, so long that I don't remember what it feels like to walk around without heaviness on my shoulders and in my gut.

Chapter 5

@gemma_cotswolds_mum Morning friends! Trying to get work done when Charlie is around is always a challenge. I thought I'd share a little tip that I use when I just need him to entertain himself: ~~Screens! All of them!~~ I go to @twinklresources and download some spelling or maths activities sheets and we play 'school'. He loves it ~~for 5 minutes~~ and I feel great knowing that he isn't looking at a screen and that he's supplementing his school learning whilst I'm getting work done. It's easy to find age-appropriate learning tools and sometimes he even takes them to school to show his teachers.
#ad #homelearning #schoolage #twinkl #twinklresources #ad #twinklparents #lifehack #parenthack #workingmum #honestmum

Mary

Thursday

Tom comes home at 3am and I'm at my desk in the company of empty mugs, wrappers, and scribbled notes. With the time spent at Rowena's and then the usual school run and parenting responsibilities, I didn't get to start my 'day job' until well into the evening. I'm dying to ask Tom what happened to Gemma (the only time he's been able to come home since the murder was for a few hours sleep and a quick shower, and the children were around) but first, I have to finish this article extolling the virtues of Hidcote Manor Gardens when it's flush with its Autumn colours.

Tom starts the lock up routine downstairs whilst I e-mail the final copy to Rosie, my Editor – oh, how that 'swoosh' can be such a relief sometimes – and we both head upstairs. Whilst we are brushing our teeth, I wait silently, but not so patiently, for Tom to tell me the details I'm so desperate to hear. He rolls his eyes at me, knowingly, and then delivers his information quickly and without emotion, in his professional capacity.

'She was dead when the first responders arrived. It was blunt force trauma to her skull – probably from hitting her kitchen island. No, Matthew and Charlie were not at home. Yes, they have been told.' He rattles off, answering questions I haven't been allowed to ask. 'Yes, it does look intentional. No, we don't have any strong leads, at the moment. And No.' he pauses here to drive home the seriousness. 'I really should not be telling you any of this.' It's also his way of confirming that information sharing time is over.

To lighten the tone, I tell Tom about my rather unconventional coffee date with Rowena. But instead, a look of concern gathers on his face.

'Isn't she married to James Boat?' he says, his brow creasing.

'Ermm ... I guess so? She said her husband's name is James but, apart from the fact that he works away in London during the week and is from somewhere in the South West, I don't know anything about him. Should I? Is he famous, too?' I'm brushing my teeth whilst Tom washes his face.

'What do you mean 'too?'' Tom asked with a wrinkled left eye (which mostly appears when he thinks I'm talking shite).

'Rowena's a children's book writer! She wrote 'Lily and the Peapod'. It's one of Charlotte's favourites.' I spit and rinse whilst Tom loads his toothbrush.

I have the sudden realisation that we are talking in two completely different planes and decide that he might actually have something rather interesting to say.

'What do you know about James?' I ask, pretending that I'm not asking about what he just told me not to ask about.

'Listen May,' using my nickname to get my attention and showing his serious face again, despite the toothpaste all around his mouth. 'The Boss has assigned me as lead on the Gemma Hatherley case. He was apologetic but he said that since DI Jackson moved to the Cheltenham team, I'm the most experienced member of MIT and he needs me.' He wasn't intending to tell me this earlier, I guess.

My eyes widen – I have quite a mix of emotions. Tom has been a Police Officer for years and getting to the rank of Detective Inspector had been quite a hard slog. He'd been assigned to the Major Incident Team only five years earlier and had been working so hard since. I am so proud that Tom is finally getting the recognition that he deserves, of course, but I am also worried. Investigating serious crime in your own village is pretty strongly against the police code and for good reason: interviewing your local garage owner on money laundering charges can be slightly awkward when you had your MOT done there the previous month. And this is a potential murder – on our doorstep! Selfishly, it also means I'm going to be lumped with a lot more single parenting in the near future.

'Of course, we are exploring the more obvious options.'

(I guess he means Matthew but he's never going say that to me.)

'but I need you to know that James Boat is currently a POI in the case. He works for West End PR which is the same firm that Gemma Hatherley was working with. Add that Gemma was killed very soon after James arrived and you have a lead. Unfortunately, I've been assigned to check his alibi.' He spits his toothpaste into the sink and heads back into the bedroom.

I am incredulous. 'Are you *shitting* me?' I ask as I follow him.

Honestly! I've managed to befriend (I think?) a normal, slightly highly strung(?), funny, famous, (OK, that's a stretch) fellow mum that makes amazing coffee, and within hours, her husband is a POI for murder? Not cool. Think, Mary!

I laugh aloud. Affected but effective. 'But Tom! That's ridiculous!'

The other half of my brain is thinking 'What if I had coffee in the house of a murderer? Or what if Rowena was the murderer?' She did seem a bit nervous, maybe unsure about something? That's my imagination, right? Maybe. It's annoying but it pays the bills.

'May, you know the score: No chatting, no running to Rowena and tipping her off. Until we can confirm otherwise, we have to treat this as a murder investigation. Like you, I think it's probably a strange coincidence but until we can chat with him ...' he says as we slide into our respective sides of the bed.

Finally, I see my chance to nip this in the bud.

'Well, Rowena mentioned that he was coming home last night; earlier than planned. He's worried about her being home on her own with a killer on the loose. Surely this proves that he's not the killer and that he would have been in London on the night of the incident. So has an alibi.'

'Possibly,' Tom says with his impossibly sexy but ever so slightly patronising smile. He always gets that look when he thinks that I'm trying to do his job for him. 'But it doesn't mean that he's not involved.'

***

I lay awake for ages after Tom's comment with my mind racing. Having Tom so close to the case could help. We rarely ever talk about his work. The reality of being an actual police officer is that 85% of what you have to deal with is thoroughly uninteresting. 5% is utterly hilarious and Tom usually remembers these stories when we are a couple of pints down. The balance 10% is categorically unpleasant and has no place being discussed in one's own home.

It's easier for him to leave it at work, as much as he can, of course, and I'm only too happy to oblige. But this is different.

Chapter 6

@gemma_cotswolds_mum Evening, Friends! We had a lovely family day at @nationaltrust. I always get ~~grief~~ asked about whether Charlie is suffering from being an only child. And I can honestly say ~~Mind your own fucking business~~ my boy is perfectly happy. He doesn't know any different and has loads of friends and cousins he can play and learn how to share with. And he loves spending time with Mummy and Daddy! Hope you all had a lovely weekend #honestmum #familydayout ~~#fuckofftrolls~~ #sponsoredpost

Rowena

Thursday

For flip's sake! Here we go again.

Every evening, I go to bed with the firm resolution to be calmer and to moan less about general parenting stuff the next day. Positive parenting, you know. New dawn, new day, and all that. And every morning, I get woken up by Alfie's whingey calls of 'Mummyyyy, Mummyyyy …' from his bedroom and I'm overwhelmed all over again.

I know, from magazines, parenting books, online forums, Instagram, etc, the right thing to do would be to set my alarm and get up before him, so I can start the day on a better footing. The problem is that he wakes at 6.11am on the dot every day and I cannot face waking up earlier than that, especially when I still have to get up at night for Eloise. I sincerely admire and envy those people who can be up at 5.30am, enjoy their coffee in peace, and have a stew on the hob, and all the laundry folded by the time the kids wake up. I am simply not a morning person, and I feel terrible about it.

So here we are again, rushing around to get ready for school. I know what you are thinking. *Hang on a second, she's been up since 6.11am, that's over two hours to get ready for school!* Well, if you're wondering that, you either never had school age kids, or you don't remember. Or you're Mary Poppins. And no matter how hard I try, I most definitely am not.

But the worst thing this morning is that James came home last night. I mean, of course, I'm happy he's home (such a relief with a killer at large), the kids gave him loads of cuddles in bed, and he did sort out Alfie's breakfast. However, by the time we need to get ready to leave (always the most challenging part of the morning routine), he is already on, a call in his study. This has two major downsides for me: 1) I can't shout at Alfie to put his shoes on, even though I have already asked five times in my best firm but calm voice, and 2) I can't leave Eloise with him, so pushing a pram and dragging a scooter (of course, Alfie has to take his scooter today, because 'It's faster, Mummy') just makes the school run that much harder.

When we make it to the school playground, despite the numerous stops to kick and jump in the autumn leaves (had to carry the scooter within 100 yards of leaving the house, because 'you can't jump in leaves with a scooter, Mummy'), I am amazed to find out the bell has not rung yet. Cue that awkward lingering on the school playground as the new mum who doesn't know anyone yet. I have spotted Mary who is talking to another mum from our kids' class, Sally, I think, but I don't dare to join them. If I was paranoid, I could have sworn she did turn her back to me just as I had started smiling at her. Thankfully, my social anxiety gets some light relief in the form of the ringing bell and I can busy myself with the daily 'Goodbye Routine' with Alfie: reassuring words, zipping up of jacket, hair ruffling, kiss, good wishes for the day, wave as he walks away, wave as he gets in and final wave again through the window.

Phew, done. How did I end up being one of those mums? I worry about what this routine means. What if I didn't do the third wave? Would he have a meltdown? Does he need that routine to have a good day at school? More troubling, do I need it? Mary is not one of those mums, she has already upped and left. Shame. I enjoyed our chat yesterday; I wouldn't have minded a few friendly words with her this morning.

As I get home, I am greeted by James in the kitchen with a mug of fresh coffee for me.

'My team meeting is over, and I have five minutes until the next one. Very important one with my main client, Impeco. They're talking about taking their business elsewhere, but I've lined up a few things that should keep them interested.' He can see that I am not that interested. 'How was the school run? Did you make any friends?' He teases in a fake patronising voice.

'Ha Ha, very funny. Well, actually, this mum from Alfie's class, Mary, dropped by yesterday and we ended up having a nice chat. Could be fun for Alfie to meet friends outside of school. I know I will also have to agree to some dreaded playdates. Alfie mentioned Ben, Mary's boy, this morning, so I will suggest something for next week, maybe.' I'm rambling now and I know James has other things on his mind.

James can hear the lack of enthusiasm in my voice. 'Don't do it if you don't feel like it, Rowe. You don't have to!'

'Well, of course, I don't but I do, really. I want Alfie to have friends and to be settled at school. And Mary seems fun. So, we could both be winners there. I'm just so tired. Making social plans just seems an unnecessary ordeal.'

'Ok. It's up to you. Got to go and get my call started. Try and have a rest when Eloise goes down for her nap. I will make us some lunch later, OK?'

I know I have a good one in James. All the more for having had to do without him before. But, sometimes, I can't shake the frustration of general parenting off. I would love to have a rest and I'm grateful that he is thinking of making lunch. But I know I probably won't rest, because the plumber is coming at 10.00 to fix the boiler and I have some laundry to hang outside as the air is warm today for November.

But just as I have decided to, at least, sit down to enjoy my coffee while Eloise is quietly playing on her playmat, the doorbell rings, immediately followed by an assertive knock on the door.

'Good morning. Mrs Boat?' As I nod, the man standing on my doorstep continues. 'Detective Inspector Lamb from Stroud Police. Could I please speak to your husband?' He shows me his badge.

'James?' As if I have another husband... The shock has turned my brain to mush. 'He is home. But I'm afraid I can't really disturb him as he is in a very important work call. Would you like to come in and I can ask him how long he is going to be?' I offer anxiously.

DI Lamb follows me into the living room, where I indicate for him to sit down while I go to get James. What the heck is this all about? I'm totally baffled as to what the Police could want from James. As I make my way to the back of the house, I try to stifle runaway thoughts of miscarriages of justice and James in prison for the rest of his life.

Before I enter the study, I grab one of Alfie's latest artworks, on the back of which I scribble with a green crayon 'The police are here and they want to talk to you?!!?!?!? How long are you going to be?!!' I quietly open the door and, making sure I am out of range of his camera, show him the message. He beckons me into the room, meaning his camera is off. I can hear his client talking on the line. He looks as incredulous as I feel and quickly writes down 'About ten minutes. Can they wait?!!'

I tiptoe out of the study, my favourite room of the house; its wood panelling and floor to ceiling bookshelves covering one entire wall were the deal clincher for me. It is big enough for us both to have a desk and I'm looking forward to having some time to work on my next book project in there. That seems like such an unreachable fantasy currently, and I have to remind myself that it felt like I would never have any time to ever sit down again when Alfie was Eloise's age. But it did happen eventually when he started nursery 3 days a week. But that was when we only had one child to worry about, no new life, oh and no police officer wanting to send my husband to jail!

I return quickly to the front room as the thought hits me that I've left an unattended stranger in my house. DI Lamb is patiently waiting on the sofa where I left him. He is a good looking man; his face is broad but attractive. His greying blond hair and lines around the eyes make me think he is about the same age as me, late 30s, early 40s, maybe? Didn't Mary say her husband was a policeman? Could it be him? I realise I don't know her surname. I'm not sure what the protocol is for making casual conversation with Police officers.

'He should be done in about ten minutes. Can you wait? Can I get you a tea or coffee?'

'I will wait if that is alright with you. I'm OK for drinks. Thank you, though.' DI Lamb looks like a serious man, but his eyes are not unkind. I relax a bit.

'Can I ask why you want to talk to James? Anything I can help with?'

'Let's wait for your husband, if you don't mind, Mrs Boat.'

After what seems like an hour of silence (but is probably only two and a half minutes), I can't hold it anymore.

'Surely it is not to do with the death in the village, is it? You know we are new here. We only moved in three weeks ago and didn't really know the victim. My husband hasn't even been to school yet or met anyone other than the next-door neighbours. Oh, and he was in London on Tuesday night.' I can hear a touch of desperation in my rambling, but I can't stop myself.

'Actually Mrs Boat, I will take that glass of water, if that's OK.' DI Lamb interrupts me. I can see he is doing it to stop me talking, but I welcome the interruption and excuse myself to the kitchen. I come back with Eloise on my hip, thinking she could be a good distraction and because she is my lucky charm, ever since she was born.

He smiles at Eloise and again I wonder if he is a father himself and whether he is Mary's husband. I will have to ask her. My train of thought is thankfully interrupted by the sound of James' footsteps.

'Good morning. I'm James Boat.' It is a fact, but it sounds more like a question.

'Good morning, Mr Boat. DI Lamb from Stroud Police. I'm sorry to disturb your work but I have a few quick questions to ask you relating to an incident on Tuesday night.'

'Tuesday night?! You mean the murder?!' James is not trying to hide the surprise in his voice. My brain is running through multiple permutations of scenarios in which James could possibly have any link to what happened to Gemma on Tuesday.

DI Lamb does not acknowledge James' question. 'We understand you work for a company called West End PR based in London. How long have you been with that company?' he asks as if it is the logical follow up question.

James couldn't look more puzzled if he tried. Mirroring my state of mind, I can see the cogs working in his brain trying to work out the link. 'Four years in March. Can I ask what that has to do with the murder?'

'The victim was working with your company. She was one of your company's number one 'influencers' from what we gather.' He looks down at his notes when he says 'influencer'. It is clearly not a job title he is familiar with.

'Oh, I see. I didn't realise that. I don't deal with that side of the business. My portfolio is very much old-fashioned media as my client base targets much older age groups: pension funds, life insurances, and funeral plans. Not so much stylish young mums ... anymore.' James relaxes a little, back to his self-assured funny self.

'Do you know or work with Antonia Parlin? She was Gemma Hatherley's main contact at West End PR.'

'I've heard the name, but I believe she is relatively new to the business. She works for Mike Hornsby, Social Media Manager. That side of the business is actually in a different building on the opposite side of the street from my office.'

'So, you have never met or worked with Gemma Hatherley?' He is clearly trying to put this line of enquiry to bed. I relax a little. This is obviously a very weird coincidence.

'Not that I recall, no. And as for here, I have yet to go to school as I work in London three days a week.'

'Were you in London on Tuesday night? Just need to close all avenues ...' he explains as he spots my budding look of indignation.

'Yes, I was. I finished work around 6.30. Then went back to our friends' house who let me have their guest bedroom on the nights I'm in London. We had dinner together and watched the *Great British Bake Off*. And then, I went to sleep. Would you like our friends' contact details to check?' he offers helpfully.

'Yes, I would, please. And then I will leave you in peace.' DI Lamb promises.

James grabs his phone and writes Julia and Libby's contact details and address down on a piece of paper that he then hands to DI Lamb who is already up and ready to leave.

As he opens the front door, he bumps into a man standing in our porch, dressed in a boiler suit.

'Hey, Tom, what are you doing here?' the plumber asks, surprise quickly turning to suspicion.

'Morning Harry. I was just leaving. Have a good day, all.'

With that DI Lamb steps into the street, leaving us to deal with potential suspicious gossip. Welcome to village life! Mental note to add being questioned by the Police on your first few weeks in a new village to my increasingly long list of reasons why this move may not be the magic answer to all our problems after all.

Chapter 7

@gemma_cotswolds_mum Morning friends! I thought I'd share with you this amazing ~~but totally disgusting~~ recipe for a cleanse. What with Christmas just around the corner and the nights closing in, it's so easy to get caught up in unhealthy eating. This is your reminder to put your health first and take care of your body! #healthymum #healthygut #mumsofuk #healthylifestyle #motherhood #honestmum ~~#utterlydisgusting~~

Mary

Thursday

Text from Tom:

14:22: Spoke to James. Fine for you to see Rowena. Off to London. Home Late.

That is Tom all over. Why say five words when you can keep it to three, right? Wrong! I have so many questions. But I also have even more sympathy for Rowena than before. Even if I didn't like her (and I do), I feel like I should make a show of being her friend to the rest of the village. Surely, they will know that I wouldn't be 'allowed' to be friends with her if her husband is a suspect in a murder investigation. Clearly Tom won't be thrilled with me spending time with anyone even remotely linked to the case, but I feel responsible for protecting Rowena and James from the judgy stares at the school gates. And anyway, it will keep my mind off the anxieties of the case itself. Suddenly, I have a plan: we will all attend the Straw Man Festival together! There's nothing more public than that until Christingle and that's ages away.

I spot Rowena at collection and make a beeline. She is scanning the crowd with apprehension across her pretty features. Her posture is too tall to match her expression, and I conclude that she is doing her best to put on a brave façade. She's uncomfortable and probably trying to gauge who knows what happened this morning and who doesn't.

I make quite a show of my support for her: 'Hi Rowena! How's that sweet baby?' Etc. etc. as we walk towards the allocated standing areas. As soon as we are mostly out of earshot (there seem to be a few more dads around now that Rowena is on the scene – or is that just me? – but they are too busy trying to figure out where to stand), I say 'Tom told me he had to pop round. Sorry about that?'

I mean, I know it is ridiculous! Where to even start? How does one apologise to an acquaintance for their husband coming around to interrogate their spouse? To be honest, it is unlikely that many people will know already, but you can bet that they will before the day is out. Judging by the faces leaning closer to each other, dropped voices and glances in our direction, it will probably be much sooner than that.

'Come to mine tomorrow afternoon for coffee? Say 2ish? I can give you an idea of what to expect at the Straw Man parade. It really is quite good fun.'

She agrees. I think she can tell that I am trying to make the best of what should be an awkward conversation, and it seems that she genuinely appreciates it. What she doesn't know is that I intend on making it a 'clearing of the Boats' name' themed event.

Friday

Drop off is manic, even more than usual. Is it illegal to surgically attach a child's shoes to their feet? Most days, I genuinely feel that I could muster something resembling a defensible case for a jury of my peers. It mostly entails me saying 'But Every. Fecking. Time!' and then looking over at a solemn group of twelve mums with primary school aged children (otherwise, would they really be my peers?) muttering to themselves 'Don't I fecking know!'

Ben finally found two matching shoes (Thank feck!), and Charlotte found her water bottle six minutes after we 'absolutely, really, genuinely, I MEAN IT! MUST leave this house." How on Earth is this my life now? I used to be cool, have fun, lead an exciting life, and travel the world! Now, I just get the 'tut' face from Mrs Dogton for being late. Feck my life.

I am in the playground long enough to see Louise and Lorna sharing gossip. They make a jarring picture since Louise's flawlessly coiffed hair and tutorial perfect make-up are such a contrast to Lorna's *Earth Mother* aura. With her expertly outlined lips, Louise leans close to Lorna's multi-pierced ear, voice dripping with the poisonous excitement of one that knows she has something interesting to say:

'Martin spoke to Harry who said that Tom was just leaving the house as he arrived. It looked like it was 'official business" The air quotes are the nasty cherry on the malicious cake. I have always hated her, really, and never more than right now.

Oh. For. Fuck's. Sake. I thought that the introduction of Netflix to a village like ours would minimise this type of discussion, but then Lorna mentioned to Vicky who mentioned to Margot that Louise didn't have Netflix. Someone, please get that girl a subscription. In fact, feck it! I'll pay for it if it gives her something less toxic to do in her spare time.

At the end of the day, they are talking about my husband, as well as someone who I hope will be my friend. Apparently, I've reached my limit. I flush with a fury that I fear might actually get me in trouble and the words fly out of me, laced with venom to match hers.

'Oh Louise, don't be so dramatic. Tom was just asking James for contact details of someone else that they want to speak to. I'm sure that the Boats have no more to do with this murder than you or me.' And then I look at her with a challenge on my face. My words have made a statement, but my raised eyebrows are asking Louise if *she* has anything to do with the murder. Louise can be nasty. She was nice to Gemma's face, but I could guess what she said behind her back. You only have to think about what she says about everyone else.

Tom is going to be so bloody annoyed. This is poor behaviour. But I can't help it. Louise couldn't wait for a bit of gossip about Rowena. She is just too pretty, too nice, too kind. Anyway, I must do better.

***

2pm is here before I know it. And by that, I mean, before I have a chance to finish tidying the lounge for Rowe's visit. At least I've given the downstairs loo a quick once over in case she needs it.

I've already decided to be honest; we need to rip this plaster off. I am hoping that coffee and chocolate will soften the blow.

'Such a beautiful house you have, Mary. Have you been here long?'

'All my life, actually. It's been in my family for a long time. My brother and I grew up here and when my Mum died, Tom and I moved in here with Dad.'

'Oh, I didn't realise your dad lived here, too?'

'Oh God, no! We all decided that he needed his own space rather quickly and now he's living his best life as the most eligible bachelor in Upper Huxley's over 55s residence.'

After the niceties, I say 'Here's the thing, Rowena. The village already knows that Tom was at your house asking questions. I'm sorry but I heard it at the gates this morning and I want you to know that I'm on your side and I can help you to clear all this up.'

Her shoulders relax a full ten centimetres to have her fears recognised and voiced from a sympathetic source.

'I have a great plan. They will know soon, if not already, that Tom is the lead on this case. For that reason, there is no way I'd be able to 'fraternize' with you if there was any chance that you or James were formally involved with the investigations. So, as long as it's OK with you, I intend to make a rather big deal of us attending the Straw Man Festival together.' I proceed to explain all the things she needs to know: children wake up early, spend the morning making their Guy Fawkes effigy out of whatever clothes are going spare, add a paper bag head, and then fill the whole thing with something that will burn. Then after a traditional hog roast lunch, the completed mannequins are placed around the village hall, their makers standing proudly beside them.

'So, it's a competition?'

I'm so pleased that Rowena is actually interested! 'Of course, Rowe! This is serious!' I show mock horror at her dismissive suggestion and laugh. 'I'm kidding, but yes, the villagers go around the hall in an organised queue. The children ask, "penny for the guy?" and the villagers offer money, starting with a penny, for each of the creations.'

I explain that they choose the amount of money offered as a way of voting for who they think is best/who they think has actually made any effort whatsoever. The parade starts at 3pm at the top of Upper Huxley Lane with the top earner at the start of the parade, second earner in second position, and so on.

'So, the children keep the money?' Rowe's brow is furrowed.

'Oh no, all the money is collected for the charity that is chosen to receive the funds for that year, this year it will be Macmillan Cancer Trust.'

I find myself waxing lyrical about the end of the parade; there is a massive bonfire on the village green. The adults take turns helping to throw the Guy Fawkes effigies on the fire, eat sausages, roast marshmallows, drink cider, enjoy the revelry and feel smug for the fact that it is all in the name of *insert appropriate name here* charity.

But genuinely, it is ace. It has been my favourite village event since I was seven and my brother Christopher and I had the proud honour of coming in second position for the parade, beat by a measly £0.13 (inflation and all that), by Paul and Sarah Smart. But I think it would have been my favourite anyway. There is something quite special about the warmth of the fire on your face after a long day working hard and competing against your friends for the good of someone that you'd likely never meet. That's the magic of charity, after all, right?

And then I realise how long I've been talking. Jesus, have I put her off completely? Perhaps I should turn this into an article for Wonderlust instead of boring the tits off my friend? I round it off with a quick quantifying 'You'll enjoy it, I promise. Not least of which because Dunkerton's is sponsoring the cider tent again this year.'

'Ha! Good, I've never been much of a cider drinker before but I'm looking forward to trying the local spoils.'

'Oh, for sure, you can't live around here for too long without drinking cider. It grows on you. That's the best I can say!' I laugh.

'How about Alfie, Charlotte and Ben do a joint submission this year? What do you think? It's completely acceptable to have multi-family submissions, especially if it's your first time. I would fully expect that by this time next year, they'll be shouting obscenities about each other's creations.'

She laughs. 'Sure! That would be great but, are you sure Mary? You seem to be almost, well ... erm ...' I can tell that she is uncomfortable. 'Looking for conflict, maybe?'

'I'm really not, Rowena, I promise.' I can feel the swell of pride with a twinge of defensiveness rise in my torso. 'There are plenty of fights around here, you don't have to look for them and I'm definitely not interested in fighting them. The only thing I'm doing is treating you the way I'd like my family to be treated if I was new to Upper Huxley. To be welcomed fairly and without prejudice. If doing our Straw Man submission together helps to achieve that, all the better!' My throat is slightly tighter than it was ten minutes ago. Besides, when I think about the Hatherleys, I know I can't just sit here twiddling my thumbs.

Chapter 8

@gemma_cotswolds_mum Morning friends! As some of you know, I live in a ~~desperately tiny~~ small Cotswolds village and, call me biased but, at this time of year, it is the prettiest place on Earth. I don't want to describe too much as we like to keep them for ourselves ~~and it's all pretty boring, to be honest~~, but we have the cutest village autumnal traditions, when our community really comes into its own. #lovewhereyoulive #communityspirit #cometogetherforcharity ~~#wouldratherliveinacity~~

Rowena

Friday

Ever since I came back from Mary's, I haven't stopped thinking about her 'proposal'.

If I'm honest, I'm uncomfortable by how worked up she seems by this whole situation. My city-dweller instinct wants to ignore it all and wait until people are no longer interested. But according to Mary this is more serious than that. What is this place? I grew up in a small Wiltshire town, but I don't remember having to worry so much about small town politics and gossip! Then again, it doesn't mean my parents didn't have to. I guess it won't hurt to do what she suggested, even if her determination seems a bit excessive, almost as if she has her own agenda. I relate part of our discussion to James when he's done with his working day.

'So, I popped out to see Mary earlier. And she wants to help save your ... our reputation as we've been the talk of the town ... village since her husband came here yesterday.' I venture.

'Hmm. OK. It can't be that bad, can it? What does it matter? We know we have nothing to hide. And by now the police have probably checked my statement. So, they must have moved on to another lead, right?'

'I agree. I'm not too worried either.' Nevertheless, I will be the one doing most of the social heavy lifting in the village and would rather avoid antagonising anyone. 'But anyway, she suggested we attend the Straw Man parade together tomorrow and get Alfie and her kids to build their 'Guy' together for the parade. If anything, it should be nice.'

'What's that all about exactly?' He may have grown up on a Devon farm but, like me, has never taken part in any other Bonfire Night festivities than a firework display.

I run him through what Mary explained to me, keeping to myself my mental images of *The Wicker Man* and The Scarecrow Festival in the BBC's *This Country*! I also don't voice my anxious thoughts about the safety risks posed by the combination of cider-fuelled adults, excited children, and a bonfire. Because as much as I hope Mary's grave concerns are unnecessary, I still want us to put this to bed and start making friends in the village.

I need not worry because James is completely sold on the idea as soon as I mention the hog roast and the cider tent. And that's all the impetus he needs to get himself into his trainers and set off for a run around the village lanes. I used to enjoy running pre-kids, but I'm far too concerned about my pelvic floor now. I religiously do my exercises every time I sit down for a meal, as recommended by my GP. I haven't had any cause for concern but I'm still too scared to risk it. And now the knowledge of a murderer roaming free is even less likely to entice me back into my running gear. Will stick to YouTube Pilates for now.

I'm about to put the kids in the bath when James comes back, in time to take over the proceedings. He is flushed from the exertion, but his troubled expression makes me ask him if he is OK. He waves it off and points at Alfie, his sign for 'Not in front of the kids.' When both kids are clean and smell of organic lavender, he comes into the kitchen with Eloise. Alfie is still upstairs, and he takes the opportunity to tell me what's wrong.

'I was running down that lane just around the corner from the pub when two blokes stopped me, pretty much blocking my way. 'Are you the London guy, the one who lives at the old Wilsons' house?' He recounts as he puts on a rough, low, mildly aggressive voice. 'They wanted to know what I was doing out in the dark. And, let me tell you, I couldn't see their faces, but it didn't sound like a friendly enquiry. What is wrong with these people? It is only 6 pm, Rowe! And I wasn't exactly sneaking round back gardens!' he rattles indignantly.

'Bloody hell! Maybe Mary is right. It does sound like people have already made their mind up about us. Or at least about you.' I concede. 'Maybe the kids' Guy Fawkes effigy should wear a t-shirt reading '*James Boat is not a murderer*!" I try to joke.

But by now, I am starting to dread the Straw Man parade. Maybe my brain is not too far off with its flashbacks to *The Wicker Man*.

Saturday

Alfie and I somehow manage to get out of the house by 9am to get to Mary's for Straw Man Parade preparations. It's bad enough during the week but having to be out and about on a weekend seems like extra torture, especially as I left James in bed snuggling with Eloise. To add insult to injury, with the boiler fixed, the house is nice and toasty, while outside, we are faced with the first frost of the year. And by the time we have made it, my extremities are frozen and Alfie, who, like most 5-year-olds, has forgotten what winter is like since the last one, is grumpy as hell.

Like yesterday, I'm struck by the charm of Mary's beautiful farmhouse, typical of the Cotswolds with its honey-coloured stone walls and slates. The mullion windows on one side of the house betray its age, but it looks like it was probably thoroughly renovated in the 90s along with some outbuildings arranged around the now landscaped farmyard. On the west side of the house, I spot a wooden greenhouse, some frost-covered vegetable beds, and what looks like a chicken coop. I bet her kids eat less food that comes out of a packet. I must get started on growing vegetables or, at least, do better at cooking from scratch.

Mary's warm kitchen is a sight for sore eyes (well, at least for sore fingers). As Charlotte takes the two younger boys into one of the barns to gather the materials for the straw man, I fill Mary in on James' sinister encounter last night. I immediately regret it when I see the anger in her eyes.

'I'm so sorry, Rowena. I am really ashamed by the way people are behaving at the moment.'

'Don't be silly, Mary. It's not your fault, is it? People might be genuinely concerned. Somebody did get killed, after all. And we are new to the village, so we are going to have to win them round. I'm sure it will all die down, no pun intended, when the murderer is arrested.' I hope I sound more confident than I feel. Within days, there's been a murder, police questioning, and now hostile villagers. Not exactly the fresh start we had in mind. I move the conversation along in an attempt to push these thoughts away.

'Is your husband here? Will he join us today? Won't it be weird or inappropriate for him?' I ask as I suddenly realise what a tricky position he could be in.

'No, he is working all day. Unfortunately, he will miss today's festivities, but it is indeed for the best this year.' She reassures me. 'It will be a weird one for sure. Gemma was quite involved in all things community, really. She and Matthew, her husband, were very much what you would call the Power Couple in Upper Huxley. Never spent much time with the two of them. But her death will certainly put a damper on things.'

'I must say I am surprised today's parade is happening considering the tragedy.' I confess, in a tone I'm hoping is coming across as nonjudgemental.

'From what I could gather on the playground yesterday, the committee wanted to cancel but most people thought that Gemma would have wanted it to go on, particularly as it would be very disappointing for the children, who wait for this year-round. It would have been like cancelling Christmas for Upper Huxley. Everyone will be putting on a brave face for the sake of the children. Also heard there will be a minute of silence before the parade. I don't know about her wanting a big party only four days after her death, but she would have definitely enjoyed a minute of silence in her honour.' Mary adds somewhat wickedly.

We head to the village green together. Next to the village hall, which looks like an old Sunday school, a giant marquee has been erected under which children will make their Guy Fawkes effigies.

Later, James and Eloise join us for the mouth-watering hog roast and to put the finishing touches on what now looks decidedly more like a scarecrow than a Catholic plotter from the Jacobean era.

A few people drop by our spot and chat to Mary, but even though I'm trying to ignore it, I can tell they are here to check us out. I'm feeling self-conscious attracting so much attention but James, a true professional, is embracing the situation as a PR challenge, supported by Mary playing her part perfectly and introducing us to a few people, especially the school parents.

Most of the villagers seem unsure of what to make of the situation. Mary is Upper Huxley born and bred. She is married to Tom. Tom is a respected police officer. And here she is with a couple of strangers from the big city who got questioned by said police officer husband about a murder only two days before. You can tell they don't want to warm to us, but Mary seems to confuse them into politeness and community spirit. I even have a nice chat with one of the school mums, Lorna, about next month's Christmas bake sale. She, not so subtly, makes it clear homemade bakes are encouraged, and I gather from her naturally greying curly bob and practical well-worn Doc Martens that she doesn't quite belong to the gang of trendy mums who were orbiting Gemma.

Just as I'm starting to think Mary's strategy is paying off, I can hear a nasty haughty voice addressing Mary. 'So, where is Tom today, then? Does he know you are playing happy families with a murder suspect and his crew?'

The woman in question intentionally said it loud enough for us all to hear. I can see James' back stiffen as he continues to help Ben and Alfie with the buttons on the Guy's jacket.

'Hi Louise, Tom is at work. And yes, he knows I'm here with Rowena and James. As I explained yesterday, James was never a suspect. Can I introduce you?' Mary's voice is overly sweet, and she is keeping perfectly calm.

James and I both come over to be introduced. Everything about Louise is loud and shouting 'look at me! I'm here!': a bright pink puffa jacket, the highest pouf hairstyle I have seen since 2006, and long sharp red nails. Even though she has totally provoked the situation, she hesitates and looks around her, clearly reluctant to be seen shaking our hands. Her claws digging in my palm leave me in no doubt she does not want to be friends.

'Yes, most unfortunate to be having the local DI visit us on our third week in the village, isn't it?' James jokes earnestly. 'I work in PR, and I would definitely not recommend it for perfect village integration.'

Louise seems surprised by this, but her smile doesn't quite reach her eyes. The man standing next to her, however, seems to find James' comeback hilarious. He introduces himself as Martin, Louise's husband, and starts chatting to James. Louise excuses herself by pretending to wave at somebody on the other side of the marquee.

I turn back to Mary, sotto voce. 'Wow, that was nasty. Who is she? Has she got kids in Huxley school?'

'Yes, her youngest is in Year 3 at Upper Huxley Community Primary and her eldest daughter has now gone to secondary school. She was part of Gemma's gang.' Mary rolls her eyes in case the encounter has left me thinking Louise was one of her best friends.

'I thought that kind of open nastiness only existed on social media nowadays. I bet Gemma didn't find it too difficult to handle the situation when she got trolled on Instagram if she was used to dealing with people like that in real life!'

'Trolled? What's that?' asks Mary, startled.

'Cyber bullies? They are rife on Instagram and Twitter. If I remember correctly, Gemma was at the receiving end of some trolling a few months ago. I can't quite remember what started it, but it escalated very quickly, and the troll ended up being attacked by Gemma's hardcore followers. Pretty horrible behaviour.'

'That's horrible! Why bother?' exclaims Mary.

'Yes, bullies can be relentless behind the anonymity of their phone screen. There was even an article on Grazia about the whole debacle.'

'Really? Do you think you could find it? Very intrigued.' she admits.

'I'm sure I can do some digging. Unfortunately, as you would have gathered by now, I waste way too much time on social media!' I hide my face behind my woolen mittens.

'Better you than me! I don't even have a SnapTok account!'

I burst out laughing. Mary takes a second to catch up with me, making me wonder just how clueless she is.

Chapter 9

@gemma_cotswolds_mum Evening friends! Autumn is in the air! Here are 5 simple Autumn outfits that will keep you warm and cute throughout the cooler weather. It doesn't matter if you are going apple-bobbing, chestnut collecting, ~~cleaning the f-ing house for the 10th time today~~ or just sitting around the fire with friends and an herbal tea, these ensembles will keep you 'in the moment.' #ad #Autumnfashion #mumsofuk #healthylifestyle #motherhood #honestmum

Mary

Saturday

"Eco-Mum faces barrage of abuse from revenge trolls."

Rowena has sent me the Grazia article that she mentioned. *"Mumfluencer* @gemma_cotswolds_mum *blasted for supporting fast fashion but supporters hit back."*

Gemma was part of a campaign for a fast fashion brand which prompted taunts from an eco influencer, @simple_ecolife, who highlighted how damaging it was to the environment. It went on for nearly a week, rallying other like-minded people by posting stories on her account. In return Gemma's cult followers decided to gang up on @simple_ecolife, reposting anything from her account that was not 'eco-friendly': her holidays, what her kids were wearing, comments she had posted years before, etc. It all seemed quite organised and some of the defenders were truly horrible. Luckily for her, @simple_ecolife had never posted anything that could identify her, or even pictures where she or her family could be recognised. After weeks of abuse, she went private, or she closed her account and disappeared completely off Instagram.

I'm not even 40 yet but I have to admit that most of what Rowena was saying about trolling and cyber-bullying had passed me by before now I also made a mental note to google 'fast fashion'. But this made for upsetting reading. For whatever you believe in – eco-living, breastfeeding, spending money, saving money, dating, travelling, staying at home – there is someone who thinks that you are an evil bitch (or bastard) for it. I mean, seriously? At least with village nastiness it's overt, not anonymous, and it usually doesn't take very long to decide whose opinion is worth worrying about.

Tom has the day off and after a well-deserved lie-in reading the article on my iPad, I make us all pancakes and bacon. Afterwards, Tom and I sit at the table in front of the warm Aga, and I catch him up on the events of the previous day.

'We had such a wonderful time. Matthew and Charlie put a beautiful wreath of white roses on the village hall door and Matthew said thank you to everyone for their kind thoughts and messages. He reminded everyone that Gemma loved nothing more than a party, which got a few laughs, and that the best way to honour her was to have the best Straw Man Festival yet. It was … hard.' I looked down at my toes. I needed half a beat to myself. 'But then Alfie and Ben were playing so nicely, and Charlotte was having a great time bossing them both around. They did apple bobbing, roasted marshmallows, and their Guy came in 16th place, and they were all chuffed to bits!'

'Seriously?'

'Yes, Tom. You remember what it's like when you are young and you can get caught up in it all; besides, it was all new for the Boats, and it was infectious for Charlotte and Ben.'

'What did Rowe and James think?'

'Loved it! As much as the children, I reckon.' I get a bit lost in my thoughts thinking about how it started out as the absolutely perfect, postcard autumn day. Dry, blue skies and cold, cold, cold. I had decided to wear my mum's favourite Fair Isle scarf to mark the occasion. She always loved the day almost as much as me. Pictures of previous festivals flashed through my mind like sappy sweet iPhone 'Memories', and I conjured all the people who meant so much to me growing up that I've since lost in all sorts of ways and then I just couldn't stop the tears. But then I remembered how the day ended: eating sausages and drinking cider until well past 10. How we walked home with rosy cheeks, full bellies, a whole new set of happy memories and new friends. Life is so funny like that, sometimes.

'Oh!' That reminds me. 'Lorna absolutely kicked off about the single use plastic everywhere! Started screaming about how it 'never used to be like this' and 'doesn't anyone care about our planet?' It was embarrassing.'

All of us have jumped on the eco-living bandwagon. We've all been working with the school to make sure that we eliminate as much plastic from our food as is practically (and sometimes impractically) possible. Our milk is now delivered in glass bottles (great!), our school dinners have to be single use plastic free (even better!), and same for packed lunches (*really* challenging!). I'm not saying I don't agree, I'm just saying sometimes, it's really quite difficult. I've actually moved to buying school lunches, so I don't have the headache. Is that terrible? But the children love the meals and at least I sleep well knowing that they're plastic free and, best of all, they aren't being eco-shamed at school. The bake sales are another matter. Lorna once disallowed some cookies because the plate they arrived in was covered in clingfilm. The *horror*!

'Well, you can't be surprised. She's *passionate!*' He puts that last word in air quotes and I'm pretty sure he means 'crazy'. His face changes to a more serious shape. 'May, I've been pulled off the Hatherley case.'

'What? I thought that was the whole reason that you weren't able to make it yesterday?'

'There's been a double homicide in Cheltenham and the current team is already overstretched. There were some mutterings about me being 'too close' to the Hatherley case ...'

He trails off as I nod fervent agreement.

'... And more questions about why I was working it in the first place.' The frustration is written in the creases across Tom's forehead. Yet another example of a total lack of organisation and poor leadership from the Constabulary, where Tom has to pay the price.

'So, who on Earth will be investigating now?'

'You'll never guess. I couldn't believe it.' His eyes wide, but lips pursed in anger.

'Erm ... Simon?' Simon Talbot is a lovely guy. A transplant from Wiltshire, he has a lovely family and is a hard worker. He would be a great choice and would do a great job.

'No, Simon's working with me in Cheltenham.'

'Fin?' Finella Falconer was recently promoted and is a genuinely nice woman. She is the most Scottish person you've ever met, and she can sometimes be a bit bolshy, but that's just how the police are sometimes.

'Nah. She's still stuck on the domestic violence task force.'

'I'm running out of options here, Tom.'

'C'mon, one more ...'

'Well, it couldn't possibly be 'Nick the Dick'?'

He looks at me out of the side of his eyes to tell me that I've hit the target. I can also see that he thinks that this is utterly preposterous.

'What in the actual fuck? No bloody way!' DI Nicholas 'Nick' Nash is an idiot. He is also particularly unpleasant and awkward for the sake of it. He and Tom have history. Nick is not too far away from retirement now, but Tom used to be a DC under Nick, so he knows first-hand just how utterly useless he really is. He is an arse-covering, arse-kissing lay-about, the worst combination of stupid, rude, and terrible at his job.

'It's so obvious to me that the Chief was doing everything in his power to avoid giving the case to Nick. But that's exactly where it's ended up!' He continues talking a little more loudly. 'More than that, I'm absolutely convinced that Nick's already made up his mind that Matthew did it and he's going to do whatever he can to get the case 'solved' quickly to try and make himself look good. His track record is absolutely crap and if he doesn't get a win soon, he's going back to patrolling the royal residence as a glorified security guard.'

'But there is no way that Matthew did it! You know that I know that!' I'm starting to get a bit worked up now.

'I know that, May, why do you think I was questioning some random that's only recently moved to the village? I think that they are still checking Matthew's story about playing squash, but even if he didn't have an alibi, you and I both know that it's just so unlikely. Matthew is a lovely guy.'

I cut him off. 'The best! And an amazing dad!' Big huge tears well up, my throat feels like it's on fire, and I feel like I might scream. Something very similar to rage is building in my chest. The unfairness of it combined with the sheer idiocy and incompetence of inept people in positions of power goes against everything I believe in. I manage to reduce my decibels to an appropriate speaking volume. 'What are you going to do, Tom?' The question is hot and pointed.

'What can I do, Mary? I'm off the case!'

The air has gone out of my lungs and has been replaced with hot treacle. I feel so panicked and utterly useless at the same time. At that moment, the anger I feel towards DI Nash, the situation, and the sheer helplessness of it all spills over at Tom. Why can't he do something? How is it possible to *not* do anything? I'm raging right into his eyes and then I have to look away before I say something I'll regret.

I have to get away. I pick up my coffee and head out to the greenhouse to play the conversation over again in my head whilst I'm clearing plants, a job that should have been done weeks ago. Lifting heavy pots is easy when you are this angry. I'm fuming about DI Nash (known by most as 'Nick the Dick' for good reason) and how his sub-par intelligence and general incompetence is going to mean that an innocent man – a good man – goes to prison and a child is left parentless.

And then I hear him say it again.

'What can I do, Mary? I'm off the case!'

Only this time, in my head, I hear an emphasis on two words:

'What can *I* do, Mary? *I'm* off the case!' And a small smile starts at the corner of my mouth.

Chapter 10

@gemma_cotswolds_mum Evening friends! Off to some ~~extremely~~ close friends' dinner party but before I go ~~I scheduled this post this morning, no way would I have time to write a post and get ready for this evening~~, I wanted to show you my latest flower arrangement ~~that I totally copied from Pinterest~~. I think the pampas add beautiful texture and warmth to it. What do you think? #flowerarrangement #creativemumsofinstagram ~~#ad~~

Rowena

Monday

What a lovely day yesterday was!

As we walked home in the dark on Saturday night, all three of us were buzzing (Eloise had given up the good fight a few hours earlier and was cosied up in her pram), filled up with delicious food and human interactions. We needed a nice family day out. It had been a while, definitely the first one since Eloise joined us.

I'm convinced Alfie's dreams that night were full of marshmallows, fires, sausages, and new friends. The first thing he asked yesterday morning (well, second, after the usual 'Muuuummmy' around 6.11am) was whether we could meet with Ben and Charlotte that day.

James and I didn't quite dream of cider and sausages, but we certainly went to bed with the happy feeling that this move might turn out to be a good idea, after all. There had been only one nasty comment from that Louise woman and few sideways glances versus lots of sincere handshakes and lovely conversations. Of course, the tragedy was never far out of people's minds and most conversations usually ended with a thought for Gemma and her family. If people were concerned for their own safety, they didn't show it, but then again, there were always some little ears around.

The day was an overall success, and we have Mary to thank for that. And we did, profusely then, and again later by WhatsApp, when I pinged her the link to that article about Gemma and the troll.

Today, my first attempt to sit down and start thinking about my next book gets interrupted by the doorbell.

I open the door to a lady I vaguely remember talking to on Saturday. It all comes back to me as she smiles and waves gorgeous pampas at me.

'Hi Marigold?' I'm not too sure I remember her name as I invite her in.

'Good morning, Rowena.' She says rather formally. I would place her in her mid-fifties, and she looks more mumsy than yummy mummy, I think unkindly. 'You mentioned on Saturday how much you loved pampas grass, so I thought I would bring some we had left over from our Guy making.'

'Oh, that is so thoughtful of you, thank you, Marigold.' I'm already thinking about where to display them to their advantage as per the cool designers I see on Instagram.

'Have you been into … pampas grass for a while?' she doesn't gesture air quotes around the 'pampas grass' but a halt in her sentence implies them.

'Hmm, I don't know. I took quite a liking to them when we were in London. They have been quite trendy around us. So eventually I jumped on that bandwagon too!' I smile.

'I see. Was it your husband who introduced you to them?' she asks, an enigmatic smile growing on her face.

'Oh, no. James would have never suggested something like that!' I chuckle at the thought. 'I suppose I saw it on social media and got inspired. I believe there are only so many times your subconscious can see something online before you end up really wanting it for yourself!'

'I'm not much of an online person,' admits Marigold. 'But I sort of see what you mean. We have quite an active 'pampas grass' community here, you know.' In addition to the invisible air quotes, she has now lowered her voice slightly, as if pampas growing was on par with cannabis farming.

'Ah OK, that's nice.' I venture, unsettled by her tone. 'What exactly does that entail? Sharing tips?' I mean I can't imagine there is that much to talk about around pampas. So niche.

'Well, you know, the usual gatherings, dinner parties, that sort of thing. I'm sure it can't be much different than in London, really. But you must join us one of these days and see for yourselves!' she suggests warmly.

I wonder how there can be that many people interested enough in pampas to build a whole community around them. But I suppose there is much less to do in the country?

'Ok, that would be nice, I'm sure. I do like to be creative.' I wish I could sound a bit more enthusiastic but it's this encounter is all a bit much.

'If you need a babysitter, my teenage daughter, Lucy, is very much in demand in the village.' Marigold assures me.

'That's good to know. But I'm sure James wouldn't mind staying with the kids.' I explain.

'But of course not!' She replies vehemently. 'Your husband must come, of course!' She winks at me.

'Oh, I'm not sure I could convince James to join us.' This conversation is getting strange now. And I'm not sure I want to have so much dealing with pampas grass anymore.

'I'm afraid our rules are very strict. It is couples only. Which, of course, is very sad when friends are suddenly no longer part of a couple.'

I am now extremely uncomfortable. Who are these people? Just because of being newly single, people are suddenly no longer invited by their friends? I need to wrap this up. I particularly don't want James to come out of his office and for Marigold to start trying to talk him into pampas grass.

'Marigold, I'm so sorry. I don't mean to kick you out.' I do. 'But I have to wake my daughter up and head out to a routine health visitor appointment.' Not true, but it could be.

'Of course. It was lovely chatting with you, Rowena. And we are very much looking forward to getting to know you both soon.' She says as she leaves. I'm sure I didn't imagine the emphasis on the 'know'.

***

I'm still confused and replaying that decidedly strange conversation in my head as I empty the dishwasher, all writing intentions forgotten.

James comes into the kitchen to make himself a cup of coffee and asks me about my visitor. I tell him about the odd conversation and suddenly, his eyes widen, and he spits out his coffee. He is now half choking, half laughing. I wait for him to catch his breath, but he keeps on laughing like I have told him the joke of the year. He can see that I am utterly confused.

'Seriously, Rowena, have you never heard of what pampas grass can be the symbol for?' he finally manages to articulate.

'No. What is it?'

He laughs even louder.

'Come on, James. What is it? What am I missing?' I gently punch his arm; he is loving my cluelessness.

'Rowena, I think, we have just been invited to join a swinging club!' he declares triumphantly.

Innocent me immediately pictures Marigold Jive dancing around a ballroom, *Strictly Come Dancing* style. But almost as quickly as that thought came to me, the reality finally dawns on me, and I try very hard not to picture Marigold anymore.

'Swinging, like swapping sexual partners, swinging?' I ask, incredulous.

'Yes! Oh my God! This is the best! This village life is getting better and better! A murder. Police questioning. And now, swinging!'

'But James, it can't be! Marigold just doesn't look the type!' I cry in denial. But immediately, all the weird air quotes and her insistence over the event being for couples only come back to mind.

'Oh, bloody hell! This is crazy! Pampas are all over Instagram. Interior designers put them everywhere. Surely, they can't all be swingers?'

'Did you say she told you Huxley had a very active community? I wonder how many of the people we met yesterday are into that!' He is having the best time.

'James! I don't want to know!' I shout, hiding my eyes behind my palms.

James leaves the kitchen, and I can still hear his laugh travelling through the house as he returns to the office. I have evidently made his day with this story.

I'm still thinking about it as I cobble some lunch together with pumpkin soup and cheese toasties when my thoughts come to an abrupt halt. what if Mary is into it as well?

I know it is hardly a big deal and certainly none of my business. And I am sure you can be a lovely person and be a swinger, but it is way too much information to have about somebody! No one wants to know about their friends' sexual practices. This new life continues to deliver in the most unpredictable ways. Whoever says nothing ever happens outside of the city?

Chapter 11

@gemma_cotswolds_mum Good morning, everyone!! Throwback to sunnier days. ~~God! Take me back!!~~ This pic is ~~carefully curated~~ from one of the many simple evenings spent in the garden when the sun doesn't set until way past Charlie's bedtime. Do you ever look at your child and you can literally feel your heart melting because you love them so much? I do. Everyday. Wishing you all inner warmth when it's cold outside.
#mumsofinstagram #motherslove #bringbacksummer
~~#fuckoffwinter~~

Mary

Thursday

The first part of the week was a blur. I don't know if it's because I was caught in the purgatory of rage with no place to focus it or if it's because we are already on the hyper-speed rocket ride hurtling towards Christmas. Probably both. Usually, I love this time of year – well, if I'm honest, I love all times of year – but the chestnut roasting, darker evenings and cold nights have always had a special draw for me. I do wait until 1st December to have the first mince pie and mulled wine but from then on, all bets are off until 2nd January (1st is usually spent nursing a hangover).

The village is absolutely beautiful at this time of year, too. It is chocolate box perfect. I know it's selfish but I'm glad that we are that bit too much "off the beaten path", which means that, bar the few day trippers and romantic weekenders, we get to have it to ourselves. I've had a Christmas dinner of shellfish fritters and creole curry on the Island of Guadeloupe and sauerkraut soup and potato pancakes in Bratislava, and I wouldn't change that experience for anything. But, as cliché as it sounds, there is nothing like being home for Christmas.

But at the moment, I feel simultaneously cooped up and frazzled. Whilst my initial panic and rage has tempered, by Thursday evening, I need a break from my responsibilities – furry, feathered, or otherwise. I message Rowena and ask her if there is any way she could convince James to do bedtime so we could sneak out to the Black Horse. I don't know if I'm ready to talk about 'it' and I'm not even sure that it's appropriate to talk to someone that I barely know about something that has affected me so deeply. I just know that I need a distraction. Her house is only a few minutes away from the pub and she replies saying that she could use the fresh air. Great!

When I step inside from the crisp cool air, I raise a clipped wave to Sam behind the bar and walk into the main seating area. I see that Rowena has managed to nab a great table just by the massive inglenook fire – thank God for layers! – and has started on a rather large glass of red. Luckily, she's made the clever assumption that I'd have the same. The pub has a lovely welcoming atmosphere, and they have already started decorating for the festive period. I feel a calmness, like a deep breath, and a jolt of warmth for my village and hope that Rowena likes it, too. However bad things seem, meeting up where people have gathered for more than 500 years reminds you that we are just a blip – that this, too, shall pass. Besides, a warm pub with a good friend is food for the soul, I'm absolutely sure of it.

The pub is busy with many of the usual faces, but I'm surprised to see Matthew sharing a pint with Martin. I feel like I might need to ask Rowena if she also sees him, as though the stress of the past week might have actually caused him to materialise in front of my very eyes. I don't remember them being close friends, but they are deep in quiet conversation about something. Despite my best efforts, I can't make out a single word. Matthew didn't see me walk in and I am disappointed that Rowena had found a table so far away from them.

I slide into my seat and remove the first of what I'm sure will be many of my layers. After exchanging quick pleasantries, I subtly indicate Matthew. I raise my eyebrows to wordlessly ask if she's seen him. I hate the idea of Matthew thinking I'm gossiping. She's obviously already clocked his presence and returns the silent question with matched raised eyebrows and shoulders thrown in. I decide to change the subject. 'Have you been here with James yet?'

'Are you kidding? We've only been here four weeks, the only night James and I have been *out* was with you to the Straw Man Festival. But let's face it, James and I haven't been out since Eloise was born. She's so young and, to be fair, we haven't really done much socially since we've had Alfie! We've never had any convenient childcare.'

'It really is so difficult without having that all important support network nearby. I'm so thankful for the special relationship between Charlotte and my dad but ever since the *Staircase Niagara Incident of 2019*, he hasn't offered to babysit, and we haven't wanted to ask.' At Rowe's request, I promise to tell her about that debacle another time.

'The rest of Tom's family, whilst less destructive, is slightly too far away to be of much day-to-day assistance and definitely not available to cover a cheeky night out at the pub.'

'We had a babysitter – the older child of a friend – that we used from time to time when Alfie was a toddler but when Eloise came along, I struggled to find a wet nurse!' she giggles and indicates her nipples with both of her pointer fingers.

'Ah Rowena, I know exactly what you mean. I feel like it was us just yesterday. Listen, if you are up for it, I'll send you some evenings when Tom is at home and I'll come look after Alfie and Eloise for the evening. You guys deserve a little downtime, just the two of you. But you'll have to express beforehand!' I add giggling.

'Really? Are you sure about that?' Her eyebrows knit with worry.

At this point I'm thinking to myself – would I trust me at this stage? I mean, we get on well but really, we've only just met. But then I thought about how desperate I was at that point to put on a bit of mascara and talk rubbish with Tom again.

'Honestly. It'll do wonders for you both, I'm sure of it!' I say, trying to exude a passing 'calm presence' vibe.

'Then yes! That'd be great, thanks!' she accepts. But she wrings her hands and scratches the back of her neck. There seems to be a hint of something more; a reason that she might be hesitant, but I can't put my finger on it and it's too soon to pry. Anyway, my train of thought is interrupted. I'm absolutely positive that I'm not imagining it, I see something akin to worry cross Rowe's face and I genuinely can't help myself. I know that I should leave people to their own thoughts and feelings but ever since I was little, I swear I can almost hear them myself and now that I'm older, I've lost the cognitive filter (or decency?) to prevent myself from asking.

'What is it?' I prod.

She blushes heavily. I'm almost giggling but it might turn into a laugh if I'm not careful. How much wine have we had?

'Honestly, nothing.' She tips her glass to empty the minuscule remnants as though it will distract me.

Now I am laughing. 'Seriously Rowena! A) you are a terrible liar and b) whatever it is that you are worried about definitely needs some air!'

'Oh God, Mary.' I'm starting to think she's a bit tiddly. 'I'm terrified to say.'

I'm not going to lie; this puts a slight chill on the warm feeling from the fire and the wine. I can almost feel myself tipping to the side of defensive.

'Rowena, come on, whatever it is ...' I cool my thoughts with the last sip of wine from my glass.

'Erm. Oh God. I'm just going to say it. Erm ... Are you a swinger? By any chance? I mean it's fine if you are ... it's ...' She is staring at her fingers which are twisting the stem of her wine glass, avoiding eye contact.

I spit/spray/spurt my last sip of Carménère across the entire table. I know. It's disgusting, terrible, adolescent behaviour but it cannot be helped. Luckily, apart from one older couple in the corner, I somehow manage to avoid the attention of the other patrons.

Now tears are streaming down my face. I still can't seem to catch my breath. I don't know if I've ever laughed so hard in my whole life. Is it possible to actually die from laughing? I put my hands up to say "I'm fine, promise. I'll be fine. Just give me a second". I'm shaking my head as I want her to know that the answer is 'no' because she's visibly worried. She starts to laugh nervously and then, realizing the reason for my reaction, joins me with a proper giggle and then a haughty laugh.

After what feels like absolutely ages, I take a deep breath. My sides and stomach are burning like I've done a legs bums and tums class for the last four hours. And here's honesty for you, I may well have lost the tiniest bit of wee.

'No, no, and no.' I can see that her relief is genuine. It's not the fact that she's asking me a ridiculous question, as such. It's that she was so terrified of the answer. I wipe my tears with a tissue from my pocket and ask her if she wants another drink.

I've resumed a normal breathing pattern by the time I return to the table with our glasses. 'Right! Spill the beans, where (or who) on Earth is this coming from?'

'Well, it would seem ...' It was clear to me that she really didn't know where to start. Something happened and she wants to protect someone from being named and shamed.

'Please don't worry, Rowena. It's fairly common knowledge that there is a thriving scene in Upper Huxley and whilst I'm neither involved, nor do I care to be, I'm aware of the fact that there are quite a few that are. But I don't know names. I like it that way. I'm not judgy about that sort of stuff. This way, I can keep my head in the sand – right where I like it – but I am definitely not a participant!' I still can't help but laugh at the idea that Tom and I would take part in extracurricular fooling around. We hardly have the time for each other!

I can see that this has provided a bit of relief to Rowena. She's obviously been concerned about betraying the confidences of anyone in the village.

'Well after I met her briefly on Saturday, Marigold Jenkins popped by on Monday morning to bring me some pampas grass.'

She pauses to check that I understand the symbolism. Once I nod my acknowledgement and stifle a laugh, she continues.

'Honestly, Mary, at first I thought it was very sweet. She's so ... mumsy. And actually, I've only just remembered! Your next-door neighbours have some pampas growing in front of their house ... Oh my God! Are they swingers, too? I'm going to see it everywhere now!' Again, her fingers are in knots, and she is now turning red.

'Ha! I'd totally forgot about that, but I seriously doubt it. Kevin has had trouble walking properly since the 80s, but who knows? That's the thing about this village, nothing is a surprise, Rowe. You'd do well to remember that.' But I, too, am having a good chuckle.

'So, did you know about Marigold?'

'No. Don't get me wrong. I find it all a bit odd. I can't possibly think about what they talk about at the dinner table during the 'pre-game'. I mean, do you talk about politics or *I'm a Celebrity* prior to the passing of the bowl of keys? I've no idea.'

'But she said something interesting, too.' Rowena adds.

I am glad it is only me that she is chatting with and the music that Sam is providing is soft enough for us to hear each other but loud enough to muffle the chat between tables. She leans closer to me, and I mirror her.

'She said that things would be different now that there are people who are suddenly single. Those aren't her exact words, but it was something like that. Who do you think she could be talking about?'

'Rowe! Do you think that Matthew and Gemma could have been swingers?' The corner of my mouth reaches up to my eyelid with scepticism.

'How would I know? But then again, does anyone ever really know what happens behind closed doors?' Rowe says with a twinge of sadness, and I see it again. The same look on her face that tells me there's something she isn't saying.

Suddenly, I realise that I'm bursting for the loo – stupid pelvic floor! I signal to Rowena that I'll only be a minute.

When I open the door to leave the toilet, it's immediately obvious that the atmosphere in the pub has completely changed. You could hear a pin drop – a tangible held breath between everyone in the room and all eyes are on a now standing Matthew and Martin. They have been joined by none other than DI Nick Nash. Nick is speaking in a voice that should be quieter to an incandescent Matthew. I look at Rowe to see if she has any answers. She just reflects my confusion back to me.

'Matthew ... quietly and we'll have a chat at the station ...' Nick's words are muffled but I get the gist.

'What the fuck are you even talking about? Why the fuck would I kill my wife?' Far more audible; piercing, really. His face flushing and morphing with rage.

'Let's talk about it a little more calmly ...'

I walk directly over to the table where they are standing without even realising what I'm doing.

'Hi Nick. Hi Martin.' Bless his heart, Martin's eyebrows point to the ceiling looking for answers. He has become childlike in his confusion and is staring at Nick trying to process his words.

As soon as I turn to speak to Matthew, Nick gestures for me to step back. 'Mary, I have this under control. This is a formal investigation. I don't need the mums brigade getting involved. Thank you.' And then he tipped his head down in a dismissive bow. Fucking prick.

I ignore him completely and offer gently 'Matthew, where is Charlie this evening? Do you need me to go and get him?'

At this, Matthew crumbles beneath the weight of responsibility. 'Oh Charlie!' he manages as heaving sobs escape from his chest. The whole pub shudders with the collective heartbreak.

I step in to hug him, which is simultaneously so natural and yet, so weird. I wonder if he feels the same, but he seems grateful in any case. 'It's going to be fine, Matthew. Tell me where Charlie is and who is looking after him.'

Unlocking from the embrace, he looks with laser concentration into my eyes. 'He's staying at Gemma's parents' house tonight. I just needed a little brea ...' He glances at Martin and checks himself before continuing. 'He's fine but could you ... Erm ...' His voice breaks and more tears appear. 'Could you go talk to them? Please tell them I didn't do it? And if he isn't already asleep, please tell Charlie I love him and I'll be home as soon as I can.'

I feel like I can't breathe. 'Of course. Is there anything else I can do to help?'

'No. Really, thank you so much, Mary. You are an absolute life saver. Thanks for helping me to sort out this mess.' The violent flip between anger, fear, and desperation have exhausted him. His face has new lines that weren't there before this evening, I'm sure.

The entire pub is stunned into silence and staring directly at him in varying shades of shock. He doesn't seem to notice. He shrinks and then starts to mumble to himself 'This is so ridiculous' then seems to grow twenty percent taller and half again as wide. He gains the confidence of being overcome with rage and shouts 'Utterly *ridiculous!*' That last word is spat at Nick.

Chapter 12

@gemma_cotswolds_mum Morning friends! Hasn't the weather been absolutely perfect lately? This is a new favourite picture from last weekend ~~hate my legs on that shot but Matthew refused to retake another one~~ spent frolicking in the garden with friends. So in love ~~like everyone else on this app~~ with this rainbow dress from @asos #ad #croquet #happydays #summerdays

Rowena

Thursday

The herbal tea is getting cold on the side table. 'Relax', it is called, and I feel like the whole box of teabags in my mug wouldn't be enough. I feel totally wound up after witnessing the awful scene of a distressed Matthew and a whole pub in shock.

James has already gone up to bed and I'm grateful for the time and space to try and process what has just happened. I'm desperate to talk to Mary but I know she will be busy getting in touch with Gemma's parents and it would feel wrong and gossipy to contact her now.

I don't know what Matthew is like, but no one could be left indifferent by his despair. The man has obviously just lost his wife and now they have arrested him. And yet, his first concern is for his son. Surely, that should be enough to convince the police that he can't have killed the boy's mum? I mean, I'm no psychology expert, but I don't think you kill someone's mum if you care that much about them. Is that too simplistic? Probably.

Could someone fake a reaction like his? Actors do that every day, I suppose. But in real life?

He looked so much calmer when Mary stepped up. I feel so much warmth towards my new friend, who knew exactly what to do and say in such a situation.

I grab my phone to try and distract myself but instead, I find myself flicking through Gemma's Instagram account.

I know very well that you shouldn't believe all the happy pictures and bright smiles you see on social media. But she was a real person: a wife and a mother to a little boy. And despite all the outpouring of love from her followers and the thousands of photos of her smiling, she is lost forever to her husband and son. And that reality has been made all the more poignant tonight.

I am scrolling through her posts, particularly, the ones about her family. I have been following her for a few years, but it would be lying to call myself a big fan. I tend to favour either aesthetic accounts or witty and genuine Instagrammers. Gemma was neither. Sure, her photos are pretty enough but her posts read as too perfect for my liking. Surely not everything in her life can have been going so perfectly. If anything, reading her posts and seeing her pictures made me feel slightly inadequate as a mum, as a wife, hell, as a woman full stop. And yet, I never clicked 'Unfollow'. I suppose if I admit it to myself, I was following her because everyone else was. Like something you have to do, in a case of FOMO. But also, maybe because she represented something to aspire to.

She was undeniably likeable online. Never too this or too that. I suppose 'Vanilla' would be the right word (insult?) to describe her account.

Never a controversy. Until that trolling incident, that is. Amongst the hundreds of perfect family photos and sponsored posts for sun cream, garden furniture, and expensive holidays, I find the post I have been looking for: a photo of Gemma playing croquet and looking radiant in a stripy rainbow dress from a well-known fast-fashion brand. I remember that dress was the it-dress for a few weeks last June and every Instagrammer was wearing it then. Like the sheep that I am, I wanted it too, but by then, I was way too pregnant to consider even such a cheap purchase.

I look through the comments to eventually find the thread I'm interested in.

@simple_ecolife: *Looking pretty as always, but don't you mind that this was made in appalling conditions in Bangladesh and that the fashion industry's carbon footprint is bigger than aviation's? You should really ask #whomademyclothes #noplanetB*

This is followed by hundreds of comments from Gemma's followers like:

@mamma_of_3_rascals @simple_ecolife *what a nasty thing to say! If you don't like what you see on here, just unfollow.*

@eat_stay_lounge @simple_ecolife *Jealous, much? Gemma does not need your negativity. This is her page and her business, and she does what she wants with it, without self-righteous people telling her what to do.*

@honest_motherhood_ntg @simple_ecolife *Go away and troll somebody else, will you?* @gemma_cotswolds_mum *is an inspiration for us all and we don't all want to wear hemp tunics and grow armpit hair. Thank you very much.*

I click on @simple_ecolife, fully expecting the account to have been deleted. But to my surprise, not only is it still live, it is also public. Meaning I can see all the pictures ever posted on that account. The last dates from August and shows a golden wheat field. I can see that even in October people were still leaving nasty comments under @simple_ecolife's pictures, despite her radio silence.

I scroll through the account full of eco-friendly tips and simple pictures. It is a beautiful feed with gorgeous and inspirational nature photos, inciting people to enjoy a slower life, while respecting our planet and its limited resources.

I am starting to seriously reconsider my lifestyle when, suddenly, I gasp at a picture of a massive bonfire and the caption *'Goodbye Straw Man. Pagan rites still going strong in the West Country.'* Behind the bonfire, I am pretty sure I recognise the discernibly unique gable of Upper Huxley Village Hall.

Oh my God. Gemma's troll was local?

I click on the link to the Grazia article I sent to Mary and slowly reread it in full. No mention of the troll's real identity or even where she came from. Whatever happened to investigative journalism?

I go back to @simple_ecolife's account and check every single one of her posts, my curiosity now seriously piqued. The pictures definitely have a South of England feel but most of them could have been taken anywhere in rural areas between Kent and Devon. Yet, there are a few with honey-coloured Cotswolds dry-stone walls. A sponsored post about a new loose food shop in Stroud confirms my suspicions. She lives around here. Could @simple_ecolife have known Gemma in real life?

I click back on @simple_ecolife's last post and there, I spot the latest comment, posted only two days ago:

@gemma_forever *What were you doing on Tuesday night last week?!*

Is this person accusing @simple_ecolife of murder? I click on that account, but it is only stock photos of Gemma. Nothing about the person behind the account. But could they have a point?

I wonder if the police are aware of what I have found. Have they investigated this before dragging Matthew to the station?

Are these flutters in my stomach exhilaration? I barely recognise the feeling. It's been so long. But I feel so ... alive.

Chapter 13

@gemma_cotswolds_mum Good afternoon, lovely people!! Check out this amazing Christmas centrepiece created by my ridiculously talented (and award winning!) ~~very close~~ friend Marigold Jenkins from @sweetpeasinapod. Her gorgeous shop located in our village is my favourite place to go for all my fresh flowers and greenery needs and is bursting with #christmasinspo. Tell her Gemma sent you for an extra 10% off. ~~since she still doesn't have an online shop~~. #ad #freshflorals #christmasflowers #floristsofthecotswolds

Mary

Very early Friday

It is gone midnight by the time I get home from the Jamesons' house, and I don't even bother going to bed. What's the point?

Telling them about the events of the evening was incredibly difficult, especially as I was also still offering my condolences regarding the death of their daughter. I'm ashamed to say that I was relieved that Charlie was already asleep. The optimist in me is hoping that this will all be sorted out by the time he wakes up but the realist in me knows how unlikely that is. I was desperate to call Rowe since she was at the pub and saw everything. I feel like chatting with her and running through the series of events would somehow make it all feel a bit less painful, but there is still so much I am not quite ready to talk about.

I'm on the couch with a knot in my stomach feeling utterly useless and helpless and all the 'less' feelings. I'm so angry with the situation that I feel like I could 'spit nails' as my grandmother used to say. And all I can hear in my head is Matthew's words: 'Thanks for helping me to sort out this mess', over and over and over again.

But what can I do?

Saturday

Marigold Jenkins opened her adorable florist about twenty years ago and somehow has the eye to keep it bang up to date. The storefront looks very 'French Cafe' with soft pastels and a beautiful green-striped awning. In the summer, it effervesces romance with hydrangeas and peonies and ranunculi galore. Today, the windows are dressed with impeccable care in seasonal greenery – holly, ivy, eucalyptus – to tempt those who are hoping to make their Christmas dinner tables that much more welcoming with an extraordinary centrepiece. I chuckle to myself that it's probably all a show for being able to procure pampas grass at warehouse prices.

'Good morning, Marigold!' I say as the bell tinkles to signal my arrival. I move quickly before intrusive images make me blush. She's just the same Marigold. Right?

She's behind the counter facing the wall and lost in designing a beautiful but modest arrangement of white roses, cedar, and berries in an antique silver compote. She puts her secateurs down to greet me properly.

'Oh, Hiya Mary! How nice to see you!' I can tell by the way the corners of her eyes lift that she's genuine. She is such a lovely person. 'That Straw Man Parade was my favourite yet, I think. Did you and your family have a nice time? How is your dad doing? And your brother?'

Marigold has been like this ever since I can remember. She is such a lovely lady, and her strong West Country lilt is unbelievably sweet, but she fires questions at you far faster than you could ever possibly answer them.

'It was lovely, wasn't it? We had a super time, thanks. Dad is great. I hear he has a new girlfriend but that was last week, so it'll probably be old news when I speak to him later today. Christopher is great, still working hard in the city. How's your Stephen?'

'All healthy, thank you! You know him, Mary. Pain in the arse but I love him all the same.'

I do know him! Marigold's children were quite a bit younger than Christopher and I, so we weren't friends as such, but we'd known their family since I could remember. I set a smile firmly on my face whilst I subtly pinch first finger and thumb together tightly in my pocket, to stifle any adolescent giggle that decides it might fester from the deep, but also to promptly quash any rogue mental images. Just because I'm happy for everyone else to do whatever the hell they want to, it doesn't mean that I want to actually think about them doing it!

'What can I do for you today, Mary?' I'm thankful that she is driving the conversation forward.

'Well, I'd love something nice to put on Mum's grave, please. Just something to tide us over until Christmas. She always loved this time of year.' All of a sudden I find myself welling up. Ah grief – you absolute bastard! I wasn't even all that upset about this Christmas. It's been three years since she passed and I keep waiting for it not to hurt but I've managed to stop crying in public, at least. It is true what they say: the big things are easier than you think they will be, it's the small things that will trip you up and set you back.

'Ah, Mary, isn't that lovely? I know you miss her every day. I know just the thing.' She starts to busy herself between the massive buckets and the fridges.

'It's alright, no rush. I could see that you were busy when I came in. I could always arrange to collect it next week …'

Marigold cuts me off and I'm embarrassed to realise that it's likely because I nearly burst into tears only a few moments ago. Dammit. 'Not at all. Rosemary's not expecting this arrangement until Monday.'

She takes out some florist's foam and a massive knife to trim it and I decide to be bold and see what I can learn about Gemma. I wonder if Marigold might have gleaned something interesting from her *encounters*. 'Marigold, can I ask you a question?'

Completely engrossed in her task, she absently mutters 'Of course, dear' like she would have done a million times in her life. Being a mum, I would know.

'Did you know Gemma Hatherley very well?' She's not at all surprised at the question. I can't imagine she's often surprised by much at all.

'I'd say I knew her pretty well, yes. Absolutely heartbreaking this business. Such a shock.'

'Matthew was taken under caution at the pub last night.'

She whips around to face me. Turns out she *can* be shocked.

I continue 'It feels so wrong. There must be something that they are missing. You and I both know it can't be Matthew so I'm just trying to learn more about Gemma.'

She gives me a pointed side-eye. 'Isn't it a bit late for that, dear? But I know what you mean – she was an interesting woman – quite the enigma. Smart and beautiful, but troubled, as beautiful women often are. She was always so confident – some would say too confident.' (At this point, she shoots me a knowing look.) 'But I did notice that there was a change in her over the six months leading up to her death. There was something that was bothering her but I'd no idea what or who it might have been.' She looks over her glasses at me for the 'who' bit and then goes back to busying herself, showing off her incredible multi-tasking skills.

'Have you told anyone about this?' I ask, even though I can blatantly tell that she hasn't. She can't quite look at me, clearly feeling guilty about betraying someone's trust. But I can also tell by her strong voice that she thinks it needs to be heard. 'Should you go to the police?' She's busy fixing some cedar along the edges.

'I'm not sure what I would say, Mary. It's not really the sort of thing you could put your finger on.' She leans down to check the angle of the boughs and sticks her substantial rear straight out behind her.

Stop it with the mental images ... Not helpful. Concentrate!

'Was it something to do with her relationship with Matthew? They always seemed so happy together.' I say even though the prod isn't necessary. You have to admire someone who can create botanic beauty whilst maintaining a serious conversation about a friend's murder.

'Mary, you know I love chatting with you. But why don't you ask him yourself? I feel sure that more than anything, he could use a friend right now. But yes, things were strained between them over the past six months.' She brushes a grey curl out of her right eye with the back of her hand and continues with her work. 'We used to see them quite often, but something seemed to have caused a bit of a rift this past summer. In June, they were having a great time and enjoying each other's company.' she pauses, looks up to the right as if trying to remember, and then dives back to her creation. 'But it seemed to change over the summer and by September – maybe about the time that school started? – you could tell that there was friction.' She stops and looks at me, ready to make her point. 'If I had to guess, I'd say that she was trying hard to hold his attention, but he seemed pretty distracted.'

'By another woman?' I say, shocked. That doesn't sound like the Matthew I know.

'Hard to say, really. The signs were there but I wouldn't be surprised if it was just a wandering eye. Things weren't very good between them at all. I remember one particular dinner party – '

Does she mean what I think she means?

"Where she got upset, and they left abruptly without even finishing their dessert!'

Oh, please for the love of God, make that a literal use of 'dessert'.

At this point she wheels around to the counter with the most beautiful flat wreath, perfect in every way. It's natural and genuine but happy and celebratory all at the same time. Tears immediately form, clouding my vision, but luckily I can still smile through them. She comes around the counter to give me a hug and says 'I'm glad you like it.' In that moment I know that Marigold can do whatever she wants in her spare time; she is still the most beautiful of souls.

I pay her the pittance that she asks for (I'm not even sure it covers the materials) and leave the shop with the most wonderful feeling of holiday cheer. I've got something festive for my mum and also a mission to find out what happened in the Hatherleys' marriage between June and September of this year.

Chapter 14

@gemma_cotswolds_mum Morning friends! Don't you just ~~dread~~ love the run up to Christmas! It's been all the more special since Charlie made us a family. Choosing the perfect present can be ~~so bloody stressful~~ a bit of a challenge, so I have compiled the perfect selection ~~copy pasted the list from the instructions from the PR company~~ for all the special people in your life and the great news is that you can find them all in one place @johnlewis. You're welcome! #ad #sponsoredpost ~~#sameposteverybloodyyear~~

Rowena

Saturday

Today, James is looking after the kids while I make it into town to get my eyes tested, an appointment which is now six months overdue.

Trying to ignore the anxiety of being away from the kids, specifically Eloise, I drive into Stroud and make it on time for my appointment. As predicted, my prescription needs updating and within 30 minutes, I leave with a new set of contact lenses. How efficient!

Determined to resist the pull to immediately drive home and enjoy my childfree time instead, I decide to make a start on my Christmas shopping. Stroud is a lovely town with a chilled atmosphere. Unlike most places, it has managed to retain some lovely independent shops full of handmade, artisan, and organic offerings, maintaining its reputation as a 'hippy' town.

I have made satisfying purchases for my sister, Dad, and a few bits and bobs for Alfie and Eloise's stockings when a shop window grabs my attention. It has been artistically transformed into a wintery woodland scene with animals and trees made out of waste materials. Nestled amidst the woodland are reusable products such as bottles and brushes and other metal food containers. It is very clever and appealing, definitely not your usual eco-shop. Beyond the display and inside the shop, I can see high wooden shelves stacked with loose food in large, attractive glass jars. When my eyes fall on the shop name, it clicks.

This is Loose People. The shop that sponsored one of @simple_ecolife's posts. Gemma's troll worked with the people running this shop!

I haven't even had a chance to mention to Mary what I discovered yesterday. I promptly walk away as I remind myself that I am no Miss Marple.

I continue my shopping, but I can't find anything else suitable. I could blame bad luck, but I know that my mind is no longer in it. By the time I have come out of another three shops empty-handed, I have convinced myself that what Mike, my brother-in-law, would really like for Christmas is one of those fancy reusable water bottles that happened to be in the Loose People shop window.

Against my better judgement, I make my way back to the shop. The interior is entirely fitted with wood, conferring upon it a warm, nurturing feel. The sales assistant behind the counter smiles warmly as I come in. She lets me have a look around for a couple of minutes before she comes over.

'Hello there. Do you need help with anything? I don't believe I have seen you here before. Are you after loose food supplies or something else?'

She is around fifty and with her long naturally greying hair, crinkly smiling eyes, and flowy upcycled handmade clothes, the best way to describe her would be "friendly witch."

'Hi.' I reply. 'I was looking at your reusable water bottles for a gift. Do they come in a box?'

'Yes, they do, actually. Which is not something we usually encourage as we are all about reducing packaging waste. But this box is made of recycled cardboard.'

'Ok, I will take this grey one then, please.' I follow her to the till. 'So, how long have you been selling loose products? Is it popular? How does it work?' I'm nervous as I want to ask other questions.

'We have been here for two years. But before that, I had a stall at the Saturday market. People were getting more and more interested, so we took the plunge to open a more permanent business. It is becoming increasingly popular. Ideally, you bring your own containers, but we always have some paper bags we can supply if you forget.' she explains as she processes my purchase.

'I've only just started to realise how much waste we are producing as a family of four and it is awful.' I admit, ashamed. One more thing to add to my List Of Failings.

She smiles kindly, in a non-judgemental way. 'It is the start, you'll see. Once you've seen it, you can't unsee it and you will want to do something about it. Next time you're in town, bring a couple of containers and you can have a go!'

'I'll definitely do that.' And then suddenly, before I can even think about it, I blurt out: 'Actually, I've been wanting to come here since I saw a post about the shop on Instagram by @simple_ecolife? A few months ago?'

'Ah yes, Lorna. We had a short partnership that did bring us quite a few local customers and followers.' *Lorna? Surely not!*

'She has stopped posting, hasn't she?' I continue, concealing the shock of hearing Lorna's name. 'I miss her posts and her gorgeous pictures.' Turns out, I can lie very easily and convincingly. Who knew? I mean her photos are beautiful, but I only found her account last night. I'm hardly missing it.

'Not sure. I think she is on a break, but she is still a customer to us.'

'So, she is local, then? That's cool!' I put on my best fangirl smile, hiding the turmoil inside.

'Yes, not far. Farmton or Upper Huxley, somewhere that way.' she replies evasively.

'Ah OK, not far at all, then.' I pretend I've lost interest in that subject, trying to keep my hands from shaking as I put my purchase in my canvas bag and bid her goodbye.

I step into the street. I am trembling.

I do know a Lorna from Upper Huxley, and she did seem very keen on the eco-life at the Straw Man Parade! Bloody hell, have I actually got a lead here?

Have the police interviewed Lorna? Could Mary find out through Tom?

I can't stop thinking about Matthew, probably still at the station, and Charlie wondering where his dad is when he has only recently lost his mum. That little boy's world has been turned completely upside down and I am not convinced that the police have done a thorough enough job. I feel bad thinking that as Tom is Mary's husband. But then again, I wonder why he was not there last night when the DI took Matthew in for questioning. I couldn't help but notice that Mary was not full of warmth towards her husband's colleague.

It was easy two days ago to dismiss my intuition, the feeling that Matthew didn't look guilty. I could reason with myself that the police had, of course, got a whole bunch of evidence to justify their actions.

But what if I have now found evidence that someone else, someone local, had a motive to want Gemma out of the way? How can I dismiss this?

Chapter 15

@gemma_cotswolds_mum Morning Friends. Is there anything better than having tea with friends and catching up on ~~juicy gossip~~ world events or even just the latest book? Whenever I get together with my nearest and dearest, I'm always reminded of how lucky we are to know people who seem to know ~~every detail of the local scandals~~ just how to brighten our day. I encourage you to comment and tag this post with your ~~#gossipqueens~~ #bestfriends who get you through the ~~village headlines~~ #goodtimes and #difficulttimes every day. Here's to you, fellow ~~bitches~~ friends! Xx, Gemma

Mary

Saturday

I finish running my errands after Marigold's and then head home in time to start dinner. I arrive in the kitchen, camel style, loaded down with the shopping (did it in one trip, though – whoop whoop!).

'Hi!' Tom is sitting at the kitchen table with a fresh cup of tea and biscuits he seems to have found in the depths of the cupboard. Now I'm gagging for a cuppa, and luckily, the kettle is still quite hot. I top it up, switch it on again and put away the items I've collected throughout the day.

He looks up from his phone by way of acknowledgement.

'What's going on with Matthew – is he still in cells?'

'Yes.' His mouth twists in disappointment.

I had already explained to him the painful scene that Rowe and I had witnessed at the pub the previous night. I broke down in tears when I told him just how desperate Matthew had seemed and how helpless I felt, so I don't think it is much of a surprise to Tom that

I am still preoccupied with the topic. 'Has Nick actually considered anyone else?'

'There were others, of course. We looked at the obvious: family and close friends, and a few who were investigated more than others. Like when I went to see James.'

'Yes,' I said, rolling my eyes. It must have been so embarrassing. For everyone.

'There was a small-time burglar that was briefly in the picture but had a solid alibi, and then a Hillary Peters. She was Gemma's agent and was investigated but she, too, had an alibi and no obvious motive. After all, Gemma was one of her main clients. Total bitch, though. I got the impression that they were pleased to dismiss her as a possibility.'

'So, do you think that this job is being worked properly?' I am asking but I've definitely come to my own conclusion already.

'It doesn't really matter what I think, Mary. The point is that I'm not on the case anymore. I may not like the way that they are conducting their investigations but it's not up to me. My hands are tied so there's nothing I can do. I'm hardly Mr Popular.' Tom has so often been the outsider in the force. Always getting results but not always toeing the party line. Doing the right thing, even when it's harder, and when the heads of the constabulary much prefer an easy life. He has had to learn to choose his battles.

'Yeah. I get it.' And with that, I know that it's something that I'm going to have to do myself. I mean, Tom's hands are tied and, without some intervention by someone, Nick is going to fuck this thing up so royally, he will make Brexit look like a roaring success. Besides, there is no way that I'm letting Matthew take the fall for something I'm absolutely convinced he didn't do. Tom is surreptitiously asking that I get involved, I'm sure of it. With that, it's clear that a change of subject is needed.

'That's a lovely wreath.'

'Thanks so much – Marigold made it to put on Mum's grave.'

'Ah that's lovely. I don't remember you ordering that?'

'Ah no, I didn't. I just popped into the shop earlier.'

'She doing OK?'

'Yeah, she's fine. Hey! Did you know that Marigold and Stephen are swingers?'

Tom just about avoids spitting out his tea. I should have learned from my own experience hearing this titbit to time the delivery better.

'Ha! Are you kidding?'

'Seriously? You think I'd joke about something like that? I'm just wondering if there was any reason to think that Matthew and Gemma were also participating in that particular flavour of entertainment. Was there anything like that uncovered during your investigation?' I immediately realise from the look on Tom's face that it was an unwelcome question so make a bid to create a diversion.

'Marigold also said that Gemma hadn't been herself for the last few months. She hinted that perhaps things between her and Matthew weren't all sunshine and rainbows.' Tom is losing interest or patience, but I can't quite decide which, so I add in a breathy Nigella Lawson voice, 'you know, like us, the *Dream Couple*.' I bat my eyelashes for effect. He rolls his eyes and pretends to be sick, picks up his tea and heads to the lounge. Ah love ...

Chapter 16

@gemma_cotswolds_mum Today I'm wearing this sunshine dress for Endometriosis Awareness Month, a cause close to my heart, having suffered from this invisible disease for a long time. Endometriosis affects 1 out of 10 women and yet, not many people have heard of it. It is the #1 cause of infertility for women and can be terribly crippling. Please talk to your GP. Your pain is valid and may not be 'just one of those things'.
Edit: Following comments, I would like to add that, yes, I have managed to have my Charlie ~~eventually~~ and no, I don't look crippled, but please accept that you don't know what is going behind closed doors and that it is my prerogative to not share ~~how much I have longed for another baby and how many treatments and surgeries I have had to go through~~ more if I don't want to. Please be respectful and help raise awareness for this disease rather than use it as another way to be mean to strangers on the internet. ~~#infertility~~ #endometriosisawareness #endometriosiswarrior

Rowena

Saturday evening

All thoughts of Lorna and calling Mary are swiftly forgotten as soon as I enter the house. It's like it's been hit by a tornado.

How long have I been gone? Surely not just three hours.

I walk my way through the devastation as I start unpacking my shopping.

The evidence of cooking and eating lunch are covering every surface in the kitchen. In the living room, all of the toys we keep in the trunk in the bay window have been taken out. I can, at first glance, count five discarded muslins dotted around the room. The changing mat I usually tidy away after each use is taking pride of place on the rug with two soiled nappies nearby.

James is on his phone, and on the sofa and Alfie and Eloise are both glued to the TV. I always turn it off when Eloise is in the room. And dare I ask if she has had a nap? Judging by the state of everything and her slightly jittery behaviour, I'm going to guess she hasn't.

But, by far the biggest offence is one of Eloise's bottles left on the coffee table, three- quarters full of milk. Not just any milk. Breastmilk. *My precious milk I spent hours expressing!* And James casually filled up the whole bottle, which she was never going to drink in full, and left it to go to waste on the coffee table.

Breathe, Rowena. I will not be listing all of his failings. Repeat after me. *I will not be listing all of his failings.* He is not used to being on his own with them, I reason. Some would say I should be grateful that I could leave the kids with him and not worry about them not being alive at the end of it. But I resent that massively. He is their parent too, and I don't have to be grateful to be allowed a few hours to myself. I know he spends most of the week away and cannot take on a lot of the parenting burden and that this was a common decision, but I feel I am still entitled to be annoyed. So, I resolve to not berate him, but I won't congratulate him either.

Instead, I settle for putting everything back in order while huffing and puffing passive- aggressively. That should do the trick. I'm not looking for a fight. If anything, I realise I have been avoiding any sort of conflict with James for a while, since we found out we were expecting Eloise. Is that even healthy?

As a result of all this, I'm not in the sunniest mood for the rest of the evening. So, soup, bread, and cheese are eaten quickly, and the children must sense the vibes because they go to sleep easily for once.

James must also realise I'm in no mood for a quiet, cosy movie night together, as part of our old Saturday routine that we had lost but have re-established since we moved here.

'I've got some work I need to ..."

He better not say 'catch up on'.

'... get ready for Monday.' His voice trails off as he leaves the room, avoiding eye contact. *Phew, close call, James.*

I take my bad mood into the front room, now looking less like a war zone. Nothing on TV is grabbing my attention so I settle for Strictly Come Dancing, but soon, I'm back on Instagram ignoring the Rumbas and Argentine Tangos. I am drawn to Gemma's account like a moth to a flame. What am I looking for? Is it voyeurism? My heart breaks further over pictures of her with Charlie. Poor child.

A post, dated 1st March, grabs my attention. She is wearing a beautiful yellow wrap dress holding a bunch of daffodils (no doubt she knew as a pro Instagrammer that it was also St David's day) and is talking about her Endometriosis diagnosis. The contrast with the rest of her light-hearted posts is striking. But more important to me is what seems to be implied in her post. She doesn't say as much but I can't help thinking that her condition has meant a complicated fertility journey. Like she added herself in her edit, she *did* manage to become a mother to Charlie, but I wonder if there was more heartache along the way. I search her face for traces of sadness in other photos. I remember reading another post, again because the tone was quite different, in which she was addressing some comments about Charlie being an only child. Maybe Mary would know. My own motherhood journey could undoubtedly be clouding my perception, but I suddenly feel a lot closer to Gemma. My indignation and sadness at her sudden early death heightened, I resolve to ring Mary tomorrow.

Chapter 17

@gemma_cotswolds_mum Morning Friends. Sharing with you my ~~incredibly bland~~ vegan chilli recipe, which is perfect after those long walks outside. At only 350 calories ~~a third of my daily allowance~~ per serving, this is the ~~most boring~~ perfect way to end a ~~most boring~~ perfect day. I suggest pairing it with vegan cheese, vegan sour cream, and Waitrose's own brand non-alcoholic wine for a perfectly healthy ~~seriously! What is the POINT?~~ friends and family gathering. #vegan #veganmummy ~~#extrabeefinmineplease~~

Mary

Sunday evening

'What's up?' Friendly but to the point. Phone is ringing and as it isn't 7pm on the dot on a Sunday, it can't be Dad. So, it's Tom. I didn't even bother looking to see who it was as I'm in the middle of cooking dinner and we aren't the type of couple for niceties, anyway.

'Oh? Er. Hi Mary!'

A female voice? I'm confused now so I look at my phone.

'Oh! Hi Rowena! Sorry – thought you were Tom. Pleasant surprise! How are you?'

'Good thanks, had a little explore in Stroud yesterday. Spot of Christmas shopping. How are you?'

'Ah fun! It's beautiful this time of year. Listen, I'm making a huge pot of chilli and Tom is at work but will be home shortly.'

'Oh sorry ... I didn't mean to interr ...'

'No, no, I was wondering if you all might like to come over and join us? An informal affair, of course. Do you all eat chilli?'

'Oh ... yes, I mean, of course we do but ...'

'Perfect! Listen, the longer it simmers, the better it tastes so just come when you are ready. Or come now if you want. We could go for a walk around the lake whilst the chilli makes itself and James can join us later? Whatever suits.'

***

Getting bundled up for cold weather with children is not for the faint-hearted and no one ever wants to do it more often than strictly necessary, so when Rowena arrives ready for the walk, I ask her to wait outside whilst the children and I wrap up. The incentive of getting to spend time with Alfie means that Ben is only moving at a snail's pace rather than his usual 'time has got to be f-ing standing still by now' pace. Charlotte is her usual efficient self, presumably excited about the prospect of a cuddle with Eloise. I grab the two Thermoses of tea that I'd already prepared, and we head out.

The 'Upper Huxley Lake path' as we refer to it in the village (I didn't say it was a creative name) is absolutely one of my favourite walks. Tom makes fun of me because it's always my default when we go for a walk. Even if it wasn't only ten minutes (and perfectly walkable) from our front door, it'd still be one of my favourites. Pulling on my trusty wellington boots and walking in and amongst the trees along the creek is beautiful at any time of year but especially in autumn. The path is muddy enough that you know you've been outside but not so muddy as to become one of those trendy fitness obstacle courses. It is windy and hilly to keep it interesting and the prize at the end of a fairly arduous amble is the beautiful lake view with the perfect bench for a Thermos lid of tea. There is even an island in the middle where the coots and mallards bustle about. I think of this bench a lot when I need a 'happy place'. What always surprises me is how few people there are on this path.

I know that Upper Huxley is only a small village, really, and there are enough footprints to know that the path is well used but, somehow, we rarely see anyone on our walks. Another reason it's one of my favourites.

Rowe and I are happily chatting about the latest 'news' at school: Mrs Fry is going to retire at the end of the year; Mr Loman is leaving to pursue a stand-up career (seriously? Or is that his first/last joke?), but it's clear by the time we've reached the bench that there is something else on her mind.

We sit down side by side, our respective stripy and spotty wellies showing camaraderie of their own, pour the tea into each of our respective lids, and I say 'Go on then?'

'What do you mean?' Her innocent 'butter wouldn't melt' face isn't fooling me one bit!

'C'mon Rowena. There must have been a very good reason why you called earlier. And it wasn't to tell me about the Christmas decorations in Stroud, although I'm sure they were lovely.'

She looks around to find where the big kids are playing and sees that they are far enough away not to hear: 'Oh fine! I know who was trolling Gemma!'

'What?' I nearly spit out my tea. Maybe I shouldn't drink around Rowena. She's already found out who it was?

She starts with how she researched the different IG accounts and how she found the connection between @Gemmaman, @simple_ecolife, and @Gemmaman_forever (sorry, but that last one is just creepy). Then she goes on to explain how she saw the shop front, went in, and started asking questions. Et voila! @simple_ecolife is Lorna!

I'm so impressed. 'So ... what does it mean?'

'No idea. I mean, I know that Lorna has strong ideals – we saw her – ahem – *passion* – at the festival.'

'That's right – but do we even know if she was upset with Gemma?'

'Well, Lorna is no longer working with the shop, and she's not using her Instagram account anymore. It could be that the behaviour from Gemma's followers has actually lost Lorna her livelihood, and perhaps even more importantly, the platform from which she shares her strong beliefs.'

'Believe it or not, you aren't the only one stumbling adventitiously into key evidence for this case! I had a chat with Marigold. In short, she seems to think that Matthew might have been having an affair.'

'But how can that be? Did she say that they were swingers, too?' Rowena shoots me a look of confusion that mirrors my own.

'She didn't, but in any case, from what I've read, there are strict rules for swingers and affairs are just as unacceptable as they are for the rest of us. Let's face it, if someone else caught Matthew's attention, Gemma would have been genuinely heartbroken.' We are both quiet and lost in thought for a minute, enjoying the hot tea and staring across the lake at the island.

It feels like a slight betrayal of Tom's trust, but I can't help telling Rowe about the conversation that Tom and I had. I explain that Tom is now off the case and the new lead, Nick the Dick, has already decided that Matthew is guilty. He is more concerned with trying to find the facts that fit his conclusion than actually doing a good job. He just needs a quick result to make himself look good, and he isn't about to let something silly like the truth to get in the way of that.

Rowe brings her hands up to cover her mouth in disbelief at the farce that this case is quickly becoming. 'But Mary, we can't let that happen!'

We chat about the fact that Tom had identified people close to Gemma personally (Marigold, for example), professionally (Hillary, her agent), and socially (media or otherwise). We bond in a way that feels more like school friends at a sleepover than grownups talking about murder. We are so pleased with ourselves and the fact that we have already uncovered more about this case, practically by accident, than the team who is supposed to be working on it.

'I am utterly convinced in my heart that Matthew didn't do it. I know it's hard because you've only recently moved to Upper Huxley, but you are just going to have to take my word for it. This family deserves the truth of what actually happened. Not some cack-handed investigation from a washed-up wannabe.' My throat feels a bit raw, and my eyes are filling from the edges.

A thoughtful 'Hmmm ...' comes from Rowe.

We sit a bit longer in silence and stillness. The cold is starting to seep into my feet, my hands, and my bum. It's so obvious to me but I just can't seem to bring myself to say it because it feels so ... I don't know? Unbelievably stupid? Ridiculous? Totally absurd? I take another sip to steel myself, turn towards Rowena, and go for it before I have a chance to lose my nerve and get any colder.

'Rowe, I know you are going to think I'm mad but if Nick is going to be responsible for the formal investigation, then we need to work together to erm ... carry out an ... *in*formal vestigation.' I'm so pleased with my cleverness regarding the word play. But then I wait for what feels like a full three minutes with my cheeks getting hotter by the second for her to respond.

Rowe makes another quick check to see where the small ears are and then says at almost a whisper. 'Mary, I think you are completely mad.' She takes a deep breath and then we are both smiling. 'Unfortunately, I also think you might be right.'

Chapter 18

@gemma_cotswolds_mum Morning Friends. I thought it was time I address the elephant in the room. As you know, one of my recent posts has created a bit of a ~~shit show~~ controversy. I am so grateful for all the support I have received on here, but I would like to remind everyone that we want to make the internet a better place where we can discuss all opinions calmly, and particularly without making it personal, and ~~hounding people~~ invading anyone's privacy. You guys are the best ~~except for the nutters~~. Let's be kind, always. #honestmum #alwaysbekind ~~#sosickofthisshit~~

Rowena

Monday

I went to bed last night with the warm glow of an evening spent with a good friend.

And yet, somehow, I wake up with a bitter taste in my mouth that has nothing to do with Mary's delicious chilli. My head is sore from the red wine that accompanied the food, but I'm not sure that is the only reason for the pounding.

The fact that I've kept Mary's suggestion that we try to solve the murder ourselves from James has made me realise that I am genuinely uneasy about it all.

The intent is very noble, of course. The idea of making sure an innocent man (if our instincts are correct) doesn't linger in prison, preventing his son from growing up as an orphan while protecting him from his parents' potentially unsavoury past does pull at my heartstrings. But how do we know that the DI in charge is going to botch this investigation? Surely there are processes and checks in place. And a justice system!

And let's not forget that we are talking about finding the real murderer. I don't fancy putting myself or my family at risk, to be honest.

This is not *The Thursday Murder Club* or *Miss Marple!* In real life, pensioners or school mums, in our case, do not investigate murders. They leave it to the professionals.

Mary's enthusiasm makes me want to follow wherever she wants to go. But I can't help wondering why she is so hellbent on doing this herself.

I simply don't know if it's the right thing to do and the decision is way too big and scary for me.

We agreed yesterday to track Lorna down this morning, but I need more time to gather my thoughts before facing Mary, so I use my headache as an excuse to send James to drop Alfie at school.

By mid-morning, my head feels much better, and I can dedicate this newly freed up anxiety slot to the woeful state of the planet, enjoying the mild November air while not enjoying sorting the recycling out in the front garden.

I am puzzling over some sorting decision when I hear a 'Good morning' coming from the lane.

I look up to see a smiling Lorna standing outside my gate, as if I have conjured her up. Is this the sign I've been waiting for? Fate is once again pointing the way, and I feel a grateful relief.

'Hi, it's Lorna, isn't it?' I pretend to vaguely remember, hoping the shock is not showing on my face.

'Yes, it is. How are you, Rowena?'

'Good, thanks. Trying to decide whether those long-life juice bricks fit into cardboard or plastic ...' It is the truth, but I also know this might be a good conversation starter with Lorna. I don't have time to question the wisdom of engaging in conversation with a potential murder suspect.

'Well, actually, it is neither. They don't get collected kerbside.' she explains.

'Really? In London, we could put them into the blue bin.'

'They will get recycled if you take them to the recycling centre or if you drop them in one of the recycling banks at the Tesco car park.' She can see from my face that I'm definitely not going to do either.

'I am supposed to go to Tesco today and I have a few things to sort there. I can take these for you if you want.' she offers kindly.

'Thank you so much. If you're sure you don't mind ...' I have already handed over the three bricks. 'Ideally, of course, I ought to look at cutting these out completely. Would glass bottles be better, do you think?' I'm so nervous, I don't even let her respond. 'Actually, I stepped into a loose food shop in Stroud the other day and they were offering to fill up bottles with apple juice. I might do that next time I'm in town.' My mouth has become independent from my reason, it seems.

'Oh, was that Loose People?'

'Not sure. Not far from the church? Lovely wooden interior?' Once again, I surprise myself with how comfortable I seem to be at pretending and lying.

'Ah yes, it is. It is a lovely place. I always go there. I even worked with them in the past.' She volunteers.

'Ah, really, what do you do exactly?' I cannot believe my luck.

'Well, I manage a baby and toddler playgroup called 'Mummy's Morning' four days a week. But I worked with that shop, promoting them when I was running my Instagram account focusing on environmental issues.' I can see from her face she is worried I don't know what Instagram is and she is going to have to explain.

'Ah, but hang on a second! I think I follow you! Are you @simplepleasures?' I mock hesitate.

'@simple_ecolife, yes.' she corrects me, looking uncertain now.

'Yes, that's it. That is so cool. I love your photos. So inspiring. I had no idea you were local! But I haven't seen any of your posts recently. Stupid algorithm.' Mentioning the much-hated Instagram algorithm is a sure way to bring anyone using it on side.

'Ah, no, it's not that. I've had to go on a break from it recently. It was all getting a bit nasty on there ...' Her voice trails off, telling me she'd rather not elaborate further. But no way am I wasting this opportunity.

'Why is that? Trolls?' I go back to my recycling box, pretending I am not that interested in her answer.

'Yes, I suppose that's what you could call them. A group of fanatic followers from a popular influencer, who didn't appreciate one of my comments on her account ...' I look up and see that she is now looking very uncomfortable.

'Wait. I read about this! Wasn't that Gemma? @gemma_cotswolds_mum? From this village?' I am smiling, trying to emulate the excitement of someone who cannot see the potential serious ramifications.

'Yes. Yes, it was.' Lorna admits sheepishly.

'Blimey, that must have been awkward on the playground!' I laugh, still aiming to keep the conversation light.

'Well, to be honest, she didn't know it was me. Initially.'

'But you knew it was her, right? How tricky when your kids go to the same school!' Yep, that's me, Rowena, reluctant detective and yet still pressing on with my questioning.

'To be fair to Gemma, it wasn't her fault at all. She never said anything against me. It was a gang of 'ultra' followers. And she did call for them to calm down when I spoke to her directly after a couple of weeks of incessant online abuse. It was all a bit awkward, but I never blamed her personally.'

'What a crazy world! Are you going to get back to it? I certainly feel I have a lot to learn. The amount of waste we generate is insane!' I point at my three recycling boxes as evidence.

'Well, don't hesitate if you have any questions. I am by no means an expert, but we are all learning as we go along! As for going back to Instagram, I am not sure yet. I was engaged in talks for a book deal, but that was killed off when this whole sorry business kicked off. The book pretty much already exists half on my computer, half in my head but with poor Gemma dead, I don't think it is the right time for me to get back on the scene. My reputation is still tarnished, unfortunately. Maybe later?'

'Hey, that's cool! For the book, I mean ... I am a writer myself, children's books. A bit different admittedly but if you need some pointers in the publishing world ...' I offer sincerely, because despite my sneaky ways to get her to talk, I have warmed up to Lorna.

She thanks me for my offer and walks away, waving goodbye with my flattened juice bricks. I quickly finish my sorting and run back to wash my hands so I can text Mary.

11:21am: Talked to Lorna (don't ask). Can cross her off from the suspect list. No gain from Gemma's death. Will ring you tonight after bedtime for full story. XX

Immediately, I can see Mary is typing a reply.

11:21am: *Wow, great job, Watson! I have news, too. Matthew has been released. XX*

Chapter 19

@gemma_cotswolds_mum Afternoon Friends. Is there anything better than discovering a new make-up product that makes your life easier and your routine faster? More time to spend doing the things you love! I can't recommend Jones Road's "What the Foundation" enough! It's AMAZING! This is not an ad. ~~But I'm absolutely desperate for a partnership and I want free product.~~ This product is so easy to use and makes me feel absolutely beautiful. Everyone deserves to feel this beautiful! #lifteachotherup #beautifulwomen #jonesroad ~~#pleasepleasepleasesponsorme~~

Mary

Monday

Before I got the text, I was starting to worry that Rowe might have come to her senses when I saw that she was missing from drop off this morning. Clearly, she saw an opportunity and couldn't pass it up. A true professional. I could definitely pick up some tips from her!

'Pending further investigation' was on the official release that Tom had read out to me from the car he was in. 'What the fuck, May? What are they playing at? They just need more evidence for the conclusion they've already made? It feels so ... shit!' he finished eloquently.

I was imagining what he would say when I told him that the newcomer to the village had identified a suspect that the police didn't seem to know about and then had subsequently cleared her from suspicion. It deserved a proper conversation, though. If I sent him a text, no matter how long, involved and detailed, I'd only get a cursory 'K' back. I generate an eye-roll emoji in my mind as my theoretical response to his theoretical text.

In my resolve to learn more about what happened to Gemma, I create a new IG account – @marylamb_travels to better understand the world of influencers! But first, the day job.

I convinced my editor to sign off on a small feature piece on the Gloucestershire Warwickshire Steam Railway (GWSR) at Christmas time (score!), so I load up my rucksack with my MacBook and camera and head to the train station. I board the train at Cheltenham Racecourse and head through the long tunnel to Winchcombe and then along the viaduct all the way to Broadway. The train journey is only an hour each way and the whole experience is so charming, the article practically writes itself. The hardest bit is trying to get some decent shots of the incredible views – steam trains are the original rickety! Just glad there are no murders on this 'Orient Express' – I think I left my little grey cells at home!

***

When I am back sitting at my desk in my comfy slippers and tatty jumper, I persuade myself that I am looking for additional copy content for the article and use my shiny new IG account to consult the lines' Instagram page – @steamgwsr. Whilst it's helpful for my piece, it also scratches the itch of learning more about the role that Instagram plays in marketing.

What a rabbit hole! I lose two hours of my life to researching steam train enthusiasts and who they follow. I have a shock when I look at the clock and realise that I am dangerously close to deadline. Like the professional I am, I polish off a perfectly decent piece, send it off to Rosie who is very pleased, and then dive back in.

I follow as many influencers as I can to try to understand how it all works, I learn a lot – many of them seem to be regular people – they have no qualifications or really, anything to offer, for that matter. They are generally just funny, or snide, or interested in interior design or make-up. Soooo much make-up! Ugh. Not my bag. I'm a mascara and lip gloss kind of girl and always will be.

By the time Tom gets home with the children, I am firing on all cylinders. I have learned that Cristiano Ronaldo has 660 million (!) followers on Instagram. Of the top 10 social media influencers, 7 are women, 6 are from the music world, and 2 are members of the Kardashian family (seriously?). But I really want to know more about influencers like Gemma. How do they get into it? How do they gain followers? How do they find their sponsors? Or do their sponsors find them?

I am keen to catch up with Tom about what Rowe discovered and to learn any more gossip. However, first we have the small undertaking of the evening routine: unpack book bags, do reading, sign reading records, rustle up the dinner, eat, bathe, brush hair, brush teeth, bedtime story. I do always appreciate it when he's around for this bit. I've never really got used to doing all of those things on my own when he's on lates.

Finally, we both collapse on the couch. He asks me about my day, so I tell him about the steam train and suggest that we take Charlotte and Ben when we get a chance. I can tell from his responses that he's exhausted. I ask him about his day, and he makes some rather noncommittal noises. Despite being so keen to chat with him all evening, I decide to let him have a bit of peace. I find the clicker, eventually, under a cushion, flip on the telly and see that there is a rerun of *Grand Designs* on. Perfect.

I pick up my phone and message Rowe:

8:10pm: Free when you are for that catch-up. Xx

8:11pm: Great – just getting Eloise settled – call you in 15. XX

8:11pm: Great! X

8:33pm: Lying on floor in Eloise's bedroom. Am stuck. Help.

Then much later, she messages again:

9:26pm: Sorry. ☹ Still awake? XX

I step into the kitchen to call her.

'Hiya!'

'Hi there! So sorry! Eloise just would not go down ...' Rowena is flustered. It has clearly been a nightmare evening.

'Honestly, Rowe, it's absolutely fine! I got to see almost all of the second *Grand Designs*, again!'

'Oh sorry! I can call ba ...'

'Ha Ha – I think I've seen this one at least twice, maybe three times. So, tell me about Lorna! How did you track her down so quickly? I'd honestly thought that maybe you'd started thinking better of our agreement to find her and ask questions when I didn't see you at drop off this morning, but then I got your text.'

'Ha! Mary! I'm such a wuss! Argghhh ... Honestly!'

'But you found her ...'

'She bloody found me, didn't she? She literally walked right up to my front door!'

I burst into laughter. 'Seriously?'

'Yes, really. You honestly couldn't make it up!'

Rowe continues to tell me about the discussion that she and Lorna had. She explains that Lorna had nothing to gain by hurting Gemma. In fact, she had quite a bit to lose. At the very least, it's put her plans for a book deal on the backburner indefinitely. Not much of a motive there.

'Did Lorna say if she was using an agent for her book deal?'

'No. I don't remember her saying anything specific about that. Why?'

'Oh no – it was just something that Tom said about an agent he'd identified when he was on the case – Hillary Peters? I wondered if influencers use agents. Hmmm. Anything else that you can think of that we should put on our list to think about?'

'I'd like to know more about swinging.'

Mock horror: 'I meant about the case, Rowena!'

'Ha Ha Mary – you bloody know what I mean. But honestly, I'm shattered now. Let's pick this up on Thursday – coffee at mine after pick-up?'

'Perfect.'

Chapter 20

@gemma_cotswolds_mum One of my recent resolutions ~~yet another one~~ has been to be more grateful, particularly for the ones who are supporting me. Of course, my family is my best support system. My beautiful husband who's always got my back ~~although not so much lately~~, my parents who are always there for me and of course, my number one, my darling boy, Charlie. But I also wouldn't be where I am without my ~~ruthless~~ talented agent, @hpetersagency. And finally, there is you, my gorgeous followers, without whom this ~~career~~ beautiful dream simply wouldn't be possible. #gratefuleveryday ~~#soppypost~~

Rowena

Tuesday

James reluctantly left for London this morning. I put on my best brave face and pretended I was totally cool about managing the kids, the house, and general life admin while a murderer was still on the loose and the police in charge were not showing an abundance of competence.

To be fair, Eloise has been more settled at night recently, except for last night where she simply wouldn't go down. But she only woke up once and I managed to settle her back without a feed. Success!

Also, I've managed to bag a space for Alfie in two after school clubs this week. From what I gathered from Mary, these are like Glastonbury tickets, and you can't waste a minute to book them when the email is sent by Jenny. So that should leave me more time on those days.

Making the most of that time, I have a big day ahead of me meeting my agent, Daisy, in Bath for lunch.

Unfortunately, because James is in London and I am still breastfeeding her, Eloise has to tag along for the ride. I wanted to take the train because years in London with no car made me extremely nervous to do longer car journeys on my own, particularly with Eloise. But the train times were no good, and I would have had to drive to the station in Stroud anyway and change at Bristol. So, I put on my big-girl pants and face the one-hour drive.

I haven't been to Bath in years and, ignoring the anxious knot in my chest, I resolve to enjoy the beautiful Georgian city all decorated for Christmas, and look forward to some adult conversation, baby permitting.

We set off as soon as I have dropped Alfie off at school. We make good time, and I enjoy the few hours walking around Bath, talking to Eloise in her stroller to keep her awake. I do a spot of shopping in some of the lovely shops on Milsom Street, and I can't resist making a detour to the Circus and the Royal Crescent before heading back down to meet Daisy at The Ivy Brasserie.

Daisy Shane, my trusted agent, is already waiting for me at our table in the corner of the main room.

'Rowena! And Eloise! I'm so happy to see you both!' She welcomes me with a massive hug. I am fully aware agents always say that to their clients, but, call me deluded, I do believe Daisy means it. We have been working together since the beginning of my writing career and she has always been most supportive, notably when fighting my corner with my publisher when I went on my second self-imposed maternity leave.

'I requested the table in the corner to give you some privacy if you had to feed the little one. Hope that's OK.' See what I mean? Being a mother of three with a successful career makes her the perfect ally to any working mum.

'Thank you. That's perfect. It's actually time for a feed, so I'll start with that if you don't mind, then hopefully Eloise will grant us a lovely long nap while we eat.' I say with more confidence than I feel. *Please don't kick off at The Ivy,* I plead silently to my daughter as we settle down on the comfortable velvet banquette. We catch up on our respective families while I feed Eloise.

Daisy demands to see photos of Alfie and deplores not having any good recent ones of her teenage boys. 'I would have to go to TikTok or Snapchat, probably ...' She rolls her eyes up to the magnificently decorated ceiling reminiscent of Wedgwood Jasperware.

We've just ordered our lunch from the waiter when Daisy exclaims 'Hillary?'

I look up to see a woman dressed in a sharp black trouser suit passing by our table.

The woman peers at Daisy through her big tortoiseshell-rimmed glasses with an expression that doesn't give much away, and I suddenly think that this is going to be awkward as she hasn't recognised Daisy. But I turn out to be wrong.

'Daisy.' That is just a statement. 'How are you? I haven't seen you in the longest time.' It sounds like a reproach.

'I am good, thank you. How are things going for you? How is your fancy world treating you?' Daisy asks warmly, clearly ignoring the coldness of her acquaintance.

'Oh, you know, ups and downs, but mostly ups. Bouncing back nicely after a recent hiccup.' she declares confidently, standing a little straighter.

'Nice, well done! Can I introduce you to my client and friend, Rowena Boat? Rowena, this is Hillary Peters. We started our careers together, too long ago.'

Hillary now looks at me and visibly recoils when she realises I have a baby attached to my left nipple. She gives me the thinnest, most insincere smile and cannot take her leave from us fast enough.

'Ah well, Hillary Peters, charming as always. I haven't seen her in years! As you've probably gathered, she doesn't work in Children's Literature!' Daisy is chuckling to herself as she imitates Hillary's face when she spotted Eloise.

While she is talking and laughing, I'm trying hard to grasp why the name Hillary Peters sounds so familiar.

'Rowena, are you OK? What is it? Did she upset you?' Daisy has spotted that I am not joining in.

'What domain did you say Hillary Peters works in? I feel like I know that name from somewhere, but I just can't place her.'

'Well, when we worked at the same agency, Philip Mayhew, she was dealing with non-fiction authors. She did that successfully for a number of years. And then, about ten years ago, she completely abandoned the world of literature and is now agenting for people on social media. You know. *Influencers.*' Daisy doesn't quite roll her eyes at the word, but I can tell from her tone that she's much happier representing authors.

The penny drops.

'Yes, of course! She was Gemma's agent!' I burst out.

'Gemma? Who is Gemma?'

'Gemma Hatherley. The influencer who died live on Instagram two weeks ago.'

'Ah yes, I read something about it. Dreadful business.'

'Wow, what a coincidence!' I exclaim in disbelief.

'Coincidence? Why would that be a coincidence?' Daisy asks, intrigued by my excitement.

'Well, Gemma Hatherley lived in my village. And, obviously, there has been a lot of noise about her death there.'

'Ah, OK. Sad, very sad.' Daisy says respectfully.

'Hang on! Hillary talked about a 'recent hiccup'. Surely, she wasn't referring to her client's untimely death?' The disbelief is clear in my voice and Eloise starts to fuss due to my agitation.

'Oh, come on, surely not. You can't call a death a 'hiccup'!' I can see in Daisy's eyes that she is mulling something over. 'Well, actually, to be fair, knowing Hillary ... She is pretty ruthless when it comes to business. We used to call her *Hill for the Kill*!' Daisy laughs now, remembering the past.

She starts recollecting other anecdotes from her time at Philip Mayhew and the subject naturally moves on from Hillary to books and eventually to my own writing. By that point, Eloise has cooperated and is now fast asleep in her car seat.

We spend the most enjoyable lunch eating delicious food and discussing my ideas for my next book, distracting me from the impending car journey home.

Chapter 21

@gemma_cotswolds_mum Afternoon Friends. Would you just look at this bake sale table? Can you believe the incredible talent ~~with a little guidance from me~~ of my amazing friends at the #UHPSPTFA? And there are vegan, gluten-free, nut-free, and lactose-free options available ~~in other words, air!~~ so there is something for everyone! Please come along to #UHPS today from 3pm and support our amazing work. #supportyourPTFA ~~#repost #copypastefromlastbakesale #saveforlater~~

Mary

Tuesday

We are running very late this morning. No, I don't know how it happened. I woke up on time, they woke up on time – it just sometimes works that way. Somewhere between waking up and now, we've gone from 'on-time' to 'very late' and it's nothing but bloody annoying.

Charlotte's hair is all over the place, Ben looks like he's been dressed by a colour-blind clown, and I have no idea what either of them has for their lunch but I'm certain that it is not Jamie Oliver approved. Whatever! I'll make something healthy for dinner, and they can read twice this evening. It's very cold outside and I make sure that at least they have coats, hats, and gloves. They may be looking a little rough around the edges and high on E numbers, but they Will. Not. Be. Cold!

'Morning Jenny! We are so very late, sorry?' I plead as I'm running up the path towards the reception office. I kiss children all over twice in the hopes that I can somehow mitigate the impacts of my responsibility vacuum with the sheer volume of my love.

When I get home, I change into my running gear and head out along the lanes for a run to clear my head and reset my morning. It's cold but it's clear and it's exactly what I need. I pop my headphones in and listen to my '2000s Pop' playlist on Spotify and run through my to do list. There is a lot there. As much as I love the autumn and all that it entails, I find the catapult towards Christmas very stressful. What starts out as the hint of cooler nights and crisp blue skies swiftly turns into very full social diaries and the familiar anxiety of Christmas Day plans and the search for the perfect presents. Don't get me wrong, I love Christmas. I just find the run up a bit hard work.

To an outdoor person like me, the shorter days increase this sense of pressure to make it all count and get it all done. Not only are the months and weeks short, but so are the days!

So:

- I need to plan the week's meals and do the shopping this afternoon – must remember stamps!
- Ben needs his football kit clean for tonight
- I need to book a table for our work Christmas party. Oh God! I am probably so late. We are going to end up going for a cheeky Nando's for our Christmas do and everyone is going to blame me!
- I need to order the turkey – argh – find out how many for dinner on Christmas day
- Charlotte needs a birthday present for the party she's going to on Saturday (thank God for Amazon Prime)

And so it continues, much like this, for 2.5 of the 3 miles.

***

By the time I get home, I'm physically and mentally tired, but running does make me feel an awful lot better. I stumble up the stairs to the bathroom and take a long shower. Showers are magical – they are the absolute best places to think. One day, clever people will be able to harness the energy of children (Goodbye greenhouse gases!), and they will manage to replicate the quality of thinking generated through 'shower thoughts' (Hello World Peace!). Until then, thank God for the humble shower.

I start to think about Gemma and her family. Who wanted to kill her and why? She was beautiful (envy?), rich (greed?), and famous (pride?). Which of these was enough to make someone want to end her life? Or was it a combination? Was there something that Gemma knew that she must never tell? Something that would get someone into trouble? Legally? Emotionally? Financially? I tried to think like the person who killed her. How was I feeling? Scared? Angry? Driven? Nervous?

I knew from my chats with Tom that Gemma had died from head trauma. On the face of it (sorry ...) you'd rule out pre-meditation. Rarely would someone go to all the trouble of planning a murder that would depend on them being in a position to bash a head against a marble counter. I swallow hard as bile threatens. So, a crime of passion! But what kind of passion? Then I start wondering about how we know that it's definitely a murder. How are the police sure that it wasn't just a burglary gone wrong? (I chastise myself for use of the word 'just' there. She's dead, after all. But I know what I mean.)

So, was the burglary premeditated or the actions of an opportunist? What were they wearing again? I think it was a balaclava and all back clothes – but I'll need to check that with Tom. But that definitely points to pre-meditation. You don't often get all dressed up in black with a balaclava in your pocket on the off chance that you might find a door unlocked (there was no sign of forced entry!) on your evening stroll. So what were they looking for? iPhones, iPads? Jewellery? Paintings? I do have a little chuckle about that to myself. However beautiful Gemma's home is (and it is!) the thought of her actually having an opinion on fine art was quite funny, never mind spending lots of cash on it. Before I could stop myself, I was imagining her picking out wall art at IKEA to go on the vast double story walls in her million-pound home. Not that I'm judging IKEA art, by the way, I am judging Gemma, and I shouldn't. She's dead.

I hop out of the shower, pull on jeans, a t-shirt, and a cosy jumper. I pretend to put a bit of make-up on – more of a nod to making an effort than an effort itself – whip up a quick bowl of porridge and head out to the Land Cruiser. 'Red' is a legacy from my dad and he announced that it 'came with the house'. I absolutely love that car. Tom has tried to get me to sell it so many times I've lost count, and he's (finally!) lost hope. I decide to head over to the Wild Boar Café before facing the weekly shop. If I'm going to meal plan, at least I should be able to do it whilst drinking one of their lovely flat whites.

I park in the small but full car park. It's right outside the village proper but the coffee is good, and the cakes are ace, so they never have a problem with lack of custom. A tinkle of the bell sounds as I open the door. The smell is excellent, cinnamon and ginger, and the warmth pulls me in – perfect on a freezing morning like this. It's absolutely packed – clearly some have walked using the old rail path from the centre of the village, otherwise I'd have never found a parking space. I squeeze my way to the counter on autopilot and then look up in surprise.

'Oh, hi Vicky! I didn't know you were working here! How are you?' Her flaming red locks are tamed in a beautiful Dutch braid that illuminates her jade eyes.

'Hiya Mary! Good here, thanks. Yeah – now that Gertie has finally started in the Early Years program, I thought it'd be fun to pick up a few shifts to get me out of the house. I had no idea it got so busy in here!'

'Ah – good for you! It does get busy in here. I think it's the locals avoiding the tourist tax from the tea rooms in the centre of town. Are you finding it OK, though?'

'Oh yeah, it's great. I really enjoy it – even if it is exhausting – and Mark is good at letting me work around drop-off, collection, and school holidays. He says, basically, I can work as little or as much as I like!'

'That sounds absolutely ideal!'

'It is – I landed on my feet. And when I'm not making world class coffee, I get to make whatever cakes I want to be able to sell alongside; only tricky bit is that he's asking me to come up with more vegan and gluten-free options. Cakes, Mary! I can do it, but I can't do it well. Not yet, at least. But I am trying. Now, what would you like?'

'A large flat white, please? It's a treat to motivate me to do some meal planning and then fuel to get through the weekly shop.'

'Sure. Anything else?' she says, eyeing the cakes.

I give a little laugh. 'Not this time, thanks, bit early for me. But I'll try next time?' I offer by way of a consolation.

'Fine. Just stay away from the gluten-free muffins.' she says, conspiratorially.

I pay and we both move to the big Italian coffee machine at the end of the counter.

'Hey Vicky – sorry for not knowing, but were you and Gemma good friends?' I'm trying to ask as nicely as I can.

'Oh, Mary, you know what Gemma was like. Friends weren't really her thing. She had more like followers. Both in real life and virtually. But I did like her. She was ambitious, of course, sometimes almost aggressively, but I always knew that deep down she had a good heart.' Vicky was avoiding my gaze, and it didn't seem to be just because she was concentrating on her coffee making.

'She could be a bit, erm, harsh to some of the other mums. I heard that she could be pretty rude in some of the PTFA meetings.' I'd heard that she'd been rude to *Vicky* on one or two occasions: about how the icing on the cakes could have been stiffer or the portions of tiffin larger but I'd never seen any of that with my own eyes.

'Ah, that's old news. Gemma would always get stressed as we got closer to the date of whatever event was currently being planned. She could be a little snappy, but everyone knew she didn't mean it.' She had finished making my coffee and placed it on the counter. When she looked at me, I could see sadness in her eyes. But I wasn't convinced it was all because of Gemma's death. I didn't remember them being so close – but am I just looking for the fall guy?

'Thanks Vicky – looks delicious! See you later?'

'Course! And if you change your mind about the cake ...' She says, but her smile doesn't quite reach her eyes.

Chapter 22

@gemma_cotswolds_mum Charlie and I upgraded the bedtime routine ~~something HAD to change as it was getting out of control~~ and it's been lovely. We now take turns reading a book ~~I choose for him from the teacher's list~~ of his choice for 15 mins and then we both share the best moment of our days. It's only been a week, but I love this moment between the two of us. ~~Cannot get Matthew interested at all.~~ Long may it last! ~~No doubt this will go out of the window as soon as I have an evening out.~~ What about you? What's your evening routine like? ~~#Idontcare~~ #gentleparenting #IGmums

Rowena

Tuesday

The long evening bath-dinner/feed-bedtime tunnel is seemingly never ending. Never do I feel more like I'm walking a tightrope than when I'm doing the evening routine by myself. One wrong step and it could all spiral out into a nightmare of an evenings. One wrong menu choice and I could end up dealing with a 5-year-old rejecting everything on his plate. The wrong bath toy or storybook could escalate into a battle of wills and a prolonged bedtime routine. All of which I can't afford, with Eloise's fuse being even shorter than her brother's. Particularly after our day trip to Bath and her screaming her way through the return car journey that left me shaking.

Tonight, however, the stars are aligned, and both kids are in bed and asleep by 8.10pm.

I crash exhausted on the sofa after shutting the door on the messy kitchen. Something for tomorrow.

As hard as the solo bedtime routine is at times, I don't dislike these evenings on my own, when I've put both kids down and I can do what I want, watch what I want on TV, eat what I want, and not have to talk to anyone else. Not so long ago, I was terrified when solo evenings suddenly became my enforced new normal, but, now that it is all behind us, I am able to enjoy the freedom of occasional alone time.

I could grab the book I'm reading (*Calm Parents, Happy Kids*) or try and work on my book. But all I want for now is a few minutes of mindless scrolling. After flicking through my Instagram feed full of motherhood and home inspiration accounts for five minutes, I can't help but look at what the internet has to say about Gemma's death. With her husband released, I haven't done any more probing. And yet, two weeks after her death no one has been charged, and suspicion still seems to be hanging over Matthew. Mary's motivation revolves around her desire to clear him. I, however, feel a loyalty towards Gemma and want to see justice done and her killer arrested.

I start by reading all the online articles reporting her death. I already read some of them when they came out but learned nothing new. The poorly written article from the local newspaper doesn't tell me much. A basic combination of pictures from her Instagram account and a few measly lines about her husband and child, clickbait aimed at pulling at all the heartstrings.

I find a couple of articles from national newspapers but again, it's more of the same, until I get to an article from an online news outlet. There, I find a description of the incident from what the audience could see on the Instagram Live.

'At around 8.42pm, the Instagram superstar is in the middle of replying to her audience's questions when a loud noise is heard coming from somewhere in the house. Gemma is startled and immediately looks to her left. She stands up suddenly and her face can no longer be seen. She can then be heard saying 'What are you doing here? Who ...?' In a frightened voice as she moves out of frame. Then follow sounds of a struggle during which only Gemma's voice can be heard. The only words that can be discerned are a plea to her followers, to 'Call 999!'

Ten seconds later, a cry of distress is cut short by a loud thumping noise. Some followers said they heard a gasp followed by some rummaging sounds for another thirty seconds. After six minutes of total silence from Gemma's house, while followers frantically asked for news of Gemma in the comments, the police can be heard and seen arriving on the scene, and they turn off the phone, stopping the live broadcast.'

I finish reading and realise that I have been pretty much holding my breath the whole time. The hand holding my phone is shaking and can feel shivers running down my spine. Reading this has really brought it home to me. There, just off camera, while hundreds of people listened, Gemma died in her own home. I go and check that my front door is properly bolted.

I get back to Instagram and go to her account. There obviously hasn't been any new content posted on there since her tragic death two weeks ago. Unsurprisingly, the 'live' video of her assault has been removed.

I click open her last post where she can be seen smiling in front of her porch, tastefully decorated for Halloween with pumpkins of all sizes, shapes, and colours. There are over 10,000 comments.

Most of them are condolences and messages of support to her family. But amongst all the outpouring of love, one message and its hashtag grab my attention:

This is tragic. The murderer is still at large. What are the police doing? #whokilledgemma

I click on the hashtag and find that there are 63 posts related to it. I open them one by one starting with the most popular. My mind is blown. There are over a dozen people that seem to be dedicating all their recent social media activity to doing what Mary and I have started: trying to find out who killed Gemma, and why?

This is incredible.

Amongst all the posts and comments, I see that some people went down the same avenue as Mary and I, suspecting @simple_ecolife. Thankfully for Lorna, none of them seem to have worked out her identity. Yet.

People have also spent a lot of time and effort retracing the timeline as described in the newspaper article, but in a more matter of fact style.

8.30: Gemma starts the live

8.42: loud noise. Gemma looks left, stands up, and addresses the intruder.

8.42.41: she moves off camera. A physical assault can be heard.

8.43.08: Gemma calls out 'Call 999!'

8.43.12: Loud thump. Gemma falls? Gasp from the intruder?

8.50: Police arrive on the scene and stop the video.

Most of the speculation from the Instagrammers is around the 'gasp' that can be heard off screen. All the online amateur sleuths are adamant it is a female voice that is heard gasping. Is it Gemma's? But all seem to have concluded that she would not have cried out, fallen unconscious (or dead?), and then gasped. So, it seems most likely that the gasp comes from the murderer!

The murderer is a woman!

My instinctive reaction is that women are not burglars. Now, I know this is probably very sexist and I'm all for equal opportunities in the workplace, but I would bet good money that the vast majority of home burglaries are carried out by men.

I am dying to tell Mary about what I've found but it is already past 11pm. My fall down the true crime rabbit hole has lasted over 3 hours!

Just as I decide to get myself upstairs to bed, I refresh the hashtag one last time and find that there is a brand-new post. I click it open and gasp. Somebody has just posted a video of the Live during which Gemma died!

Over seven minutes of video, there for me to watch. Before I even question the morality of it, I press play with a shaking finger. The video is of terrible quality as I realise that somebody has filmed the Instagram Live on their phone with another device.

The video starts with Gemma already off screen and struggling with the intruder. My heart thumping, I watch and listen in horror as all that I read about only minutes earlier unfolds on my screen. I know what is coming but I still jump in fright at Gemma's anguished cry and stifle a scream at the loud thump that immediately follows. I don't hear the gasp because of my loud breathing and the blood rushing to my ears.

I need to watch it again, but I'm not sure my nerves can take it.

Then, my brain kicks in because I realise that Instagram is probably going to take down that video in no time as it must violate their ethical policy. Inspired by the post itself, I quickly grab my iPad and use it to film the video playing on my phone. If the post gets censored, I will still have a copy of it on my iPad. I will worry about the legality of this later.

This time, because I have put the volume on maximum, I can hear the gasp, which is indeed feminine. I continue filming for the next six minutes until the police arrive onscreen and turn off the recording. I stop my own camera and try and to slow my heartbeat down.

I can feel the adrenalin rushing through my veins and I suddenly have to run to the bathroom to be sick. It was bad enough reading about the details of her death, but listening to it is so much worse.

I need to talk to somebody about this. I know she won't reply this late at night, but sending a message to Mary still feels like sharing and unburdening. I decide not to mention the video as such, as again, I'm not too sure how legal it is.

11.34pm: Mary, found a lot of info about what happened to Gemma the night she died. Got to meet up tomorrow morning. Please. Call me when you see this.

I check all the doors and windows again and get into bed, but my brain is running in overdrive. I am still trying to calm down when Eloise wakes up demanding a feed to be soothed back to sleep.

Never have I been so grateful for a night-time feed. Holding my baby in my arms while she makes her little sucking noises works wonders on my exhausted nerves and I fall asleep as soon as I've put her back in her cot.

Chapter 23

@gemma_cotswolds_mum Morning Friends. Happy Small Business Saturday! Just a friendly reminder that your favourite influencers (including me!) often rely on their social media accounts for income to support their families. So, your likes, follows, and shares mean a lot to us. Even better if you go on to support the products that we advertise and tell them you heard it here first! #smallbusinesssaturday #supportsmallbusinesses #likefollowshare

Mary

Wednesday

I pick up my phone to turn off the alarm and the second thing I see is a text from Rowe. Even from reading those few words, I can tell she's upset.

6:30am: Sorry, Rowe, just saw your message. I'm free after drop-off? Xx

6:30am: Great! See you at school. Xx

After we drop the children off, we amble back to Rowe's house talking almost exclusively about superficial news items – weather, latest from school, impending holiday plans. I can tell from the way that she is avoiding my direct gaze and keeps surveying our surroundings that Rowe is dying to tell me something but is clearly saving the headline act for when we get to hers.

Once we are both in the kitchen, she busies herself with the coffee machine and I decide I can't take it anymore. 'Ok, spill it! What's up?'

'Oh Mary. I found the video!' She waits for my reaction. 'The video of Gemma's murder!' She switches quickly to hiding her face in her hands. 'I wasn't trying to find it because I wanted to watch it or anything.' She puts her hands down, palms facing upwards in exasperation, and looks straight at me with pure innocence. 'I'm not a sociopath, after all. But I was doing some research on Instagram, and I actually found the video. The original one, of course, has already been taken down, but there was a version that someone had obviously filmed from another device.'

I can tell that she is really winding herself up about this. I feel the need to interrupt her train of thought before she becomes completely overwhelmed.

'Oh, my goodness, Rowe.' I'm putting on my calm voice now to give her something to concentrate on. 'That must have been harrowing to watch. Are you OK?'

'Yeah, I'm alright.' She's starting to become calmer now. 'It was just really upsetting to watch someone ... well ... you know ... to watch someone's last moments.'

I feel for her. She didn't want to say the words 'to watch someone die'. Again, it really hits home that whilst we are playing Miss Marple, there is a real victim here. Rowena resumes making the coffees and we chat a bit about menial topics.

After a while, she asks if I want to watch the video.

'I mean, yes, I think so,' I say tentatively. 'Really, I just feel like I need to – I mean, this is the most important piece of this whole puzzle so far, right? This is the best possible chance we have to clear Matthew. Surely, it's the sort of thing that detectives dream of? An actual video of the murder.'

She opens the video on her iPad so that we can watch it together and then, there it is. All of the sudden, it's Just. So. Real. It's seven minutes of 'not an awful lot' on the face of it but when you know what's coming ...

After it's finished (and I was secretly praying for it to hurry up and be done) I feel sick. I'm glad I haven't had a big breakfast as my stomach definitely does a little roll.

Rowe looks at me, questioningly. 'Well?'

I take a deep breath and pause a second to make sure I trust myself to speak without vomiting. 'Horrid. Truly.' The muscles in my hands are screaming from having clenched them together so tightly. And I hadn't been breathing properly for some time. I feel lightheaded.

'I know ...' she says.

'Honestly – that plea from Gemma to 'Call 999!' sent ice through my veins.'

'You can see why I've been preoccupied.' Rowe says, and I can see that as horrible as it is, it's a relief for her to find someone to share the experience with.

We watch the video again, pausing often to discuss specific details – to try and understand what is visible, audible, discernible, and what (if anything?) is missing (always much harder).

After that Rowe starts explaining what she's learned from the comments section, that there is a whole group of people in the process of doing what we are doing – trying to find Gemma's killer. She explains that they even have their own hashtag and everything.

'Obviously you get some wild unrelated conspiracy theorists but some of the points that they are making are valid and interesting. Like we noticed, one part of the group is focusing on the fact that the gasp that is made by the 'burglar' is almost surely female.'

A flash bursts in my brain. I stand up and shout 'This is it, Rowe! If it's a female, then it's not Matthew! How can this have been missed by the police? Or even worse, dismissed! What the...?'

'You are right, Mary.' She pauses thoughtfully. 'That's it, I'm in!' The confidence in her voice is matched by the resolve on her face.

'In for what? The investigation? I thought you already were?' I look at her out of the side of my eyes in mock chastisement.

'Well ...'

'Never mind. However it happened, I'm glad you are fully on board now, especially since you've been doing all of the investigating so far!' I laugh – buoyed by the recent revelation. 'What about we make a list of questions that need to be answered?'

I find one of Ben's party bags thrown in the junk drawer with a microscopic notebook in the shape of *SpongeBob SquarePants*. To complete the look, I find a hot pink pen with a huge fluffy monster on top. Columbo never had this style! We both start blurting out questions and I write as quickly as I can, trying to keep a semblance of legibility, eyes burning from the terrible contrast:

- What are the possible motives for a woman breaking into a house?
- If she's the burglar, does that also mean she is definitely the murderer? Or could it be a coincidence that both were happening around the same time?
- Was she working alone or with someone else?
- Was she the only other person in the house?

- How did she get in the house since it wasn't forced entry? Doors unlocked?
- What did she take? OR – did she take anything?
- Did she come to the house with the intention of killing Gemma?
- Did she recognise Gemma?
- Do the police have any idea about this woman or who she might be? Is she under investigation?
- Are the police following up on the online thread of #whokilledgemma as well? Could the murderer be following it?
- How are we going to be able to find the answers to these questions without looking like meddling weirdos?

That last question was mine.

Chapter 24

@gemma_cotswolds_mum Morning Friends. Big kitchen reveal! I know I have been teasing you for weeks ~~this has been the longest redecorating ever~~, but it's finally time to share my new favourite room. love to sit at the island with a cup of herbal tea, and I love my new white cabinets from @dreamkitchensuk. I cannot praise the quality of their cabinets and finishing details enough, ~~out their customer service is appalling.~~ and I'm ecstatic to be offering a huge discount code of 20% off their ~~very~~ limited range of @dreamkitchensuk. Use code GEMMAKITCHENDREAMS at checkout. #dreamkitchens #lovemyhome #interiors #bigreveal

Rowena

Wednesday

I feel so much better for watching the video with Mary, mostly because her reaction wasn't unlike mine.

Contrary to me, however, she did manage to keep her breakfast in. Seems like I deep cleaned the toilet for nothing this morning!

I know I shouldn't be laughing about this. But I don't know what else to do.

All of my reticence around this investigation has vanished at some point during the different viewings. It is totally unlike me, but where I should feel an all too familiar anxiety eating at my insides, I feel a burning rage and fierce determination to see justice for Gemma and her family. And yet, I feel I have to share my last bit of concern over what we have done.

'Mary, I should have mentioned before, but it sort of slipped my mind ... I was so focused on sharing what I had found out with you ... Basically, I don't know how legal it is that I have this video on my iPad. I checked the hashtag earlier and the video we've just watched has already been taken down by Instagram. This makes me very nervous. And even more so for you as Tom works for the police. What do you think?' I blurt out nervously.

'Ah, I see what you mean. Not ideal. I guess you should delete it. How could anyone find out you have this video, though? You didn't save it straight from Instagram, did you?'

'You're right. I only watched it twice on there. And then, I filmed it on a separate device. I haven't emailed it to anyone. So, once the video is deleted, there is no way to know I have done this.' I say, slightly reassured.

'Ok, before we delete it, we should watch it a couple more times to make sure we haven't missed anything!' Mary says enthusiastically, as if I needed any more proof that she is the brave one in our duo.

The most frustrating thing about the video is that it starts after the intruder enters the house and when everything is happening off camera. Nothing new comes out of our 1st or 2nd rewatch, except the shocking realisation that you can very easily become numb to the most horrific things. After four watches I certainly don't feel the nausea, I felt last night. I'm almost starting to lose interest when Mary blurts out:

'There! Pause!'

'What? What is it?' I can't hear anything new and there is nothing to see other than what seems to be Gemma's home in the background.

'In the mirror! Look!' Mary shouts excitedly.

I look intently as the quality of the video is appalling, and then I see it. There is something or someone moving in the mirror at the back of the room.

'Do you see the black shape? That looks like someone! Is that the murderer?' Mary asks urgently.

'Yes, I can see it. I've seen screenshots of the Live from just before the incident and Gemma was not wearing black. She had a red top on. So, it can't be her! It has to be the intruder!' I join Mary in her excitement, only for her to burst it like a balloon, seconds later.

'Oh, hang on, I've just remembered. I'm an idiot, really. I already know that the burglar was dressed in black. I'm sure Tom mentioned it and said that he or she was wearing a balaclava.'

'I guess this is how they know. The police must have got hold of the original video from Instagram. It must have been a better quality version for them to be able to discern a balaclava when we can only see a vague shape ...'

'But wait!' Mary shouts 'It is a vague shape, but can you see that jerky movement just before the loud thump?'

I strain my eyes and yes, I can see it.

'It looks like the intruder's arm. Looks like it is whacking something down ...' Mary trails off.

'Oh Mary, something or someone down. Could it be when the murderer ...' I can't find the right word and the only one that comes to mind is too violent.

'When the murderer forcefully hit Gemma's head onto the marble counter?' Mary tactfully finishes my sentence. 'Yes, it really looks like it.'

'This doesn't look like Gemma fell onto the counter, then, really. This was definitely not an accident!' I feel furious on Gemma's behalf all over again.

'Yes, I think this is what the police have also concluded. That video is probably the reason why.'

I don't know why I feel disappointed, really. It's not as if we can really solve this mystery ourselves, is it? This is police work.

As if Mary has read my mind, she says in a quiet voice: 'I think I'm going to have to tell Tom I've seen this video. Just to broach the subject with him, if anything. I probably will also have to tell him about the hashtag. Those internet sleuths might help with the investigation.'

'Do you think he will be cross with us?' I ask sheepishly.

'Oh, I won't tell him we have been actively investigating, Rowe! I'll just say we have stumbled upon this info. Probably you, actually, if you don't mind. He knows I know feck all about social media.'

She finishes her coffee in a hurry, and mumbles something about work deadlines and a vet appointment for Norman. Before she goes, however, I delete the video off my iPad and cloud. I feel like I need a witness to do that.

I close the door to Mary feeling drastically lighter. A problem shared is always a problem halved. Well, to be fair, with Mary, sometimes, a problem shared is a problem multiplied.

But not today.

Chapter 25

@gemma_cotswolds_mum Morning Friends. Thank you all for participating in my Happy Autumn Live event last night ~~(except those shitty comments asking if I was drunk!)~~. It was so great to hear from some of you and these things are always so ~~terrifying~~ fun for me. Getting to know you all is ~~bloody annoying~~ such a privilege. Congratulations again to @mrsmummysmith who won my prize draw ~~by liking and tagging, such a challenge~~ for the beauty bag and @maureen.grace47 who was the winner of the pamper hamper! Friendly reminder to take care of yourselves on the run up to the most wonderful (but ~~ALWAYS~~ sometimes stressful!) time of the year! Xx Gemma #gemmacotswoldsmumlive #supportsmallbusinesses #likefollowshare #mumfluencer ~~#hanginthere~~

Mary

Still Wednesday

What a day. I'm absolutely shattered. First, all the excitement with Rowe about the video. Then, I had to pound out a decent 500 words about the Straw Man Parade. Norman had to go to the vet, Charlotte had ballet and then Ben had football. And frankly, it's evenings like this when I bloody wish that Upper Huxley had a McDonald's! Can you imagine? At this rate, I'd settle for an overpriced kebab but no such luck. You can grab a quick chicken basket at The Green Man but that's not quite the same as Chicken McNuggets® so it's fish fingers for the children (again!) and then I somehow get them in bed by a decent hour.

I'm sitting on the couch with Norman curled up at my feet, surfing the internet for information about domestic burglary (just until Tom gets home, of course), and how prevalent women are in that particular line of work. Disappointingly, there are no 'Women in Burglary' groups advertising their list of members. Equally, there are no annual awards dinners with accolades for the 'Contribution to Advancement in Burglary' celebrating their female constituents. So, I'm pleased when Tom finally comes home. In my line of work, research is usually a lot easier than this.

I do a lovely (if quick) dinner of salmon and green beans, and we chat about the usual daily details. I am keeping a little bit (OK, OK, a lot) back about my visit with Rowe but after a sufficient amount of time has passed, so that he won't think I am all that bothered, I broach the subject of the video. I tell him about how Rowe had managed to find a video of *the* video and when we watched it, we saw the person in the mirror, wearing black, slam Gemma's head into the kitchen counter and how we saw that it couldn't possibly have been an accident. I realise I am getting quite excited and have so much more that I want to tell him.

I not only have the confidence to tell Tom what Rowe and I have really been up to, but actually feel like I have a responsibility. I blurt it out quickly in the hopes that if I say it rapidly, Tom won't think that the way I've been behaving is ridiculous. I tell him everything. I tell him about how we've found out that Lorna was trolling Gemma (after a brief detour to explain what trolling is) and then that Lorna was trolled herself.

'Mary, slow down!' He's interested but chuckling in amusement, too. 'I'm getting lost – trolling and counter-trolling? Should I alert MI5?'

'Tom! Listen!' I huff.

I explain how we've found out that Lorna is unlikely to be responsible for any harm coming to Gemma as the murder actually postpones her public recovery from a spat between the two. I tell him about how Gemma had been acting very strangely for the last six months and how we've realised that there is another person in the video that is definitely not Gemma and that there is a gasp which we think sounds distinctly feminine. This gets his attention.

'Enough to make you think that it's definitely a woman?'

'Yes! Now you are finally getting it!' My throat is raw from both the talking and the frustration.

I round it all off with the excuse that I am doing all this for poor Charlie with his dad in prison, and what on Earth is going to happen when he is 15 and he finds these articles about how his parents were swingers, if that's even true, of course?

The whole time I am talking – quickly and barely pausing for breath – Tom is listening calmly and watching my expressions without an awful lot of his own. I wonder if he is using his police skills on me. I hate that thought.

After I am finished, he is quiet and then he takes a deep breath. I am waiting for him to have a proper go at me about how silly it is to be running around like Miss Marple and how if I want to be the crazy woman in the village, I could at least choose something that won't jeopardise the case – or his career, for that matter. It won't be a good look when Gloucestershire Police find out that Tom's wife has been investigating murder as a side hustle.

I am not breathing, I notice. But he doesn't have a go at me. Instead, he looks at me and says 'Oh May, I knew that you were clearly upset about what's happening to Matthew. For one, you seem to be bursting into tears quite often when that's not normally your style.'

'I can't sit here and do nothing.' My fucking lip wobbles all over again, proving the point he's only just made.

He smiles the warmest of smiles and takes my hand over the table to give it a little squeeze. 'I get it. I'll make you a deal: if you can promise me that you won't do anything silly, put yourself or anyone else in danger, or do anything that will jeopardise a conviction, I'll tell you whatever I hear in the office. I'm not going to interject myself into the investigation but whatever I do hear, I'll tell you.'

'But why would you do that, Tom? I mean, thank you, of course, but why?'

'Because, Mary, I think that you and Rowe have done some stellar work so far. You've managed to find out information that the team of 3 DCs have missed, and they are on this case full time. I also think that it's something that you feel passionate about for all the right reasons. You are right to worry about Gemma's name, how she'll be remembered, that Matthew is the main suspect even though he's very unlikely to be the perpetrator, and, lastly …' He scrunches up the right side of his face like he does when he's either trying to remember something or deciding on whether or not to say what he's really thinking. 'Because Nick is a Dick.' And with that, he stands up, picks up his plate, and heads to the dishwasher.

Chapter 26

@gemma_cotswolds_mum Morning Friends. Not much to report today ~~I don't know what to post about anymore~~, but I had to have this beautiful flower arrangement on my grid. It was made by my talented friend, Marigold, the owner of @twopeasinapod ~~#sotiredofthis~~ #slowday #flowersofig

Rowena

Thursday

James is returning from the city this evening and my self-inflicted guilt is nagging at me because I feel I have nothing to show for my week. Well, apart from keeping the kids alive, that is. Of course, Mary and I have made some significant progress in our 'informal vestigation', but I'm not planning on telling James about that just yet.

If I didn't fear introspection, I would spend some time asking myself why I feel I have to justify my time to James. In all honesty, I'm scared to analyse why I am no longer an open book with him. Why do I still feel this reserve? I put a stop to my spiralling thoughts before I fully contemplate the question of whether James is also keeping some things from me.

Unlike me, Mary owned up to Tom last night. Surprisingly, instead of being cross, he was quite supportive and admiring of our amateur detective work. I am trying hard to put a lid on any silly sense of pride. Getting any sort of enjoyment from this feels wrong in many ways.

In a last-ditch effort to have something positive to tell James about my week, I have booked Eloise and myself into a music session at the Upper Huxley Mummy's Morning that Lorna runs at the village hall today. I used to attend a selection of baby classes with Alfie in London, on top of my NCT coffee mornings. Eloise, as your typical second child, is now almost six-month-old and has yet to attend a single class.

First World problem, I know. But the mum guilt is real!

I know we as good as discounted Lorna from our suspect list, but I can't help watching her as she distributes the instruments, wondering what kind of relationship she really had with Gemma. I wonder if Gemma had ever attended such classes when Charlie was a baby. I struggle to imagine her sitting on the flimsy, stained floor cushions with parents from all walks of life. If she did, I doubt she posted about it online, as the faded village hall decor wouldn't quite have fitted with 'aesthetics'.

The music baby group turns out to be fun. If anything, it's a good real-life reminder that not everyone is nailing this whole parenting thing, contrary to what social media would like to make us believe. Indeed, most parents (only one dad here today) are looking just as tired as I feel. Some mums are showing great enthusiasm in singing along, but I can see quite a few that are just there so they can let somebody else entertain their brood, while they smile with a vacant look, no doubt looking forward to the chance of finishing a hot drink before it turns cold. The music bit is quite an oversell, to be honest. But if the haphazard shaking of maracas and banging of drums combined with a big dose of baby whingeing is music to your ears, then this is the right class for you.

Unfortunately, our fun is slightly spoiled when Eloise kicks up a fuss five minutes before the end. I hate it when that happens in public. I'm the last one to judge parents when their kids have a meltdown, but I always worry about what everyone else is going to make of me when my kids start crying.

With the class over, I'm trying to wrestle Eloise into her winter suit when one of the mums who had been making friendly eye-contact with me during the class comes over with a sympathetic smile.

We chat for a while about our kids, of course. *What else?*

We're enjoying a cup of coffee when Lorna comes to check if we're having tea. 'Please remember to put all teabags in the special container for composting!'

The friendly mum, Justine, rolls her eyes, clearly used to Lorna's obsessions.

I decide to explore the village and some of the lanes around the village green, hoping that the motion of the pram will soothe Eloise to sleep. Autumn is now in full swing and most of the trees are now completely pared down to their naked winter skeletons. As much as I'm looking forward to our first spring and summer in the Cotswolds, there is an undeniable charm to nature in autumn, especially the beautiful stone cottages with their smoking chimneys. It just feels so cosy. I am fully aware it is also a complete cliché. But I couldn't care less; it actually feels lovely to be living in a beautiful cliché world.

Murder aside.

I've come to the row of shops just off the village green, beyond the Red Lion pub. We've been here over a month, and I have yet to explore the limited retail offerings of Upper Huxley. The first traditional wooden-fronted shop is a pretty florist. As I look through the beautiful Christmassy window display to assess how busy it is before going in with my big pram, I spot Marigold with a tall brown-haired man. He has his back to me and the two of them are doing a sort of a to-and-fro with a bouquet of flowers. Marigold's look is what I would describe as determined as she pushes the flowers onto him. In apparent defeat, his shoulders sag and his arms drop to his sides. Immediately, Marigold envelops him in the biggest hug.

As she lets go of him, Marigold spots me looking through the window, smiles and beckons me in. Now, this is embarrassing. It looks like I was being nosey. I have nothing to be ashamed of as I can't have watched for more than 30 seconds and yet, I can feel my cheeks flush. As I faff with the pram to give my face time to regain its normal colouring, the man who was hugging Marigold steps out of the shop and I recognise him immediately from the horrible scene at the pub. This is Matthew, Gemma's husband. Widower.

We politely nod hello at one another as he holds the door to let me in before striding away, a look of total exhaustion in his eyes.

'Good morning, Rowena!' Marigold welcomes me warmly.

Her shop is utterly delightful. Simple but tasteful. No garish roses or tulips in the middle of November here. This shop certainly wouldn't look out of place in trendy Spitalfields or posh Greenwich.

'Hello Marigold. How are you? I didn't know this was your shop. This is stunning!' I'm so enchanted by it that I have forgotten my earlier embarrassment.

'I'm good, Rowena, thank you. And who have we got here?' she asks as she leans into the buggy.

'This is Eloise. I'm afraid you are not meeting her on a good day.' I mutter apologetically.

'Hello Eloise.' She puts her hand on Eloise's chest and starts making those soothing sounds that only mothers know.

Immediately, Eloise quietens and focuses her eyes on Marigold's smiling face.

This lasts a whole minute and when Marigold turns her attention back to me, both my daughter and I feel much quieter.

'Well done. That has worked a treat on her. Thank you.' I say shyly, embarrassed at my parenting fail.

'Oh, don't mention it. She is a poppet. Bit tired, I bet.' She really seems like the loveliest lady. But then the whole swinging thing comes back to me again and I can feel myself blushing. This is ridiculous, I have nothing to be uneasy about. And I also don't want her to feel embarrassed.

'Listen, Marigold. I feel there may have been a slight misunderstanding.' *Understatement of the year!* 'You see, I am only interested in pampas as plants. Not for anything else.' I manage to say with as much confidence as I can muster.

'Yes, I figured that out after our conversation. You looked utterly confused by the end of it and it dawned on me, as I left, that we were not on the same wavelength at all.' she replies kindly, with a twinkle in her eye.

'Ah, OK. Good. Great. Just wanted to clarify ...'

'Of course. It's absolutely no problem. We don't have to talk about it anymore.' She shows no sign of awkwardness, and I find that I like her even more. It takes a strong woman to show such confidence and grace in ignoring my embarrassment.

'Ah well, looks like Eloise has given up.' She tactfully changes the subject.

My baby is now peacefully asleep, looking completely angelic in her white winter hat.

'Oh, you're right. It looks like your magic has worked, Marigold.' I suddenly feel very comfortable with her.

'Now, are you after some plants? Flowers?'

'I was just having a nose around the shops, but I will actually take this bunch of eucalyptus, please. Maybe I can make my own wreath this year ...' I muse.

'Ah, if you are thinking of making your own wreath, you must come to our workshop at the village hall! £10 for the school PTFA and all the greenery, ribbons, and ornaments are provided. It's usually great fun. And Vicky makes a mean mulled wine,' she adds with a wink.

'Ah, that sounds great. When is it?' I ask, crossing my fingers it is a night that James will be around.

'Next Friday. 7pm. Shall I put your name down, then?'

'Oh yes, please! James will look after the kids. Thank you.' I reply enthusiastically.

I move to the counter to pay for my eucalyptus and notice the credit card receipt that the previous customer has left on the counter. I think nothing of it until Marigold clocks me looking at it and quickly swipes it away from sight.

But I have had time to read, written in bold letters: DECLINED

Chapter 27

@gemma_cotswolds_mum Morning Friends. Craft time!! ~~Lord help me!~~ Check out this beautiful Christmas ornament that you can make with your little ones. ~~This is the 18th one we made, the others had to be burned.~~ Things you'll need ~~excluding the buckets of patience and wine~~ and full instructions are in the comments section. Please post yours with #gemmascrafts so I can see your gorgeous creations. #mumsofig #influencermum #craftymum #craftwithme

Mary

Thursday

Text from Rowena:

17:43: *Hi Mary. I saw Marigold today – she mentioned the Wreath Workshop at the village hall next Friday. I've put my name down. Did you know about it? Were you planning to go? Xx*

17:55: *Hiya Rowe. I did know about it but Tom is working late on Friday, so I wasn't planning on going. ☹ That's why I forgot to mention it to you. It's great fun! You should definitely go. I might ask my neighbour if she can look after the children and then I can join you. I'll let you know. Xx*

Oh, I do love the wreath workshop! It's the perfect excuse to chat with loads of people, listen to proper cheesy Christmas music, and drink lots of Vicky's fab mulled wine. And it's close enough to Christmas that the wreaths are still fresh and beautiful, even on the day. That is, of course, if you are any good at making wreaths. Which I am not! I embrace my lack of talent in the crafting arena. I'm always too busy chatting and laughing, anyway. If I get something that looks half decent and won't confuse the neighbours about which season I'm celebrating, I'll be more than happy. I need to speak to Anne and ask her if she wouldn't mind putting the children to bed and watching telly with Norman (her favourite) just until I get home next Friday.

Friday

Fuck! That alarm is so annoying on mornings like this. You know the kind of mornings where the very sound of the alarm makes you angry to your core? Whilst I'm pulling on my leggings and my sports bra (is it that little bit tighter? Or is that my imagination?) I try to think of things that I'm thankful for or something that I'm looking forward to so that I can clear the 'in a funk' vibes but all I can do is repeat 'I'm so tired. I'm just so tired' in my head, over and over again.

Tom is awake before me. Despite the fact that he didn't get home until 2:30, he's all bright-eyed and bushy-tailed and sitting at the kitchen island with a steaming hot cup of coffee, having already got the children up and ready for school. People like him are so annoying. I love the mornings, I do, but I also love sleep. Tom is one of those rare people who doesn't seem to really need sleep. Like I said, annoying.

'You OK to take the children?' I ask loud enough for Tom to hear from the boot room. I'm really only asking to be nice. If he said 'no' I'd be well pissed off.

'Sure.' He's on lates again and I'll see him later, so I give Ben and Charlotte kisses and cuddles and ask Norman if he wants to go for a ride.

'Oh Muuuummmyyy! It's not faaaaiiiir! How come Norman gets to go?' cries Ben.

'Oh Ben, firstly, it's 'Why does?' not 'How come?'. I know you want to go but you have to go to school – we'll do something special this weekend, OK, I promise?' Mental note to try and think of something special to do this weekend. Charlotte has her nose stuck in her most recent Lottie Brooks novel. She's such a clever girl and loves her reading. I think again about how lucky I am – it seems that the morning time funk is already receding – probably at least in part because I know I don't have to do the school run.

I put on my running shoes, do the phone, keys, wallet, and ancillaries (headphones, phone strap, lead) check, open the back door and head with Norman towards Red. I climb into the front, put the keys in, and she cranks up straight away. I then notice that the petrol light is on, and the needle is looking precariously close to the E. 'Bollocks! Who drove this thing last?' I wonder aloud, knowing full well that it was me. Tom's not a fan. Why is it so nice to have someone else to blame sometimes?

I text Tom before I leave:

8:37am: Need anything from the shop?

We drive out of the way so that I can fill up at the Tesco on the edge of Stroud.

Deo, pls. x

Ugh. Now I have to go in.

I park as close as I can to the side of the building and promise Norman I'll be right back (he couldn't care less) and dash inside. I pick up the deodorant for Tom and a few other things (French stick to have with the soup I'm planning to make later, some broccoli and some avocados). I go through the normal queue where you actually interact with someone and then I am back in the car, making a fuss of Norman.

I drive over to the petrol station and pull up to the pump. After paying, I climb back in. I put my wallet back into the glove compartment and looking up, I see that there is a note under the windscreen wiper. Huh?

It's not a garish flyer – surely I would have seen that earlier. And I can't imagine anyone handing out flyers in the Tesco car park this early in the morning, anyway. Now that I'm holding it, I can see it's normal lined A5 notebook paper folded in half. On the front it says 'Tom.' Instinctively, I look around to see who might have put it on the car and then I quickly realise that no one has put it there whilst I was refilling. They must have done it before. But when? When I was in the shop? And why is it a note for Tom? Everyone knows that I'm the only one that drives this car. I open the note and am shocked to see what is written there. My ears fill with the sound of my pounding heart.

'Matthew is a cheating bastard!!'

My hands start shaking and I look around me again. My heart is beating so fast as I fumble in my pocket for the keys – forgetting that I've already put them in the ignition. Norman starts whining, sensing my anxiety. I can't get away fast enough. I put the note in the glove compartment. I presume that it will probably need to be dusted for prints at some point? Shit. The thought scares me all over again. I abandon my plans for a trail run and head straight home.

I'm glad that Tom is on the school run when I arrive back home. As much as I need to see and talk to him, I am glad that the children aren't there to see me so shaken. I put my gloves on to retrieve the note from the car to minimise any unnecessary handling, and then I find a new plastic bag to put it in. I put the note inside, unfolded so that you can see both sides of the note, and I wait for Tom to get home.

Chapter 28

@gemma_cotswolds_mum Morning Friends. It's BBC Children in Need Day today! Not an ad. Just something close to my heart. So many children are not as lucky as my Charlie, and we love to do our bit at our local school and online. So please let me see your spotty outfits and don't forget to donate @bbccin

Rowena

Friday

One day I will tell you about a day where everything has gone perfectly as planned. I promise. But today is not that day.

James came back late last night from London. As a result, Alfie is super excited at breakfast and can't stop telling him all about his new football club. No amount of nagging from me can get him to hurry up through the whole morning routine. By the time he is repositioning the Velcro straps on his shoes for the third time, I have used up all my gentle parenting tricks and am ready to scream the house down.

But, of course, I can't because James is already on his team meeting in the office. So, I have to be quiet or at least, pretend I am not a completely inept mother.

Focus on the cup of coffee you will have when drop off is done. Focus on the coffee. I repeat in my head like a mantra.

We do the school run in its literal sense. Well, as much as a pram and a five-year-old allow me to run ... I am ready to breathe a sigh of relief as the bell rings just as we turn into the school lane, only to realise that no one is wearing a uniform this morning. Oh no they are all wearing Pudsey ears or spotty clothes.

My heart sinks. Shit, it is BBC Children in Need Day.

Of course, there's no fooling Alfie.

'Oh Mummy, it's Pudsey Day today!' I don't need to look at him to predict the imminent tears.

Sure enough, five seconds is all it takes for him to start wailing. Sure enough, everyone is looking at me. I want to cry too. Time to activate the full-on Mary Poppins mode.

Focus on that coffee.

'OK, OK, darling. Calm down. Let me talk to your teacher to see if I can go and fetch your spotty hoodie and the Pudsey ears we had last year.' I try in my best conciliatory voice, pretending to ignore everyone staring at us.

That coffee is going to have to wait a bit longer.

As I get ready to leave the playground without making eye contact with parents who have all remembered about non-uniform day, I fall into step with Tom.

'Wow, Children In Need is clearly a big thing in Huxley!' I'm trying to pretend I'm not feeling completely deflated by my parenting failure.

'Ah yes, Upper Huxley loves it.' he explains with a smile, trying to pretend he didn't witness Alfie's meltdown.

'Right, got to dash home and get all the spotty things, then!' I know I sound slightly unhinged. But I feel TOTALLY unhinged so, not a bad effort.

Focus on that coffee.

I don't bother trying to be quiet for James this time.

I bang open the front door, run up the stairs, slam the wardrobe door, and open several drawers and toy chests.

Where are those stupid bear ears?

Meanwhile, Eloise has decided that it shouldn't be all about her brother this morning and has started crying in her pram in the hallway.

I finally locate the bear headband in a Lego toy chest and run downstairs as James comes out of the office.

'What is going on? I'm in a meeti …' His voices trails off as he sees the murderous look on my face.

'Don't.' Is all I muster as I head out of the door again.

***

I barge into the school office and drop the items onto Jenny's desk. The receptionist has clearly decided not to cut me any slack today, despite my flustered face and crying baby.

'Do you have your pound coin, please? Do you not receive the school messages?' she asks in that uber efficient voice that admin people in positions of power love to adopt.

'Oh, I do. Huxley Primary school messages is all I seem to receive these days!' I can't help my sarcastic tone as I slam the pound coin onto the counter.

'*Upper* Huxley' she corrects as she notifies me I can leave by turning back to her computer.

I am fuming.

'*Upper* Huxley! *Upper* Huxley! Where the fuck is *Lower* Huxley, anyway?' I'm talking to myself like a deranged person as I turn into the lane, only to bump into Louise. This is all I need. The one and only person who has openly been hostile to us since we've moved here. Well, apart from Jenny just now, that is.

'Oh, hi, Rowena. How are you? Had to dash home for your Children In Need things, did you?' She enquires with a gleeful glint in her eyes.

'Hi Louise. Yes, I had to. How has your day been so far?' I ask, even though I don't care. But I've already been rude to Jenny today and I don't particularly want to upset the chief-bitch mum. At least, not today.

I want to get home and drink my coffee in peace.

'I'm good, thank you. Busy, busy, you know. Helping with prepping the wreath workshop for the PTFA and supporting poor Matthew with funeral arrangements.' She stands a bit taller when she volunteers the last bit of information.

'Ah, do you work for a funeral director, then?'

'Oh no no. Just helping a friend. Matthew and I are *very* close. I mean, Gemma was a very good friend of mine, God rest her soul.' She adds quickly, like an afterthought. 'I'm only doing my bit to honour her memory and support her poor family, really.' Clearly well-rehearsed words. 'But Matthew really needs a close friend right now and not everyone is that loyal, you know.'

This last sentence is obviously loaded, and I don't usually give space to gossip but sleuthing is 50% listening to gossip, 50% I'm not sure what else, or we would have already found Gemma's killer.

'Have Matthew's friends not been very present since Gemma's death?' I sound sceptical as I've seen him with Marigold and Martin.

'Well, your new friend has not, considering ...'

'Mary? She did help after he got taken to the police station.'

'Sure, but you expect a bit more from childhood best friends, Rowena!'

'Childhood best friends? Mary and Gemma?' I can't hide my surprise, and Louise looks like a cat who got the cream. I feel like I've been punched in the gut.

'No, Mary and Matthew, of course! Surely, you know those two were totally inseparable all through their school years, until Matthew met Gemma, basically. Didn't she explain?' The malicious glint is back in her Claudia Winkleman-esque eyelinered brown eyes.

I try to compose myself and conceal the whiplash I feel at the high speed in which my brain is rearranging the facts.

'Ah yes, of course she did. Sorry, thought you meant Gemma. It's been a bit of a morning already! Ha Ha.' Cue nervous laugh. She is absolutely not fooled but allows me to save face and pretend that I'm not completely shocked and feeling totally cheated by my new friend.

Mary's connection to the Hatherleys is much stronger than she'd ever admitted to me. Why hide it? Why lead me on this investigation and not give me all the facts? What else is she not telling me? The Rowena of three weeks ago would have cut her losses and just stayed away from Mary, but today, I feel I need answers.

Chapter 29

@gemma_cotswolds_mum Morning Friends! A gin and ~~slimline~~ tonic will always be my go-to cocktail, regardless of the season. One of my favourites ~~which would be my only favourite if they paid me more~~ is the fantastic gin from @siblingdistillery made right here in our beautiful Cotswolds. Their autumn edition with fresh apples and blackberries just screams English Countryside but I love the other options, too! Impress your friends by serving this up at your next gathering.
#ad #ginisfordrinking #buylocal #buycotswolds #siblinggin #siblingdistillery ~~#mothersruin #shouldhaveaskedformoremoney~~

Mary

Friday

By the time Tom gets home, I have calmed down considerably. I am sitting at the kitchen island with a cup of coffee and staring at the note. It totally freaks me out to think that someone has actually stopped, written a note, waited until I'd gone into the shop (maybe?), walked over to the car, and placed the note under my wiper blade. I mean, I was in that spot 12 minutes max and in the shop for 10?

Tom walks in through the back door and removes his shoes. 'I don't think Rowena's having such a great morning!' he says as he walks into the kitchen from the boot room. 'Oh dear!' he stops, startled when he sees the look on my face. 'What's the matter?'

'Umm ... a fucking psycho killer has put a note for you on my Red!' I spit/screech in Tom's direction.

'What? What happened, Mary?' He looks a little concerned now, even though I see him make the mental adjustment to account for my propensity for dramatics.

So, I tell him exactly what happened.

After we run through the timeline of the events, we start listing the extrapolated facts:

- Clearly, the note-writer was someone that just happened to see me, an opportunist. Even I didn't know I was going to Tesco until this morning
- It was someone that knew Tom, knew me, and my distinctive car (a fellow UpHux?) and
- It was NOT someone that was doing the school run

Not so sures:
- Is it related at all to Gemma's death?
- If it is related to the case, did the person that put the note there know that Tom had previously been working on the case?

Totally unknowns:
- Is it true?
- WHO PUT THE BLOODY NOTE ON RED?

I ask Tom if we should tell Nick about all this. He gets a visible flash of inspiration and says: 'Not quite yet, I just want to check something myself.'

He grabs the keys to his old Golf and makes like he's leaving. The worry must be showing on my face!

'Where are you going? Could I, at least, come with you?'

'Not right now, May. I promise that I'll tell you what I find out, if anything, as soon as I get back, but I don't want to get your hopes up.' With that he dashes out of the door. I'm standing there a little bit flummoxed even as I hear the car leave the drive.

I text Rowena:

10:07am: *Hi Rowe, I've got absolutely loads to tell you. Are you free for a coffee? X*
10:08am: *Hi Mary, how about now? Mine, please.*

Her message looks a little clipped to me. Am I being summoned? Maybe something exciting has happened?

10:08am: *On my way. X*

I've never been so happy about leaving my house. I send Tom a text.

10:11am: *Gone to Rowe's. Norm in boot room. Please let me know if you are going to be any more than a few hours.*

10:13am: *K*

I make it to Rowe's in about 12 minutes. At least the speedy pace of the walk there is helping to burn off some of this excess adrenaline. Maybe I will go for that run when I get back home, after all. And it is only then that I realise that I am still in my running kit.

'Hi,' I greet Rowena as she opens the door. Her hair is distinctly dishevelled – and not in her normal accidentally beautiful way. If I didn't know better, I'd think that she isn't exactly over the moon to see me That's not quite what I was expecting.

'Hiya. Thanks for agreeing to coffee." She closes the door gruffly and immediately sets off towards the kitchen without a gesture.

I'm guessing I'm supposed to follow? It's awkward in a way that it hasn't been between us before but I'm clueless as to why. I try to get the conversation going. 'Tom told me that you weren't having the best of mornings.' I had totally forgotten that until this exact moment. 'I hope everything is OK?' When we get to the kitchen, she finally turns to look at me.

'Yeah! It was a bit awful and that was even before Louise dropped a bombshell!' she spits in my direction. It's clear that Rowena is having a terrible day!

I can't help but rub my hands together in anticipation. What has Rowe unearthed now? 'Oh excellent! What is it? Spill it!'

She gives me a look that I can't quite decipher.

'Well – that you and Matthew used to be best friends. Totally 'inseparable'.' She uses air quotes to emphasise the point. There is an uncomfortable silence and then she continues 'Why haven't you mentioned this?'

'Ah.' Now the indecipherable look makes sense. It's defiance and hurt I can see on her face. I should have anticipated this discussion. Fuck.

'I can see how this looks. The truth is that we haven't been friends for such a long time. But yes, it's one of the reasons that I'm so convinced he didn't do it ...'

'Then why didn't you say? Why did you imply that you didn't know the Hatherleys?'

'Because I don't!' I insisted, then corrected myself. 'I didn't know the Hatherleys! I knew Matthew before they became the Hatherleys. And that feels like an absolute lifetime ago. But yes, you are right, my nostalgia for the guy I used to know has been the main drive behind wanting to investigate.'

'Exactly, Mary! Why are you asking me to investigate this murder with you when you haven't told me all the facts? And you made me look stupid in front of Louise!'

'Oh Rowe, I'm really sorry. I definitely should have told you. But you see what I mean. I wasn't purposely keeping it a secret. It's common knowledge within the villa—'

'But I'm not from *Upper* Huxley!' I can tell that Rowe is terribly hurt. Not only does she feel betrayed, but she must also feel like a total outsider. 'You've let me make all sorts of assumptions about Matth—'

'Rowe, like I said, I don't know Matthew. I know 18-year-old Matty who used to be my side-kick and best friend. We left school. I went travelling, he didn't, we didn't keep in touch much after that.' The lump in my throat and the embarrassment prevents me from telling her more.

As if on cue, Eloise screams through the baby monitor. Rowe mumbles an apology and heads upstairs. Should I leave the room? Or the house, altogether? I'm wondering if she still even wants to be my friend. I fear I've seriously fucked up here. Talking and thinking about how close Matthew and I used to be and how painfully it all ended is so hard and yet, here I am trying not to lose another friend.

Rowe appears with a swaddled and freshly changed Eloise. She looks tired, but her face has softened, and she sighs. I can tell that she's decided to believe me, but I probably need to be a lot more careful now.

She puts Eloise on her playmat and joins me sitting at the kitchen island.

'So go on – what was so bad about the day before you decided you might want to hate me?' I ask, trying to put on my very best 'please forgive me' face.

'Oh, it's just that stupid Pudsey Bear.'

'Oh, I know – he's an absolute twat! I heard that he was seen spray painting penises all over the village telephone box!'

Rowena looks at me with confusion and then bursts into proper belly-laughter, which tells me I might be forgiven. For now, at least.

I laugh and that makes her laugh harder, and me, and so the spiral goes until both of us are crying and laughing but for quite different reasons. I feel lighter for having let it out and I can see that she is looking a load better, too.

'Oh, thanks Mary. I needed that. Really. I nearly told you I was busy this morning as I was just so pissed off with everything and you! But I'm so glad I didn't.'

'Erm – thanks? Not going to trust you now if you ever say you are busy.'

Rowe gives me daggers. 'Let's not talk about trust just yet, Mary.'

'Touché.' She's forgiven me, but she's not ready to forget.

Then I proceed to get Rowe up to speed. I tell her all about the note on my car and I find it much easier to recount the story the second time – especially after having got most of the emotion out of my system. I explain all about the list that Tom and I made. Finally, I tell her what a prick he is for then flitting off without giving me any clue as to where he was going. And, most importantly, she agrees.

Chapter 30

@gemma_cotswolds_mum Morning Friends! Today is our 10th wedding anniversary and we have never been happier ~~if only that was the truth~~. Happy Anniversary to us! Matthew is not only my husband and the father of our beautiful boy, ~~the only thing holding us together~~ but also my best friend! ~~I wish I had another best friend I could confide to~~. Love this montage of our wedding. What a beautiful day that was! #lovestory

Rowena

Friday

Mary tells me all about the note on her windscreen and my first thought is to wonder if it is even true. Could she have written the note herself? But I suppress the notion as soon as it bubbles up. I'm still rattled but I do trust her, and I'm now mostly annoyed she made me look stupid in front of bitchy Louise.

'Wow, Mary. That is a lot of information.' I say slowly.

'I know, looks like Marigold was right about the affair. I can't quite believe it, to be honest.' Mary says pensively.

'Oh! Now that you mention Marigold!' I suddenly remember something that might have some bearing in this discussion. 'I ended up in her shop yesterday. And just as I was going to step in, I saw her hugging Matthew in there!'

'Hugging how? Did it look like a romantic embrace? Did you talk to them?' Mary is rattling through her questions.

'Actually, Matthew left and let me in. Neither of them looked particularly shifty about it, to be honest. But …' I want to share the other thing I witnessed but Mary cuts me off.

'But he could have been buying flowers for his mistress, then!'

'Well, he did leave with some flowers, but ...' She is barely listening, and I can feel my frustration rising as I'm desperate to get my point across.

'I can't actually imagine Marigold having an affair with Matthew, to be honest. She used to babysit him, for Christ's sake!' Mary looks disgusted.

'Oh Mary, just stop! I'm trying to tell ... Hang on, what?' I just registered what she is saying. 'Eww! Surely, they can't have been swinging together then? That would be way too creepy!' I wish I didn't have to bring this back up again.

'Noooo!' Mary is covering her eyes, shaking her head.

'Now, listen.' I grab her shoulders to bring her back to the room. 'There was something else interesting about their interaction. Before the hug, Marigold looked like she was forcing him to accept some flowers. And I saw a card receipt on the counter. It said 'Declined'. The only customer in the shop before me was him.'

'Money problems?' Her eyes are shining at the idea of a fresh angle.

'He did look like he was carrying the weight of the world on his shoulders.'

Mary's face collapses. 'Well, his wife being murdered, being the main suspect and worrying about his son would do it, really. But add money problems and that would be impossible to bear.' I can see now all that I've missed before, she is genuinely hurting for her estranged friend.

'What does Matthew do for a living? I don't think I've ever asked.'

'Last I heard he works in Aerospace, some sort of senior management position. Somewhere in Gloucester or Cheltenham.' Mary explains.

'Well, I would have thought there is a bit money in that industry, wouldn't you? And Gemma was quite successful in what she was doing, I think. But then again, how can you tell? It is all so fake on social media.'

'Indeed. But if you think about it, with Matthew being employed by a company, his salary must be fixed and not vary in time. Gemma's, however ...'

'Yes, you're right. If the financial difficulties are confirmed, it might be that her income had reduced. Not a reason to die though, and that definitely wasn't a suicide.'

'Hang on. There is a reason why her death could help the financial situation ' Mary blurts out. 'What if they had a big life insurance policy?'

'Matthew would definitely be the beneficiary of that! Good point, Mary. But don't you think the police would have spotted that when they looked into their financial situation?'

'Tom didn't mention anything like that. I supposed that could be the reason they arrested him in the first place. Strong motive rather than opportunity?' Mary says, looking worried again.

'What about an alibi? I never asked but does he have one?' I ask, knowing full well that is the first thing the police would have checked.

'Yes, Tom said he was playing squash in Stroud with Martin. But they still dragged him for questioning.' Mary says, looking confused.

'Hmm, indeed. How can he be a suspect if he had an alibi?'

'That would explain why Tom is fuming over the whole botched investigation and why Matthew has been released.'

Feeling like we have exhausted the whole money side of things, my mind moves back to the note that was left on Mary's windscreen.

'So, until you told Tom about the note, he hadn't said anything about an affair. Their investigation hadn't brought it up at all?' I take a sip of my coffee and find that it has turned cold. I lift my cup to Mary and point to the coffee machine as an offer to make another one. She nods and continues with her flow of thoughts.

'No, but let's not forget that Tom was taken off the case early in the investigation. Nick the Dick is no doubt keeping his cards close to his chest. Regardless, the message seems to corroborate Marigold's suspicions …' Mary visibly shudders, and I wonder if she is again thinking of Matthew and Marigold having an affair.

'Don't. It can't be Marigold. Why would she have mentioned the affair if she was the lover herself! And I have a more fitting suspect, actually!'

'Seriously! Who? How?' Mary's face has lit up again.

'Well, just before Louise dropped her big revelation about you,' Cue sheepish look from Mary, 'she boasted about helping Matthew with the funeral because they are 'so very close'! And she did insist on the 'very'.'

'Really? Eurgh, she really is a piece of work … But would she boast if she was having an affair?'

'Yeah, I did wonder. She strikes me more as wanting the attention.'

'Absolutely. She wanted to be centre stage and to be honest, she never quite could because Gemma was hogging the attention most of the time. Louise was mostly eclipsed by her.'

'Having an affair with her husband would be one way to get one up on Gemma.' I venture, unconvinced.

'Or ... killing her?' Mary suggests reluctantly. 'I mean, she is awful, but would she really kill to be the new Upper Huxley Queen Bee?'

We both silently mull over what we have just discussed, drinking our fresh coffees. As if she can pick up on the serious mood, Eloise is quietly playing on her playmat.

'You were right when you said about not knowing what is going on behind closed doors. Gemma and Matthew, Marigold and Stephen, Martin and Louise. So many secrets.' Mary thinks out loud.

'Yes, you should never take things at face value. Trust me.' I reply sadly.

'Rowena? Are you OK?' Mary asks, her voice full of concern. I can see she is still worried about our earlier confrontation.

'I am, really. It's just that ... Well, it's not been always happy families in the Boat household either.' I don't know how to phrase it.

'Rowe, you don't have to explain anything. I'm sorry for asking.'

'No, I want to, really.' I take a breath before I continue. 'A year after Alfie was born, we decided to try for another baby. Have them close in age, you know, get the baby years out of the way. But like all best laid plans ...' I take a moment to remind myself that this is all behind us now. It still feels so raw.

Mary grabs my hand, but she remains uncharacteristically, quiet.

'I don't want to go through all the details and heartache, but there were months of disappointment, a couple of early losses and finally, two failed rounds of IVF. These left me broken. I can't describe it any better. And I hated feeling like I wasn't completely there, mentally and physically, to look after the one child we did have. Alfie was three, by then. And the guilt, Mary ...' My voice shaking, I look at my daughter to remind myself again that it is all behind us.

'The guilt consumed me. And it overtook my desire for another child. So, I decided to put a stop to it. James wanted to continue. Just one more go. I refused. And as much as he wanted to be understanding about it, it really put a strain on our relationship. We tried for months to recover but, in the end, we were left with only one more thing to try: separation.' I swallow, remembering the awful day we admitted defeat.

'So, we did. But we couldn't reconcile ourselves to something definitive. So, we both kept living in the flat, but we would take turns to sleep over at friends' houses so we would never be there as a family of three anymore.'

I can't look at Mary, but she is keeping very still in my peripheral vision. I continue.

'Anyway, to cut a long story short, after a few months of that limbo family set up, one night, James had nowhere to stay at the last minute, so offering him the sofa seemed like the sensible solution. I mean, we were very civil about it all and it was still his home at the end of the day. Anyway, a few glasses of wine later, we found each other. And you've guessed it ...'

'Eloise.' Mary whispers.

'Yep. The irony. When we weren't trying at all. We had split up because of this missing second child. So, now that she was on the way, we had to give our marriage another chance. And we have been trying ever since. Moving to the country felt like a way to start again with a clean slate. That's it.' I look up to Mary and her smile is all kindness.

'Oh Rowe, I don't know what to say.' But it turns out she does! 'I'm so sorry you've had to go through all this. Thank you for confiding in me. I really hope this is the fresh start you have been looking for. And I get it now when you said you didn't need drama! I'm sorry.' Mary looks at me with one of her sheepish smiles.

'Hey, don't worry. I'm in too deep now! To be honest, it's that experience that's drawing me to investigate Gemma's death since I read one of her posts about her endometriosis diagnosis. She doesn't say as much in her post but that and other references to Charlie being an only child have made me wonder whether she went through a similar infertility journey.'

'Oh wow, I had no idea. Poor Gemma. And Matthew.' Mary looks sad.

'So, was there anything else Tom mentioned? Who else did they interview?' I ask, keen to move the subject away from me.

'Gemma's parents. They're devastated, of course. They were babysitting Charlie that night. Terrible.' She shakes her head to push the thought away. 'Then, all their neighbours confirmed that they hadn't heard anything until the police cars turned up. There are eight properties down that lane, so someone would have heard a car driving there.'

Mary is trying to remember everything that was said by Tom.

'They also talked to people in London and Bath. People she would have worked with. They interviewed Gemma's agent at length, Hillary Peters. She was on a Zoom call at the time of the murder – which has been corroborated – so I don't think she's a person of interest.'

'Yes! Did I tell you I met her in Bath?'

'You what?'

'I was having lunch with my agent, and they used to work together. So, she stopped for a chat.'

'But how did you know her?' asks Mary, puzzled.

'Well, I didn't at first but then I remembered the name. She is not a likeable person, let me tell you. You should have seen the revulsion on her face when she spotted I was breastfeeding in the middle of the Ivy!' Mary laughs. 'She mentioned a recent hiccup and I've got a horrible feeling she was referring to Gemma's death!'

'Nooo! Surely not?'

'Well, I can't be sure. At that point, my brain hadn't joined the dots. But Daisy used to work with her years ago and her nickname was Hill for the Kill, for context.'

'Interesting nickname. Ruthless enough to actually kill someone? I know the 'formal investigation' discounted her as she has a solid alibi, but it might be good to get more info about her. You never know what we could find out.'

I agree to ask Daisy about Hillary when I get the chance.

Just then, Mary's phone chimes in with a message.

'That's Tom. He's back home. Must dash.'

'Let me know, please! Very intrigued.'

'You and me both!' she shouts, as she heads home at a jog.

Chapter 31

@gemma_cotswolds_mum Morning Friends! How do you shop for food? I mostly order our weekly food shop online, from Ocado. So practical. And if we need a mid-week top up, I will go to Waitrose. ~~you won't see me dead in Tesco.~~ Love their café ~~always someone there for gossip~~ for PTFA meetings and you can get a free coffee to take away if you shop. #notanad ~~#iwish #noinspiration~~

Mary

Friday

I am not even embarrassed to run home. I mean, at least I have my running kit on, right? The exercise is helping but I still have so much pent-up anxiety and a lot to process from what Rowe's shared. I'm so pleased that she's trusted me with her struggles. I hope that I can be a good friend to her. And then I edit the statement – a *better* friend to her. Ugh. The guilt of not sharing everything weighs heavily on me. But I just can't.

As I slow and pass through the back gates, I check Red to see if there are any more stupid notes on the windscreen, but the likelihood of someone coming into the yard behind the house to leave another note is improbable at best. Surely, they would just put it through the letterbox. I make a mental note to consider one of those virtual doorbell thingies.

I come through the back door, pull my shoes off in two swift movements and head straight to the kitchen. I am a woman on a mission.

Tom is in the process of making himself an extremely tempting bacon sarnie, replete with proper toasted bloomer bread and HP sauce. Men are so lucky – they seem to live in a perpetual state of university-age thinking and metabolism. How can he cook at a time like this? I think again to myself about how life just isn't bloody fair.

I look the question straight into his eyes when he looks up at me. 'So?'

He is clearly miles away. Probably thinking about re-roofing one of the outbuildings in the yard that we've been talking about.

'Where were you?'

'Oh right! Yeah.' He's back on the topic at hand. 'I went to Tesco to find out what CCTV they had from this morning.'

Bloody hell. Why didn't I think of this? I remind myself that he is an inspector in the police, after all.

'I wanted to go quickly. Anything that they might have had would have been taped over if we didn't get in there soon after the fact. I've spoken to the security manager there, Mike, a hundred times for exactly this sort of information over the years. Normally it's so boring. For both of us! I pretended that it was something equally as boring this time.'

'And?' My voice is ¾ of an octave higher than it should have been and there was more than a hint of anger.

'Yeah, alright!' My lack of patience is testing his. 'So, unfortunately, the cameras weren't facing quite the right direction so there aren't any smoking guns, exactly. But there are four people that we were able to identify in that part of the car park at what I calculate to be about the right time.'

'Anyone we know?' Again, my tone is not the kindest.

He is starting to get frustrated with me now. I suppose that his colleagues aren't always quite so desperate for whatever intel he's managed to garner.

'May ' It is a warning.

'Sorry, sorry'. I am not. I really am not sorry in the slightest, but I am afraid that he might decide that I am sufficiently wound-up and reconsider his whole approach. And I definitely couldn't cope with that. Not at this stage ... I feign being calm. I'm a terrible actress, heart on my sleeve and all that, but I can do what is required in a pinch.

He looks at me with a considerable pause. Obviously makes up his mind to continue and takes a breath 'So, the first one was Mr Jameson.'

It is clear to him from my face that this data point is completely lost on me.

'Oh May, you know him. Mr Jameson.'

"So you said", I think very unkindly. "I still don't know!" I manage to keep my mouth shut.

'Paul Jameson He's the one that used to run the Thursday Night bridge games. He's married to Elizabeth Jameson – one of the teachers at school. She's active in the WI.'

You can practically hear the cogs in my brain clunking through the years of detritus stored there – and then I am able to place Mrs Jameson exactly. She's one of the helpers – maybe Year 2, and then suddenly I have her husband in my mind, too! The neurons find the path they were looking for – Mr Jameson. Probably late 60s now A lovely bear of a man with eyebrows that it seems could keep the majority of his top half warm and the kindest disposition you could imagine. I can't possibly fathom him even using the word 'bastard', much less writing a note and putting it on my car. But as soon as I dismiss the possibility that it might be him, those same cogs grind out a morsel: I remember that he is Gemma's uncle, but I can't remember whether or not they were close.

'Oh yes! I remember him! He's Gemma's uncle, right?' I'm not even sure if Tom would have known this. He doesn't know all of the fascinating spider web connections of our village.

I can tell by the cartoon frown and high eyebrows that Tom definitely did not know this. I ask him how we might find out more details about the family tree without having to ask so obviously. He says he'll find out and let me know.

'OK. So who was the other person?'

'Vicky Clarkson.'

'What, seriously? That can't be right!' I'm absolutely gobsmacked.

'Why?' says Tom. Clearly, he wasn't expecting this reaction.

'Well, for starters, I'm absolutely shocked that she wouldn't have been doing the school run. She's only just started working at the Wild Boar Café and she was saying that her boss lets her work around the school schedule. Secondly, she and Gemma were at least friendly, but I wouldn't have said that they were best friends? Why would Vicky want to drag Matthew's name through the mud like that? Unless she thought that he was guilty of something else? I mean, the note suggests that whoever wrote it was angry about something. That they had somehow been wronged ...' My mind is working at 100 miles an hour now.

'Not sure, May, but you've managed to turn both of these characters into viable suspects. That's a bit annoying.'

'Tell me about it.' I am distracted but something niggles. 'Who were the other two?'

'There was one male teenager on a skateboard dressed all in black without a bag.' (This detail was important, Tom explains, because it would be unlikely that he would have access to notebook paper and a pen.) 'And a Tesco employee,' he consulted his notes 'Petra

Grabens, who normally works in the café. She went for a smoke break right about the right time but it's a slow time for the café, so it wasn't exactly an odd thing for her to do.'

'OK. Well at least we've got some interesting stuff to go on for now. Very interesting ...' My thoughts are solely focussed on Paul and Vicky. Both are a shock, but Vicky is totally unexpected, especially after our recent chat. If she is the one that put the note on my car, what does it mean? Is she the 'other woman' who has been scorned in some way? Or does she know that something was going on behind Gemma's back and just wants to set the record straight? Surely, if that is the motive, then the note wouldn't be quite so dramatic? And maybe could provide some more intel by way of evidence? Or at least the prospect of a meeting so that the evidence could be shared? Oh my God. Who knows? I think to myself, yet again, 'How the hell did I get here?'

'What do we do now, Tom? Do I need to share this info with Nick? Do I need to submit the note as evidence? Do we need to hand over the info that you got from the CCTV?'

'Let's leave it for now. We don't want to send anyone off on a wild goose chase.'

I honestly don't know whether he wants to keep all that we've learned from Nick out of spite, or whether he's worried that I'm going to look like a person doing their best impression of someone going a little bit nuts.

Chapter 32

@gemma_cotswolds_mum Evening Friends! How do you exercise? I have been wanting to share my exercise regime with you since I started 3 months ago ~~but there was always a chance I would stop after a week~~. It comprises of: Yoga every other morning before Charlie gets up, walking 10,000 steps daily, and Pilates classes every Thursday evening. Add onto that a squash game with Matthew whenever he can ~~wants, i.e. hardly ever~~. It goes without saying but I feel so much better for it, physically and mentally ~~but still feel shit most of the time and cling onto exercising for dear life~~. #fitbodyforbettermind #exercising

Rowena

Still Friday

Because Children in Need is huge in Upper Huxley, the school has invited the whole 'school family' after drop-off to build the longest school family human chain. It's a bring your grandparents/great-uncles/third cousin once removed/step-nan type of event.

Thanks to Mary, our heart to heart, and a renewed interest in our investigation, my mood has significantly improved since this morning, when I was ready to boycott the whole thing.

Don't get me wrong, I genuinely think it is an amazing charity that does so much for children who need help. But I also feel slightly pissed off that said children have to rely on charity and I always feel that if, as a country, we had better social care, they wouldn't have to be paraded on TV so much. However, I have to admit that community spirit is a beautiful and powerful thing, and raising awareness and encouraging empathy is never a wasted opportunity.

So, for the first time since we moved here, James and I both make our way to the school along with Eloise in the baby carrier. We, unfortunately, do not have any family, even in the loosest sense of it, to invite to the school. At least, not at such short notice. However, my mum should be coming over especially for Alfie's nativity play in three weeks' time. It will be nice to have her around, helping with the kids and around the house, just to get a bit of a break from adulting.

The playground is jam-packed. We manage to fight our way to the Year One area, where we collect Alfie. He is visibly chuffed to see both of us here. His two parents on the playground is a first here and was not a thing in London either. I crane my neck to see if the Lambs are around, but the crowd is too thick.

As Alfie is starting to grow restless, Mrs Dogton starts addressing our little Year One group.

'Hello, thank you everyone for coming. If you don't mind waiting for another five minutes, Mrs Mearle, our headteacher, will be addressing everyone explaining what we have to do. We've had a lovely day in our class, and we did loads of Pudsey activities. Children, maybe you can tell your grownups about it all as we wait for Mrs Mearle to kick it all off.'

That seems enough to keep Alfie's mind off the crowd, and for the next five minutes he tells us all about the colouring he did and the *Pin the Ears on the Bear* game they played in class.

I still haven't spotted Mary, but James is now engaged in conversation with Martin, Louise's husband. My quick scan around lands on none other than DI Nick the Dick only a few meters away from me, attempting to have a conversation with Mrs Mearle. A lull in the noise around me enables me to hear part of what is being said.

'Listen, Inspector …'

'Detective Inspector,' he corrects her, standing a bit taller.

'Detective Inspector,' she has put on the voice of a teacher who has to deal with a difficult child 'as you will have gathered, now is really not a good time. I will happily answer your questions when all the children and their families have left the school.'

'But …'

'Or you will have to come back on Monday. Now, if you'll excuse me …' She placates him as she turns on her microphone to address us. His face is registering the shock of being so firmly rebuffed.

'Dear school family, thank you all for coming on this special day. As I am sure they have already told you, the children and the team have been very busy today, celebrating Children In Need with many fun activities. We are now ready to start our annual school family human chain! Please hold hands with the two people next to you as soon as I shout 'Go!'. Please proceed calmly, we do not want a stampede. As in previous years, once the chain is fully formed, Mr Bartwood, our esteemed caretaker and our wonderful Jenny will be coming along the chain to count each and every one of us and collect our £1 donations. As a reminder, last year we managed to form a 956-person-long chain. Let's hope we beat it this year! And go!' she shouts in the microphone. There is a palpable level of excitement emanating not just from the children but also the adults. All voices raise at once as everyone gets hold of a nearby hand, just as the sun is setting over the trees in the Forest School area, the hues of pink and mauve announcing a frosty night.

My left hand is already holding Alfie's and the lady next to me (one of the kids' grannies, I presume) grabs my right hand. Alfie has managed to get hold of his dad who has paired up with Martin while they continue their chat.

'... really want to get back to it ... used to play it ... workmates ...' I can only hear parts of what James is talking about because of the general brouhaha. Despite that, I can clearly hear Louise loudly interrupt her husband.

'Ah well, I'm sure Martin wouldn't mind playing squash with you. He plays all the time! Mostly with poor Matthew, of course, but I'm sure they could fit you in, too!' She clearly wants as many people as possible to hear how special Matthew is to her.

Martin appears suddenly quite uncomfortable, which I'm sure I would be too if Louise was my wife.

I stifle a laugh as I spot Mrs Mearle firmly holding onto Nick the Dick's hand. His furious yet resigned look tells me that it wasn't his charitable heart that made him join the chain.

Finally, Jenny and Mr Bartwood have made their slow way to us. Martin seems to have lost the pound coin he was given by Louise, as we all now know because of her loud reproaches. While the caretaker waits for the pound coin to be located, Jenny moves over to collect our donations.

'Hmm. What about the baby, then?' she asks briskly.

'Eloise? Well, she's asleep and she can't stand anyway ...' I venture incredulously.

'No need for that. You hold her hand ...' She grabs Eloise's hand that is hanging out of the baby carrier, and places it in mine, which she has already removed from the old lady's.

'And then, Mrs Mortimer, you hold the baby's other hand. Every little person counts! That will be £2 then.'

Thankfully, I have the right change, or I can't imagine what scene would have unravelled.

I'm too new to know if 'wonderful' Jenny is always so curt or if I have upset her this morning with my rudeness. I'm going to have to be generous for Christmas. Chocolates can go a long way.

This is taking forever now. I'm trying to see where Jenny and Mr Bartwood have progressed to but there are far too many people. Eloise is stirring and I'm hoping she won't wake up in a bad mood. That would be bad enough in itself but my bladder has also decided to play up, no doubt enabled by the cold temperature.

Two minutes later, I have resorted to rocking on the spot, while Mrs Mortimer is having a conversation with Alfie, who was getting restless until she mentions she lives on a farm and starts naming all her animals. James is still chatting with Martin who seems to have cheered up again now that Louise is talking to a school mum on her left.

I breathe a sigh of relief when Mrs Mearle's voice can be heard again on the microphone.

'Children, Ladies and Gentlemen, our school family human chain is now complete! I'm deeply honoured and proud to announce that we have beaten last year's record with 1,011 people! Congratulations, everyone! You can all let go of your hands and give yourselves a massive clap!'

A huge cheer engulfs the playground accompanied by a loud round of applause.

'Well done, everyone. If we add it up to the additional donations that the children brought this morning for wearing spotty outfits, we have collected a whopping £1,460. This will make a massive difference, and you can all be very proud!' More cheers from the crowd. It really is a heart-warming event. Or it would be if only I didn't have an unsettled baby and a full bladder.

Mrs Mearle then gives instructions on how to make the best orderly exit from the playground without crushing any little people, and another ten minutes later, we are finally on the way home, where I will be able to relieve myself and feed Eloise.

Alfie and James are typically totally oblivious of Eloise's annoyance. They are chatting ten to the dozen about how cool the human chain was, and James is trying to tell me something about playing squash but I'm not listening as I just want to get home.

Chapter 33

@gemma_cotswolds_mum Morning Friends! Helpful service bulletin: for those of you that haven't finished your holiday shopping, then you'd better get your skates on! ~~Yeah, right, like I've got mine done!~~ I like to have mine done in plenty of time, ~~but it doesn't mean I do,~~ especially for those last-minute items that have to come through the post. You never know what delays ~~strikes or other crap~~ might be in store! Happy Holidays! #helpfulhints #mumsofig ~~#wishitweretrue~~

Mary

Saturday

We were so lucky with the weather yesterday. Even to do that chain thing. I know that it's all for a fantastic cause but I'm going to have to take out a loan to be able to afford the £1 events that the school puts on! Never mind the bake sales where I have to buy the cakes (or worse, *make* them!), remember to take them to school on the correct day, and then give my own money to the children so that they buy the same stupid cakes back! I mean, seriously, can't we just have an opt-out option?

My idea is this: at the beginning of the year, the PTFA decide on a colour of t-shirt for that year. It couldn't possibly just be 'blue'. Oh no! Not at Upper Huxley Community Primary! It would need to be cyan or chartreuse or something ridiculous like that. Anyway, t-shirts in that colour are all printed for the children with the words: 'I support Upper Huxley Community Primary School' and the year. These shirts are (wait for it!) £150 EACH! I know, I know … just bear with me for a minute. But here's the thing. The kids can wear them to *every stupid event* all year long. They don't have to dress up or wear PJs or buy stupid lanyards or bracelets. They don't have to wear socks on their hands or choose a character for Star Wars Day. They each get one cake/ice cream/lolly at each event based on the premise that it would have already been paid in advance. It would be worth it just to avoid my yearly parenting fail shit/show that is World Book Day. Take. My. Money. £150 is a steal! 100 children at UHPS = £15,000. Awesome. Job done. No more £1 days and no more sorting out PTFA fundraisers. But we can keep the Pop-Up Pub Quiz in the hall. I like that one.

Anyway, it was a lovely day but honestly, by the time I'd got home, I'd had enough of Friday, and the week, and lots of other things, too. I think bored. Bored and annoyed. Annored? Bannoyed?

I wake early and struggle to get back to sleep. I listen to the rain pounding on the windows. I'm not a fan of inclement weather when I'm planning to go for a run, but I do love the sound, especially when I know I don't have to get out of bed straight away. I look over at Tom sleeping peacefully and wonder how his evening was. The funny thing about living with a policeman is that you really have no idea what they would have been dealing with at 2 in the morning when most of us are sleeping all snug in our beds.

I remember reading about how ancient societies used to have 'sin-eaters' whose job it was to eat a meal containing all of the sins of a recently deceased person so that they would be able to go to heaven. I often think about how the police are the 'sin-eaters' of our modern societies. They deal with all of the things that the average person doesn't want to know about or see that exists within our society so that we don't have to. Obviously, I'm biased, but I don't think that we give them enough credit (or money) for that particular aspect of their service.

After this cheery thought, I revert back to my normal rhythm of thinking – 1) what do I need to do today? 2) What do I want to do today? and 3) What meals will we have? Once the anxiety of the to-do list surpasses the serene sound of the rain, I quietly crawl out of bed, put on my slippers, find my ancient aubergine dressing gown (mental note to ask for a new one for Christmas), and head downstairs. Norm trundles along behind me. There is nothing quite like sitting by the Aga on a cold rainy morning. Norm agrees.

I pull out my phone to find out what I've missed since yesterday afternoon both in terms of general world events (BBC News App), my new carefully edited world (Instagram), and then my immediate close friends and some carefully select family members (WhatsApp).

There's a message from Dad:

7:51: *Hi Darling. I hope you are all doing well. I'm writing to ask if you are still available for lunch tomorrow? Love, Dad*

Shit. That one didn't come up in my mental dress rehearsal of the weekend. I check my diary and see that I have written: Sunday, 24th Nov. 12:00 Lunch with Dad – The Flying Fox.

9:12: *Hi Dad, we're good, thank you. Definitely still on. Did you want us to pick you up or will you walk? X*

9:19: *Hi Darling. Yes, that would be perfect. X*

9:19: *Which, Dad? Do you want a lift? Xx*

(...)

He seems to be typing forever. I can actually feel myself reverting back to petulant teenager.

9:22: *Hi Darling. I'll walk there. The fresh air will be good for me. What's all this about Matty? I hear he was taken down to the station? Would you be available to give me a lift back to Tall Oaks afterwards? X*

Only people of that generation would split the content of a simple text with difficult questions. I should have known that Dad would be worried about Matthew. He was practically Mum and Dad's third child for a while – especially reflected in the weekly food bill. Dad was also particularly heartbroken when our friendship came to an end. I suspect he secretly hoped that Matthew and I would get married one day but that was never going to happen for us. Sadly, society has decided that girls and boys can never just be friends.

9:23: *Perfect. We will see you there at midday. We will chat about Matthew. If you change your mind about wanting a lift, just send me a message. Love you, M Xx*

Ah, that's lifted my mood. My dad and I have always been close. I would like to go see him on my own one of these days. We just don't seem to get the time to chat properly when Ben is asking him about which of the Star Wars characters he knows (none!) and Charlotte is explaining the most recent STEM topics they are discussing at school (he's much more capable of intelligent exchange in this arena). If I was brave, I'd ask myself why it is that my mood needs to be lifted. But I'm not. Not yet.

It's almost 9:30 by the time Charlotte comes down from her bedroom. Is this the beginning of the horrible teenage years? I remember when she used to be up at the crack of dawn. Far earlier than I wanted to be, that's for sure, raring to go and planning all of the activities for the day. I'm comforted by the fact that I know she had probably been reading since about 7:30. I haven't lost her down the rabbit hole of adolescence yet – after all, she still has to learn to eat properly with a fork! She comes and sits on my lap in her sleepy little way and for the millionth time since she was born, my heart feels very much like it might just burst into a trillion star-like pieces. I cuddle her, put my head on hers, smell her hair, and kiss her like I've done since she was born. I'll never stop unless she tells me to – and probably not then either.

'We're having lunch with Grandad tomorrow.' I tell her.

'I know, it's on the calendar.' she says with a lovely sleepy smile. She's as excited to see Dad as I am. They, too, have a special bond. I'm looking forward to seeing him, but I'm also interested to learn what gossip there is in the retirement home about Gemma's death, and to ask him more about Mr Jameson. I'm fairly certain they used to be friendly, but I can't remember why. What I really want to know is: could he have been the one to leave the note?

Chapter 34

@gemma_cotswolds_mum Morning Friends! Spent the ~~wettest~~ best day at the Gloucestershire Farm Park @glosfarmpark. Charlie didn't let the weather dampen his spirit~~, I did~~. We were invited ~~but I wish I had been paid for it, unfortunately they are not interested in having me as an ambassador~~ to test their new forest trail where the children can learn all about the local forest wildlife and endemic tree and plant species. ~~It was absolutely not my thing, but~~ Charlie loved it. Give it a go~~, if you don't mind mud all over your brand-new car~~! ~~#givemeastiffdrink~~ #ad ~~#givemesomesponsoredjobs~~ #lovewhereyoulive

Rowena

Tuesday

James is back in London again today.

Unlike me, he truly enjoyed the whole school family event last Friday and last night took up Martin's offer to play squash together. He loved it, particularly because he 'demolished' Martin (his words, not mine), who is apparently quite rubbish for someone who plays so often.

I am pleased and relieved James is also making friends here. I was worried it would be awkward for him as he shares his time between here and London, and that it would feel like he is always 'visiting' in both places. Of course, the children and I are anchoring him here, but making friends and taking part in the village social life will help.

I feel lighter to see this other block slot itself into the foundations of our new life. We really need this to work for us.

Feeling like I'm winning at motherhood today after successfully putting Eloise down for her morning nap, I confidently sit at my desk in our beautiful study with a steaming hot mug of coffee.

While nursing Eloise the other day and reminiscing about the Straw Man Parade, I got excited over an idea for my next book featuring a scarecrow as a main character.

Fifteen minutes later, I've jotted nothing other than 'Scarecrow comes alive at night' and 'little Robin friend'. The more I try to concentrate the more I find my mind wandering to the investigation.

Who could have killed Gemma? Why aren't the police making any new arrests? Is Matthew still suspect #1? Nothing much is slipping out into the press.

We have now completely discarded the idea that trolling could have been the motive. At least Lorna herself seems completely innocent.

I look at my notes and on the next page of my notebook, I have written:

'GEMMA'S MURDER – LEADS'

Seriously? Leads? Who do I think I am? This is ridiculous.

But then, something that I said to Mary on the first day we met comes back to me. About what a shame it is that we don't write murder mysteries. I have always wanted to write a novel one day. Our 'investigation' could be the perfect source of inspiration! This is not being a busybody like Miss Marple, this is work!

That is all it takes to appease my already weakened conscience.

With renewed energy, I write down:

Lead #1: Instagram troll. Lorna has no actual motive. Any other lead linked to her influencer job?

Lead #2: Husband's affair – swinging?

Lead #3: Money problems

How do we find out more about #2? Do the police now know about this? As for lead #3, money is always a good contender for motive. I'm mot sure either of us are qualified for bank account hacking, though. That is the sort of thing the police will definitely get into.

I suddenly remember how I could try and gather more info about lead #1. I grab my phone and find Daisy's name. I'm sure it's down to years of experience, but Daisy always makes it sound like you are exactly the person she wanted to talk to whenever you ring her.

We speak for a bit about the sales of my current books and what I am planning to do with my next one. She runs by me the possibility of talking at next year's Cheltenham Literature Festival, which is very exciting seeing that it is so local to me and also the oldest literary festival in Britain!

'That would be really cool, Daisy. I could even get Alfie to come and watch me. He would be so proud. Talking about local festivals, what about Huxlit? It's not as big as Cheltenham, but it's still pretty good, I hear.'

'Ok, let me try and get more info on both gigs for you.'

'Thank you so much, Daisy.'

'My job, darling!'

'Talking about agenting. Remember that old acquaintance of yours? Hillary Peters?'

'Yeess?' she replies, intrigued.

'Well, I coincidentally heard about her again the other day.'

'Really, how so?'

'Remember I mentioned her client, Gemma Hatherley, who got killed live on Instagram? She lived in my village.'

'Ah yes, have they found the killer, then?'

'Well, they have arrested the husband but then released him. I don't know him, but people here are not convinced. Anyway, it made me curious about Hillary. She struck me as such a ... What's the word?'

'Bitch?'

'Well, maybe. Is she really like that?'

'As I explained to you on Tuesday, she had quite a cutthroat reputation when I used to work with her.'

'Yep, Hill for the Kill, you used to call her, right?'

'Indeed. But she actually wasn't always like that. We started together as part of a small graduate scheme our agency had launched. There were only three of us and work for at least six. She was working for one of the senior agents. He's quite well known so let's call him 'P'. She was lovely and what can only be described as a bit of a pushover then.'

'Really?' I find that impossible to imagine.

'Yes, she never said no to any of his difficult requests. She was giving her all for that job but was also a great friend to have around. She was very supportive of the two other graduates, i.e. me and this guy who had just arrived from Cornwall and was utterly lost in the big city.' I can hear the nostalgia in her voice. 'She was a great team player, particularly for the team she formed with P, her mentor. She had a nose for unearthing the small promising writing talent, but she also had the interpersonal skills to reel these talents in and soon, she was building a nice little list of promising writers that she was managing for P. Of course, because she was so junior, none of the commissions were for her, but she didn't seem fussed about it. She was there to read the manuscripts, find the next big one, bring in the business for the agency and hone her craft in the process.'

'Wow, that sounds like such a different person to the one I met in Bath.' I say, incredulous.

'Well, it is not the same person you met in Bath.' Her voice sharpens.

'How so?'

'Because after Hillary had given her everything for two years, bloody P left the agency and took not only his entire list of authors but also hers with him. He somehow managed to go behind her back and convince all the promising writers to come with him to an even bigger agency, where he was offered a partner position.' She still sounds so angry for something that happened so long ago.

'Oh dear.' I'm lost for words.

'You could say that. She went MIA for a week after that. We all thought she had resigned or lost her job as her mentor had left.'

'But no, the following Monday, she came back, and she was a completely different person. Like she had put a wall up. She worked just as hard if not harder, but she was no longer a nice person to be around. No more friendly chat or supportive help. She focused her entire being on her job. She was a woman on a mission. Within two months, she had managed to get all the clients on her list back under her representation. But she didn't stop there. She made it her goal to get P's writers too and she snatched most of his big names. Some said it was unethical, and the agency's name suffered along the way, but she stuck to her guns and eventually left to set up her own agency.'

'Where she didn't have to be a team player?' I venture.

'Yes, I suppose so. Where she didn't have to deal with others. She pretty much ruled out other people after that.'

'But surely to be an agent you have to work with other people all the time.'

'Oh, she was terrific with her writers. She would get the best for them, as ultimately the best for them was the best for her. I'm sure she is the same with her influencers.'

'Wow, sounds like the betrayal was a wake-up call.'

'The change was so brutal. Coffee machine amateur therapists, aka some of our colleagues, put it down to an earlier trauma, something about her father leaving the family overnight. I mean, I don't know the details but that can't have helped. Regardless, I really got to miss the Hillary I used to know and love.' She sighs regretfully, but she quickly bounces back to her chirpy self. 'But such is life, and the world of publishing can be ruthless.'

I wind up the call soon after that, desperate for a bit of free time to process what I have just learned. I am not sure this would be enough to make me like Hillary now, but I can certainly feel some sympathy for the young girl she used to be. Unfortunately, none of this helps with our investigation.

Chapter 35

@gemma_cotswolds_mum Morning Friends! Had the best autumn picnic with Charlie at the weekend. ~~Absolutely not my bag. Wish I was on a beach in Dubai instead.~~ We had the best selection of local products from @cotswoldfarmers. My favourite was the apple crumble tart and Charlie loved his @greenvalleyorchard apple juice and the sausage rolls. ~~you wouldn't see me dead eating one of those. Charlie refused to sit still and within minutes we were covered in mud and we couldn't wait to get back inside.~~ #lovewhereyoulive #eatlocal ~~#givemethebigpartnerships~~

Mary

Tuesday

I wake incredibly early but also super excited. I spent a few hours last week finally convincing Rosie to let me do a piece on local food as a Christmas Ideas spread. She basically acquiesced on the promise that I would get at least one of them to book some ad space – but I'll worry about that later. I've already lined up visits with a local gin distillery, an apple orchard that makes juice and cider, a cheese maker, and a local boutique charcutier. I'm positively electric with the excitement of showcasing what our corner of the country has to offer ... Oh, and stuffing my face full of delicious food and drink.

I also managed to book our gorgeous photographer, Marco, for the whole of Tuesday to travel all over the county with me. I'd never admit it to Rosie, but I'd booked his time and all of the appointments even before I approached her about the article. Sometimes I feel like my true calling is persuasion and that writing is just a hobby. He arrives at my house at about 6am for an early start. It seems a silly decision when it doesn't get properly light until about 8 but I can't believe how lucky we are with the weather, and I am ever so glad when we are already at the orchard just as the sun is pushing its way through the trees. Rosie will be very pleased. I hope!

The atmosphere in the orchard barn is incredible. In one of the corners of the ancient oak structure, there is a dedicated seating area and a beautifully rustic farm shop. It has old chesterfields and cosy blankets, and the effect is enhanced with a faux ceiling of miles of warm twinkly fairy lights. There is a huge wood burner that keeps the chill at bay and a bar that exclusively serves cider, juice, tea and coffee. The smell of hay and freshly sawn wood is unmistakably barn-y but (in the absence of animals, I guess) fresh and welcoming in a sentimental way. It would be the perfect venue for weddings, and I mentally congratulate the owners, Ulyana & Griff, for creating such a 'story' behind their product. They may be selling cider and juice but there is a large helping of hygge that comes free with purchase.

I am writing lots of notes about what they were doing prior to buying the orchard (hedge fund manager and A&E nurse in central London, if you're interested. They're an unlikely pair on paper but seem to be blissfully enamoured with both each other and the new life they've created/adopted) and it gets me thinking about people who have such a drastic career change in their lives. As is so often the case these days, my mind drifts back to Gemma. She wasn't always a successful influencer.

The owners and I are sitting at a huge farmhouse table (in anticipation of the product tasting to follow) whilst sexy Marco is climbing all over the barn like a Russian gymnast to find interesting angles to capture. At least he's putting those incredible abs to good use.

Despite the fact that I should be listening to the differences between the tart apples that are good for making cider and the sweet apples that are good for juicing, I find my mind is desperately trying to hunt down the information about Gemma's previous occupation. And then I remember! She worked in HR at the same company where Matthew still works. I know very little about HR. Not surprising as a writer who works almost wholly autonomously (except for when I have the pleasure of being paired off with Marco for the day).

I chide myself for the fact that I cannot focus on the different fermenting processes for sweet and dry ciders, all the while thinking on whether Gemma left her job because she wanted to or because her family needed her to. Obviously, life is never that simple. The reality is a continuum of all of one's hopes and desires. If Gemma was anything like me, she would have been desperate, after a suitable time, of course, to challenge her brain again and get back to some sense of responsibility outside of the day to day running of a household after she had her child. But then, she might have been absolutely nothing like me – in that respect, at least. There are plenty of women who decide that working outside the home is no longer an attractive prospect after starting a family.

'Marketing is complicated these days.' Ulyana explains, bringing me back to the present. 'Yes, you still have your branding, identity, and USPs; all the things that we talked about when I was in business school, but all of the traditional ways of getting that message out to your target demographic have changed. Think about how you watch television. People don't want adverts anymore. Even on streaming services where adverts still exist, we know from recent studies that people tend to ignore these and use them as a prompt to go to the kitchen or for a comfort break. Obviously, we would never be able to afford television advertising, regardless, but I'm just using that to show you how we have had to completely change our thinking.'

'So, who *is* your target market?' I realise that this isn't exactly the direction that I should be heading if my goal is to write a 'Cosy Cotswold Christmas List.'

'Well, in fact, we have two completely separate markets; one is for the juice, and one for the cider, which is tricky for a small business our size. All of our products are completely organic and farmed using permaculture methods, so even though there is a range of consumers, we have two that we focus on. For the juice, we target the 'Yummy Mummy' set.'

'Ulyana! Don't say that!' Griff interrupts rather gruffly and shoots a stern look at me. 'Please don't use that label in your article.'

'Ha Ha. No, of course not.' I confirm. I'm used to people being somewhat cautious but it's clear to me that Griff is the sensitive one here. 'How about 'conscientious parent'?' I proffer.

'Yeah, that's better. Thanks.' He is more nervous about this interview than I realised. I guess when you have a small business, the pressure is on to make the most of any opportunity for promotion but the expense of a faux pas – especially one that might alienate your market – could be costly.

'Course.' I say rather dismissively. I'm not belittling his concerns – 'once something is in print ...' I often think, but I also don't want Ulyana to lose her flow.

Ulyana rolls her eyes almost imperceptibly. If Griff is the heart of this operation, she is most definitely the brains.

'The cider is very much aimed at foodies who like trying lots of different types of ales, beers, and ciders. The great news is that we are extremely popular with this demographic, so the reach is wide but the quantity that they buy is often small. These tend to be people who will try lots of different brewers and will rarely become loyal to a single brew house. So, the pressure is on to continuously increase our reach.'

'And how do you manage that?' I say, allowing Ulyana to take a breath. Her passion is contagious.

'Various methods, but recently, we've been spending more time using social media. Of course, we have accounts on all the major platforms, and we spend a lot of time creating content for these. Lately, we've been using more competitions to get exposure, especially in conjunction with other accounts.'

'Like with other similar brands?' I realise that I'm for sure out of my depth here.

'More like complimentary brands. Like Pete's Meats.' This is the charcutier that I plan to visit later. 'Along with his charcuterie, he does an awesome line of pork scratchings that go brilliantly with our dry cider.'

'Oh nice!' Is my mouth watering? That's embarrassing, it's only 8:45am, but I do love pork scratchings.

'Yeah – and the follow, like, comment, and share method gets us higher up the Instagram algorithm.'

'Uh-huh.' Erm ... What the fuck is she talking about?

'But it's not as effective for our juice. That needs more obvious endorsement so we've starting using some local influencers and hiring them to create content.'

'Oh really? Anyone I would know?' Who am I kidding, the only influencer I know is ..

'Gemma Hatherley before her terrible ...' If it weren't for the fact that Ulyana goes on to list two others, I would swear that I only said her name in my head, but her words came out perfectly synchronised with my thought.

'Did you say Gemma Hatherley?' I feel the blood rush to my ears again.

'Yeah – did you know that she recently passed? A terrible situation ...'

I can't bear the fact that she might actually start to tell me what happened. It would just be too awkward, but I also can't quite figure out how to tell her that I know without making her feel uncomfortable.

'Yes, absolutely terrible. Our children go to the same school, and we were friendly.' Honestly, it is like Gemma is finding her way into every aspect of my life. Everywhere I go, there is some sort of connection to her or this terrible murder.

'Oh, I'm so sorry to hear that, Mary.' Ulyana may be the brains, but she does have some heart. 'I'd never spent much time with her, but she did do some wonderful work for us and always seemed so helpful, unlike her shark-like agent. She had great suggestions for content and clever ideas.'

'Ah, that's nice to hear. Obviously, I didn't know her in her ... ah ... professional capacity.' All of a sudden, I find that I don't feel much like drinking super sweet apple juice and tasting three different types of cider, but I steel myself for the task ahead.

I also learn that advertising through influencers is expensive! Ulyana tells me that depending on the number of followers, one single post can cost them as much as £5k! She also says that Gemma was their most high-profile endorser so I guess that must have been at least somewhere near her rate. If Gemma was making

£5k for a quick post, surely that's more than she would have been making in her HR role?

  Marco confirms that he's got what he needs and packs up the car. I stand up from the table for the first time in too long – a credit to the excellent interview, I'm sure. I'm pleased that it only takes me a second to confirm that my legs are wobbly from sitting, not from the scrumptious cider. I thank Ulyana & Griff for their time, wish them all the best for a busy Christmas season, and we head towards our next stop: the cheesery. Marco and I resume our customary banter: taking the piss out of each other's accents and him teaching me the rudest words in Spanish. But really, I am calculating Gemma's annual salary in my head and wondering if I might be able to take up being an influencer.

Chapter 36

@gemma_cotswolds_mum Evening Friends. Just this beautiful picture of lilies, my favourites. Nothing to sell, nothing to say, just have a lovely evening. Love, Gemma.

Rowena

Thursday

Today is the day of Gemma's funeral.

I wasn't going to go because 1) I only met her a couple of times at school, and 2) I didn't have anyone to look after Eloise.

But James came home last night, and Mary was insistent I had to go because of our 'informal vestigation', and also persuaded me that I kind of knew Gemma better than she did, through social media.

Feeling like a fraud, I resolve to make myself very small at the back of the church.

I'm lucky to say that I have not been to many funerals: only my grandparents and a great-aunt. And it is one thing to say Goodbye to an elderly person who has had a full life, but quite another to a 38-year-old mother with a lot left to live for.

As a result, I am dreading it and am ready to turn around for home when I bump into Mary, and she grabs my arm to guide me into the church. Forget my idea to find myself a pew at the very back; Mary drags me into the middle section of the church, where I recognise a few parents from school.

Once I am over my initial embarrassment, I start looking around the little church. It is clearly ancient, but I wouldn't venture a guess at its age. The aisle, made out of uneven flagstones weathered by centuries of worshippers, is flanked by oak pews each decorated with a small bouquet of lilies, matching a magnificent arrangement near a blown-up picture of Gemma by the altar. We are still waiting for the family and coffin to arrive (I shudder), so I turn my attention to the congregation. The church is absolutely full. The whole village is probably here but I discern a group of people who stand out from the local crowd. They look significantly more polished than the rest of us and I can recognise some quite famous influencers who would have been part of Gemma's virtual gang. They look solemn, but cynical me reminds me that appearances are their bread and butter.

A few rows ahead, I spot Gemma's agent, Hillary. She is elegant in a sharp black suit and is the picture of dignified grief, sitting absolutely straight with big sunglasses hiding half her face. I discreetly point her out to Mary.

The music starts and the coffin comes in, followed by the family. I keep my eyes resolutely facing ahead because I don't want to make a spectacle of myself when I barely know them. One look at the poor little boy and I will be going down in floods of tears.

I wish I could blame the hormones but even when I'm not pregnant or breastfeeding, I've always been a weeper. Films, adverts, animal documentaries; I will cry at anything. Since I have become a mother, it's got much worse and anything affecting children is sure to bring on the tears.

I keep my head down, but my side vision tells me that Mary is holding her composure together much better than me.

I'm pretty sure it is a lovely service, but I zone out for half of it as I keep oscillating between focusing my mind on something mundane to prevent the tears and returning to the occasion out of respect for Gemma and her family, only to start thinking about my shopping list when my eyes threaten to fill up again.

The family has organised a wake at the Black Horse, and we are all encouraged to go by Reverend Peter. Again, I am ready to make my excuses, but Mary has decided otherwise. Not one to make a scene but also secretly curious to see how it will all unfold, I find myself drinking a merlot at the pub, ten minutes later. While Mary has gone to say a few words of condolences to Matthew and his family, I have bagged us a small table nearby, in a prime location to see all the mourners presenting their best wishes to the widower.

Martin and Louise spend quite a bit of time with him. Louise is busy making it loudly clear that she was very involved in the whole wake preparations when Hillary Peters approaches Matthew. As soon as she has dispensed the formal sympathies, she tries to engage him on the subject of the fallout following Gemma's death and his arrest and starts to suggest some proposed PR steps to recover the situation. It makes for cringe watching and Matthew doesn't seem to know how to react. He's clearly not engaging and mumbling some short answers, sending some desperate looks around him.

'Rowe, go and get her. He's desperate. You met her recently, you can save him, and that will be our chance to have a chat with her. Go!' Mary whispers as she pushes me up.

Oh, bugger. I make my way towards them. 'Hillary?' I venture. 'So sorry to interrupt. I'm Rowena, we met in Bath last week, with Daisy, my agent?' Her eyes are shooting daggers at me for my interruption. 'Can I offer you a drink maybe?' I turn to a grateful Matthew, murmur 'My most sincere condolences,' and lead Hillary away towards our little table.

'Hillary, can I introduce you to my friend, Mary? Mary, this is Hillary Peters, Gemma's agent.' Mary puts on a convincing show of not knowing who Hillary is. 'Hillary, can I get you a glass of wine or something else?' I ask.

'I will take a gin and tonic, please. Light tonic. No ice. Lime. Not lemon.' She is clearly used to getting her way.

When I come back five minutes later with Hillary's drink of choice, she and Mary are in an animated conversation about the future of magazines.

'I don't believe the younger generation will be willing to pay £4 or £5 to read a magazine when they can read great quality free content directly on their phone. If I were you, I would move onto digital immediately.'

I can see Mary bristling at the patronising tone, but she hides it by putting on her best helpless schoolgirl voice.

'But how does that work, Hillary? Who is going to pay me to write a post on Instagram? People can read it for free, surely.' Mary is playing dumb, and Hillary actually rolls her eyes at Mary's feigned lack of knowledge (which two months ago wouldn't have been faked at all).

'Of course, they can. But the more people read your posts, the more brands will be interested in sponsoring your posts, your stories, your reels, and this is how you will make your income. Hotels, restaurants, tourist destinations will invite you and pay you to review what they have to offer.'

Before she turns to me, I can't help but notice that she doesn't seem to be displaying any emotion about the funeral. Gemma's shocking and early demise seems to have been put at the very back of her mind. More interestingly, as she was talking animatedly to

Mary, she took off her sunglasses and her eyes aren't showing any signs of redness. Not much of a crier, then.

'Do you do social media, Rowena? Daisy is quite old school but even she would advise you to be present on social media platforms, I hope.'

'Hmm, yes, I'm on Instagram. I write children's books, so my audience is mostly mums like me.'

'Ah yes, that audience is my bread and butter. My clients are mostly mum influencers. That is a very lucrative market, which attracts sponsors from a vast array of different industries: fashion, toys, education, beauty, tourism, home décor, tech, you name it. And mums who are supposedly *so busy*,' she fake whinges 'seem to have a lot of time on their hands to hang out on Instagram.' She chuckles to herself, forgetting who she is talking to.

Ok, now, I hate this person. I cannot say that I hate very many people, but she truly is detestable. I have to remind myself of the betrayal she suffered years ago, but attenuated circumstances don't seem to weigh in enough for me today.

Mary gives me a discrete kick under the table as she can see me getting annoyed.

'Ah yes, I understand Gemma was very much in that market, then?' she asks candidly.

At the mention of Gemma, Hillary seems to suddenly remember where she is and her whole face falls as she grabs one of these mini napkins from the metal dispenser on the table, flinching as the stiff paper wipes at invisible tears.

'Yes, she was. Poor Gemma. Awful, sad business. She was my best one. We were more than agent and talent, the two of us, you know.'

Mary is making all the right noises pretending we believe her act, but I can't help it anymore.

'Ah, really? You weren't referring to Gemma's death when you mentioned a 'hiccup' to Daisy on Tuesday, then?'

Mary suddenly turns to look at me, with an odd look in her eyes. Is that admiration mixed with surprise?

'What? I never said that.' Hillary denies firmly.

'Ah, OK, I must have misunderstood then.' I say, looking at her directly, hoping my eyes convey the message 'I'm onto you. I'm not falling for your BS'.

I don't know where this is coming from. When my marriage was crumbling, I somehow lost confidence in my voice, and since I have mostly shied away from confrontation. But recently, as with Jenny in the office and when I confronted Mary, I have found that I have things to say and am no longer happy letting those things go unsaid. What I am doing here with Mary may seem silly, but it is important. Gemma died and the murderer needs to be found.

After that dig from me, Hillary signals her desire to leave by finishing her drink and grabbing her bag, but she stops and gasps as Lorna enters the pub.

'What is it?' asks Mary.

'I can't believe she has the guts to show her face here today.' she spits out, her eyes full of vitriol.

'Lorna? Do you know her?' I can't hide the interest in my voice.

'I do know her alright. She caused some PR issues for Gemma when she attacked her on Instagram from her environmental moral high ground. I had to do major damage limitation.'

Aware of the potential valuable intel, I try to stay calm and keep the flow of revelations going. "Oh?" I ask, hoping to find the balance between showing the right amount of interest and interrupting.

'Yes. But, beyond the business side of things, it really upset Gemma when, after some investigating, I told her who was behind the Instagram account. She couldn't believe it was someone she knew and met every day at school.' She looks smug at the memory of her revealing this to Gemma.

'You mean, Lorna never came clean to Gemma herself?' Mary blurts out. I shoot her daggers. A question too specific might make Hillary clam up.

'Well, she did when Gemma confronted her ... She was all apologies and put on a proper sob story to Gemma because, against my better judgement and advice, Gemma ended up calling on her followers to stop the nastiness against Lorna. Thankfully though, things calmed down after that. Gemma came out on top and Lorna pretty much retired from the field.' If her victorious tone is anything to go by, not coming out on top is not an option for Hillary.

Despite an apparent calmness, I know Mary is, as I am, doing a lot of rearranging of the facts in her head. Does it change anything for Lorna? Does it give her a motive? Why did she lie to me about going to Gemma to confess she was the troll?

Chapter 37

@gemma_cotswolds_mum Morning Friends! I couldn't wait to show off my new Radley wallet that Matthew bought me ~~after I begged~~ as a 'Happy December' gift. He even put a ~~single pound coin~~ crisp £50 note in it so he wouldn't have to give it to me empty. He's so thoughtful that way. If this is how we start the month, I can't wait to see what's under the tree with my name on it! ~~But I'm sure I can guess since I sent him a very detailed spreadsheet.~~ Xx
Gemma

Mary

Thursday

As crude as it sounds, this is the most engaging funeral I've ever been to. Luckily, I haven't been to many but when I have, the overwhelming emotion was sadness. This one is sad, of course – such a young and promising life cut short. But it is also mixed with intrigue and speculation. And that is even before we found out that Lorna lied!

As I walk into the vestibule, Gemma's electric smile and beautiful Disney princess eyes are staring back at me. Her incredible photograph has been blown-up to larger than life size. Rather uncharitably, I think to myself about just how 'Gemma' it was to have headshots done (and updated regularly?), just in case of the event of her untimely death. No one ever takes pics of me. My phone library hardly thinks I exist; it is full of the children, Tom, Norm (too much Norm), but like any typical mum, almost none of me. If I die any time soon, I fear they are going to have to cobble together pics from the most recent Wonderlust Christmas do where I might be blurred (and more than tipsy) but at least I'll have on lipstick!

But then my heart breaks all over again when I see Matthew sitting on the front pew in a dark suit putting on a brave face for Charlie. I can't see Charlie properly but his grandparents, Gemma's mum and dad, are constantly reassuring him. How lovely to have such a close connection to your grandchildren. I know that they say that burying your children is the worst pain (I hope I never find out), but there must be some solace in knowing that you have a piece of them that will live on in the form of a child.

Directly behind this pew are Matthew's parents, who I resolve to speak to after the funeral is over, and Paul & Elizabeth Jameson. Paul is Gemma's uncle, and he is also the one that was in the car park during the time of *The Note*. He looks at Elizabeth a few times but, most importantly, he reaches forward and puts a strong hand on Matthew's shoulder with a supportive squeeze. Matthew brings his hand up to rub his eyes in response. Not the behaviour of someone who, just a few days before, might have labelled Matthew a bastard. But then, anger makes people behave very strangely.

The other two possible note-writers are Vicky (present and accounted for, sitting in the flock of mummies) and the Tesco employee (Paula? Polly? I couldn't quite remember her name) who isn't at the funeral, but no surprise there.

I am, however, royally annoyed to see Nick the Dick. Not surprised, of course, but very annoyed. I imagine he is desperately trying to glean cheap intel that he can't otherwise be bothered to work for. He is glancing around, staring uncomfortably long into the faces of people he thinks might be 'of interest' and, worst of all, jiggling his knee in anticipation – it implies something more akin to excitement than reverence.

However, ashamedly, I find myself doing pretty much the same. I try to observe any particularly interesting reactions without being overtly obvious. Unfortunately, subtlety has never been one of my virtues. I am also looking for anyone who might be conspicuous by their absence – surely anyone in the village that isn't at this funeral would need a good reason not to be there – but none of those came to mind either. There is a tiny bit of my brain that was just being downright bitchy – e.g. Who is this group of fashionistas with large sunglasses and haute couture? Seriously! This is Upper Huxley, not Paris.

I was so glad I'd hoodwinked Rowe into going to the pub for the wake afterwards. Not only for the intel but also for the general craic. And Gemma's agent proved to be thoroughly entertaining and full of useful information. I do love a good wake. I started to feel a bit wistful that I would end up missing my own!

Gemma's close friends are fairly young and as carefree as you can be when you have kids. More to the point, many of them had probably arranged babysitters to give Gemma a proper send-off.

***

Rowe and I leave before the crowd gets too rowdy, but I am certain there will be many a sore head tomorrow. On the walk back to her house, Rowe and I quickly dispense with the niceties, 'lovely service', and all that and get onto the more interesting bits.

'Can you believe that Lorna lied?' I can't decide what would motivate her to lie about something that seemed so trivial. What difference does it make whether Gemma approached her about the trolling or whether she owned up first? It makes me realise that we shouldn't be taking everything that's said to us at face value. What a couple of amateurs!

'So strange. Should we confront her about it? Would she normally bend the truth like that?'

'It's pretty out of character. Lorna doesn't give much of a shit about what people think of her, generally.'

'Oh Mary, I'm trying to remember the exact words she used. What if I just assumed that she was taking the moral high ground and came clean first?'

'At the end of the day, we haven't managed to find a real motive for her and it's still true that she's lost more than she's gained through Gemma's death. Let's hope that we get a chance to clarify with her.' I'm trying to reassure Rowe, who's looking a bit anguished now, and decide to change the subject.

'Poor Matthew.' It comes out of my mouth without my realising, like more of an expelled thought than a statement. I can't help but think that for someone who has had a few weeks to get used to the idea of life without Gemma, he seemed a little bit like it was hitting him for the first time. But then that just seems to happen to people at funerals sometimes.

'I know what you mean.' Rowe has twigged the sheepish 'of course' look on my face. 'I think it's even harder for him being the centre of attention all by himself – even more so now that he's been so publicly humiliated by the arrest in the pub. And, of course, now the whole of Upper Huxley will know about it.'

For all that they were the 'it' couple, I knew that it was always Gemma's wish for them to be so high-profile. Now everyone else would know that, too.

'Did you see Paul and Elizabeth Jameson on the second row? She's one of the helpers at the school but, remember, he is Gemma's uncle?' I encourage.

'Oh yes, I mean, I saw them but I'm not sure that I would have put two and two together. Was Gemma's family tight knit?' Rowe asks.

'Erm ... I'm not sure. You remember that he was one of the ones that showed up on the CCTV camera during the time that Red was parked at Tesco?'

Rowe nods her head, remembering the list.

'Well, when I saw my dad for lunch the other day, he told me that the word on the street at the retirement home was that Mark's daughter, Jess – you know Mark, right, he owns the Café? – well, his daughter, Jess, spotted Paul and Matthew having dinner at the Red Lion pub two weeks before Gemma's death. Don't you think that's a bit odd? Why would they be having dinner just the two of them? Going for a drink would be perfectly explainable, but dinner? It seems so formal; planned, maybe? Like they had something specific that they needed to discuss.' I'm talking so excitedly, I finally have to stop for breath.

'Well, surely that removes Paul from the running for leaving the note, right? I mean, on the one hand, Paul is willing to discuss something specifically over a dinner with Matthew and the next minute, he's leaving story-telling notes on your car?' Rowe's wheels are turning fast.

'I don't know. What if they had a falling out during this dinner? Jess said that they were engrossed in some documents. What kind of documents would you take to dinner to chat with someone about?'

'What did Paul do before he retired?'

'He was a mortgage advisor. He helped my mum and dad with some of their accounts when my grandmother died.'

This supports the theory that Matthew and Gemma were having financial difficulties. Is it enough to be a motive for Matthew?

Chapter 38

@gemma_cotswolds_mum Evening Friends! Feeling wonderfully festive as I spent the evening with friends making this beaut. I am so proud of our little village community ~~despite how useless some people are~~. We had the best evening making our own Christmas wreaths, everyone in their own style. ~~I would really like to brag as mine was definitely the classiest~~ #lovewhereyoulive #handmadewreath

Rowena

Friday

Following yesterday's sadness and drama, I've had a quiet day trying to invoke my Christmas spirit in preparation for tonight's wreath workshop. I continue to marvel at this community's ability to carry on with the festive season after such a tragic event. 'Life Goes On' is certainly a motto here.

The upcoming workshop brings back my fondest childhood memories of foraging with my grandparents for moss and holly in the woods near our house to decorate for the holidays. My mum would organise the best Christmas crafternoons with my older sister, Becky and me.

For the last couple of years, I have tried to emulate these with Alfie, but I have found them incredibly stressful and frustrating. The last one ended up with two very sorry looking paper angels, an extremely bored child, a stressed mum, and glitter in every corner of the flat. I was still finding some in August! We will see if I feel brave enough to try it again this year. If I ban glitter, it should be easier.

By the time I set off for the village green, I've managed to keep my Christmas mood to a reasonable level, despite some serious whingeing over the food at dinner (Alfie) and some tears at bath time (Eloise).

Since Marigold's visit, I've had to scrap my idea of integrating pampas into my wreath like the cool ones I had pinned on my Pinterest board. Way too risky in this village! Don't want any Carol Swingers knocking at our door!

The village hall is shining like a beacon on the dark village green. Inside, even though I am one of the first to arrive, the warmth and fragrant spice of what I'm guessing is the mulled wine only enhances my festive mood.

Marigold is standing behind a small table collecting the participation fees. She walks around the table to welcome me with a hug. After we've exchanged the usual greetings and I have handed my tenner over, she points me in the direction of the mulled wine stand.

The table is (wo)manned by Vicky, who, I remind myself, was identified by Tom and Mary as a potential suspect for leaving the slanderous note on Mary's windscreen.

She doesn't particularly strike me as vindictive, but neither does Mr Jameson, to be honest.

'Hi Rowena. We met once at school, but I don't expect you would have remembered everyone. I'm Vicky. Would you like a cup of mulled wine?' Her green eyes are shining, enhanced by the subtle shimmering powder she's applied on her freckles.

'Hi Vicky, yes please. It smells delicious! Did you make it yourself?' She nods as she starts pouring the wine into a glass punch cup. 'Oh, this is nice. In a glass cup no less!'

'Ah yes, we have been making a lot of effort for the environment in the PTFA. Trying as hard as we can to stay away from disposable plastic.' She explains, but I detect a note of irritation at what I have no doubt is Lorna's influence on the matter.

'This is great. Bet it tastes nicer, too!' I say hoping to sound encouraging.

'It does but it also means a lot of washing up, unfortunately ...'

'Happy to lend a hand with that later.' I offer as I take my first sip of what is probably the best mulled wine I've had in a long time.

'Great. Thank you, Rowena. We always need more hands.'

The hall has started to fill up with about a dozen people and the tables have been laid out with all the greenery and materials. I'm settling my things as I spot Mary making a beeline for me, perfectly in time with the beat of 'Little Drummer Boy'.

'Evening, Rowe. You OK?' She looks flustered and is rapidly scanning the room.

'Mary, are you alright? What's up?' I ask, concerned.

'Yes, yes, I'm good. Just something ... Is Louise here?' she whispers.

'Hmm, I haven't seen her yet.' I reply as I start discreetly looking around. 'Why?'

'Probably nothing, but as I was on my run earlier, I saw Louise's car parked on Matthew's drive.' Her eyes are still darting around the room.

'Well, what time was that?'

'About 6.45. Why?'

'Well, that's not exactly what I would expect to be the perfect time for an illicit affair. Matthew's son would still be up, and we know they are friends, anyway. Possibly the whole family went for dinner there.'

'True. Very true. It's probably nothing. Ignore me. Bit hormonal today. Hence the last minute run. Had to get out and burn some frustration over an article that I just couldn't write.'

'Oh, I know the feeling. I've had a massive case of blank page syndrome recently. Not a word ...'

'Still, very weird.' Mary interrupts me. I don't even feel annoyed as I know Mary is simply obsessing over this development. 'Louise doesn't usually miss this event. It's kind of her baby project she initiated years ago.'

'Hmm.' I indicate with a nod to stay quiet as Marigold has made her way to us to check if we have got everything we need.

We spend the next hour chatting with the ladies around us and making our individual wreaths.

I'm nowhere near finished when Mary stands up and declares that she's done.

'Not my best one, but I really can't spend any more time on this! Rowe, refill?' She picks up my cup and walks towards the mulled wine table.

I'm busy fiddling with my glue gun to stick some pinecone to my greenery base, when Mary comes back with our drinks.

'Rowe, mince pie?' She asks in an urgent tone, that I would have picked up on if I wasn't concentrating on my creation.

'No. Thanks. Not now.' I reply without raising my head.

She kicks my chair, forcing me to look up. 'They look so tasty, come and check them out.' She sounds weirdly insistent.

I get the message and follow her. When no one is watching, she drags me towards the toilets.

'Mary, what is going on?' I ask eagerly.

'It's Louise. Vicky said she called in sick!' She is visibly excited by the news.

'Wow. But maybe she just popped to Matthew's for something. She may genuinely be poorly and tucked up in bed now.'

'Maybe, but maybe not.' She adds meaningfully as she heads back into the hall.

I follow her and we remember to pick up some mince pies before going back to our wreaths.

Having clearly abandoned her wreath, Mary is chatting to everyone in the hall. Considering how quickly she cobbled the wreath together, it actually doesn't look bad at all. She glued some gingham ribbons, pinecones, and cinnamon sticks to a fir base, giving her wreath a lovely rustic charm. Very *Little Women* aesthetic.

I'm now finding it hard to concentrate on my own crafting. I can't help wondering if Mary is right. What if Louise is having an affair with Matthew?

What does that mean? Surely, she can't have murdered Gemma because of it! That is too sordid. But murders are hardly ever pleasant, I remind myself. Matthew is still suspect #1 for the police, and an affair would be a good motive, but what about his alibi? I wonder if Louise had one.

Eventually, I manage to find enough brain space for my creativity, and I am chuffed with my wreath. I have gone for what I hope is an understated sophisticated style, using slightly gold-sprayed hydrangea heads, antique gold baubles, and eucalyptus branches.

Mary and I leave together after helping with the washing up (me) and tidying up (Mary).

'Right, well, that was lovely. I really enjoyed that. I'm off this way, then.' I point in the direction of my house.

'Oh, no, I don't think so. I think we need to walk the mince pies and mulled wine off.' She winks at me as she grabs my arm and drags me in the opposite direction.

'What? Why? Where are we ...' She quietens me by putting her finger to her mouth.

'Let's go and see if Louise's car is still parked at Matthew's house.' she whispers.

I can't exactly make a fuss as there's a group of PTFA mums who have gathered outside the hall to say their tipsy goodbyes. Resigned but irresistibly curious, I follow Mary with my wreath in my canvas shopping bag, feeling like an inadequate grown-up member of the Famous Five on the way to a stake out.

Chapter 39

@gemma_cotswolds_mum Evening Friends! Would you just look at the new chandelier I designed for our atrium? Isn't it stunning? ~~And will never be this clean again!~~ Thank you so much to @amandapdesigns, NY ~~that's New York in case you were wondering, darlings~~ for her guidance. She was amazing ~~at doing exactly what I said~~. I am in LOVE! #loveyourhome #designerlights #notanad ~~#amandabetterlikethis #andsuggestacollab~~

Mary

Friday

I mean, don't get me wrong, part of me does feel like a bit of an idiot sneaking around pretending Rowe and I are ridiculous characters from some rubbish 1980s PI story, but the other part of me is absolutely exhilarated. I feel like I have electricity coming out of each of my fingers and toes.

For an outsider, it's not a big deal that Louise wouldn't show up for the annual wreath making event. It may be the season of good cheer and ugly jumpers, but it's also the season of flu, cold, and everything else that the germ breeding grounds muster. It's not unreasonable to think that Louise is actually sick – except that there is no way that Louise is sick at Matthew's house. It's also way more fun because, let's face it, Louise is a total bitch. I also can't believe that Matthew would even be interested in her but then, I wouldn't have guessed he would go for Gemma, either. I would love to catch her out and see the stupid look on her beautiful (if a bit gormless) face.

Rowe is playing along but I can tell that she's really not into this at all. She's feeling more stupid and less invigorated than I am right now. I need to think of something to fire her up, to motivate her to commit to the task. I decide to play the sympathy card.

'C'mon Rowe. Do you think that anyone down at the police station knows that Louise has called in sick to one of her favourite activities in the Upper Huxley holiday calendar? Do you think that they have any idea that her car was parked at Matthew's house? What if Louise is literally getting away with murder? Without us, who is going to stop her?' I want to add 'and wipe that look off her stupid face ...'

'That's right. No one working the case would know about what's happening tonight at Matthew's. And especially not Nick the Dick.' she states.

Excellent. She is coming around to the idea, but I still walk faster in the hope that she will be less likely to change her mind.

Unfortunately, imitating professional power walkers has the unintended effect of making us look even more ridiculous than before. Luckily, we both have on faux fur hooded coats to hide our raucous ugly Christmas jumpers (Meredith won the evening's contest for the 4th year running – where does she find this hideousness?), but that's where the hiding ends. I have on my handknitted elf hat because, apart from the fact that it's festive, it's also warm, and my red sequin high top Converse. Rowe is wearing a lovely white knitted bobble hat that is still rather conspicuous, even if it is very on-trend, and gold lamé ballet slippers. Whilst Rowe remembered her tote to bring her wreath home, I, of course, forgot mine so I'm also half wearing my wreath under my arm sort of handbag-style. I also note with a sense of worry that I'm feeling the slightest bit tipsy, which might go some way to explaining the exhilaration. Damn Vicky and her glorious wine! And I'm pretty sure the fast walking and fresh air is making it worse instead of better!

We round the corner onto Lambeth Close, and I can see the Hatherley home 4th up on the left. These are the new 'executive homes' just on the edge of the village and they really are beautiful. There are only eight in total, and they are all nearly identical to each other. It almost has a gated community type feel to it. They are made to look like barn conversions – I imagine this was in a bid to get the planners to agree that they are 'in keeping' with the surrounding area. They all have a double height atrium in the middle of the house visible from the street and most have a feature light fixture. One has a waterfall type chandelier, and my favourite looks like a lighted allium with warm white lights at the end of each spoke. Matthew and Gemma (or do I just say Matthew now? So awkward …) have a series of glass globes around a filament bulb, all set at varying heights. The effect is pretty but it's the only way I can remember which house is theirs (his?) – oh, and Gemma's BMW X5.

How should we play this? We need a reason to be here, right? The problem is that it's a cul-de-sac, of course. So, we need a *good* reason to be here. I come up with something, but I know that Rowe is not going to like it. At all. Never mind, it hasn't stopped me yet. If I tell her beforehand, she'll run, so I walk purposely up to number 1 and whisper out of the right side of my mouth: 'go with it.'

Luckily, Ben made a very 'homemade' Christmas candle holder out of a Pringles can at school that day that is still in my vacuous handbag. I whip it out at the last minute, throw in the change from my purse, ring the doorbell and in my strongest churchy voice, begin to sing 'We Wish You a Merry Christmas' with vigour. If we are going to be conspicuous, we are going to embrace it.

Rowe looks at me with a look that can only be described as a mixture of 'Are you Fucking Kidding Me?' and 'Eat Shit and Die'. I was right. She is *not* happy about this, but clearly, hiding behind the manicured box hedge is not an option here. I'm not sure I would have come up with this idea without the wine.

Luckily it isn't too late, but the occupants of Number 1 are surprised, nonetheless. After we finish the song (some singers more committed than others) I hold out the fire hazard candle holder and in my most convincing voice say: 'We're carolling to raise money for the Village Christmas Dinner. Would you have £1 to contribute?' They are generous and give quite a few pound coins. They must be more surprised when we then dash off after one measly song, but something tells me that they are also partially relieved. I make a mental note to sort out the donations later. I can't risk getting a reputation as a thief over this crap.

We walk quickly to Number 2 where they've even put ivy and lights on the For Sale sign for festive bonus points. I am not sure that I am ready to find out if Rowe is still speaking to me, but luckily the Patels heard the commotion and have already turned on the front porch light. There is no turning back. If Rowe hates me, she is doing a good job of hiding it, and she follows my lead more quickly when I start the same song again.

The Patels are even more generous with a £10 note and even happier when it is obvious there will only be one song. I've always thought I was a decent singer – perhaps I am wrong?

By the time the door is shut behind us, Rowe makes a stifled noise that quickly turns into a giggle, which makes me do the same, and then a laugh turns into a chortle and by the time we've got close to Number 3, I can hardly make my legs move properly from laughing so hard.

She is angry, but she thinks it is also hilarious. 'Is that the only Christmas song you know?'

'Ah, Rowe, it's a tradition with my uni friends. We all live miles apart, but we always get together at Christmas. We do a rude Santa, and we sing this song for each person in turn as they open their gifts. It's not the only song I know, but it's definitely my favourite.' Warm glow. I'm definitely pissed.

'Ah OK. In that case, you are forgiven.'

'What, for dragging you along on this escapade?' I venture.

'Oh no – I forgive you for getting that song stuck in my head on repeat for the next month. I'm never going to forgive you for this ridiculousness.' She responds, and we both fall into fits again.

By the grace of God, Number 3 is out and whilst it might not seem like it, both of us are doing a fairly good job of keeping our eye on Number 4 the whole time – Rowe better than me, probably because she's not as drunk. Thankfully, Louise's car is still there, and no one has come in or out of the house in the time that we've been mucking about. Probably more importantly, the pattern of the room lights hasn't changed either. So, whoever is in the house isn't moving around much. There is one light on upstairs on the top right – it's dim, more like a bedside table lamp, but I'm surprised that the curtains aren't drawn. My guess is that this is likely to be Charlie's room. Kids always forget to turn off lights. The chandelier in the atrium at the front is on and there are no curtains there.

All of a sudden, my confidence has left me, and I panic about whether or not we should approach the house. But Rowe seems to have found her courage, and we head towards the door.

She says 'You wouldn't want people to avoid you like some sort of pariah, would you? And, like you say 'embrace the conspicuousness'.' I know that she is right.

I pretend to be confident, hoping that the real thing will follow shortly and push the doorbell, Pringles can at the ready. We start to sing but my voice is a little more tentative, so Rowe takes the opportunity to squash my foot with hers, just enough to *bloody fucking hurt*. Instead of a scream, I belt out the rest of the verse. She's singing and facing the door so I can't see her exactly but she's definitely laughing inside.

Before too long, Matthew appears on the landing at the top of the atrium and heads down the stairs looking what can only be described as 'ruffled.' He is running a hand through his tousled hair. It wasn't wet, so he wasn't in the shower. His clothes are freshly re-applied and are a bit rumpled – like they may have been on the floor. He's clearly been interrupted. Perhaps he heard the singing and knew that the lights on in his house mean that he couldn't pretend he's out.

Finally, he opens the door. His surprise causes us to stop singing.

'Mary? Erm ...'

'Hi Matthew.' I'm immediately sober and we are both lost for words.

Then he looks towards Rowe. 'Hi, erm?'

She answers for him 'Rowena. Hi.' She looks down at her shiny shoes. He's confused but he's not coming across as embarrassed. Maybe he really is a cheating bastard? After an awkward exchange explaining our noble charity work, he locates his wallet on the hallway table and gives us £20. We exchange the typical never-ending 'goodbyes' that English people do so well, culminating in childish waves before crossing the street towards Number 5.

'That's a lot of money!' I say to Rowe as soon as we are out of earshot. 'Do you think he was paying us to shut the fuck up? Or maybe to just get the fuck out?'

We giggle and move on to the next house – in for a penny, in for (hopefully quite a few) pound(s). I'm just glad that there are only 8 houses in total.

Chapter 40

@gemma_cotswolds_mum Morning Friends! This video is your step-by-step tutorial on how I decorated my #christmasmantlepiece this year ~~take three!!~~. I'm so happy with how it ~~finally~~ turned out. My top tip is to ~~spend a bloody fortune and take 2 days~~ embrace what is already there. If you have to buy something buy local! All of my foliage comes from my trusted @sweetpeasinapod! Not an ad. ~~#stillnoonlineshop #stillwontsponsorme~~ Make use of the structure and highlight the elements that you like about it ~~and use greenery to hide everything else~~. Make this #Christmas your most #aesthetic yet!! Happy decorating! Love, Gemma xx #decoratinginspo #beautifulhomes #cotswoldvibes #decomums

Rowena

Friday

I get home one hour later than originally planned and James is, thankfully, already asleep because I couldn't face telling him what we did.

I would like to say that I am fuming at Mary, but I'm still chuckling to myself every time I recall our carol singing down 'Posh Avenue'.

I may complain, fret, stress, and drag my feet, but I must admit I am enjoying being pushed out of my comfort zone. Tonight's adventure was definitely one for the memory box.

I can feel the adrenaline rushing through my body. I make myself a 'Good Night Sleep' herbal tea and take it to the snug where I take to brain dump onto WhatsApp all that I couldn't debrief with Mary because she had to relieve the babysitter.

11.42pm: *No way is my adrenaline-filled brain going to allow me to sleep. What do we do now? Somebody needs to know what we found!!! Do we need to go to the police? Should we talk to Tom?*

I'm half-expecting Mary to be asleep as she was quite tipsy, but she replies within the minute.

11.43pm: *I think we need to let the police know but I'm not sure I want to involve Tom. His wife playing amateur detective wouldn't do much for his career.*

11.44pm: *Agreed. So, we can't just turn up at the Police Station, right? (Not that I want to, believe me. No one needs to know about our carolling.)*

11.44pm: *I blame the mulled wine. Totally deny any responsibility.*

11.45pm: *OK, so how do we get our intel to Nick the Dick? Anonymous letter?*

11.45pm: *Bit cliché*

11.47pm: *Mmmm, yes, but we're not looking to be original. How else? Not as if we could call from a telephone box, using a fake voice. Mobile phones can be traced and that would be even more embarrassing than the singing!*

11.47pm: *Mortifying!*

11.48pm: *So, anonymous letter, it is then.*

11.49pm: *OK, can we talk in the morning? Really struggling to keep my eyes open*

11.50pm: *Of course, night night, Mary Bublé!*

11.51pm: *Lol, Goodnight!*

I'm still not feeling tired at all. Damn, I need to sleep or tomorrow is going to be another arduous day with the kids.

But I also know that my brain is going to spend all night drafting different versions of our anonymous letter unless I dump it on paper now. I grab my laptop and start typing.

To Nick the Dick

Hmm, I am going to have to find out what his last name is, before we send this.

To Inspector Nick [..]
Matthew Hatherley is having an affair with Louise O'Leary. Look into it.
Anonymous

Seeing it on paper, I am forced to admit that it is weak, as we cannot present any evidence. I worry it sounds spiteful more than anything and will be dismissed as idle gossip. Furthermore, for all we know, this may have no link to Gemma's death. Matthew and

Louise may be having an affair, but that does not mean that one or both of them killed Gemma. I am no longer so sure about informing the police about our hard-earned intelligence.

The worry has consumed all the adrenaline, and I now feel a bit deflated.

I can't help thinking about Gemma whose husband was cheating on her.

The honest truth is I haven't told Mary everything when I explained why all this business was rattling me.

I've kept quiet about my strong suspicion that James had been seeing somebody else just before I realised I was pregnant with Eloise. Just after I said to him that us sleeping together that one night did not mean we could start again. Just after I rejected him. I'm not proud of it but, at the time, I felt like one night together did not mean all our problems were magically solved. And to complicate matters further, in the months James and I were separated, I had, myself, grown close to someone else. Nothing physical had happened between us, but the connection we made, beyond that of mere school parents on the playground, was undeniable. But fate took the decision out of my hands when Eloise miraculously chose me as her mum, and I have zero regret.

All the while, of course, James might have used that time with someone else. And I can't blame him. I only have to look at myself and these feelings I was developing for a man who was not him.

So, I've never asked. Some signs were there, but I don't think I want to know, especially not now that we are giving our marriage another chance. I know I can't call it an affair, and I am absolutely in no position to be jealous. If anything, even without my fling that never was, I was always on Team Ross. I mostly agreed with his 'We were on a break!' plea. And yet, when I imagine James with another woman, I feel more and more like I am now on Team Rachel. And Team Gemma, whose husband is evidently finding comfort in somebody else's arms, so soon after (or even before) her death.

***

The next morning, I am granted a lie in as James gets up with the kids. I can hear their chattering downstairs and I'm luxuriating in the quiet of my bed. I feel more serene than I did last night. Everything always looks brighter in daylight.

I grab my phone and, after browsing all my usual social media feeds, I remember to go and check what our amateur Instagram sleuths have discovered on the #whokilledgemma hashtag.

I click on all the latest posts and read nothing new, until I get to the fourth one posted yesterday.

After the usual speculations (the husband, an actual burglary gone wrong, etc.), I spot a new comment:

@truecrimeluver562 *Probably nothing to do with her death, but it looks to me like @gemma_cotswolds_mum was on a downward slope career wise. The last three partnerships were with businesses local to her. She used to partner with all the big names, from TUI, to M&S and BMW, but recently it was more Local Orchard and Cotswold Wellie boots … Was this intentional or was she struggling to attract big names? Was her engagement with her followers decreasing? Does anyone know? How can we find out?*

@poppycanon52 *Going back through her feed, we can see that she celebrated her 200K followers milestone back in April. And she only posted about reaching 100K in March. Her account is currently on 215K, but we can't say whether some people joined* since her death ... Regardless, that's not a big progression, when she was doing so well in the spring. Anyone know?

@mumofthree89 *Long-time follower here and Gemma did complain in the summer about the lack of engagement on her account. She was blaming the algorithm but also asking her followers to really engage with her content (commenting, resharing, etc) and not just lazily like her posts.*

These guys might have explained why the Hatherleys were having money problems! If Gemma was no longer getting the big lucrative partnerships, their income would have shrunk, and that house I saw yesterday and the two big expensive cars on the driveway would have come with hefty monthly repayments!

I'm considering calling Mary when I hear Alfie running up the stairs calling 'Mummyyyyyyy!'

My time is up. Mary will have to wait.

Chapter 41

@gemma_cotswolds_mum Morning Friends! My love and I have just come back from the best weekend away in Brighton ~~literally had to beg him to come away with me~~. Shopping, romantic meals, and early autumn walks on the ~~fucking~~ pebble beach. It was ~~such hard work~~ so lovely to spend some time just the two of us. #romanticweekends #notanad

Mary

Saturday

I feel quite a sense of relief when my eyes open – I am tentatively waiting for the realisation that I have a headache and feel a bit quamish – alas, I believe that I may have just got away with it. But I could do with another 10 hours or so of sleep. Never mind, I've felt like that since Charlotte was born, and I've resigned myself to the fact that I probably always will.

I still can't believe Matthew is having an affair – and so blatantly. It just doesn't feel very 'Matty'. I know our friendship was such a long time ago, but do people change *that* much? Is there anything that we are missing? Any way that we might have the wrong end of the stick? I mean, we didn't see Louise there; perhaps she just dropped her car off (when she was supposed to be sick?). It was definitely her car – it's easily identifiable because of her naff private plate: LOU15E O.

1) I dread to think how much that would have cost and 2) why would you take this car to go around philandering? I know she is a total bitch, but I couldn't remember her being that stupid.

I start thinking about how on Earth we are going to be able to get this information to the police without causing all sorts of problems and then I remember the note that was left on Red. Instead of an anonymous letter, could we just use the actual note that was left for me/Tom?

Over breakfast, I get Tom up to speed on the events of the night before. He will find out soon enough anyway, so it might as well be from me. When I mention the impromptu carol singing, Tom rolls his eyes as only Tom can.

I tell him about my plan with the note. He says that he isn't sure – what happens if they trace it back to someone that can't have left it at the time and place we leave it? Or what if they trace the note back to me? I don't want to just go to the police station and hand it in! I don't want anyone in the police to know what Rowe and I are doing. For starters, I might be a bit embarrassed but more importantly, I don't want to open either of us up to any unwanted attention from the murderer.

We talk about the possibility of posting it from a post box on the outskirts of town (where there isn't any CCTV). I'll mention this to Rowe later. Whoever wrote the note in the first place intended for it to be given to the police (Tom) anyway – it's just made a slight detour! I make a mental note to speak to Rowe about it later – but something still doesn't add up. People have affairs all the time. It doesn't always result in someone dying. I guess the question is – did Gemma know that Matthew was having an affair? Who would know? Or rather, who would know that would also speak to me? Suddenly, I realise I know just the person.

I tell Tom that I need to go pick up some presents. I hint that they will be for the children so that he will be obliged to let me go by myself. It was a half-truth. I do need to get some presents, but they are far more likely to come from Amazon than the village these days. I'll have to pick something up whilst I'm there and make good use of the time that I've been granted.

***

There are a few people chatting and browsing in Marigold's florist when I arrive so I pop to the bookshop to see if there is anything that Rowe might like for Christmas. I decide on *Live Green: 52 Steps for a More Sustainable Life* by Jen Chillingsworth. It looks great – and I'm hoping that she might lend it to me after she's finished. Cheeky?

By the time I've perused the shop and made my purchase, Sweet Peas in a Pod is empty apart from a rather busy looking Marigold.

Ting-aling

'Hi Marigold!'

'Oh, hello there, Mary! So nice to see you. How are you?' She looks back at her wreath that she's putting finishing touches on. A beautiful version of 'The Holly and the Ivy' is playing softly in the background. I adore cheesy Christmas music – all of it – but it's also lovely to walk into a shop at this time of year and not hear Mariah Carey.

'I'm great, Marigold. Haven't you had enough of wreaths?' I say, trying my best to broach the subject fast.

'Oh, heavens, no, Mary. I'll get tired of making wreaths about two days before Christmas; handy, as no one wants them anymore!' She has a twinkle in her eye. I never know whether she's being serious or not.

'Listen Marigold, I wanted to chat with you about something serious, well, about Matthew.'

She stops what she's doing and looks up at me. 'Oh yes, dear. I'm not at all surprised about that. But you know what I'm going to say.

If you want to know what's going on with Matthew, you should go and speak to him yourself.'

'You know we don't talk, really. Not in that way.'

'Yes, I know, but you are adults now. You should be able to talk about difficult things.'

'Oh no. Not that …' Apparently, I didn't manage to get that out fast enough.

'He was so heartbroken at the time.'

Oh God. My stomach is turning over. I can't talk about this. I've managed to go years without having to explain myself to anyone. I always brushed it off and made excuses and I'm not about to change that now. I try to laugh it off.

'Oh Marigold. That was a lifetime ago. I was young and he was stupid.' I give a loud guffaw full of joviality I don't feel. I'm hoping to use humour to deflect the pain and to get her off the subject, my age-old trick.

'Mary.' Her voice is quiet and full of love and the lump in my throat grows. She's way too smart for my tricks.

'Marigold!' My feelings are hurt, and I feel raw and hard done by. 'He broke my heart! Not the other way around. Why are you taking his side?' I'm full of powerful feelings but shrinking from the sting.

'Oh Mary. You know very well that there is no such thing as sides in real life. I love you and Matthew both! I have no doubt that he hurt you, badly, too.'

"Too'?' WTF? He totally sold me out for his shitty five-minute shag!

'That letter that you wrote hurt him more than you'll ever know.'

Oh, for fuck's sake. That shitting letter. I was so mad. I was heartbroken. And I was also 18. Surely the stupid shit that you do when you are 18 can't follow you around for the rest of your life?

The shock and confusion are all over my face. How would Marigold know about that letter, anyway?

She answers the question that I didn't get a chance to ask. 'Gemma showed me that letter. I think she felt threatened by your relationship. He loved you, in his funny little Matthew way, and as much as he was smitten with Gemma at the time, he never ever would have hurt you by bailing on your plans if he didn't think it was the only option.'

My heartbeat is so loud, I can hardly hear the rest of Marigold's sentence. Why did Matthew show Gemma the letter in the first place? It was nothing to do with her! And why the fuck did Gemma show it to Marigold? Was this some sort of vendetta? A way to poison Marigold against me? God! Even dead she's a fucking bitch.

Clearly my eyes ask her the questions that my brain and mouth can't quite deliver but her only response is: 'I've said too much. Talk to him, Mary. No more assumptions.'

Chapter 42

@gemma_cotswolds_mum You guys got so enthusiastic ~~you sad bunch~~ about my last cleaning video, that I thought I would also share with you how I keep my shaggy rug looking good as new, despite all the demands of a busy family home. ~~Charlie is not allowed food or drinks anywhere outside of the kitchen, anyway.~~ My super tool is the latest VAX cleaner, which really does all the work for me. ~~I wish.~~ So satisfying. ~~Can't believe the only content I seem to be getting engagement on these days is cleaning videos!~~ Thank you for the love, friends! #cleaningvideos #rugcleaning #cleanersofinstagram ~~#somethinghasgottochange~~

Rowena

Saturday

This morning's lie in is long forgotten. The kids have been driving me crazy all morning. Parenting when tired is such a bad combination, but what's the alternative? Relinquish all social life and go to bed at 9 every night, to hope for a better parenting day? Especially as it is never guaranteed even when I'm not tired. I might as well have a drink or two and go carolling once in a while!

James has gone to Stroud to play squash with Martin (again!), and I'm trying to juggle settling Eloise down for a nap, keeping Alfie busy, and tidying up the lounge to make space for the Christmas tree we are getting this afternoon! Unsurprisingly, Alfie is beyond excited. I'm doing a better job at hiding my anticipation, but this will be our first Christmas in our new home and one of the first things I could visualize when we viewed it back in July was where a magnificent Christmas tree would be going in the front room, by the bay window. I loved our cosy little London flat, but there was never enough space for a big tree, and we also never bothered with a real one, as we always spent Christmas day at my parents' house or with James' parents. This year, because it is our first as a 'complete' family with Eloise and in our new life here, I want to make this Christmas really special and go all out decorating for the holidays. The wreath I made last night has already got pride of place on the oak front door and is looking rather lovely, if I say so myself.

I am busy filling up a box with all the toys cluttering up the lounge when James returns from his game.

'Good match?' I ask, as I am trying to wrestle a stuffed panda into the box.

'It was fun, thanks. Martin is a great guy. Hilarious.'

'Ah brilliant. Glad you're making some lovely friends.' I say in my best mocking mum voice.

He winks at me. 'Ah, and I now know why he is so rubbish at squash.' He chuckles.

'Hmm.' I'm barely listening as I'm trying to reach a Lego piece that has lodged itself in the furthest corner under the sofa.

'Yeah, I was waiting for him at reception as I'm not a member yet and got chatting with the employee there. I don't know Martin's surname and he couldn't really place him based on my description, which is weird for someone who plays so often. It's only when I mentioned that he plays often with Matthew, the guy whose wife got killed on air, that he knew who I was talking about.' James continues, laughter still in his voice.

My ears prick up at the mention of Matthew. 'Oh, yes?' I ask casually.

'Yeah, the guy said he'd been talking about the poor man with his colleagues after they recognised him from the newspaper articles.

But he said that Matthew hadn't played squash there since the summer.'

My head still under the sofa, my heart skips a beat.

'So, yeah, turns out Martin hasn't been playing squash for quite a while. Not sure why his wife seems to think he plays all the time. Probably goes to the pub with his mates! Ha, Ha!' He laughs to himself.

My brain is shouting 'Oh my God!!!!' But I don't want to let James see my inner turmoil. It's a good thing he can't see my expression as I am still face down on the floor. I have never mentioned my budding detective career to him and I'm not sure I want to start now.

James is totally oblivious and takes himself off to the kitchen still chuckling to himself. He has unknowingly dropped an absolute bomb!

Matthew has not played squash with Martin, or anyone else, since the summer. But he told the police that's what he was doing at the time of Gemma's murder! How is that possible? Surely the police would have checked? Did Martin corroborate his alibi? If yes, why would he do that?

I put the tv on for Alfie (needs must!) and run into the study to call Mary.

'Mary, hi. It's me. Can you talk?'

'Rowena, are you OK? You sound very agitated.'

'I am, but I have just found that Matthew's alibi is a lie! He wasn't playing squash, with Martin or anyone else.'

'What? But how do you know?'

I relate as best as I can what James has told me.

'OMG!' Mary shouts.

'My reaction exactly! Well, except, I didn't tell James that.'

'But the police must have checked!' Mary sounds indignant.

'That's what I thought too! Did Martin confirm Matthew's alibi? Is there another place you can play squash around here?'

'Good point. There might be. But if Martin is a member of this one, why would they go somewhere else? Still, we better check it.' Mary says reasonably.

'Should *we* check it? I think this is big enough that we need to let the police do it. Surely this is one for the professionals.' I venture.

'No.' Mary sounds panicked. 'There must be a mistake, we can't just drop Matthew in it like that. I can't.'

'I'm sorry, Mary, but no alibi and a motive is pretty damning.'

'Oh Gosh, I can't believe it, Rowena. This is too awful. Poor Charlie.' I can hear Mary getting upset on the other end.

'I know. It doesn't bear thinking about, really. But we have to let the police know what we have found.'

'Maybe. I don't know. Can we talk about this tomorrow?' Her voice is hard.

'Mary, are you OK? I know this is upsetting but the sooner we do something the better.' I'm using my most reasonable voice.

'Yes, I'm fine. Listen. Gotta go. Will talk tomorrow.' She cannot hang up fast enough.

Well, that was weird. I was fully expecting Mary to get upset about finding evidence against Matthew, but the way she blew me off at the end is making me feel very uncomfortable, like I have unknowingly done something wrong.

I cannot believe that we are back to square one with Matthew as our main suspect. After all of our efforts to protect him from arrest, what we've found is only going to make it more likely.

I collect myself as best as I can and join my family, thinking that my festive mood is now truly ruined.

Chapter 43

@gemma_cotswolds_mum Morning Friends! Do you still send snail mail? Ever since I was a little girl, I have been obsessed with stationery and letter writing sets. I would write to my cousins and pen pals weekly and come home from school with trepidation hoping to find a new letter on the hall table. With emails and phones, I can't think of the last time I wrote a letter to someone. I have decided to restart this tradition and I will select one of you at random in the comments below to receive a handwritten letter from me. #snailmail #writingletters #igmums

Mary

Sunday

Shit, shit, shit. This is not at all going to plan. I'm trying to make sure that Matthew doesn't get caught up in this and I've somehow made it worse for him. Through our snooping, we've blown a hole right through his alibi. And why is Martin covering for him? What's in it for him? Does any of this have anything to do with what Marigold brought up? (Still so annoyed.)

I hardly sleep a wink. And when I do, I dream I'm in Gemma's house on that fateful evening. I enter her kitchen and then I wake with a start and sit bolt upright in a cold sweat. I finally give up on sleep and head downstairs at 5:40. On autopilot, I head towards the coffee machine, empty the grounds from yesterday into the compost bin, and start the process again. It's so comforting in its 'every-day-ness', but it also gives me a chance to think properly about the facts with the lights on – where it seems easier to organise my thoughts.

I look down at my phone and see that I have a message from Rowe:

8:56 – I've drafted up a note to send to the police. Can we meet up so I can show you and we can talk about it?

Shit! I need to try and talk her out of this – or at least delay her until we can find out what's really going on.

8:58: *Sure! Play date this am at mine – bring the kiddos? X*

9:07: *Sure. Be there for 10:30? Eloise can sleep whilst we're there. X*

9:10: *Perfect. X*

As soon as Rowe arrives, the boys run upstairs and start playing Star Wars. And no, I don't know how you play – all I know is that they were where I couldn't hear them. Win. Charlotte has spent the previous hour making a bed for Eloise, so she is keen for her to see it straight away and then to fall directly to sleep! Charlotte asks Rowe fifty questions in the first ten minutes that were a variation on 'why isn't she asleep yet?'. Poor Rowe is looking harangued.

I explain to Charlotte that sometimes babies will become interested in new places with new faces and voices, and that one of the best ways to get her to drift off was to be very quiet. Obviously, it is true, but the main purpose is to get her to stop talking for five minutes. Somehow, it doesn't seem quite right to discuss a possible marital affair and bloody murder in front of Charlotte, so Rowe and I chat about general news and information until Eloise finally falls asleep and Charlotte gets bored. Eventually, she announces that she is going to see if the boys need a Rey. Mission accomplished.

As we settle into a comfortable position on the couch, Rowe shows me the draft of the letter she's written to the police.

To the person investigating the death of Gemma Hatherley,

It has come to my attention that Matthew Hatherley has made a false statement regarding his whereabouts on the night of Gemma's murder, and that Martin O'Leary has also lied in order to corroborate his alibi.

Signed,

A Concerned Citizen

Ugh. I need to think of ways to convince Rowe to at least hold off. 'Let's not rush into sending something to the police. What if it's just a red herring? Nick is hardly capable of sifting through spurious information – if it's wrong, and I really think it is, then he'll be off on another tangent.'

'Yes, but this is evidence, Mary!' Rowena springs up with her arms in flying squirrel position behind her, stopping just short of stamping her foot. 'You don't just get to pick and choose what evidence you are going to consider.'

'Nick seems to be incapable of being neutral here. He's desperate to pin the murder on someone, anyone, quickly. Once he has this, he'll stop looking.' I'm trying to calm Rowe down.

'Yeah – but what if Matthew actually did it?' Rowe is practically doing laps around the coffee table.

'Rowe. First – sit down, you are giving me a headache. Secondly, I'm absolutely convinced that he didn't do it. But either way, we know that we are capable of finding out why he lied about his alibi. I'm just not convinced that Nick is.'

'Oh, I don't know, Mary.' She has her palms on her temples, and I wait for her to continue.

'The problem is that I'm not usually the best person at making decisions. The truth is, since James and I went through our rocky patch I've lost the ability to trust my own judgement and make big decisions.'

'Oh Rowe, that's quite a difficult way to go through life.' The frustration I felt with her begins to melt.

'Tell me about it! I end up relying on signs or letting fate decide for me. I know how ridiculous this sounds but it's been working for me so far. James' company introducing a remote working policy just when we needed to start afresh, walking into Loose People in Stroud, Lorna turning up at my door right as I was trying to decide whether to join your investigation ...'

'My investigation?' I repeat, trying to hide how pleased this makes me.

'Let's face it, Mary, you are definitely calling the shots here, but I need signs that tell me I am doing the right thing, and James telling me about the alibi feels like a sign. I have to act on it. Now.'

For the first time since I met her, I'm wondering if everything is OK with Rowe. I know that she has had some difficult times, but she's come across as a sensible soul. Sensitive, yes, but rational. With this recent behaviour, she seems a little, well erm ... irrational.

'Absolutely! I totally agree! But not the police. At least not yet. I just can't.'

I can tell Rowe is still really uncomfortable with the situation. In an attempt to placate her, I pull out my phone and google all the places that the Matthew and Martin could have been playing squash within a 50 mile radius. I'm sure there is something we are missing – and even more sure that we can find it. I just need to keep Rowe on board.

Chapter 44

> @gemma_cotswolds_mum Evening Friends! Following my story post yesterday about our Elf on the Shelf, I got ~~a couple of~~ soooo many DMs asking for tips from overloaded mums ~~don't blame you~~. Don't panic, but if, like me, ~~you wished you had never started that tradition,~~ you're in need of inspiration, I've put together a little carousel of pictures of our ~~f....~~ Elf adventures in years gone by. Enjoy ~~the mess and sleepless nights~~ the magic in your kid's eyes! #elfontheshelf #mumsofinstagram #igmums

Rowena

Monday

Gosh, I'm so nervous you'd think I'm trying to deal drugs to schoolchildren. I feel stupid pretending to act normal as I shakily drop the letter in first and then the Christmas cards I am posting. Thank goodness for winter as my leather gloves would look damn suspicious in June.

The mission accomplished, I feel the weight has lifted off my shoulders and landed in the pit of my stomach. How can you feel so wrong for doing something that you know is right? Mary said *she* didn't want to post a letter, she never said I shouldn't do it, I reason with myself. Who am I kidding? She might as well have done. Have I betrayed her by going against her wishes? I can barely explain to myself why I have posted the damn letter. Certainly not rationally. I have become incapable of ignoring the signs the universe is giving me. I know Mary is loyal to Matthew and that their old friendship is pushing her to continue the investigation herself, I mean ourselves. But as my brain refused to succumb to slumber last night, memories of Louise telling me about Mary and

Matthew being childhood best friends came back to me, her voice played on a loop in my head: 'Didn't she explain?' Again, I suppress the doubt that Mary could be involved at all. None of it makes sense to me. Beyond Mary's resistance, I can't help wondering what this all means. Martin is married to Louise. Louise is most likely having an affair with Matthew. So why would Martin cover up for his rival? Could it be some sort of *ménage à trois*? Maybe that is a thing in the swinging community. Are they all swingers? Unless they played squash somewhere else, and the alibi has already been verified by the police. I'm now hoping it has.

I'm grateful the letter will remain anonymous because a) I could totally be wrong about this and b) maybe Mary will never find out I sent it.

I wonder how long it will take for the police to receive, review, and do something about the letter. Why is this whole investigation taking so long? Gemma died almost four weeks ago, and nothing seems to have happened since Matthew was released.

Mary and the kids have now made their way over to us and I go through the motions of the morning greeting routine, all the while wondering if Mary can tell how sick with nerves I feel. Alfie excitedly tells Ben and Charlotte all about his Elf on the Shelf (Ælfie)'s latest prank as they make their way to their respective classrooms.

Mary grabs my arm and squeezes tight. 'Oh Rowe, you didn't.'

I wince as my heart sinks. *How the hell does she know? Did she see me?*

'What are you talking about?' I ask nervously. I am already regretting posting that letter. What if I lose my only friend here because of it?

'You got an Elf on the Shelf?' she whispers with a mix of disappointment and worry.

I laugh somewhat hysterically, in relief. 'Yes, first year! Alfie loves him, and he was so excited this morning!' I reply enthusiastically to hide my earlier terror.

'Of course, *he* was! But *you've* signed up for miserable Decembers for the next ten years, at least with Eloise!'

'What do you mean 'miserable'? Don't you have one? It's fun!'

'Oh, yes, it's fun. For the kids. But parents have to come up with and deliver 25 innovative ideas and personalised letters every year! For years! And no, we don't have one despite the kids' annual lobbying. I hate his miserable polyester guts.' She is dead serious.

'Ha Ha Ha! It can't be that bad, Mary!' I laugh nervously now.

'Oh, it is. I've seen mum friends cry over the added mental load, Rowe. Late nights to prepare the stupid pranks, the mess they then have to clean and tidy. One year, my cousin actually resorted to writing an apology letter from Father Christmas saying the Elf was on a special mission and couldn't come because she just couldn't face another 25 days of it.'

'Oh well, too late now.'

'Indeed. I wish you had mentioned it to me before.' Mary says, her voice full of regrets.

We are now on our way out of the playground along with all the other parents, when we turn around to respond to the voice greeting us.

'Morning, Ladies' says Louise in a tired voice. She looks exactly as she sounds, with dark marks under her eyes.

'Morning, Louise' we reply in unison.

'How are you? Feeling better?' Mary enquires in what I now recognise as her 'investigation' voice.

'Slightly. But not quite there yet. Martin couldn't do the school run, so I had to drag myself out of bed but I'm heading straight back under my duv ...' She is interrupted by a nasty chesty coughing fit.

Mary gives me a surprised look. Louise does look really poorly.

'Did you have a good time at the wreath workshop?' Louise manages to ask once she has caught her breath.

'I loved it, thank you. Such a shame you couldn't join us, Louise.' I say innocently.

'Oh, tell me about it. Absolutely gutted. First time I've had to miss it in twelve years.'

'Yes, it was great fun. We even finished the evening doing carol singing to raise some money for the Village Christmas Dinner. You should have heard us!' I can't believe Mary is daring to broach the subject!

'Ah OK, lovely. Good idea.' Louise does not show any unease at the mention of the carol singing and even seems quite disinterested as she has now started shivering.

'Louise, you'd better get yourself back home, in the warm.' Mary encourages her, despite her disappointment at Louise's lack of reaction.

As soon as we are out of earshot from other parents, Mary exclaims: 'She did look very unwell, Rowe!'

'I know! She didn't look like she was faking it at all.' I acknowledge reluctantly.

'She could have developed a cold over the weekend ...' Mary suggests unconvincingly.

'Or she could have been unwell at Matthew's ...' I venture, with as much doubt as Mary.

'And she did not react at all when you mentioned the carolling!'

'I know! Surely Matthew would have mentioned it was us at the door on Friday night?' I exclaim.

'Hmm. Curiouser and curiouser.'

Unfortunately, we cannot continue to discuss this any further as Mary has a meeting with her editor.

I head home and, despite my guilt and my fear of antagonising Mary, I feel a glimmer of excitement as I catch a glimpse of the Christmas tree that we decorated yesterday through the window. I decide that, Eloise permitting, I'm going to use the day to finish decorating the lounge to distract myself from our investigation, which is getting more confusing and tangled. This is no longer an exciting adventure, and I feel like I could lose a lot in the process.

Chapter 45

@gemma_cotswolds_mum Morning Friends! Do you know how to keep your kiddos safe online? Do you talk to them about the potential dangers that they might face? This is your reminder to make best use of parental controls on whatever screen they are using: iPads, iPhones, games consoles. There are loads of great resources available online to help you understand how best to do this. If all else fails, ask one of your IT savvy friends to help. Let's #keepourkidssafeonline #onlinesafety #internetsafety #kidsafety #cybersecurityIG

Mary

Monday

'Rosie, I know nothing about the world of social influencing. I actually had to look it up when it was mentioned in the reports of Gemma's death. Yes, I dabble in Pinterest – mainly to save recipes that I'll never actually make – but the world of social influencing is really rather foreign to me.' I'm trying to sound like a willing participant in Rosie's most recent hairbrained idea and not the exasperated mum who is rather busy doing her actual job, raising two children, and just about managing not to commit her own criminal act in the run up to Christmas.

In addition to that, what I really want to be doing is working to understand Matthew's alibi (or lack thereof). I hate those weeks when work and parenting responsibilities get in the way of the things that I really want to do. But when that activity means the difference between an innocent man going to prison or not, it makes the draw even stronger.

Anyway, this meeting is not going as intended. I had hoped to talk about the stories that I am working on, pitch out five or so in the hopes that she will bite on three, and then I can go back under my rock and write for a while until Tom brings the children home from After School Club. Then, I can concentrate on solving a murder. But no. No such luck today. Rosie (who I adore, please let the record show) has got a bee in her bonnet about how we can get a placement for our magazine in a post from one of the bigger travel influencers to try and increase readership.

I try the logic argument – the fact that we rely on people to subscribe and read an actual physical mag is testament to the fact that our target readership is probably unlikely to know what an influencer is.

Her counter: 'People are now engaging with Gardeners' World via app and online engagement.'

My counter: 'But not via snap-tok or whatever.'

'There is potentially a whole new market for us if we *were* able to crack it.'

Now, I'm just trying to get out if it, if I'm being honest. 'You told me that readers of rags can move to online engagement (Gardeners' World), but there's no evidence that they will move the other way. Are young people who are mainly engaged on online platforms going to go 'backwards' and buy physical content?'

Her turn for exasperation. 'Just do it, Mary. We need new readers, and the board is all over me to 'think outside the box'. To be perfectly honest, I couldn't give a shit whether it works or not. At least, I can show that we are exploring new avenues. And besides, the worst that can happen is that we don't gain any readers, right?'

Checkmate. 'I'll do my best, Rosie, you know I will. OK – speak again on Wednesday. Love to Oscar!'

I'm not annoyed at her. I know that she wouldn't ask if she didn't think that it was what needed to be done. And I know why she chose me to be the tea boy on this one. The other writers on the team are fantastically talented – some more so than me, it pains me to say – but none of them have the loyalty to the rag that Rosie and I have. I know that she trusts me to find someone whose values match ours, and our mag's – even if that person has to be an influencer (eyeroll emoji). But I also really cannot be fucked. I've got a murder to solve and a friend to save from prison.

Text Rowe:

13:20: *Hiya. Do you remember that obnoxious agent lady from the wake? Hillary something? Rosie wants me to try to engage the services of a travel influencer – hoping that she might be able to help me. You wouldn't know how to get in touch with her, would you? X*

13:35: *Hi Mary. Of course – how could I forget?* 👻 *Her surname is Peters and she and Daisy used to work at the same agency – Philip Mayhew, I think? I should be able to find her in no time if you want.*

13:36: *Oh, yes please. You are so much better at this stuff than me – thank you!!!!!!*

13:39: *Right – Managed to find her e-mail address <u>Hillary@HillaryPeters.com</u>. She is currently working on her own (not within a larger agency) and she also has a slick but rather basic website – HillaryPeters.com.*

13:40: *Crikey, Rowe – that was quick. Thanks so much!!*

13:40: *No problem. Everyone has their talents 😉. See you at collection?*

13:42: *Not today – kiddos in ASC and Tom collecting. But see you in the morning! Xx*

13:42: *Sure. Good luck with Hill for the Kill! Xx*

I decide to draft an e-mail to Hillary. I find a mobile phone number on Hillary's website but then remember how Type A aggressive she was at the wake, so I can only imagine what she's like in her professional life. I decide that being able to tell Rosie that I'd sent an e-mail would at least be something.

From: Mary Lamb <Mary.Lamb@wonderlust.co.uk>
Sent: 02 December 2021 13:58
To: <u>Hillary@HillaryPeters.com</u>
Subject: Travel Influencer needed – Wonderlust magazine placement

Dear Hillary,

I hope this finds you well.

My name is Mary Lamb – I'm not sure if you remember me but we met at the wake for Gemma Hatherley. I found your e-mail address on the web

I'm a writer for Wonderlust – a travel magazine. My editor is keen to explore the possibility of engaging a social media influencer for placement advertising and I thought that either you might be able to help me or, if not, point me in the right direction of someone who might?

Thanks so much,
Mary

Mary Lamb
Senior Staff Writer
Wonderlust

From: Hillary@HillaryPeters.com
Sent: 02 December 2021 14:02
To: Mary Lamb <Mary.Lamb@wonderlust.co.uk>
Subject: Re: Travel Influencer needed – Wonderlust magazine placement

Mary,

No, I don't remember you.

I don't currently represent any travel influencers but if you give me your budget and a synopsis of your target audience – are you tents or luxury hotels? – then I will find one.

Hillary.
Sent from my iPhone

Christ, she's even worse in print! What a cow! I mean, all she had to do was click on the link in my e-mail to have a look at our website – this would tell her whether we were 'tents or luxury hotels'. If I was being totally honest, I'd admit that I'm jealous of anyone that goes through life with that kind of confidence.

How is this my headache? I can't quite remember so I decide to text Rosie:

14:20: *Hi Rosie. Have found an agent who will find us a suitable influencer. What is our budget?*

14:25: *No idea. How much can it cost? £500? £1000?*

Oh God – I should totally have asked Rosie this question beforehand. I'm convinced that Hillary is going to eat me for lunch now.

14:26: *I think that we are going to be looking at a bit more than that. I'll let you know how I get on. X*

She only gets one kiss for putting me through this rubbish.

From: Mary Lamb <Mary.Lamb@wonderlust.co.uk>
Sent: 02 December 2021 14:45
To: Hillary@HillaryPeters.com
Subject: Re: Travel Influencer needed – Wonderlust magazine placement

Hi Hillary,

Thanks for your message.

Wonderlust is mainly experience driven adventure travel. Our readers are looking for outdoor adventures and unique experiences – Icelandic off-roading, African Eco-safaris, Pearl diving experiences in Tahiti. They tend to have above average disposable income, spend a lot of money on travel (obviously), but book their travel themselves and expect to get top notch service for a fair but reasonable price.

Our budget for this project (which will be a pilot for us) is £1,000.

Thanks,
Mary

Mary Lamb
Senior Staff Writer
Wonderlust

From: Hillary@HillaryPeters.com

Sent: 02 December 2021 14:49
To: Mary Lamb <Mary.Lamb@wonderlust.co.uk>
Subject: Re: Travel Influencer needed – Wonderlust magazine placement

It will be at least £5k for anyone decent inclusive of my fee.

Terms attached if you wish to proceed.

Hillary.
Sent from my iPhone

Attachment: HillaryPetersTerms.pdf

Ok – that's it. I've reached my max quota for overt rudeness today. I forward Hillary's e-mail on to Rosie and ask her 'how she would like to proceed' and resolve not to open any response from her until tomorrow. I only have three hours now until Tom gets home with the children, and I'd like to spend some time doing some actual writing ... and maybe finding out more about what is going on with Matthew!

Chapter 46

@gemma_cotswolds_mum Evening Friends! Just wanted to share with you the outfit that I've been wearing non-stop recently. The perfect school run outfit, comfy but smart. These @whitecompany hoody and trousers are 100% cashmere, so they are like secret pyjamas. Pair that with my leopard-print @veja trainers and shades for style and comfort. What is your secret pyjama outfit? ~~Please don't tell me any of my followers actually take their kids to school in their pyjamas.~~ Not really an #ad but I worked with the White Company before. #~~wontsponsormeanymore~~ #ootd #mumsofinstagram

Rowena

Tuesday

It's Tuesday and I will not bore you with the details of my now-typical solo parenting nightmare morning routine.

All you need to know is that we somehow make it to the school playground, on time and alive.

I am having some sort of negotiation with Alfie about whether or not I will bring a snack for him at pick-up when I hear a conversation behind me.

Vicky is saying to one of the school dads: 'Yes, the police came last night, and they took Martin away to the station.'

My heart rate jumps up to alarming levels.

'You mean, he was arrested?' Responds the incredulous dad.

'Well, I wouldn't know. He wasn't handcuffed or anything. So it could be only for questioning, really.'

It's fascinating how, thanks to crime TV programmes, everyone seems to be an expert in the police procedure department.

'Is he back home now?' The man asks, his curiosity (and mine) now clearly piqued.

'I'm not sure. I haven't seen either him or Louise this morning. But I haven't exactly kept watch, as you can imagine. Private business and all that. Not sure their kids are here this morning, actually.'

'Oh gosh. Do you think it has to do with Gemma's death?'

'Well, I can't see how Martin could have anything to do with it but then again, what else could it be about?'

While they have been talking, I have tied and retied Alfie's shoelaces about three times with shaky hands, and he is now fussing as he wants to run around with his friends while we wait for the bell to ring.

Mary is fast-walking towards me, so I stop my eavesdropping and let Alfie run away.

From the bewildered look in her eyes, she has already heard through the grapevine and put two and two together. The moment I have been dreading is finally here, and I feel like I'm going to be sick.

'What have you done, Rowena?' she asks with no preamble, getting straight to the crux of the matter. She pulls me to a quiet corner of the playground, away from prying ears.

I could try and pretend I don't know what she is talking about, but I respect her too much for that. I look at my feet and feel like a child about to be told off.

'You sent the letter, Rowe? I can't believe it!' I look up to her and she is furious, her cheeks flushed, a hard stare in her eyes.

'It was the right thing to do, Mary. You know that.'

'Do I? Do I know that? We could have looked into it ourselves. I thought we agreed that's what we would do.'

'You declared *you* wouldn't do it. I never agreed. And the police can check the alibi and save everyone some time.'

'But Matthew is going to be arrested again, if he hasn't already!' She is so angry she can barely look at me. I am also very aware that we are on the playground and the teacher has just called the kids in.

'Well, what if he did it?' I say defensively, as I wave Alfie goodbye.

'He didn't!' she hisses, turns around, and leaves with a thunderous look on her face.

I am left rooted to the spot. What have I done? That is why I shouldn't make decisions by myself. I've ruined everything. I manage to contain most of my emotions as I exit the playground, holding on until I can get some privacy.

As I turn into the lane towards my house, in the same place as I bumped into her the other day, I see Louise hurriedly walking away. She has her hood on and has clearly no intention of stopping to chat with anyone. She must have dropped the kids at school and is understandably avoiding anyone who would want to ask about Martin.

I am ashamed to say that my curiosity makes me forget my inner turmoil and I try keeping up with her. Unfortunately, she gets into her car before I reach her.

I'm expecting her to drive away immediately but surprisingly, the car remains parked and is still there when I get to it.

I've decided to feign ignorance of the rumours of Martin's arrest and knock at the window to initiate a chat. However, as I get closer to the car, I can hear heartbreaking sobs coming from inside.

I feel too raw myself and so guilty that I walk on pretending I haven't heard anything. A true detective would stop and find out why Louise is crying so much but it feels too wrong today.

Evidently, whatever happened last night has been devastating for Louise. Has Martin really been arrested then?

What have I done? Mary is no longer talking to me. Martin has been taken by the police. Louise is heartbroken. All because of me.

I make it to my house, get Eloise out of the pram and her winter suit so she doesn't overheat, place her on her playmat with a kiss, take myself back to the hallway where Eloise can't see me, and finally allow myself to collapse on the doormat in a heap of tears.

Chapter 47

@gemma_cotswolds_mum Afternoon Friends! What activities do you all do to stay fit? I've recently taken up tennis (well, taken it back up – I used to play in secondary school). Anyone know any exercise tips for strengthening my backhand? ~~I can't afford proper lessons.~~ I'm hoping to be able to enter the Gloucestershire Ladies Tournament in the spring, but I don't know if I'll make it. #rootforme #tennis #wimbledon #womenstennis #sports

Mary

Tuesday

I don't think I've ever got home from school so quickly. It's easy to walk fast when you are pissed off. I was surprised that Tom was still asleep when we left as it's such a rarity for him, but I didn't hear him come in, so I have no idea what time he finished. Luckily, he is awake by the time I get home.

'Hello darling,' I say in my breeziest manner possible. I wonder if he can tell that I'm slightly out of breath from having practically sprinted home and trying to ignore the anger in my throat. Luckily, the fast dash home has dialled the rage down a few levels. I'm still reeling from what Rowe has done. I feel slightly betrayed. I knew she wasn't 100% on board with *not* sending the information to the police but I didn't expect her to do it straight away. And it really does feel like it was behind my back. I didn't ask her to keep the information from the police, I just asked her not to share it yet. Apparently, that was just too much to ask! Guess I'm going to have to salvage the situation by finding out as much as I can from Tom.

'Morning.' He grunts a greeting from behind his coffee cup.

'Be Cool Mary' I say to myself – if he realises how determined I am to pump him for information then he will roll his eyes and go back to bed – or worse, tell me how silly I am. I decide to open the fridge to make myself a glass of apple juice, so I don't have to face him for a minute.

'You must have got in very late last night.' I say to the leftover lasagne.

'Ugh – got pulled into helping with a tricky situation in Cheltenham.' Tom is so reticent to talk about work. As I've said, he likes to keep things compartmentalised. I'm always interested in what's going on and if he wants to talk about stuff, I do my best to be an excellent listener. But not right now. I can't contain my curiosity.

'Oh? Anything to do with Martin O'Leary being arrested?' I purposely make a risky assumption that Martin has been arrested (even if it's unlikely) as it will force Tom to either confirm with a silent acceptance or correct me. Either way, I get to find out if he was or not – and quickly.

'Christ! That Upper Huxley telegraph is on good form. He was only bailed at about 3am! He's probably still asleep, for fuck's sake! And not really, no, I was helping out on another case that was going smelly. Time was running out to be able to charge and there were some tricky decisions ...' He looks into my eyes and straight through my soul and then trails off. 'But you just want to know what's going on with Martin, right?'

I'll never get an Oscar. 'Oh Tom, I do care. Please can you tell me about it properly later? I'm dying to know what's going on with Martin! Is he a suspect? Why was he arrested? On what charge? Did the police find out about the affair?'

'Mary! I'm not supposed to be telling you anything. At all.' He's being serious. 'Is this because you and Rowena are running around looking into everything and making general gits of yourselves? It's like a tv show or something! Two Miss Marples!'

I look at him unblinking for a minute with my biggest innocent eyes. I'm not exactly sure if he's expecting me to answer the question or if I'm being told off and reminded that this is his actual job – not just a hobby that I can go around mocking.

'Seriously, Mary, don't you think it's a little bit silly? I mean, I told you I would let you know what I hear but isn't this a bit silly? Do you think you can uncover … the …' I can almost see the lightbulb ignite over his head.

'Holy shit! That note! It was from you two, wasn't it?'

He can clearly read the guilt all over my face – even if my guilt is one of association rather than being directly culpable. 'Well, technically, it wasn't me.' I am nearly batting my lashes in a bid to be declared innocent.

Thankfully he's chuckling now. 'Oh my God. I can't believe it. You two are the anonymous 'Concerned Citizen'.' His expression changes to a question. 'Really? 'Concerned Citizen'?' Air quotes. 'That's so unimaginative, May. You are both writers for goodness sake.'

'Actually, we talked about it, but I *thought* we'd agreed not to send the note. I'm absolutely sure that Matthew didn't kill Gemma, but this most recent discovery blew a hole in his alibi. I was trying to convince Rowe to investigate further with me to find out the explanation before sharing this latest development but, clearly, I failed.'

Even though it wasn't my idea, and getting Martin arrested was definitely not part of the plan, I'm glad that the information that Nick received has been taken seriously.

In the meantime, Tom has decided that it's all just too hilarious. 'You two should have a proper name for yourselves. 'Mother Hubbard's Detective Agency' or 'Two Twats Go Murder Solving'.' Erm. Rude! 'Oh! I know! The Anonymums!' At this he is both most pleased with his pun and on the verge of pissing himself. I am neither but I would, under duress, admit that it is fairly clever.

Despite the fact that I was against sending the note, I find myself properly defensive of Rowe — and me, by association. 'You can make fun of it all you want, Tom, but we were the ones, actually, it was Rowe, who found out that Matthew's alibi was rubbish! I wasn't ready to go to the police yet but that doesn't change the fact that the work being done by them is subpar, at best!'

'OK, OK, OK.' He takes a deep breath to gather himself. 'You do make a good point. How did you two debunk Matthew's alibi, anyway?'

'Well, it's a bit of a long story but basically, it turns out that Martin is shit at squash, considering that he and Matthew play 'all the time" (my turn for air quotes) 'and then James found out that neither Martin or Matthew had been to the club for months — even though they both said that they were going all the time and that they were there at the time of the murder.'

'Right.' He pauses to give his thoughts a chance to organise themselves. 'I mean ...' This is painful for him to say, I can tell. 'Well done you two!' Wry smile. 'I can't believe that you two have blown holes in a case alibi that the force is currently on week 4 of investigating. If anything, I would expect Nick to be motivated to incriminate Matthew much faster! Surely even Nick can't be that incompetent!'

'So?' He's had his fun, I want the intel that I now feel I've earned.

'Soo …' I can see that this information is no longer particularly interesting for him – he proceeds to tell me the rest of the update on Gemma's case in the flat, almost bored tone that only an officer with 18 years in the force can. I will never understand how he can relay this type of incendiary detail of someone's private life without particular interest or concern, but I imagine it makes him exceptionally good at his job. He's just about finishing his last sentence when I grab my coat and make towards the back door. 'Holy shit! Holy Shit! HOLY SHIT!' Is running through my brain on a hyperspeed loop.

'Oh? Where are you going?' he pretends to ask, rolling his eyes – he knows exactly where I'm going. 'Be sensible Mary, do *not* get me into trouble. Only Rowe is to know what I just told you and you must ask her to keep it to herself.'

'Of course, darling.' I go to kiss him goodbye on the cheek.

'And, by the way, I think that Nick is trying to keep that note a secret, you know. He only showed it to me because I was working the case before and asked if I had any idea who might have written it. I told him I hadn't a clue – thank fuck I didn't know it was you – and he asked me to keep it to myself. So you need to put that on the list of things that you don't know.' Again, with the eye-rolling.

***

I get to Rowe's just in time. I have never ever been so full to the brim with something to say in my whole life. It is almost the same feeling as when you are absolutely desperate for the loo – a feeling I know all too well. I am laser-focused straight ahead on the way as I am genuinely concerned about how I will maintain a semblance of normality in the face of seeing any friend or acquaintance. I wouldn't be tempted to spill the beans to just anyone, but I might come across as someone whose senses have taken temporary leave.

I knock on the door and whisper out loud 'Come on. Come on.' I thought they only did that in the movies. It's taking too long so I knock again (so rude! Would never normally behave so terribly) and after what feels like ages, Rowe finally opens the door. I don't wait to be asked in.

'Rowena, couldn't do this on the phone. You are not going to believe this!'

Her beautiful eyes are the size of saucers but red from crying. She looks sheepish and worried that I might continue my accusations.

'Rowe? Are you OK?'

'I'm sorry, Mary. I shouldn't have ...'

'Oh Rowe. Whatever – it's fine. I know you were just doing what you thought was right. I think it could have backfired massively, but, as luck would have it, it was just the thing to do! We now know why Matthew was lying!'

'We do?'

'Yes. It turns out that Martin was arrested for perverting the course of justice for providing a fake alibi to Matthew for the night of Gemma's murder.'

'What?'

'Because of this, Matthew was also re-arrested!'

'Oh no!'

'But, on further questioning, the police discovered that the fake alibi was not to cover for the fact that Matthew killed Gemma. The alibi was to hide the affair.'

'What?' Rowe pauses and stares at me in utter confusion. 'Mary. That doesn't make any sense. Why on Earth would Martin be lying to cover up an affair between his wife and Matthew?'

'That's just it!' My gesticulations are larger than life. 'The affair isn't between *Louise* and Matthew – Louise isn't involved! Matthew is having an affair with *Martin*!'

'Whhhaaaaaatttt?' Her mouth seems to get stuck in a comedy 'O' shape that you see in the movies.

'I know! And I've obviously had ten more minutes than you to think all this through, but it totally makes sense! Matthew seemed to be a bit distracted according to Marigold. Louise was sick on the night of the wreath workshop, but her car was at Matthew's, and ...' I trail off. There is something on the end of my tongue. '... it perfectly explains why Martin was so rubbish at squash! Because they were busy at something else!'

Rowe finally gathers her thoughts. 'Oh my God. That's just crazy. I'm ashamed to say that I don't think I would have seen that coming. I wouldn't have guessed that.'

'Oh no way!' In truth, I never would have guessed it either.

'Well, I suppose that Louise was a much more fitting candidate. Oh! That definitely explains ...' She's almost talking to herself at this point then she turns to look at me again. 'I nearly forgot to tell you! I saw Louise get into her car after drop-off but when I got up beside the car, I heard the most heart wrenching sobs. It was awful! I guess the affair was news to her. Oh, I feel absolutely terrible. I know she's such a righteous bitch but for your friend to be murdered and then to find out that your husband was – or is? – having an affair with her husband. Christ! That's one crazy school term.'

'Completely agree! Poor Louise.' We hold an honorary moment of silence for her.

Rowe's the first to speak. 'But now we need to think about what this means for the case!'

I go on to explain to her the rest of what Tom told me. That once they'd determined that Matthew did have an alibi for the murder – that it was Martin, just not in the way that they'd originally professed – that they were both released on bail without charge and sent home. Obviously, corroborating an alibi that is so private in nature would be difficult, but they seem to be satisfied for now. That they'd recontacted Matthew who would be coming in for some additional questioning – clearly the presence of an affair calls into question some of the other information that they have and could, theoretically, strengthen Matthew's motive for murder, although, I don't buy it ... And that Nick showed Tom the note that he received to find out if he had any idea who might have sent it. But that Nick is keen to keep its existence rather schtum. And, most importantly, that Tom has a new nickname for us – the Anonymums. Twat.

We decide that we need to make some notes, so Rowe starts a fresh pot of coffee and grabs some paper and pens. I am *really* glad that I am not working to any deadlines today.

Chapter 48

@gemma_cotswolds_mum Evening Friends! Not every day is a glamourous one. Some days you just have to be the adult and sort through these cupboards! Decided to tackle one that I know will make a difference to my mental health: my beloved pantry. So much was out of date ~~because I buy stuff for the cook I want to be and not the lazy one that I am,~~ so I have been able to make loads of space. It feels so good for my head to see all this beautifully sorted and arranged. ~~You don't need to see all the mess that is behind me out of shot.~~ Instantly makes me want to get cooking! Show me your pantry, guys! #kitchensofinstagram #lovemyhome ~~#somuchclutter #runningoutofpostideas~~

Rowena

Tuesday

As I go into the study to quickly grab some pens and paper, I pause for a second. What are we doing here? We are clearly not very good at this. Mary says we are back on track and declares she has forgiven me for going rogue but I'm not sure what we are actually achieving. If I'm honest, I'm also annoyed at the nickname given to us by Tom. The Anonymums detectives! It sounds so twee and ridiculous.

I walk back into the kitchen, grabbing Eloise from her playmat on the way, and share my doubts with Mary, who is now bouncing off the walls. My excitement has subdued a little in the 90 seconds it took me to bring back stationery (and my baby).

'What do you mean by 'what are we achieving?' Tons, of course. If it wasn't for us, well you, the police would be none the wiser about this development!' cries Mary indignantly.

'Well, would that truly be a bad thing? Neither we nor the police are any closer to finding out what happened to Gemma, but her family's private business is now going to become public knowledge. I have indirectly outed two people today and families are hurting.' I lament, thinking of Louise.

'Fair enough, but how do you know we are not closer to finding out what happened? Maybe it is linked to Gemma's death!'

'Mary, are you sure you still want to go down that route? Remember where it led us before. Yes, Matthew has a strong motive as we now know for sure he was having an affair and that they were having money difficulties.' I reason vehemently.

'True, but he has an alibi!' She is back to her desperate defence of Matthew.

'An alibi provided by his lover who has already lied once to the police. Mary ... How reliable is that?' I remind her.

'Mmmm, you're right. But the police will now check it in more detail and Martin and Matthew must know that.'

'Well, Matthew could have an alibi and could still have orchestrated Gemma's murder ...' I venture hesitantly.

'How? Surely, you don't mean a hitman? Do they exist in real life? Where would you find one in Upper Huxley? The dark web?' she asks incredulously.

As we have our heated debate, Mary has been making notes and a whole page is now filled up with scribbles.

'Well, yes, I know. It sounds completely far-fetched. And we know it should really be a hit woman, right?'

'Indeed! That's just another thing that leads us away from Matthew!' Mary sounds utterly relieved.

'See, this is what I mean. We are going round in circles, just stirring up trouble. First, we could have got Lorna in trouble, now

Matthew and Martin. And there's no need to remind me that I sent that letter, and you didn't want to. I feel so bad about all this. We have no method, and we're just going with the flow, ignoring collateral damages.'

'That's neither strictly true nor fair, Rowe. We didn't report anything about Lorna the troll or the supposed affair. As much as I hated you doing it, you only contacted the police regarding something absolutely essential: a fake alibi. It was your citizen duty, I know that now. We may not be following a process, but we are being careful about the implications and who could get hurt. We never mentioned anything about the swinging to make sure Charlie wouldn't hear about it.' Mary says reasonably.

'OK, fair enough. I'm still kicking myself for doing it the way I did. This is so unlike me. And I suppose I am also disappointed we didn't see this coming. Martin and Matthew, I mean.'

'How could we? I mean, I know it is the 21st century and same-sex relationships are hardly big news material, but both of them were married to women and Louise was the ideal mistress. No way could we have considered Martin when Louise was acting like such an obvious candidate. And I've known Matthew for most of my life, even if we grew apart in recent years, and I never realised! But I suppose you're right, we need to question everything, not just stick with what seems obvious or fitting.'

'OK, but next thing we find out, we need to be absolutely sure of it, and I promise to listen to you.' I concede eventually.

'Deal.' Mary extends her hand.

'Ok, so where do we start? We must have missed something.' I say as I shake her hand.

'Let's start with the victim.' Mary titles a whole sheet of paper with Gemma's name. Name, age, profession, family situation, and then we move onto listing all of her possible issues/complexities:

Money problems? Reduced income and struggling social media engagement?

Marital problems? Were they definitely swinging? If yes, was it her idea or Matthew's?

Matthew's affair. Did she know he was gay/bi? Did she know he was cheating?

Leading figure in the village. Did she have enemies?

Leading influencer. Any enemies there? How do we find that out? Only known troll was Lorna. Initially discounted, as no obvious motive. But then found out she lied to us. Why?

Once we have dried out on the subject of Gemma herself, we move onto the murder scene.

Unfortunately, we no longer have the video to refer back to, but we can rely on the Instagram sleuth posts that summarised the incident.

8.30: Gemma starts the live.

8.42: loud noise. Gemma stands up, looks left and addresses the intruder.

8.42.41: she moves off camera. A physical assault can be heard.

8.43.08: Gemma calls out 'Call 999!'

8.43.12: Loud thump. Gemma falls? Gasp from the intruder?

(We now know that it was not a fall, and that Gemma was deliberately pushed, but it looks like no one else had spotted it.)

8.50: police arrive on the scene and stop the video.

Also, there on Instagram, we refresh our memory with some screenshots of the main moments of the video. We are trawling through them, making some notes, when Mary stops me by grabbing my wrist.

'What is it, Mary?'

'I'm not sure. I can't quite remember their kitchen layout. But I would have thought the doors were on the other side. I mean, I would have said that the patio doors were on Gemma's right.'

'Ok, but does it matter? We don't know that the intruder came in through the patio doors. They could have come in through the front door or a window, even?'

'For sure, but the thing is I'm almost sure there are no windows and only three doors into the kitchen: the massive folding patio ones, the one that comes in from the atrium, which is behind Gemma on the video, and one that leads to the walk-in pantry.'

'And where is the pantry one?'

'I would have said it was on Gemma's left. Where Gemma actually looked and addressed the intruder ...' Mary is clearly puzzled by this.

'Could somebody have come in through the pantry?'

'Well, I've never been inside the pantry as such. But from the couple of times I was at Gemma's, on the few instances I stupidly accepted the PTFA meeting invites, I would have said that the walk-in pantry was a blind room.'

'What does that mean?' I ask as I fail to comprehend the problem.

'I don't know! I must be wrong because how could some intruder come in from inside the house?'

'Indeed, it doesn't make any sense ... Unless they had broken into the house earlier and been hiding in there? Why would they come out when Gemma was clearly talking to somebody?'

'We need to check this, Mary. This could be crucial.'

'No way can we barge into Matthew's. Not me, not now.'

'Indeed.'

'I could ask a few people who knew Gemma and her house better than I did. But again, that would look a bit suspicious.'

'Hang on. Didn't you say all the houses on their street are exactly the same bar the light fittings in the atrium and the front door style?' I exclaim.

'Yes, they are! Some are mirrored but the layout should be the same. But I don't know anyone on the lane well enough to invite myself into their pantry.' Mary muses.

'Maybe not, but isn't one of them for sale? Didn't I see a For Sale sign the other day?' I grab my phone excitedly.

'Yes, the Patels are downsizing! Still. I could hardly pretend I want to buy their house. And you've only just moved here. Even the estate agent would know you. Small village and all that.'

'Of course, Lydia would remember us. But we don't need to go and view the house! Look!'

I push my phone right into Mary's face.

'OMG! Of course. Well done, Rowena!'

Together, we scrutinise a detailed floorplan provided free of charge by Rightmove!

There on my phone screen, we get the confirmation of Mary's inkling: the walk-in pantry off the kitchen is an internal room with no other access than the door to the kitchen.

'Wow! This is potentially really important. But before we get too excited, we are going to need to check whether the Patels' house is a mirror image or not. I cannot remember. And I don't fancy doing any more carolling.' Mary confesses.

'Again, Mary, we don't need to move from this kitchen to do our investigation! Have you never heard of Google Earth and Google Streetview?'

From Rightmove, we click on the Google Streetview link and make our way along the lane virtually. A few more clicks to double-check on the satellite image and we have our conclusion, that Gemma was indeed sitting with the pantry to her left.

Her murderer came into the kitchen from the pantry?

Chapter 49

@gemma_cotswolds_mum Morning Friends! I love being able to work from home but sometimes I do miss that "being in the office' feeling ~~of not wearing joggers everyday.~~ I ~~never would have thought it but~~ miss saying good morning to my fellow colleagues each day and always having someone to chat with at lunch in the canteen. ~~OMG – Am I lonely?~~ #luckytowfh #setyourownschedule #newwaysofworking ~~#mycolleagueisakettle~~

Mary

Tuesday

I have some errands that I need to run before collecting the children so, unfortunately, Rowe and I have to cut our chat short. Shame, because I feel like we were really getting somewhere. My mind is whirring – concentrating on the weekly shop is absolutely impossible. The good news is that the excitement of the new information and the relief at being able to clear Matthew's name (again!) means that the anger and betrayal I felt towards Rowe has dissipated. I did, however, make a mental note to talk to her about this "give me a sign" bullshit. That path leads everyone to misery, I'm sure! In any case, everything I will eventually get home with from the food shop will be a complete surprise and next week's meals will be creative, at best.

When I get home and into the kitchen, completely laden with full and heavy bags for life, I notice that Tom's lunchbox of leftover lasagne that he is surely planning to take to work for his dinner is on the kitchen counter by the sink. Knowing that he won't have time to nip out for anything – and certainly not anything healthy

– I resolve to drop it off for him at the station before going to collect the children from school.

2:05pm: *You've left your dinner here. Accident?*

2:07pm: *Y*

2:07pm: *Want me to drop it past? Can do it before collection?*

2:12pm: *Pls? X*

Christ! A kiss and everything. He must be desperate.

We dash to the truck and Norman is only too happy to take up his usual space – excited for yet another adventure. We head straight to the police station and I park up, explain nicely to Norman that he is just going to have to wait for a bit, grab the lunch box and head in.

There are the usual faces on my way in – Martha on reception buzzes me through the main door to the offices.

'Mary?' A voice I can't quite place calls out to me from one of the side rooms. It's where the vending machines and water cooler are and where the officers hang their work coats, so I do a 180 towards the voice and come face to face with none other than Matthew Hatherley!

I try not to look as shocked as I feel. Not only is it one of those situations where seeing someone out of context is just so jarring, but I'm also flooded with so many emotions. I'm slightly embarrassed now that I know about his affair with Martin and feel terrible for him about having lost his wife, but the overarching emotion I feel is anger. It's truly fascinating how quickly the human mind can work – especially in a stressful situation.

'Matthew?'

'Mary!' He beams a genuine and familiar smile at me – even through the dark bags under his eyes and the newly developed wrinkles in his forehead. He is somehow also shorter and slimmer. I wish I was happy to see him. But I'm not. I'm so angry still after the revelations from Marigold and I can feel myself getting worked up all over again about the betrayal. I can tell he can't quite read my expression so the 'How are you?' comes out a bit hesitantly.

Deep inhale. I turn around to gather my thoughts and see the open door as my perfect excuse. 'Let me just shut the door for a second.' When I turn back to face him, he looks terrified. 'Matthew. Let me start with how terrible I feel about your wife having died and the fact that you are getting tied up in all of this.'

'Thank y …'

'I'm not finished. I could go on about the ridiculous way that you dropped me 20 years ago without any thought or explanation, but I've made my peace with that. Or at least I thought I had. Until I find out that all of Upper Huxley is reading the stupid letter that I wrote to you when I was an upset teenager!' My hands are shaking and I'm having to concentrate to keep my voice steady enough to be heard through the pounding in my ears.

'Huh?' More wrinkles appear in his forehead, and he subconsciously crosses his arms in defence.

'The letter? The one I sent you after you totally abandoned me and I had to go travelling to the other side of the world all by myself. The one where I poured my heart out to you about how hurt I was and wondered if our friendship meant anything to you.'

'I know what letter you are talking about, I just don't understand what you mean about everyone in Upper Huxley having read it? I haven't seen that letter in 20 years! That whole situation broke my heart, too! Why would I show it to anyone?' His arms have resumed their position at his side and his palms are facing me in curiosity. But now huge tears are forming in the corners of his eyes and are threatening to spill over – his voice so soft it hurts my ears.

'Well, Gemma showed it to Marigold and fuck knows who else? She might have posted it on Instagram for all I know?' I can't get the thought out of my mind of groups of people (including Matthew and Gemma) standing around in conspiratorial circles laughing at my expense.

'What? Mary, I have no idea what you are talking about! I never showed it to Gemma! I would never have done that to you. I felt bad enough as it was!'

'You felt *bad*? Not bad enough to keep your promise! You bailed on me three days before we were due to go! What was I supposed to think?'

'Oh Mary. I suppose it doesn't matter now. Gemma didn't want ...'

'Yeah! I know! She wanted you all to herself. Typical selfish Gemma!'

'She was pregnant, Mary! She was 18! We were terrified!'

'What do you mean? How can she have been pregnant? Charlie is only 8.' I'm so confused that I look down at my fingers to check my maths. Why lie about this – I can fucking count!

When I look up again his face tells me everything I need to know. I can see the heartbreak there and my own heart breaks all over again.

'We found out five days before you and I were supposed to go on our trip. We'd only been seeing each other for two months, but what was I supposed to do? I couldn't leave her. But before we had to make any decisions, she lost the baby. By that time, you were in Phuket and no longer speaking to me. Rightfully so.'

There is a black hole where my stomach used to be. I don't know what to say. I turn around to open the door. Matthew stops me and turns me around to face him.

'I kept that letter because I always wanted to find a way to explain to you what happened. I thought that you deserved that at least. But when you got back, you made it clear that you wanted nothing to do with me, so I left it. I figured that was the kinder thing to do.' He's desperate for me to understand his side.

I turn around again to go. I can't bear to face him and the colossal fuck up I've made. I was too wrapped up in myself to wonder if there was anything that could have made him behave that way. I also don't want him to see all the tears. I don't want anyone to see them.

'Mary, don't go. I need a friend.'

'I don't feel like a friend. What kind of friend behaves like that?' I say to the door, still unable to face him.

He pulls me around for the second time. 'I don't blame you, Mary, how can you possibly have known? Gemma didn't want me to tell you at the time. I couldn't figure out how to tell you without betraying her.'

The room is silent whilst I process everything that he's told me. I rearrange all the pieces of the last 20 years in my mind, and it seems so different and all just so sad.

'Friends?' he asks in an inappropriately cheery way, and I see my Matty back.

'Friends.' I resolve to find out what went on with this stupid letter but now is not the time. 'Right. How are you? And what are you doing here? Have they brought you back in? Any progress?'

'No, I've come here voluntarily to try and help. No progress. Can you believe it? Still no closer, really. Or at least not that they are telling me – who knows, that could be part of the agenda.' He looks down at his toes and for that split second, he truly looks like a broken man.

'I just don't understand why she wanted us out of the house. Did she know what was going to happen? But then that would make it something resembling suicide, surely?' He looks for reassurance.

'Oh Gosh, Matthew – I cannot think for a second that Gemma would have planned for something horrible to happen to her.' I guess being desperate for answers makes you consider all possibilities, however unlikely.

'No, no, it's just not possible,' he says, doing his best to convince himself and me.

'So, Gemma wanted you out of the house on the night of the murder?'

'Oh, she was adamant. She wanted me and Charlie both out of the house! Charlie was sent to his grandparents, and I was told to make myself scarce.'

'Any idea at all of the reason behind this – was this something that she normally did?'

'No! She would ask me to do all sorts of crazy stuff for her IG page. I took hundreds of stupid photos, videos, I even helped her with the editing. I know that things weren't quite as good recently as they had in the past.' he pauses here and looks out of the corner of his eye at me. I wonder if he knows that I know but I have to collect my children at some point today – we've covered broken friendship, dead wives, miscarriages. Sexuality revelations and extramarital affairs will have to wait until next time, I'm afraid, so I keep a neutral face.

'But it doesn't explain why she would want me out of the house for her broadcast." he continues.

'What about Charlie? Would she normally have sent him away?'

'It wasn't uncommon, but it was so strange this time. She originally asked my mum and dad to have him, but Mum had to cancel last minute – very unlike her – so I just told Gemma I would cancel my plans. But she was adamant! She got rather cross and said that she would just have to ask her parents to have him.'

I can tell by the way that he's saying it that he has clearly answered this question before – probably to others and himself, countless times, and it still doesn't make any sense to him.

'She had to have been planning something.' He absent-mindedly raises his left index finger to his mouth to chew the edge of his nail.

'What could she possibly be planning that needed you guys out of the house? Almost like she was protecting you from something? Or maybe it was a surprise for you?'

'I literally have no idea. She seemed to be laser-focused on increasing her number of followers. That was her main goal in everything that she did lately. She was feeling the pressure to generate better engagement so that she could start to land jobs with the big names again. But why would that require us to be out of the house?'

'Oh Matthew, I'm so sorry. I know that Tom isn't on the case anymore, but he was working really hard to try to get some answers. And I feel sure that Nick and the team will be doing exactly the same.' I catch a sly frown from him at the mention of Nick's name. Crikey – does anyone like that man?

I make a purposeful glance at my watch and mention the school run. I ask if someone is collecting Charlie and he confirms that his parents have been doing the wraparound care for the past few weeks, but thanks me for my offer.

I rush out the door to the car and text Tom:

14:50: *Lasagne in your staff fridge*

14:55: *??*

Meh – he can wonder … I'm in a mad dash to collect the kiddos on time and I have way too much to digest.

Chapter 50

@gemma_cotswolds_mum Evening Friends! Join me on Tuesday 5th November at 8.30pm UK time for a Live event. I will talk you through all my favourite tricks and products to cope with the dark days of winter, but more importantly, I will do a general Q&A. So ~~please please~~ come and join me for a great night in together!
#q&a #igmums #iglive

Rowena

Tuesday

As I'm leaving the school with Alfie, I almost bump into Mary who is running (late) into the playground.

She has no time to stop but breathlessly throws a cryptic 'There's more. I will call you later this evening' as she rushes to pick up Ben and Charlotte.

How much can happen in one day? How can there already be more? It was only this morning we found out about Matthew and Martin. Thankfully for them/Louise, people don't seem to know the details yet, as I heard more whispered suppositions and questions on the playground, and I saw no signs of Martin or Louise this afternoon. Probably trying to lie low for now, even though it is inevitable something is going to come out at some point.

I spend the evening with my mind only half-dedicated to the kids, waiting for Mary's phone call. As I guessed she would, she calls around 8.30pm once out of the dinner/bedtime tunnel.

We agree that face-to-face would be easier and thankfully, Tom is home from his day shift, so I only have to wait another fifteen minutes to hear the latest development.

Once settled on my sofa, she fills me in with her conversation with Matthew. Or at least, the parts that are mostly relevant to the investigation. She doesn't hide what a big deal this long overdue conversation with her old friend is to her and I can tell they have talked about a lot more than just the night of the murder. But she can tell me more about that when and if she feels ready.

'Wow, Mary, you should hang out at the police station more often!' I exclaim as I try to digest this new information.

'I know, right? So, what do you think it means?'

'You mean the fact that Gemma wanted to be home alone?' I paraphrase.

'Yes, it is a bit weird, right? She could have just asked Matthew to stay in his study and Charlie would have been asleep anyway.'

'Yes, so why didn't she want them in the house? Surely it is not because of the nature of what was going to be discussed on the Live broadcast, because Matthew could have listened to it. So, she was hiding something else.'

'Was she waiting for someone? A lover? Could she also have been having an affair? Both of them?' Mary suggests incredulously.

'Yes, I suppose that is a possibility, but it is not a great way to hide it. Do you really kick your husband and child out so you can have your lover over?'

'Hey, don't ask me. I haven't got a clue how people who are having affairs do it. How do they even find the time with a job and a kid?' Mary exclaims, her arms raised in disbelief.

'Very true. What else do we know? She was determined to improve her Instagram engagement. A Live event would have been important to her. You said that according to Matthew, it was all she was thinking of, that she was obsessed. So, it sounds like she didn't have much time to spend on an affair.'

'Yes, good point. Let's park the affair for now.' And Mary writes 'AFFAIR' on the side of the same notepad we used this morning.

'Hey, what about what we said this morning, that the intruder/killer was already in the house? Tom said there was no forced entry. Maybe they came earlier, unnoticed, and then hid in the pantry? How does it tie up with her wanting to be home alone?'

'Did that person know she would be on her own? Or did they arrange with her to come, only to actually kill her? But if so, why were they in the pantry? Were they hiding in there? But why hide if Gemma had made sure she was home alone so they could come?' Mary rattles through all the questions.

'Indeed, I can't make sense of it either.' It is all so illogical that it is giving me a headache!

'Now, let's go back to what we wrote this morning. What else do we have? Her money problems. I don't suppose Matthew mentioned that, did he?' I ask hopeful.

'No, not exactly. He only talked about how Gemma was obsessed with improving her engagement so she could land big partnerships again. But he didn't say they were struggling, as such.' she admits.

'An Instagram Live is probably a good way to engage with your audience. But enough to justify kicking your family out on a Tuesday night ...' I'm still completely at a loss.

'Hey, crazy idea! Could she have borrowed some money from some dodgy people, and they came for a repayment?' Mary shouts in excitement.

'I suppose that's possible. Seems a bit like something from a bad crime TV programme but I guess it must happen in real life too.' I concede. 'Shouldn't they have cut one of her fingers off first or something?' I chuckle to myself. 'Sorry, not funny. Let's put that on our list.'

Mary writes 'MONEY LOAN SHARK' on the notepad and we stay quiet for a while.

'Hey!' Mary jumps off the sofa. 'We forgot the intruder is most probably a woman! Surely, they wouldn't be both having same sex affairs, at the same time. What would the odds be?'

'Unless it was all part of the marriage 'agreement'. Like they were both gay and they got married to have a child?'

'Mmm. Seems unnecessary in the 21st Century, to be honest. They could still have had the child without having to go through the whole traditional family set up, surely! As far as I know, they are not particularly religious either.' Mary argues.

'Ok. Seems unlikely then. So, the affair can go to the bottom of the possible reasons for wanting to be alone that night. I suppose women can also be loan sharks ...' I sound as unconvinced as I feel.

'Mmm. Shit, Rowe. None of this makes sense. Why would she want to be alone on the day that someone decides to come and hide in her pantry? Is it just an awful coincidence?' Mary rages in frustration.

'Ok, we are not getting very far. Let's go back to the suspects.' We start listing them.

Matthew – motives (money, affair), but alibi (possibly weak), and not a woman. Hitwoman?

Martin – motives (affair with her husband), but alibi (possibly weak), and not a woman.

Louise – no particular motive other than she seemed to fancy Matthew and Gemma always used to steal the spotlight. Alibi?

'Well, if Martin was with Matthew, Louise would have been home with the kids. Surely, she wouldn't leave them alone.'

Mary nods. As mums, that seems a watertight alibi to us, but who knows.

'And you don't book a babysitter to go and murder your best friend, do you?'

'Too obvious, I would have thought.' Mary concedes.

We add Lorna, Vicky, and Marigold to our list.

'For Vicky, I can't imagine what the motive would be. But then, she could have placed that note on my windscreen.'

'Woman scorned? Could she have had an affair with Matthew before Martin?' I don't like that I seem to be the one bringing it all back to affairs.

'And how did she know about Martin? We also don't know if she had an alibi …' Mary tails off, clearly running out of steam on the subject of Vicky.

'Now, Marigold. She is clearly close to Matthew. It looks like she could be a confidante to him. Hard to imagine she could be driven to murder. But then again, I would have never said she was a swinger either.' Mary cringes as she reminds us.

'Mmm, I can't see it. But what do I know?' Maybe I'm too soft but I really like Marigold. I don't want to imagine her being a murderer.

Keenly, we move on.

'Lorna. She had a motive. Sort of. Her being trolled by Gemma's followers. She lost a book deal because of the whole sorry business.' Mary reminds us.

'Yes, but like she said herself, Gemma's death was bad timing for her, just as she was planning to come back to social media.'

'As she said herself! That could be it! Maybe she is covering up how much she hated Gemma and what happened to her following the trolling. And remember, she did lie to you about confessing to Gemma!'

'Well, I'm still not sure about what she said exactly. Did she actually say she confessed unprompted to Gemma? I can't remember exactly. But, oh gosh, do you think we were too quick to dismiss her?' I say horrified.

'I don't know. It could be that we were on the right track from the beginning.' Mary furiously circles Lorna's name with a red pen.

'Oh dear. I feel terrible. I'm the one who took her defence at face value.' I add weakly.

'Rowe, don't. It may be a completely wrong lead again. But we ought to double check it. We ought to have done that after the funeral, but we both got so caught up in this affair business.' Mary reassures me.

'OK, I will try and talk to her. I can approach her with talks about her book or tips about recycling.' I volunteer, keen to redeem myself.

'OK sure. I will take on Vicky. I'm not sure how yet, but we will see where that leads.'

Before Mary goes home, we add Hillary Peters to our list just because we don't like her, even though that is no motive.

Chapter 51

@gemma_cotswolds_mum Evening Friends! Mindfulness has become such an important buzz word for so many of us. But what does it really mean? To me, it means being more present with my family. ~~And I bloody hope it makes them more present with me.~~ I have started a self-led plan to learn to meditate in order to help me be more mindful. Once I have done a few more sessions ~~and find out whether it actually works or not~~ I'll happily share the details with you. ~~With any luck, they'll also sponsor me.~~ What do you all do to practice mindfulness? #mindfulness #meditation #bemorepresent #presentmum #happyfamily

Mary

Wednesday

Matthew has dropped an epic bombshell and, frankly, I don't know where to start on how I feel about it. I need time and space (a few miles) to process this information so I start my day off with a run. Was Gemma, Ms 'my whole life is online for all to see', the one who it seems has never eaten a meal without posting how well she cooked it or what perfect pub served it, really so private that she didn't want Matthew to tell me, his *real* best friend, about their struggles? I wonder if he realised at the time that she was really asking him to drop our friendship altogether. I still wasn't sure how I felt about how quickly he was ready to do that. I'm not surprised by his ability to be such a loyal person, I guess I just took for granted that I would be the receiver of the loyalty.

Norman is ecstatic with the proposition of a jog and drools his excitement halfway down my left leg. That's going to hurt when we hit the cold air. It's early enough that I should be back before either of the children are awake and, of course, Tom is there if there's an emergency.

Off-brand ear buds in place, trainers laced up, and we are out the door. And I was right, on top of being still very dark, it is also absolutely freezing. Seeing my breath in the outside spotlight means that I get through my stretching routine way too fast to do any good. My steps crunch through the grass on my way to the footpath.

As usual, after the first 10 minutes (downhill, thankfully) of thinking I've completely lost my mind, I hit my stride. By the time I get to the entrance to the lakeside path, I can focus on the real priority of today: either ruling in or ruling out Vicky Clarkson as a suspect in Gemma's murder. I run through our meeting at the coffee shop again. There was something that she was definitely sad about when I saw her. And then there is the possibility that it was her who wrote the note, but that note was written by someone who was angry. Anyone can be both of those things, of course. Sometimes people can be both of those things at the same time. I decide to play mental "what if" where literally everything is possible and must be considered. I start with the obvious:

What if Vicky found out that Matthew was having an affair and wanted to alert the police after Gemma died in case it was an important factor? Definitely doesn't feel right. If she knew something that she thought would be important and might help, surely she would just go to the police station and tell them. After all, we know that she wasn't the partner in the affair ... Or do we!

What if Matthew was having two affairs? One with Martin and one with Vicky? Unbelievably unlikely. I can't think of any situation where someone in Upper Huxley would be able to get away with two affairs at the same time and not get caught with his trouse ... ahem.

What if Matthew was having an affair with Vicky but dumped her to have an affair with Martin? Plausible, yes, but likely? Would definitely explain the sadness plus the bitterness in the note.

What if Vicky was jealous of Gemma and decided to try to steal Matthew away but wasn't successful? Would definitely explain the bitterness in the note but perhaps not the sadness?

I pause the game to get a reading on exactly where I am. I have to be careful when thinking this hard whilst I'm running – especially because I know these roads so well, I could end up in Stroud before realising that I was late for the school run. I'm outside of the commons, and the sun is just starting to show itself. I decide that it's a good place to turn around. Norman couldn't agree more. He loves going out with me, but he also loves sitting by the nice warm fire.

Right, back to the game.

Would Vicky try to steal Matthew away? Doesn't really seem like her. She is always the one that is willing to help – even when the rest of the mums are trying to pretend that they can't hear the request for someone to stay after and sweep up. I'm not saying that helpful people can't be murderers, just that it's probably less likely. I realise that my whole thought process so far is relying on the assumption that Vicky left the note on my car.

I decide that before I do anything else, I have to find out if it was her. But I'm not sure how to do that without 1) challenging her in a confrontational way and 2) blowing my cover as an Anonymum (I've decided to wear the label with pride). I don't want anyone to know what Rowe and I are up to. I decide to go to the coffee shop later this morning and hope that inspiration will strike me en route.

I get Rowe up to speed quickly at drop off about my morning plans and tell her I'll call her when I'm leaving the café. She looks at me with a bewildered look and gently nods in understanding, even though her eyes are showing anything but comprehension.

***

I walk into the warm and cosy coffee shop which couldn't have been more welcoming – and then I get a whiff of something cinnamon with a hint of ginger and correct my assessment. Now it couldn't be more welcoming!

A smiling and engaging Vicky is behind the counter. She is chatting with a few of the regulars and is deftly operating the fancy machines and serving up cakes as though she's done it for years. It is good to see her in her element. I stand in the considerable queue for some time until, finally, it is my turn to place my order.

'Hi Vicky!' I smile my friendliest smile.

'Oh! Hi Mary! I didn't see you in the queue. Busy, isn't it? What can I get you?' The din of the shop means that she is having to speak rather loudly. Despite the shouting, she seems like she's enjoying her work and is happy enough to see me.

'I'd love a large flat white, please.'

'Your usual, then!' She beams a proud smile at me.

'Very well remembered!' I am truly impressed.

'Any cake this time?' I'm very keen to keep her sweet and her Ginger Cake looks fantastic.

'Go on then, a slice of Ginger Cake would be great, thank you. Does it come with a satisfaction guarantee?' I'm trying to buy a little time, but I quickly resign myself to the fact that there is no way, with all these people and noise, that I'm going to be able to have a meaningful conversation with her.

'Great!' She puts everything into the till, I tap my card, and we move to the end of the counter.

I decide that I'm just going to have to come out with it. 'Vicky, do you get any kind of break this morning? I'd like to ask you something, but I'd rather do it where it's a bit quieter.' I gesture to the full café.

She darts her green eyes straight at me and for the tiniest of seconds, I feel like a stalked animal, but it's gone so fast that immediately I wonder if I've imagined it.

'Sure! I go on my break in ten minutes.' She says with hardly a second thought. 'Meet me out back, if you don't mind, and I'll let you in the kitchen door. Mark doesn't like us having our break with the rest of the punters as it looks like we're slacking.'

I'm surprised that she hasn't even asked what I want to talk about, but I think that maybe she is just glad to have someone to chat to on her break.

**

Vicky calls to me as I'm almost finished with my coffee and motions towards the back of the café. I swig the last bit and put my cup down on the table. I rewrap myself in my many winter layers and head outside towards the kitchen entry.

I knock on the big metal door, and it opens immediately. I realise quickly that I'm quite uncomfortable and I don't know how to start the question. I make a big deal out of getting to see 'behind the scenes' and the shiny stainless-steel kitchen. I set my bag and coat down on a stool by the door. I leave my bobble hat and scarf on – it's barely warm in the kitchen – clearly there aren't many hot meals being prepared for lunch today.

'This is cool. Do you make your cakes here?'

'Sometimes. Mark doesn't mind if I make them at home and bring them in, though. It's much easier than trying to bake between customers.' She takes a pause. 'I'm glad to tell you all about working at the Wild Boar and making cakes, but I'm not sure it's what you wanted to ask me about?'

'Absolutely right, Vicky. Well deduced.' I give her a 'fair enough' look. 'I actually wanted to ask if you left a note on my red truck outside Tesco a while ago?' I'm deliberately vague about any more detail. I mean, she either knows what the hell I'm talking about, or she doesn't. I also realise quickly how very alone we are in this kitchen. The realisation makes my extremities tingle and my heartbeat significantly faster.

Again, she turns her huntress eyes on me and her demeanour is completely different than it was not ten seconds previously. 'Yes, Mary, it was me.' She spits the words in my direction. The hatred is radiating off her. I can't tell if it is directed at me or someone not in the room. It makes me feel cold but then my curiosity gets the better of me.

'What happened?' Shut up Mary! Just grab your coat and go! Butt out! Instead of doing what my brain was telling me to do, I hear myself say 'What made you leave that note?'

Her pupils are dilated. Her face contorts into hard angles and sharp points, and I take three steps backwards.

'She didn't deserve him! She never realised what she had!'

It is at this point that I realise that she is closing the distance between us as fast as I can make it. But it doesn't make sense. The note said 'Matthew is a cheating bastard!' That sounds like she was angry at him! The journalist in me was desperate for the story.

'Were you in love with Matthew, Vicky?'

She looks at me for a beat and then turns away so that I can't see her face. I take the opportunity to reverse imperceptibly towards the door – knowing full well no one would hear my scream for help. No sudden movements, and all that, isn't that the advice?

'I still am.' She sobs into her hands. 'I fell in love the first time I saw him at the parents evening before Charlie and Jack started school. It was as though the rest of the world just dissolved and all I could see was him.'

She turns to look back at me. 'He was so in love with Gemma. Stupid idiot! And she was just pretending, I could tell. So, I made friends with him. It was so easy. I could tell that even though he spent so much time with Gemma, he was really lonely. We met for coffee and lunch and, I don't know why no one seemed to gossip but I think that people just assumed that we were friends because of Gemma. When, in fact, it was nothing like that. She was a cold-hearted bitch who was only out for herself. I was only ever pretending to be her friend – just like she was pretending to be mine – and everyone else's! Gemma's never had a real friend in her whole life. She wouldn't know what one was!'

She starts shaking and the flush of rage reappears in her cheeks. 'And it was *me* who convinced Matthew that he deserved better. That he could have a happy life if he could just be true to himself. Discover what made him happy – not just spend his life being responsible for her! And that's when it happened! He fell in love with Martin! It wasn't supposed to happen this way. He was supposed to realise that he could only be happy with *me*!'

She is moving ever closer to me, shouting but pleading at the same time. 'I was his true friend. His only true friend. The only one that cared about Matthew as a person, instead of just 'the other half of Gemma & Matthew'. It was supposed to be me!' In a swift movement, she grabs a rolling pin that is just to her left and she raises it over her head.

'What are you doing, Vicky? What are you *doing*?' I'm terrified and I can't get away. No one will hear me if I scream. I feel the panic rising and my eyes are searching for something to use in my defence but there is nothing. Fuck! What have I done? Why did I goad her? She is holding the pin high by her right ear and pushing me towards the door. 'Vicky! Seriously. Think about this. Stop it!'

I shout 'HELP!' as loud as I can and I have just managed to pry the door open half an inch when Rowe comes bounding into the room and punches Vicky square in the nose, sending her flying.

'Mother fucker!' Shouts Rowe shaking her right hand and then holding it in her left. 'That hurt!' Not only is my new best friend beautiful, clever, and funny; she can also throw a mean punch and swear like a sailor.

When it's appropriate, Rowe asks me 'Did you get it, Mary?' She is referring to the fact that I told her I would record the conversation with Vicky on my phone.

'Every. Bit.' I say panting out each breath.

Vicky has managed to get herself back up to a sitting position on the kitchen floor, and blood is pouring out of her very likely broken nose. The sobs she is emitting are also creating a slurry of snot and tears that are mixing in a terrifying stream down her mouth and chin.

Once my heart calms down to a reasonable rhythm, I am so thankful. I am thankful that Rowe hadn't been a second later. Thankful that I'd picked up on the tiniest of looks that Vicky gave me earlier when I was ordering. I am thankful that it gave me the idea to text Rowe whilst I sat at the table drinking my coffee and asked her to meet me at the kitchen entrance ASAP. But mostly, I am thankful that I have excellent judgement in choosing my friend.

Chapter 52

@gemma_cotswolds_mum Evening Friends! Here is a picture of the cupcakes we ~~slaved over~~ quickly whipped up with my Charlie. He ~~was absolutely not interested in~~ needed a bit of encouragement for the baking part, but he went wild for the decorating ~~still cleaning up the sprinkles and edible glitter off every surface in the kitchen~~. All organic and gluten free. Don't they look amazing? ~~Couldn't tell you what they taste like, they are not on my paleo diet list.~~ #igmums #honestmum #bakingwithkids

Rowena

Wednesday

The day is not panning out as planned. I had expected to go food shopping and then take a trip to the library. Instead, I'm at the Wild Boar Café, waiting for the police with an ice pack around my sore knuckles.

Talk about a turn of events! Whoever killed Gemma would need to have a very violent streak to be able to physically hit her head on the marble counter, and we now know Vicky ticks that important box.

One of my first thoughts is that I'm going to have to tell James about this. Up until now I have kept my involvement in this investigation under wraps, but I've never had to lie. I just didn't tell James about it. Not that he would be particularly cross. If I look introspectively, I do recognise that there is a part of me that still wants to keep this to myself. Before our temporary separation, I would have shared these sorts of adventures with him. My only worry would have been around him laughing at my silly new hobby. So why am I keeping part of myself out of our relationship? I know James is all in, but am I?

I have looked hard within myself, and I no longer think about him. Akin. I don't. But sometimes my mind does wonder what could have been if I had not taken a pregnancy test that evening. Hypothetically.

Is this healthy? But how else can I move on? I know I do want us to be a family unit. But the question I am too scared to answer is whether I still want us to be a couple? I thought we (well, I) were doing so much better. But I guess, I worry at the first sign of trouble.

What a mess!

What if Vicky sues for assault? I can't claim self-defence because she wasn't attacking me.

And what are we going to tell the police? There is no time or opportunity to confer with Mary before they arrive as Mark, Vicky's boss, joined us in the back kitchen when he heard the commotion and is now keeping an eye on Vicky until the police and paramedics arrive.

Thankfully, she was never unconscious and is now sitting very still in the corner of the room. After a spell of uncontrollable crying, it seems the fight has left her completely. Her head resting on her chest, she is looking utterly beaten down. Literally, I suppose. I'm still shocked I have come to blows with someone. I never knew I had that in me, but as I gently stroke Eloise's head, I can't help feeling proud knowing that I would do anything to defend the ones I love.

Mary must have had the same concerns as me as she says: 'Thank you, Rowe. You saved me here. Good thing I told you I was round the back. I think we will have to reconvene for our coffee date. Ha

Ha Ha.' She sounds light-hearted but she is looking right into my eyes, meaningfully, her voice unnaturally loud.

'Sure.' I reply, hesitantly, but equally loudly. 'I was going to wait outside but I heard you shout. No idea what's happened here.' I know it sounds more like a question than a statement, but Mary is nodding, and I know we have agreed on our versions of events. Me pretending like I know nothing of what happened and why sounds like a cop out, but we both know it is the best way to not contradict one another when we get questioned. And, of course, we also don't want them to know that we are both actively investigating the murder. Mary asking questions about the note that was left on her windscreen is understandable as it is personal.

The police arrive within ten minutes. Thankfully, it's not Tom. That would have been extra awkward for all involved.

Unfortunately, however, they have sent DI Nick Nash instead. I don't dare look at Mary.

He walks into the back kitchen with an air of self-importance, which could have passed as self-confidence if it hadn't been for his rudeness to us, and for the huge tomato stain on his mac, which has long since seen better days.

'Ok, what's happened here, then? Housewives' fight? Did you fight over leftover cake, then?' he laughs to himself as if this is the best joke he's ever heard.

Another sexist joke and I might forget that my fist is hurting. I'm not sure where all this rage is coming from.

Mary starts talking first. 'I met Vicky here in the kitchen for a chat and she got angry and started coming at me with the rolling pin. She would have hit me if it wasn't for my friend, Rowena, who stopped her.'

'Rolling pin? Ha Ha Ha! This is hilarious!' he babbles, slapping his thigh this time. The man himself is a joke.

'It was not hilarious, DI Nash. It was actually really scary.' Mary chastens him.

He seems to recover a tiny bit of professionalism.

'Ok, Jones, you interview this lady here.' he addresses the young lanky PC he arrived with, pointing at me.

Jones couldn't look less enthusiastic if he'd tried. 'Is there an office or quiet space we can go?' he asks Mark, who had introduced himself as the manager.

I follow PC Jones outside to the car park. He takes my details and asks me to recount the incident. I try to stay as succinct as possible: 'I was due to meet my friend, Mary, for a coffee. She called to say she would be round the back of the café. So, I was waiting outside when I heard her shouting in distress.'

'How did you know she was distressed?' PC Jones asks astutely. I have to reassess my initial dismissal of him because of his incompetent DI. Better keep my wits about me.

'She shouted Vicky's name and then said 'Think about this. Stop it!' followed by 'Help!'.' I use my most matter-of-fact voice, because I think Mary's words speak for themselves.

'What did you do then?' He looks up from his little notebook, in which he is dutifully writing my answers.

'I went in and when I saw Vicky was going to hit Mary with the rolling pin, I punched her. I'm not proud of it, but my friend was in danger.' I hate hearing how shaky my voice sounds at the memory.

'A rolling pin? I'm sure it hurts but it wouldn't have done much damage to your friend, surely ...' PC Jones argues, with a hint of patronising tone.

'It was one of these stone ones. Marble? That could have killed her or caused serious damage,' I reply indignantly. I am in no position to make a fuss, but I don't appreciate the implication that I was an 'hysterical female'.

'Ok. Was Vicky knocked unconscious?'

'No, she wasn't. But I think the shock must have calmed her down and made her realise what could have happened. Her manager came in and has been keeping an eye on her.'

'Do you know what they were arguing about?' PC Jones asks, just as I think I have done pretty well, and it is almost over.

'No, I don't.' I consider saying more but sticking to the minimum is probably the safest option.

'Do you know this Vicky person?'

'Yes, I do know her from school. Our children are in Upper Huxley Community Primary together. And we met at a couple of PTFA social events, that's all.'

'Ok, that will do for now. But we might call you in for more information.' he concludes, clearly keen to wrap this up and to move on to questioning Vicky.

By that point, Eloise, still in the baby carrier strapped to my chest, is hungry. The café has been shut for the day following the incident, so I'm left with no choice but to go into my car to feed her. Once settled, I text Mary to let her know we are in the car, so she can join me for a debrief. I can now add physical violence to the list of stupid things I have done recently. The rage and all the pent-up anxiety of the past few months are bubbling up and I find myself dropping a few tears on my baby's head.

Chapter 53

@gemma_cotswolds_mum Morning Friends! How handsome is my coffee date? Charlie and I went to the @wildboarcafe for a special afterschool treat today. They do an amazing Oat Milk Chai Tea Latte ~~that I only ever drink half of – who can spare all those calories?~~ and Charlie loves their 'Loaded Hot Chocolate'. ~~Shame it turns him into a sugar fuelled nightmare afterwards.~~ If you haven't been lately, I would recommend a visit. ~~Not going to wax lyrical if I'm not being paid to~~ #shoplocal #wildboarcafe #coffeedate ~~#somanycalories~~

Mary

Wednesday

I am so glad that Rowe and I have had the 'conversation' about our story. But even so, my mind is still racing at a million miles per hour. How the hell am I going to explain winding (an apparently already fairly highly strung?) Vicky up over a note left on my truck that I knew full well might be related to a murder that Nick was investigating? Shit! Tom is going to be very annoyed, too. I hope this doesn't get him in trouble.

'What the hell is he even doing here, anyway?' I think to myself. 'Unless he wondered if this might have been related as well?' These calculations are whirring around my head like protons around a nucleus. If I'm not careful, I am going to end up with a case of cerebral nuclear fission. Or is it fusion? I can never remember which it is, but my head is already starting to ache, regardless.

Either way, his flippant dismissal of the situation as being something utterly hilarious is really starting to grate. The only thing emerging through my fog of confused thoughts is a reminder of just how much I am truly not a fan of this man.

Somehow, I find myself sitting in a very uncomfortable chair in a tiny little office off the kitchen. I presume that we were guided in that direction, but I honestly don't remember. Nick the Dick has made himself comfortable in the considerably plusher chair behind the desk. Clearly, he needed to make the point that he was in charge here. Mental eye roll.

'Ok Mary, what is going on here? I had you down as more of a lover than a fighter.'

I swear to God, I better be imagining that attempt at a twinkle in his eye. Otherwise, I'm going to lose that coffee and ginger cake right here on the office floor. I make a quick decision that I am going to have to play the innocent to be able to get through this quickly – and with a bit of my pride still intact. Besides, I am going to have to do my best to protect Rowe from any formal complaints.

I ignore his comment and decide to get it out efficiently. 'Simply, I came here to meet my friend, Rowena Boat, for coffee. When I arrived, I saw Vicky, who I know as our children both go to Upper Huxley Community Primary.' I pause to ensure that I am ready for the next few sentences and decide to make Nick more of an active participant in the conversation:

'I'm not sure if you are aware,' *of anything at all, ever* 'but someone left a note on my car a few weeks ago about Matthew having an affair. I had no idea who'd done it.' (True!) 'And then I remembered when I saw Vicky behind the counter today that I'd seen her in the vegetable aisle in Tesco on the morning that the note was left.' (NOT true. I saw her on the recovered CCTV, but also I saw her coming out of the shop with some carrot tops hanging out of her bag for life, so I extrapolated. No way can I tell

Nick that Tom helped me get CCTV from that time.) 'So, I decided to ask her about it.'

He is half-listening, and that is giving him the benefit of the doubt. 'Yeah, OK. But that doesn't explain how you both got to the kitchen.'

Ignore him, Mary. Just be calm and measured. I say 'That's right,' *you pig-headed moron* 'the coffee shop was busy when I arrived. I didn't think that it was necessarily something that should be discussed within reach of lots of villager ears. I asked her if she would have a break and she told me to join her at the back door soon after that. I called Rowe as I didn't want her to think that I had stood her up for the coffee and told her that I was chatting with Vicky around back.' I kind of shrug my shoulders as if to say 'that's it!'.

'Wait for him, Mary' I think to myself. And I do. And it feels like a long time. He is writing notes in his stupid little notebook when he isn't chewing on the end of his pencil and searching in the air for answers to questions that no one has asked. God, he really is very irritating.

I am still trying to decide whether or not to tell him that I recorded our conversation. I doubt seriously that Vicky would have heard me tell Rowe that I'd managed to capture it and I can't decide whether it would be better or worse for Rowe to admit that I have it. I am mostly concerned that it might make the whole event look a little pre-meditated. I nearly scoff at the idea – as there is no way that I would have been able to foresee these events – but then remember that (theoretically, at least) my every reaction is currently under scrutiny and that scoffing probably isn't a good idea right now.

'So then, you asked her about the note back here?'

I decide to be wilfully simplistic and deliver only the facts that I know to be true. 'Yes. She admitted to leaving the note on my car. She said that she wanted the police to know that Matthew had been having an affair because he'd broken her heart and she was very angry with him.'

I realise that even as I'm saying this, I'm not exactly sure why she wanted the police to know about the affair? Was she hoping to cast suspicion on Matthew as a suspect? Was she trying to suggest that Matthew somehow had a motive to kill Gemma? Or was she just temporarily psychotic with rage and jealousy and hadn't given it an awful lot of forward thought? And if so, is she prone to these sorts of outbursts?

'Why do you think she became so angry with you?'

I pause for thought. 'I don't think she was angry with me, per se. I think that she's just very angry with the situation and I was probably the only person that had ever asked the right (wrong?) questions. It was all very raw.'

'Is it your intention to pursue a complaint of assault against Mrs Clarkson?' he asks, looking at his notes.

'I will agree not to if she agrees not to pursue any complaints against Rowe?' I surreptitiously ask him with my eyes if this is the done thing in these situations. He visibly rolls his eyes. For the first time in our whole conversation, I sympathise with him and how he must perceive this situation to be a huge waste of everyone's time.

'I'll let you know what she says. In the meantime, I will consider the matter to be still under investigation. Please make yourself available for any additional questions that may be required.'

'Of course, Nick. Sorry, DI Nash.'

Well now I've made my bed. I haven't shared the recording, so I very much hope that it won't come back to bite me. In the meantime, I can't wait to get home, have a hot shower and maybe a little cry, with Norman, about the whole thing. I'm dreading, however, that Tom and I are also going to have our own debrief whilst I sit there and take my telling off. I take out my phone and see a text from Rowe:

11:53: *In the car feeding Eloise. Will stay here until you are done.*

I quickly change my mind and decide that I'd far rather have a full debrief with Rowe – assuming that wouldn't look too suspicious? I'm not sure why I feel so guilty but I'm sure it's something to do with the fact that we are still investigating a murder that we shouldn't be, and it seems like it's getting a little more dangerous every day.

I might still pencil in that cry later, though.

Chapter 54

@gemma_cotswolds_mum Evening Friends! Throwback Thursday to last year when I attended the most amazing event at London Fashion Week ~~Can't believe I have to resort to reposting things now~~. That was certainly a highlight of my year! So much fun and glamour with our little gang of 'Fashionista Instamums' @glamourousmum @lovekidslovefashion #londonfashionweek ~~#invitemeagainplease~~ #tbt

Rowena

Wednesday

'When you told me that Martin hadn't been playing squash for months, we had to inform the police that Matthew's alibi was fake.'

After understandable concerns over the café incident and mine and Eloise's safety, I've now had to reveal to James how he contributed to finding out that Martin and Matthew are having an affair. What should have been a cosy evening between the two of us, in the warmth of the woodburning stove and the glow of my adored Christmas tree, is turning into a difficult confrontation.

'Who the heck is 'we'?' Mary didn't even want to send that letter, so maybe I should have said 'I'.

'Mary and I. We didn't get involved as such; I sent an anonymous letter. The police questioned Matthew and Martin, and Tom told Mary about their relationship.'

James is looking at me as if he doesn't know me at all. 'How long has all of this been going on, Rowe? Matthew could still be the killer. Or this Vicky?'

'Mary is adamant that Matthew would never have killed Gemma.'

'How does she know? I thought she wasn't super close to Gemma.'

'Well, that's the thing, she wasn't. But she's known Matthew for a long time. They used to be best friends.'

'Used to be?' His voice is now keen rather than angry.

'They had a row years ago when Gemma came into Matthew's life and have barely talked since, apparently.'

'So, you're telling me that you've been helping someone you've only just met to prove that their ex-best friend didn't murder the wife he was cheating on?'

I nod and we let that statement hang in the space between us.

'Rowe, do you trust Mary? From what you told me before, there was no love lost between her and Gemma, and now you're telling me that she lost her best friend when Gemma came into his life? How long have you known about her friendship with Matthew?'

'A few days?' I say confidently, trying to act as if his questions are not raising valid points.

'And since when have you been helping her?' He has the voice of the lawyer who's ready to make the killing argument.

'A few weeks ago.' I try to keep my voice steady to show I am the one in control of this conversation.

'So, you're saying that for weeks, she didn't tell you the truth about why she wanted you to help her find a murderer!' He is getting agitated again.

'True, but I do trust her, James. I don't know for sure why she didn't tell me, but it is common knowledge in the village as everybody knows that they were estranged. They were supposed to go travelling the world together before uni. They had planned it since they were kids but 3 days before they were due to leave,

Matthew announced he wasn't going as he didn't want to leave Gemma, whom he'd been seeing only for a few weeks.'

'So, he chose Gemma over his promise to Mary.'

'Something like that.'

'She must have really hated Gemma!' Eurgh, it does look terrible from the outside!

'I guess she did back then, but she was so young. Only 18. She's an adult now.'

'But she had a motive!'

'For murder, you mean? Come on, James, that was 20 years ago! Why would she wait so long? And for what? Revenge? That's ludicrous.' I know logically James' accusation is solid, and I have had these doubts myself, but not anymore.

'How do you know she is telling the truth? She spent weeks lying to you!'

'It wasn't lying as such! James! You cannot seriously be suggesting that Mary could have killed Gemma?'

'Well, somebody did. She didn't like her, and she is going round asking questions and accusing other people.' I feel like now is not the time to tell him about Mary not wanting us to inform the police about Matthew's affair.

He continues 'How do you know Mary didn't leave the note on her windscreen herself?'

'Well, Vicky admitted to it.' But as soon as the words leave my mouth, I'm not sure anymore. She didn't admit to it in front of me. Mary told me she did, but I didn't get to listen to the recording. Not yet. Still, I refuse to believe Mary could be playing me.

'Rowena, I know you're really taken with Mary. And I really liked her too the few times I saw her. But I just want you to be careful. We don't really know her, and she could be using you. Sending anonymous letters to the police, punching people ... that is not you.'

Is it not? I feel despondent. I haven't felt so much like myself for months. Ironically, when I am with Mary and we are working on our 'vestigation', I don't feel the anxiety that has been plaguing me for months. I don't question my life choices and whether I am in the right place or with the right person. For once, I want to trust my instincts. They have proven quite sound so far, in the investigation.

'It might be best if you keep your distance from Mary, really.' James would never tell me what to do and I know this comes from a place of worry. Our newly reestablished marriage needs honesty, but I feel like we are so close to finding out what happened to Gemma, so I say nothing. Uncomfortably, I realise that my silence sounds too much like agreement.

***

'James? Are we OK?' I ask later, when we are in bed.

'Well, I'd much rather you took on Pilates instead of boxing with Eloise, if that's what you mean!' I can hear him stir on his side of the bed.

'That's not what I'm talking about, James. Are *we* OK? Generally. As a couple.'

He must have heard the anxiety in my voice as he immediately pulls himself up and turns his bedside lamp on. My heart breaks a little as I see his wounded and surprised look.

'What are you talking about? Of course, we're good. We're great. Look at us, we have never been happier. Here, the four of us.'

'Yes, our family is great. Complete with Eloise. And I love our new life here. Murder aside. But I can't help worrying about us as a couple. Are we together because we want to be together or because we make sense as a family?' I can't look at him. He grabs my hand, forcing me towards him.

'Rowena, I love you. I was miserable when we lived apart. Not just because of all those pregnancies we lost, and that baby we had to stop hoping for. But because I wasn't with you. I missed *you* and you know I didn't have to hear of the unexpected pregnancy to want to try again.'

I wish we could talk about that period and whether he had started seeing someone else But I couldn't face it if he told me what I don't want to hear. And I would feel like I had to come clean too, even if nothing happened with Akin. I'm not sure where starting that conversation would take us.

His reassuring words are so soothing to hear and maybe that is all I need. The past is best left in the past, they say.

'I love you, too.' I mean it, of course, but why do I keep questioning our relationship?

Our embrace mercifully puts a stop to my incessant worrying, and I allow myself to be reassured that we are still good together. Very good, indeed.

Thursday

Yesterday was eventful and emotionally draining, and between that and the mounting pressure to get on with Christmas preparations (only nineteen shopping days until the Big Day!), I need a rest. But with Gemma's killer still unidentified, I also know that we need to plough on with our 'informal vestigation'.

I wonder what the police found while interviewing Vicky. Mary and I talked through it all when they were done interviewing us, and yet, I've been running through the same questions in my head since yesterday.

I'm not convinced that Vicky being in love with Matthew and her rage at him for having picked Martin over her constitutes a motive for murdering Gemma, but weirder things have happened. She is clearly unstable and I'm hoping the police get to the bottom of it, even though my confidence in Nick the Dick has reached rock bottom.

We can't, however, make the same mistake as with Matthew and the affair and drop all our other lines of enquiry until that one delivers or peters out. So today is Lorna day!

To that end, I have made plans to meet with Justine, the mum I met three weeks ago at the Mummy's Morning.

I decide to go in early to grab a chance to grill Lorna and find her busy laying the floor cushions out when I step into the village hall.

'Good morning, Lorna, how are you? Did you enjoy the wreath workshop last week?'

'Yes, was fun. Did you?' she asks.

'Loved it! So much fun. I was very pleased with my wreath. Can I give you a hand? Eloise is quiet for now.' I offer, pointing at the stroller parked in the corner of the hall.

'Ah yes, thanks, Rowena. If you don't mind laying out the music bits and bobs.' She hands out a box full of drums, maracas, tambourines, rainmakers and other rattles.

I get on with the job for a bit, before I start my subtle probing.

'So, how is the book going? Have you been working on it again?' I ask casually as I carry on without looking at her.

'If intensely thinking about it constitutes working on it, then yes, I have!' she replies with a chuckle.

'Ah, still concerned about the whole Gemma business, are you?' I am now faffing with the floor cushions.

'Yes, I am. I think it's best for the murderer to be found and for the interest to die down, before getting back on social media.' she explains matter-of-factly.

'Ah yes, do you know how the investigation is going? I heard there was an issue with her husband's alibi and that somebody was arrested?' I venture innocently.

'Really? I don't pay much attention to gossip. But I did see Matthew drive through the village this morning so the police can't be too worried about him anymore.'

'It's a funny thing an alibi, isn't it? Unless you're the murderer, you never know you are going to need one, do you? Like the night that Gemma was murdered, James was in London, and I was alone at home with the kids who were asleep. Not sure how I could prove my alibi if asked ... Apart from the fact that I would never leave my kids alone, of course?' I keep it light to hide the questioning.

'Ah yes, I was thinking the same thing, the other day. I'm glad I haven't been asked for my alibi that night because I was sewing in the summerhouse at the bottom of the garden, while the rest of the family was inside. So that doesn't really make for a solid one, does it?' She laughs to herself, and I join her, while making a mental note that, while her alibi is indeed flimsy at best, why would she offer that information if she was the murderer? Unless it is a twisted double bluff thing that only a psychopath can understand.

We are now busy arranging coffee cups and drinks on the side table when I decide to go back for more.

'I know you were not exactly close, and your target audiences were different, but did you and Gemma ever talk together about your influencer jobs? Like sharing tips? I know I love to talk to other authors ...' I am keeping my tone light but I'm aware that I sound like I'm questioning her.

'No, we didn't. As you say we were quite different. For her it was all about money and growth, while mine was much more around raising awareness for a better future. I mean, don't get me wrong, I was starting to do quite well and was overjoyed about being asked to write a book about it, but I wasn't doing it for the partnerships or the money.' she explains calmly.

I nod and think about what else I could ask when she starts again.

'Actually, that's not quite true. She did come to me with questions about my agent and how much percentage they were taking when I had partnerships.' she clarifies.

'Ah OK. What would they take. 50%? 5%?' I ask innocently.

'Well, I told her that mine takes a 10% cut on all my contracts. And she looked shocked. She didn't say exactly, but it sounded like hers took a much bigger cut. She requested my agent's details. But frankly, I don't think they would have been interested because Gemma didn't fit their portfolio.'

I gulp and carefully think about the appropriate tone for what I am going to ask. 'Ah OK, was it a long time before she died?'

'Not really, no. She asked me at the school Halloween disco. So not long at all.' She turns back to unstacking coffee cups.

I go and pick up Eloise to buy myself some time to muse over what I have just heard. Gemma was considering changing agent. That could have been a big loss for Hillary. I wonder if she knew about it. I would love to ask why Lorna told me she confessed to Gemma, when Hillary told us it was the other way around. But, if Gemma did indeed come to Lorna for advice recently, there clearly was no animosity left between the two women. Who to believe? The only person who could tell us would be Gemma herself.

Chapter 55

@gemma_cotswolds_mum Morning Friends! Tell me about a time when you had an e-mail that wound you up. ~~This is a desperate attempt to drum up engagement.~~ Who was it from? What did it say? How did you respond? Did you regret it later? ~~I really couldn't care less, I just want some of you to like and comment this post!!~~ #email #tellmeaboutatime #shareyourstory ~~#likecommentandfollowFFS~~

Mary

Thursday

Rowe called me as soon as she got home from the baby group and told me everything she'd learned. We are supposed to be eliminating suspects, and it seems that all we are doing is making the people that we've previously dismissed stronger candidates.

Now, we need to investigate this agent business that Lorna mentioned. So, I need an excuse to talk to Hillary, and it turns out that I don't have to look too far.

Text from Rosie:

10:54: *Hi Mary. Have you confirmed with Hillary that we want to proceed? Nigel is asking for an update.*

Shit. Nigel is head of Mag. What have I missed? Rosie should know that I don't check my work e-mails like normal people.

Sure enough, I fire up the laptop and there is one waiting for me – from Monday! And we are now on Thursday:

From: Rosie Lynx <Rosie.Lynx@wonderlust.co.uk>

Sent: 02 December 2021 16:23
To: Mary Lamb <Mary.Lamb@wonderlust.co.uk>
Subject: Re: Travel Influencer needed – Wonderlust magazine placement

Dear Mary,

Finance have agreed to allocate £5k to this project. Please explain to Ms Peters that this is a fixed budget for the whole engagement and that Wonderlust expect to see some significant returns on this investment.

Legal have reviewed the terms and will revert with comments.

Thanks so much,
Rosie

Rosie Lynx
Senior Editor - Wonderlust

I check the rest of my mails to find some comments from legal on Hillary's Terms document. Great, no excuses, now I have to deal with that dragon again. For a second, I wish that I had her mobile number, but then I decide that she is very likely one of those people who are constantly glued to their mobile phones in a manner of self-importance and answer all e-mails the instant they come in. I find her last e-mail and send a quick reply.

After some further curt exchanges (especially on her part) we agree to a 3pm Zoom call where she will explain the process and the timeline. I'm not sure how I ended up being the project manager from our side, but I figure with my recent distractions, I could probably use something to put me in Rosie's good books. I might even be able to get some more information on what Hillary is like as an agent. I mean, I can't imagine why Gemma would be wanting to stop working with such a charming individual (internal eye-roll).

I dial in two minutes early and wait in the 'lobby' until exactly 3pm. I get the impression that even if she wasn't busy immediately prior to the call, that she would certainly pretend that she was. She is just that sort of person.

It is interesting to see Hillary in her own surroundings. She has the obligatory bookcase behind her – I guess she can't bear the naff fake backgrounds – but, unsurprisingly for such a private and cold person, it is blurred. I'm not sure I would have noticed except that I would love to know what Hillary Peters reads for fun in her spare time! How to Cheat on your Taxes? How to make Enemies and Piss People Off? 50 Best Recipes for Cooking Small Children?

'Hi Mary. Nice to see you again.' I feel distinctly like she might be reading that off of a cue card.

'Hi Hillary. And likewise.' I am having quite a bit of fun with my word choice in spite of her miserableness. She proceeds to explain everything that will happen next regarding the placement. She tells me which influencer she has chosen and why and how we will measure the effectiveness of her campaign. I am surprised but impressed with how professionally she approaches what I understand to be social media nonsense. We go through some additional details regarding payment and what will happen if we decide we want to engage the same influencer for a follow-up post.

After a brief exchange of details, she asks if I have any questions and I say 'no, thank you.' At this point, she awkwardly changes topic and asks me if my children attend Upper Huxley Community

Primary School. The surprise must have shown on my face. I am in work mode and the shift is so abrupt that it truly catches me off guard.

'Yes, I have two children at Upper Huxley.' I say.

'Ah, in that case, I imagine you'll be at the sodding nativity play on Saturday.' she replies.

I am not used to 'sodding' and 'nativity play' being in the same sentence – but OK. 'Yes, I will?'

'Great. In that case, could you please bring along a copy of the most recent Wonderlust? I'll pass it to Marcie early next week.'

Now I really am confused. 'Does that mean that you will be there?' I ask.

'Yes, unfortunately.' And in typical Hillary fashion, that is the end of the topic. It is clear that she won't be offering any more about that.

After an interesting, if brutally efficient call, I fire off an e-mail to Rosie, detailing the next steps and showing her that I am in control of the situation.

Work is sorted, for now, but there is something niggling in the back of my mind. Something that just doesn't sit right – doesn't add up. I can't quite put my finger on what it is.

I go to the kitchen and boil the kettle. Tea helps everything. Based on the recent discussions we've been having about the environment and 'doing your bit' I decide to forego my standard PG tips and make myself some loose-leaf tea.

I grab my rainbow mug and walk to the under stairs cupboard that we've repurposed into a fully fitted food pantry. As I open the doors and turn on the light, all the pieces fall into place. I hear the mug smash on the stone floor and my ears are ringing, but not because of the sound of the mug shattering. My heart is racing – I move to the chair by the Aga and sit down. I can't trust my legs. I fumble my phone out of my hoodie pocket. My fingers are shaking so badly, I can hardly operate the screen. I call Rowe – without even texting first!

'Hi Mary – all OK?'

'Hi Rowe.' I can't be bothered with more niceties. 'I've figured it out.'

'What?'

'I know who did it! And I think I know how. When can we go on a walk?'

'A walk? Can you not tell me now? Is your phone tapped?'

'Rowe! Don't be ridiculous, of course my phone isn't tapped!' Trust Rowe to take the edge off with her anxious ideas. I nearly laugh but we have things to do! 'We need to test a theory!'

'Mary! What have you figured out?' The sharpness in her voice betrays her frustration.

I explain everything, exactly how the fog lifted and everything came into focus, and how I think the killer committed the murder and has (so far!) done such a great job of getting away with it. Rowe is silent.

'Rowe? Still there?'

'Yeah. Here. I just can't believe it.' Her voice gets quiet, and I hear her take a big breath and then she practically shouts 'So what do we do now?'

'Well Rowe, we are going to catch the villain!'

After a few more seconds of silence (it seemed appropriate), we decide what we will need for our adventure: dark clothes, a torch, welly boots, and a waterproof (just in case). I am going to see if I can find the night vision binoculars that I bought Tom ages ago to look at the wildlife around us, but I don't hold out much hope.

I spend the afternoon on Google Maps trying to calculate the clearest route from Gemma's house to the layby, then the fastest, then the most surreptitious. I check the weather reports for the last week and for the week prior to the murder. I decide that I should make a big pot of tea and bring two thermoses. It might be a long and cold night.

***

We arrive at Lambeth Close at about 8pm, trying our best not to look too suspicious and probably failing. I have brought Norman by way of an excuse, but our collective movements would be very suspicious to anyone that is paying anything more than a passing notice. There is a handy footpath that goes just between numbers 2 and 3 towards the fields to the rear. It is far enough away from Number 4 that we won't be suspected of nosing around anything related to the murder, but close enough to be able to calculate timings fairly accurately.

Luckily, we haven't had much rain lately, so the ground isn't too churned up. I also notice that we aren't leaving footprints – I am glad for that, even though I have to keep reminding myself that we aren't doing anything wrong. If anything, we are definitely doing something right! I am fairly sure that this experiment could prove that our suspect had opportunity, but I want cold hard evidence.

I get my torch out and open the clock app on my phone. We start the timer and wait for about a minute and a half to adjust for the distance between the back of Gemma's house and where we are standing. The cloud cover means that we need the torch tonight but on a clear night and with a bright moon (as on the night of the murder), you could easily do this without one.

We make it in plenty of time, and, most importantly as far as I am concerned: we couldn't be seen unless someone was specifically looking for us. Yes, we had to cross over two fields with three stiles in total before we got out onto a very convenient layby off the main road towards Stroud, but it is easily do-able, and the footpath is well marked. I make a point to look at how muddy our wellies are – hardly muddy at all! The footpath comes out onto a proper pavement.

We are convinced. It is definitely possible – and actually, pretty easy. That's means and opportunity marked as feasible. And Rowe and I agreed that we have a motive tied up.

More than ever, I am convinced that we have this solved. I am flooded with so many emotions: anger, sadness, relief, pride, worry, and so many more.

Next question is: what on Earth do we do next to make sure that the murderer is caught?

Chapter 56

@gemma_cotswolds_mum Evening Friends! Doesn't my Charlie look amazing in his Joseph ~~when you think his teacher initially casted him as a shepherd – the cheek~~ costume. He was the star of the show #proudmum
Do you remember as a kid having to use a tea towel to dress up as shepherds? Well, none of that anymore here! ~~I, all by myself~~ Our PTFA did some fundraising, and the school has now been able to invest in these amazing costumes, which will be worn proudly by our village kids for years to come! #ptfamum #schoolnativity

Rowena

Saturday

I am so nervous I think I might be sick.

My only reason should be that Alfie is on the stage later as shepherd #2. This is the excuse I give for my agitation to James and my mum, who has come especially for the occasion, when they see me fidgeting and looking nervously around the school hall. The main part of the venue has been taken over by rows of uncomfortable chairs and benches in which parents and family members are sitting in an array of festive jumpers and glittery tops.

The Victorian school hall wooden panels have been adorned by swags of festive greenery, and a majestic Christmas tree is taking pride of place in the front left corner next to the piano, where Jenny is playing a lively rendition of "Jingle Bells".

In true mum fashion, the guilt is real as the only thing I should have on my mind is whether Alfie is going to remember a) his two lines 'Look at this bright star!' and 'Let's follow the big star, friends!' and b) not to wipe his snot with his sleeve.

And I do worry but, in truth, I'm on tenterhooks because Mary and I are now 99% convinced we have cracked the mystery of Gemma's death. Unfortunately, we are not 100% sure because our theory can only be confirmed by a check that only the police can carry out (or a confession would do the trick, I suppose).

So, this time, Mary was on board with tipping our 'friend' Nick off through another anonymous letter. If our suspicions and logic are correct, Mary is convinced we can realistically expect an arrest tonight. I'm just hoping they will wait for the Nativity to be over before they proceed. The kids, teachers, and families would be devastated if that was interrupted.

Once again, I scan the room for Mary, but the Lambs have not arrived yet.

As I look around, I spot a slightly sheepish Matthew Hatherley accompanied by his parents and Hillary Peters. I suppose she was invited because Charlie is due to read a poem dedicated to his mum. She is not talking to anyone and is rudely immersed in her phone. I'm surprised she has come at all. I wouldn't have said this was her scene. I'm just hoping she isn't planning to use Charlie's poem for social media.

On the opposite side of the hall, Martin and Louise are sitting together but the atmosphere between them is looking frosty, even from a distance. Yet, Louise is putting on a brave face, smiling at everyone who looks at her, but not talking to Martin at all. As far as I know, the rumours about the affair have not gone around yet, despite everyone still talking about Martin being arrested on Tuesday.

Another sheepish face in the assembly is Vicky. Some people would have heard about the incident because Mark had to close the café early on Wednesday while waiting for the police. I'm relieved to see she is showing no sign of bruising from her encounter with my fist. I would take no pride in having injured her.

I don't know the details of what happened afterwards, but Vicky hasn't pressed any charges against me since Mary also agreed not to take things any further.

James has not mentioned me staying away from Mary again since Wednesday, and I didn't mention that my 'mental health' walk on Thursday was really a reconnaissance field trip with her. I feel uncomfortable about being economical with the truth. He still only knows about 50% of what we got up to, but it will hopefully be all out in the open in a few hours, now that we have pretty much solved this murder double-handedly. Tonight, I am incredibly thankful for his calming presence next to me. Maybe this is more than just enough for the future of our relationship. Maybe this is fundamental.

In the row in front of us, I can see and hear Lorna getting loudly agitated about the use of glitter on the stage backdrops that have been artfully painted (and glittered) by one of the school teaching assistants. Something about micro-plastic ending up in the sea.

Receiving compliments and thanks from all for donating all greenery garlands and other mistletoe arrangements, Marigold is standing by the double doors with who I can only guess is her husband, Stephen. I can't help watching them in fascination. My somewhat narrow mind is still astonished at the fact that this middle-aged couple have unusual sexual practices. Whatever I may think, they seem very much in love and as long as no one gets hurt ...

Out of the corner of my eye, I see Mary and Tom enter the hall. They are accompanied by an older gentleman, who I guess is Mary's dad.

She seems more excited than nervous. She spots me and gives me a little wave and discreet thumps up.

My heart swells at the incredible friendship I have found with clever, funny, and fearless Mary. Who would have thought only six weeks ago that I would get so close to someone I would be ready to throw a punch for her?

A friend to go fake carol singing with and trudge across muddy fields in reconnaissance adventures. A friend to solve a murder with.

At least, we can only hope we have solved it, and that the murderer will be sleeping behind bars tonight.

I shudder at the thought that in this lovely festive setting, on this joyous occasion, a murderer is here while their victim has been deprived forever of watching her little boy in his school Christmas play.

Someone Gemma trusted and invited into her home that night.

Someone who was not where they said they were.

Chapter 57

@gemma_cotswolds_mum Evening Friends! I have realised that I never share with you what book ~~is on my bedside table~~ I enjoy reading. ~~I don't read much but booktok is huge and I need some share of that cake.~~ Currently obsessed with Hercule Poirot ~~tv series~~ books. I always try to guess the ending, but Agatha Christie is far too clever for me! What do you like to read? Kindle, Audiobook, or paper? #bookstagram #booktok ~~#booktwitter #booksnap #bookeverybloodyplatform~~

Mary

Saturday

My heart is pounding. I try to play cool, but we've already established that I'm a terrible actress. Mostly. Tom notices the fact that I'm fidgety, but I play it off as being excited about the nativity. Turns out that being in the room with a murderer is a bit ... erm, is 'exciting' totally inappropriate? One look over at Rowe tells me that she feels it as well. Nothing is getting past her tonight, either.

The play is great, as usual. The children have done a wonderful job, and you can feel the collective breath of the audience being held each time a child speaks. Ben manages his line 'All the way from Bethlehem' almost perfectly but Bethlehem comes out a little more like 'Bemtheldem'. He looks straight at Charlotte, and I follow his gaze to see her giving him the most encouraging smile and thumbs up, and then his corners of his mouth life up to mirror hers. I'm just so proud of them both I could burst. My heart is so happy and lifted that it isn't until Charlie goes up on stage to read the poem for his mum that I remember what I was so anxious about earlier.

The teachers lead the children from the hall in an orderly queue towards their classrooms where they can change out of their costumes (and the school can ensure that they get to keep them). The parents, grandparents, and other press-ganged members of the audience pick up their coats, stack their chairs and move them to the side whilst the PTFA members are setting up the tables for the Christmas Fayre. The teachers will later bring the children back to the hall to be reunited with their gushing family members.

The adults mill around the hall congratulating each other on the performance of their little ones, generating a dull thrum of conversation. Had I not been looking for it, I would have missed the appearance of Nick the Dick entering through the side door. He is in plain clothes, and I wonder whether that is on purpose. There are two constables with him that remain by the external door. He locates Mrs Mearle, the headteacher, and gestures for her to lean in so he can whisper something. Luckily, she remains facing me, so I have the best view to watch her face start with curiosity and then contort through concern all the way into pained confusion. I can practically hear her thinking 'Seriously?' despite the fact that she is across the room from me. She takes a step back out of his proximity to face him properly, and he makes a gesture with his hand towards the stage. She then raises her hands, palms up, as if to say 'OK? If you really think that's best?' Knowing full well that whatever he is suggesting is definitely *not* best.

He makes his way to the front of the hall and bounds up the two stairs with the pomp of a royal guard but none of the grace. A shadow of utter dread and embarrassment washes over me. Whatever Mrs Mearle worried was about to happen, I am sure that

I now share her feeling. My heart starts pounding and I feel nauseous.

Nick pauses in the middle of the stage with his hands clasped behind him in the manner of a 4-year-old with something important to say. 'Good evening, Ladies and Gentlemen,' he announces in a voice far too loud for the circumstances. The hall is immediately silent. Eyes shifting from person to person. Faces full of questions but you can hear a pin drop.

'My name is Detective Inspector Nick Nash.' Luckily, he has adjusted his volume. All I can think about is that this is a rather unconventional way of making an arrest, but perhaps he found the pub performance a little too pedestrian – lacking in a bit of *je ne sais quoi*.

'As you will all know, the most unfortunate of tragedies unfolded in Upper Huxley with the MURDER of Gemma Hatherley on the evening of 5th November.' The emphasis on the word murder was somehow both pantomime-esque and sinister. 'My investigation has been both thorough and exhaustive.'

Erm ... What the fuck is happening here? I wanted so badly to shout 'You messed up not one but two alibis, you total fuckwit!' I shoot a worried look over at Rowe with a slight shrug of my shoulders. She mirrors my panicked gesture. I sneak a look at Tom, whose eyes are each as big as Christmas puddings. I have no idea what is happening, but I'm scared to miss even a second of this absolute train wreck, so look straight back at Nick.

'We have considered all of the possible suspects.'

No. My mind is racing ahead of this.

'And there have been many.'

Oh nooo.

'Some of the members of the village you would think *most* unlikely.'

Oh, my good God. This cannot be happening. Hercule Poirot you are not, my friend. This will not end well. Please stop.

'Take, for example ... YOU, Mrs Mortimer!' He is pointing aggressively at one of the sweetest old ladies I know, and the eyes in the room follow his finger. It is no exaggeration when I say I hear a record scratch sound effect in my brain. What the fuck? When was Mrs Mortimer a suspect? And why?

'You used to do your weekly shop on the same day as Gemma, no?' Do I detect a hint of accent now? 'I distinctly remember hearing you say that Waitrose was far too busy on Thursdays and that you wish some people would change to another day.'

'Well ... yes. Yes, I did say that.' She straightens up and pulls her shoulders back, radiating a bravery I'm not sure she feels.

'Enough to kill Gemma Hatherley?' There is a collective gasp from the crowd. I look over at Hillary and Matthew. Unbelievably, Hillary seems to be checking e-mails on her phone whilst Matthew has turned white as a sheet.

'That's preposterous!'

'Answer the question, Mrs Mortimer.'

'No, of course not, Officer!'

'No indeed, Mrs Mortimer. It was not you.' Nick turns his attention away from her as she whimpers with relief.

'Jenny Moore?' Nick lifts his chin like someone with something incredibly intelligent to say. 'You secretly hated Gemma Hatherley.'

'I don't *secretly* hate anyone!' Jenny snaps. The emphasis on 'secretly' makes me want to laugh. She's not wrong there. But, to be fair, I have never noticed anything particularly acrid about her interactions with Gemma. She is just being Jenny, as far as I am concerned.

She continues 'Gemma was a bit full of herself, but she always had the school's interest at heart. Of all the people I'd like to ...' she trails off, realising how wholly inappropriate her comment is going to be. 'Anyway, I certainly didn't cause Gemma any harm.'

I look at Tom, whose face is the picture of professional neutrality, but I spy his poker tell of clenched fists and white knuckles.

Nick acquiesces 'Quite right. Quite right.'

With this, he reaches up and strokes a beard that does not exist.

Deciding that standing on the stage isn't quite dramatic enough, he moves to the front edge where he squats down and then awkwardly shuffles himself off on to the floor, gathering angel glitter into a shiny half-heart shape on his sizeable arse. This takes much longer and more effort than he has planned, and he can feel that he is losing the momentum of his ridiculous charade.

With a final 'HMPH' he makes his way to the front of the throng. Like oil passing through water, the crowd makes a circular space around him, and he has somehow managed to maintain everyone's attention. He turns and heads directly at me.

'Mary?'

I look at Tom and then Rowe. They are both as confused as I am but Tom mouths 'be calm' to me. It doesn't work.

My face betrays the shock, anger, and ridiculousness of it all and my mouth starts speaking before my brain can catch up. Unfortunately, it comes out all in one breath.

'Oh of course! Everyone seems to think I hated her. I know this would come as a big shock to her if she were here, but it wasn't about her! I thought she had stolen my best friend! And even though it turns out that wasn't the case, she did go around showing everyone a very private letter that I had written to *him* about it. I wasn't her biggest fan, but, for goodness sake, I didn't KILL her!'

The rage is coming out of me in waves. I look at Matthew to make sure that he believes me. He looks horrified, but luckily, he doesn't have to think on that for very long.

'Erm.' The pause and confusion on Nick's face betray the fact that this was not at all the direction he was heading. 'I was just going to ask you if you could hold my coat.'

If ever there was a time for the floor to swallow me whole, now would be ideal. I snatch his coat and do my best to slink into the crowd to make myself invisible. I'll worry later about how I'll face anyone ever again.

This is now an utter farce. Tom can't stand it anymore, and he makes a purposeful advance towards the middle of the circle, which startles Nick. Perhaps Nick didn't realise that he had a fellow policeman in the audience for this ridiculous show.

But the dramatic crescendo dissolves miserably when he fails to spot his actual target quickly enough to point to next. His short tubby stature means that he actually has to rise onto his tiptoes to identify his true target. He adds the audible pause to buy some time which further undermines the effect that he is trying so desperately to achieve.

'Erm ... Where is ...?' He spots her.

'Hillary Peterson!'

'Peters, you idiot!' I feel like she has said this many times before and it comes out as an automatic reflex, but it rattles him.

'Ah yes, sorry. Hillary Peters! It was you who killed Gemma Hatherley.'

'What? This is crazy!' Looking to the wider audience, she pleads for support. 'This man is crazy. He's talking rubbish!' Facing him, she asks, 'Who's next, *Sir?* Ms Scarlett in the library? Ha Ha Ha.' But she is the only one laughing.

'No, Ms Peters. You are the murderer. You were Gemma's agent and ...' he trails off whilst he rummages in his pocket for something.

Despite the incredible tension in the room, I have to stifle a giggle. This clodpole has actually forgotten the motive! He is being outperformed by the reception-aged children who commanded this same audience half an hour before.

Taking out a ragged notebook with pages sticking out everywhere, he opens the cover, licks his thumb in a most repulsive manner, and turns the pages until he finds what he was looking for. Without a shred of dignity or self-respect, he unfolds the anonymous note that Rowe and I had written and reads an extract aloud.

'You were Gemma's agent, reliant on the income that she generated for you, and had reason to believe that she might be looking to replace you.'

This is too much for Hillary. Her pride can't take it. 'I didn't need her shit commissions!'

Mrs Mortimer gasps at this and makes a comment about how she is glad the children aren't still in the hall.

'She was an amateur! And her sponsorships were insignificant and getting worse! I was planning to drop her to concentrate on my more lucrative clients but then she started sniffing around looking for another agent and asking about commission rates! Like she was the one in charge! Gemma never had a single idea of her own. She was a blank canvas with an appreciation for pretty things. That's ALL. I made her a success and then put my career on the line to increase her engagement and she thinks she can just drop me? First my father and then that BASTARD! Well – not again – and definitely not Gemma Bloody Hatherley. NO ONE will ever dump Hillary Peters again and get away with it!' She is screaming by the end of her monologue. Her entire body is trembling, her fists are clenched, and her eyes are wild with uncontained rage. She looks like she might actually explode.

The hall is absolutely dead still – completely silent.

And then I hear the quietest 'Fuck' from Tom. I ask with my eyes. He whispers 'She's said all of that without being under caution.'

Nick's eyes widen almost imperceptibly, as if he has just had the same thought. 'Hillary Peterson.'

Like something out of a pantomime, the entire audience shouts 'Peters!' but only Hillary can be heard adding 'you FUCKWIT!' at the end.

'Hillary Peters, you are under arrest for the murder of Gemma Hatherley. You do not have to say anything, but it may harm your defence if you do not mention when questioned something which you later rely on in court. Anything you do say may be given in evidence ...'

The rage that was all-consuming just moments before seems to have exhausted Hillary, and she goes peacefully.

Nick and the two constables guide her out of the hall. I am surprised that he decides not to use handcuffs. Not because they are required, but that everything else seems to be for dramatic effect – it looks as though he's missed a trick. My guess is that they are probably still in the car, forgotten.

I give Rowe the side-eye and we sneak out of the back door to the playground, where we stand unseen to watch Hillary being bundled into the back of the panda car. I feel like we've earned the right to be spectators in this last scene. We are quiet until the car drives off and then for a beat longer. I don't say anything, but I just give Rowe the biggest hug and then I start laughing. I am not laughing because murder is funny. I'm definitely not laughing because someone is dead. I am laughing because of the intoxicating euphoria of relief. I am so proud of us for relentlessly pursuing the truth and even putting ourselves and our reputations on the line to try and find out what happened to Gemma Hatherley. I know that Rowe feels exactly the same as we do a silly little hug dance. The laugh turns to a bit of a cry for both of us which then turns quickly back into a proper laugh.

I laugh the hardest I've laughed in years, and it makes me realise how often that happens with Rowena. I realise all of a sudden that I had no idea what I was missing until she came into my life.

I stop and say to her 'Thank you.' She looks at me confused and I don't want to explain the happiness that she has brought to my life right now. I'll wait until I can find the right words. 'I'll tell you another time. Thank you.'

She offers a cheesy grin and says 'You're welcome?' And that's all I need for now.

We turn to head back into the hall, but I know we'll never really be the same after that night. Tom and James have come looking for us and meet us just outside the doors. We make plans for the Boats to go to their house, get the children settled in bed with Rowe's mum on babysitting duty, and then the Rowe and James will come over to ours for a late dinner. Rowe and I promise that if they can wait that long, we will tell them 'Everything'. Although, I very much doubt our story will include everything.

***

I kiss my gorgeous children even more fiercely than normal at bedtime that night, even through a chorus of whiney 'Oh Mummys!" I will never again take it for granted that I am lucky enough to be able to kiss them goodnight every night, and that they are lucky enough to still have their mum around to do it.

Rowe and James arrive just as I am coming downstairs, and I fetch the first of many bottles of wine that will be drunk that night. We sit down to a wonderful meal of sausage casserole and Rowe and I take turns relaying all, no, most, of the exciting things that we've been up to over the last six weeks.

The carol singing episode is even more hilarious on the re-telling and there are plenty of details spared regarding speculation about who is and who isn't in the swinging group. But Tom is most interested in how we figured out that Hillary was the killer.

'We'd interviewed her when I was still on the case?' He is bordering on the defensive and rightly so. 'She had an alibi – she was on a Zoom call right around the time of the murder.'

'Ah yes, but Hillary uses a blurred background for her Zoom calls.' Rowe says. I am glad she is jumping in here. Somehow, she makes it less combative.

'OK, but what does that have to do with anything?' Tom says.

I jump in – switching back and forth makes the exchange seem much less serious. 'She has a bookcase behind her chair in her office that is lit from above. From the direction that Gemma was looking when she was talking to her attacker, Rowe calculated that Hillary was coming into the kitchen from the pantry rather than from an outside door. This meant that the attacker had to be someone that was already in the house.'

Now it is Rowe's turn again. 'When Mary saw Matthew at the police station, he mentioned that Gemma was desperate to get everyone out of the house that night, so she had to have invited Hillary specifically and known that she was in the pantry. Which begs the question 'Why was Hillary in the pantry?"

I take over the story again. 'It was to have a Zoom call with someone at the time of the 'break-in', but then Hillary put it to use as her alibi for the time of the murder.' I pause for dramatic effect and see both men have looks of utter confusion on their faces.

I give a quick nod to Rowe to reveal the genius of it. 'The shelves with the food on them, lit from above and then blurred, would look very similar to the bookcases that are behind Hillary's chair in her office. So, the background for her call would look almost the same as it usually does in her own office. Whether this was something that Hillary had planned beforehand or utilised on the spot will be something for Nick to sort out.'

'But why was Hillary there in the first place?' I can tell that James feels a little bit like he's been transported to a parallel universe, but he is looking at Rowe with a startling mix of adoration and fear.

Rowe continues 'Given the fact that Gemma wanted everyone out if the house that night, that no one saw Hillary or her car, and that she had her Zoom call in the pantry right beside Gemma, we think they had planned something dramatic to rescue Gemma's career. Something no one should know about.' She pauses to make sure everyone is still following.

'Our theory is that the break in was planned as a publicity stunt, and Hillary was going to act as the intruder. As a result, she couldn't be seen at Gemma's, and she needed an alibi. She planned the perfect murder: one where the victim helps the murderer plan their own death.'

'Unbelievable.' James is truly lost in the gravity of what's happened. Tom chooses to mark the revelation in silence. I think there might be some embarrassment beneath his silence, but I hope he knows that it doesn't belong to him.

'Indeed, we're pretty convinced Gemma was faking it for her followers when Hillary came into the kitchen wearing the balaclava, even when she called out to her followers to call 999. What we don't know is at what point she realised Hillary wasn't acting and was there to actually kill her. We can only hope she didn't have enough time to realise she was about to die.'

'All of this was circumstantial and sort of psychological guesswork until we could get evidence.' I add.

'That's when we needed the police to check Hillary's phone location. We guessed that she wouldn't have been stupid enough to use Gemma's Wi-Fi, but we thought that maybe she would have used her phone as a hotspot for her call and that would be traceable.' Rowe explains. She holds out her hands as if to say "that's it!"

'The arrest tonight confirmed we were obviously right.' I added, to drive the point home.

'But if Hillary was trying to increase her 'engagement' then why the fuck did she kill her?'

I jump in. 'Because Gemma was looking to get rid of Hillary as her agent. I get the impression that 'Hill for the Kill' is more than capable of riding the waves of fortune and misfortune with all of her clients. She realises that some of them will have good times and bad times. I'm also sure that she knows how to help them when they are struggling – like devising this publicity stunt. But what her ice-cold ego cannot abide is being fired or replaced.'

'But it was more than that, wasn't it, Mary?' Rowe interjects. 'It was likely a response to the trauma that she suffered as a child and then again at a critical stage in her career. At the risk of sounding like an armchair psychologist, I would venture to say that this was about way more than just Gemma.'

I think to myself about the huge mistake I made by jumping to conclusions with Matthew and not taking the time to understand the situation fully. Again, Rowe is bringing that sense of perspective, reminding me to stop and consider others' points of view.

She continues 'In any case, we think that once Hillary got wind of the fact that Gemma was looking to replace her, the wheels were put in motion to kill Gemma and make it look like a robbery gone wrong.' she pauses. 'Hillary used the secret nature of the publicity stunt to make sure Gemma kept quiet, so no one would ever know that Hillary was at her house. She then killed Gemma and snuck across the fields to a lay-by further outside the village where she might have left her car – although we can only speculate on that particular bit.'

My turn again. 'And that, our lovely husbands, is how Hillary Peters killed Gemma Hatherley!'

Tom clearly cannot help himself. 'And she would have got away with it, too, if it weren't for you meddling Anonymums!' he says, but I can tell that he is quite serious in his sentiment.

James still looks like he's seen a ghost. 'Did Rowe tell you I actually thought you might have been ... well ...' He has lost his nerve and looks to Rowe for reassurance. She returns a stern look that I can't read.

'Spit it out, James?' I challenge.

'Well, I thought you might have done it!'

'Done what?'

'Killed her.'

'Gemma?'

'Has someone else died?' He looks worried.

'James! Are you being serious?' I steal a glance at Rowe which answers my question. 'If I didn't like you, I'd be offended.' I'm finding it funny even though I should be more offended. 'Sure, I was angry with her when I was 18 because I thought she stole my best friend just for the fun of it. But I got on with the rest of my life. She was annoying because she was ubiquitous, but I was fairly indifferent. I gave her a wide berth and she reciprocated. I definitely didn't hate her and certainly not enough to kill her!'

'Well, I'm sorry, Mary. I realise now how wrong I was. And, for the record, I like you, too.'

'Well thank goodness for that.' I give him a cheesy grin and then roll my eyes conspiratorially towards Rowe.

What I didn't realise was just how much Rowe had been keeping from him. I suppose that she was still trying to convince him that moving to Upper Huxley had been the right thing to do and maybe keeping him up to date on our risky escapades wasn't quite the right method of doing so. But he's also full of admiration and I can see the love that he feels for Rowe written all over his face. Every couple has their challenges, but I'd love to think that these two are going to be just fine.

The situation is poignant. Gemma's life on Instagram was fake on almost every level. The glamourous, luxurious life that was splashed all over her feed hid serious financial troubles, and the happy marriage and power couple smiles were plastering over incredible sadness and a broken marriage. Even the last moments of her life were faked in an effort to create a false truth that would generate more interest in her.

Social media is a pretty illusion and Gemma ended up dying for it.

In almost uncomfortable contrast, I can't remember a time when I have been prouder of either myself or my wonderful new friend. I feel like I'm able to recognise now that Rowe is filling a hole that I didn't even realise existed. It's been such a long time since I felt that connection with a friend – a real friend. We are quite different and we definitely don't agree on everything but she's real with me and I'm real with her. And that's so valuable. I guess the last true friend I'd had was Matty. And being dumped (like I thought I had) made me think that I didn't need a best friend. I'm sure that Matty and I will make amends, and I'd like to think we can be good friends again in the future. But right now, I am positively beaming at my new friend, and she is beaming, too. The feeling is made all the more potent by the heat of the fire and the warmth of the wine, but I know I've found something truly special in my new friendship with Rowe, and we've used that special bond to help do something genuinely good for the world.

And that feels ... well ... pretty damn good.

Epilogue 1

Tuesday 5th November – 8.32pm

This is going well, she thinks.

So far, it's the most engagement she's had on a Live for the last five months. Turns out she is not the only one who has nothing to do on a boring November evening. As the kids only went back to school yesterday after half term, no doubt people are waiting for the weekend to attend bonfire festivities, like the Upper Huxley Straw Man Parade on Saturday. Charlie is very much looking forward to this and has been making plans for his Guy for weeks. She loves seeing him so excited but wishes she could share his enthusiasm. Matthew has tried to excuse himself from the event, but she is not having it.

He thinks she doesn't know what is going on, but she is not stupid. However, if he thinks she will confront him and give him the opportunity to leave her, he's got another thing coming.

Whoever he is seeing at the moment, that bitch won't win him over. This is not the first time she and Matthew are going through a rough patch. They are solid and will recover from this like they did from all their previous difficulties. She just knows it.

Back to what she's doing. She really needs to concentrate. She is so nervous she is overdoing it on the cheeriness to mask it. She hopes the viewers don't think she is drunk. To be fair, she has been overdoing it on the wine for a while now, but she doesn't think her followers have noticed. Except for the ones who have unfollowed her. In droves. And made her lose so much income. As a result, they are now struggling to pay back their credit card bills, loans, and mortgage. Matthew has been making noises about downsizing. Over her dead body. She's worked incredibly hard to get to where she is and refuses to compromise. Of course, she could be more like Mary Lamb, who doesn't care about driving that old banger around like it is an absolute treasure. But she loves the power she feels at the wheel of her BMW X5. And she would love to be naturally beautiful like that newcomer, Rowena Boat, but she hates her own natural mousy hair colour and only feels herself with her face fully done up in expensive make up.

Eurgh. This is the reason she and Hill have come up with this elaborate charade. She needed something that would give her that immediate step up in visibility and engagement. So, Hillary cleverly came up with this fake burglary plan. She must admit, as annoyed as she is with her agent for bleeding her dry with her commission, she is utterly grateful to her. She doesn't know anyone who would take such drastic and risky steps for their clients.

So, although she had started putting out feelers for a new agent, there is no way she can leave her now. She will need to have a frank discussion with her about her percentage. Particularly if their stunt yields the results they hope for, then she will be in a stronger position to negotiate. As much as she hates the idea of blackmail, after this evening they will be stuck together forever, as they could both end up in serious trouble if they get found out. Hill is very clever and is always thinking two steps ahead of Gemma, so it won't be easy to get her to accept a cut to her percentage. But surely, she'd rather have that than lose her client.

She can see the number of viewers has now reached the figure she and Hill have agreed on to start their act. She can hear the faint noises coming from the pantry and she knows she is now on her way. She feels sick with nerves. She was pretty good at Drama at school, but this is next level. Thankfully all of it will be off camera. It's the aftermath that will necessitate her best acting skills.

The pantry door has opened silently, and Hill comes into view on Gemma's left. She has to remind herself that it is her because she looks quite scary with her balaclava on. As agreed, she loudly pushes the pantry door shut.

Gemma startles and looks at her. She stands up and moves off camera, putting on her most frightened voice: 'What are you doing here? Who ...?'

She is smiling at Hill as they pretend to tussle like kids. She can only see her eyes through the balaclava, and she is not giving anything away. Gosh, Gemma is going to have to do it all of the acting here!

'Call 999!' she shouts in pretend anguish to her viewers as she winks at Hill.

Christ, that's it, no going back now. The authorities are on their way.

If she ever gets caught, she hopes that Charlie and Matthew will believe that she did this for them. For all of them.

Epilogue 2

Rowena

Last day of term

We've made it to the end of term. And what an eventful term it was! New life, new village, new house, new school, and a new hobby! I'm not sure murder investigating can be classed as a hobby, but it's most definitely not a job for me.

Tonight, Mary and co. have joined us for an end of term celebration: just our two families and a menu solely comprised of nibbles, canapés, and other delicious finger foods. Oh, and loads of cheese, of course. The children are loving it, and we congratulate ourselves in creating their own little buffet or there wouldn't be anything left for us to eat within two and a half minutes, especially as Tom is expected later, when his shift finishes.

We are going away visiting our families from Sunday until New Year's Eve, so we thought we needed a proper celebration with our friends who have made us feel so welcome in our new life.

Call me sentimental, but I would love for this to become a new tradition: The Lamboats' End of Term Christmas Canapé Party!

The house is beautiful this evening. Somehow in between school events, buying all the presents for all the people, a teething Eloise, and a murder investigation, I have managed to finish decking the halls, with help from my mum when she came two weeks ago.

Admittedly, two months on from our arrival in Upper Huxley, we still have loads of boxes in the garage that need to be emptied and organised, but the house is glowing with candles and fairy lights –

the epitome of Christmas cheer. I let out the biggest exhale. I feel settled. All the anxiety, uncertainty, and heartache that had been hanging over us for the past two years seems to have vanished.

Watching from the sidelines as Mary rekindled her friendship with Matthew has been an unexpected stocking filler bonus.

Predictably, the kids have hoovered up all their food in two minutes flat and are now putting the finishing touches to the gingerbread house they baked with Mary and me after school. Of course, that was infinitely more stressful than they make it look on Instagram. Anyone who has ever baked with kids will know what I mean.

I'm busy making a sloe gin cocktail for Mary, when James returns from fetching some logs for the fire, exclaiming: 'It's snowing!'

The children (and myself too) shriek and rush to the nearest window. It is snowing hard. In the front garden, the grass is already covered by a thin layer. The fairy lights that I got an unwilling James to adorn the front of the house with are casting a beautiful glow over the swirling snowflakes. It truly looks magical, in the cheesiest possible way.

'Daddy!' shout an excited Charlotte and Ben as they spot Tom making his way up the front path.

'Happy Christmas, everyone!' booms Tom in his best Santa voice as he steps into the house, shaking the snowflakes from his hair and coat.

A few minutes later, after the kids have returned to the kitchen and we, the adults, are enjoying a quiet drink and some delicious food, Tom fills us in on his day.

'Ladies, you are not going to believe this. Guess who is getting a special distinction over his 'exceptional' handling of the Hatherley case?' asks Tom, using his fingers as air quotes.

'Surely not!' exclaims Mary. 'Nick the Dick? Or should it be Nick the Thick? Both nicknames are a great fit!' Her cheeks are flushed, and her eyes are narrow and hard.

'The very one! And all thanks to you, Anonymums!' Tom declares while mock applauding.

'Noooo.' I wail. 'So, I guess no one knows about the anonymous letters which delivered him this case on a silver platter, then.' As much as I am relieved no one will now trace these back to us, I also wish Nick was not profiting from all our hard work.

'The letter he had the cheek to read out loud during his knock-off Hercule Poirot drawing room denouement!' Mary interjects.

'Trying to forget about this. But nope. Only I know about the letters. But of course, he didn't show me your latest one this time. And I can't very well ask him about it. I did try to ask a few questions on how he came to suspect Hillary, and he pinned it all down to checking her phone location on the night of the murder. But he won't be drawn on how he worked out the motive and the whole fake break in – that Gemma organised herself.' Tom reasonably explains, sounding amused by the ridiculousness of the situation.

'Oh gosh, we didn't foresee we would be helping him in his career! He is absolutely useless, and so rude as well!' I agonise, my head in my hands.

'Indeed. So, Anonymums, for your next case, could you please make sure I'm the one who ends up with a promotion?' He winks at us.

'Next case? We won't be making a habit of this!' I shout indignantly.

I turn to Mary, and I swear there is a glint of excitement in her eyes as she raises her glass to me.

Acknowledgements

If you've made it this far, thank you! We hope you enjoyed reading it as much as we enjoyed writing it.

What started out as a seed of a silly idea back in 2012 when our firstborns were tiny and evolved into a lockdown project, soon turned into an all-encompassing passion.

While we wrote (and re-wrote many times) this story together, this book could never have come to light without the support of many people.

Firstly, we would like to thank our mums for their love and genetic predisposition for crime book appreciation and our dads for always being there, too.

Despite our tongue and cheek dedication, we are grateful to our husbands because we do love them, really.

This book simply wouldn't exist without our biggest supporters, the loves of our lives, our children; our endless source of inspiration and motivation for continuously asking for 3 years "Is it published yet?" (in the familiar, if slightly irritating "Are we there yet?" tone).

This book would still be a messy draft without the help of our editor, Reassuring Rachel and our book cover designer, Patient Patrick.

We hold a very special place in our heart for our first reader, best buddy and full-time supporter, Diyana.

We also want to thank Tonton Max and Auntie Rachel, two of our earliest readers. Your encouragement meant so much and we hope you enjoy the latest version even more.

To Alessandra who's been a huge supporter to us, Audrey and Bridie, fellow writers and beta-readers: your encouragement and input has been so invaluable to us. We cannot wait to see the good things coming your way.

Special mention to our online writing community friends, and their constant cheering in our phones, too many to name but you know who you are. We cannot wait to see you at the next festival.

We cannot forget all our real-life friends, who responded so enthusiastically when we 'came out' as writers and told them about our silly hobby. Thank you for your support and for wanting to read this even if it's not your bag.

Lastly, we want to thank each other. There is absolutely no way we could have done it without one another, the highs and lows are more fun and bearable respectively when we're in it together. Can't wait to see what comes next for Mary and Rowena.

Inspired by their friendship, their countless parenting fails, and a lifelong passion for cosy crime, Emilie and Eve write *The Anonymums* book series.

They both live in Gloucestershire with their respective families (and a cat called Tom) but still slightly too far away from each other.

Like a lot of modern duos, they met at work but bonded over sore nipples and sleepless nights when they simultaneously became first time mums.

This first book, *A Bloody Merry Murder*, has been recognised in several writing competitions: longlisted for the 2024 Flash 500 Novel Opening Prize and for the Crime Writers' Association Emerging Author Dagger 2025 and shortlisted for the Killer Twist Pitch prize and the I Am Writing Competition 2025.

Their next *Anonymums* book, *Murder At The Lit Fest* (working title), will be out early 2027.

Follow them on social media for updates (and stupid reels).
Instagram: @the_anonymums_writers
TikTok: @the.anonymum.wri
www.theanonymums.com

Printed in Dunstable, United Kingdom